ECHOES

L.G. WRIGHT

First published in Great Britain in 2023 by L.G. Wright

Copyright © L.G. Wright 2023

The right of Lyndsay Wright to be identified as the Author of the Work has been asserted by her in accordance with the Copyright, Designs and Patents Act of 1988.

All rights reserved.

This book is a work of fiction and, except in the case of historical fact, any resemblance to actual persons, living or dead, is purely coincidental.

No part of this publication may be reproduced, stored in a retrieval system or transmitted in any form or by any means without the prior written permission of the author, nor be otherwise circulated in any form of binding or cover other than that in which it is published and without a similar condition being imposed on the subsequent publisher.

For Mum and Dad, with love

Wednesday

Chapter One

London. 8th September 1976

The pavements of Baker Street are shiny with long-awaited rain. As The Globe's landlord re-locks the door behind me, the cloying smell of rain on overheated concrete rises up to meet me. But thank God, the humidity has broken at last.

The streets have sloughed off their tourists, leaving only a handful of stragglers and those, like me, ejected from the pubs. The streetlights hum and buzz, louder than I've noticed before. Their eerie orange, mirrored in the wet pavement, sets an unnatural glow against the barely dark sky, clear now but starless against London's never-silent night.

As I turn into the more sedate side road housing my hotel, the sounds of civilisation become muted and indistinct. I love the city at this time of night, emptied of its daytime hubbub.

The Globe's bitter must have slowed my mind as I'm already eight paces past the alleyway before I register what I've seen. I turn and am four paces back again before I even consciously catch up with my intent; my reaction is pure instinct.

'Hey!'

Adrenalin shoots through my veins as I call out. Fight or flight. Instinct or rational brain. Put this one down to having three sisters at home because there isn't much rationality involved. At least a belated stab of self-protection makes me hold back at the entrance to the alleyway.

As the more analytical side of my brain catches up, I realise it isn't an alleyway at all but an entrance to a cobbled courtyard, wide enough perhaps for a horse-drawn dray. Older than the neighbouring Edwardian terraces, certainly.

Another part resolves the two figures at the end of the courtyard into a man and a woman, weakly lit, pushed up against the wall, the blind end of the first terraced house.

At twenty feet away, it's the stance of the pair that tells the threat: the man's aggression articulated in the right hand pressed flat against the wall by her head, in the left clenched at his side, in the shoulders hunched over her cowering frame, in how she's shrunk back against the brickwork, face turned away and shoulders raised in protection.

They're both from the same world to judge by their clothes. Long hair, bell-bottomed jeans. The world of the students littering the sun-drenched grass of the Backs at home. Just an alcohol-fuelled lovers' tiff in all likelihood. Hopefully.

'Piss off, mate. Ain't no business of yours.'

Home counties accent, trying to be East End.

'Are you alright?' I nod in her direction. A glance from her to the man, ignored.

'I said,' turning towards me now, 'piss off.'

A louder tone, the words more enunciated to hide the slurring. A broad man but not tall, younger than me. I draw myself up: my wiry frame won't intimidate but I can use my several inches' height advantage.

'I will once I know the lady is OK.'

'Lady? What lady?' he sneers.

It's her chance to step away from the man, but she doesn't. Come on, come on. *Move.*

But it's the man who moves, turning towards me, both fists now clenched at his sides.

'Either,' one step closer, his face disappearing into shadow, 'you walk away right now or you get what's coming to her.' Another step nearer and he comes into the shadows of the timbered entrance to the yard. 'Right now.'

'Don't, Dan.' Her whispered denial and the hand on his upper arm have no impact.

'I told you, piss off. This ain't your business.'

'Dan, leave him alone. Please. You don't want any more trouble.' That's the right kind of accent for the neighbourhood.

'I can't leave until I know she's safe.' No jacket to conceal a weapon. Cigarettes in the shirt breast pocket. Bulging back trouser pocket likely contains nothing more than an over-filled wallet. Slim rectangular outline in the left front jeans pocket, though: a knife or just a lighter? Left-handed.

'And what are you going to do about it?' Two steps forward. Deliberately menacing, but he allows himself to be held back by the woman's hand on his elbow. His eyes scan me up and down, assessing me as I did him.

'I'm going to wait here until you leave.' Same tone: rational, light, unemotional. I keep my arms loose at my sides, palms open, unthreatening.

The guy glances at the woman. Uncertainty: that's my advantage.

A nod from the woman and she releases his arm, dips her head as she steps back. The left hand drops to the jeans front pocket. A light touch, index and middle finger only. Sizing me up, he seems to think better of it.

He takes a final look at the woman and a step towards her that brings him right over her again. Grasps her chin and twists her face at an awkward angle. A word in her ear but his eyes are fixed on me at the other end of the alley. Her eyes lower towards the cobble floor, every part of her body submissive. He thrusts her chin away, then broadens his chest as he strides fast down the alley, wanting to get away now. Hands open, eyes straight ahead; the swagger of the beaten arrogant.

It's as he passes me that I make my mistake.

Drawn by the movement of the woman as she slumps back against the wall, I take my eyes off him a moment too soon.

From the corner of my eye, I see the punch coming just a fraction of a second before I feel it, a direct blow to the stomach from that left hand as he passes my shoulder.

All the air is driven out of me and I double up, fire burning in my stomach, eyes closed, focused on the site of the attack.

I try to straighten up, knowing I need to defend myself, and force my eyes open. Just in time to glimpse the fist that is aimed at my face, the arm at right angles, the downwards slant putting the full force of the shoulder behind the strike.

It drives my head down and rocks it hard, ringing through my ears. It actually feels like my brain bounces off the inside of my skull. Pinpoints of light dance across my vision. The blow seems to ripple through my whole body until my legs give way and I crumple to the floor.

Hands on each side of my head draw me up onto my knees until I'm looking upwards into the man's face. I see the fist drawn back, the shoulder at full rotation and can do nothing but wait for the blow.

My head snaps sideways. No longer held up and unable to break my fall, the other side of my head smacks hard against the wall. The pinpoints of light became one massive flash that, in an instant, collapses into the distance. Darkness overwhelms me and my senses disappear.

Gone before my body hits the floor.

Buzzing. Sounds of people around me. Talking, words, but not connecting. Hands on my face, testing my neck. Turning my head. Prising open one eyelid. A flash of piercing, blinding light. Then again. I groan in the back of my throat. Pressure of hands on my skull. Intense shooting pain beneath. A silent scream. Blackness.

The hum of many voices and fluorescent lights. Bright against the inside of my eyelids. Gone. Then again. Gone. Then again. Laid flat. Wheels rolling. People on either side of me, crammed around. A thumb pulls my eyelids up again, one, two. A round dot of light dances across each eye. Behind it, polystyrene ceiling tiles, square, pock-marked, off-white, water-stained. A corridor. Surgical green walls. Too bright. Too loud. Too harsh. The darkness creeps back in from the edges and I welcome it with relief.

White light. Softer now. Filtered through cotton. Muffled noises on the ward. Warm beneath blankets, tightly tucked, cocooning me. A shaft of sunlight spilling between the curtains. A presence to my left. Auburn hair flaming red where it catches the sun.

Sam? It can't be.

Tightness around my head. Stabbing behind my eyes. Retreat is easy.

Thursday

Chapter Two

London. 9th September 1976

'OK, that's enough. Time to come back now, Eoghan.'

There's pleasure in hearing her say my name again, soft and breathy on her tongue. Like the Welsh Owen, but spelled the Irish way, I tell people.

Her hand is on mine where it rests on a blanket, a familiar roughness beneath my fingertips that reminds me of childhood.

Warmth from that hand. Then pressure, closing around my fingers and squeezing. Encouraging but also asking.

There's a flood of relief at the sound of her voice. Of joy, almost. But there's still resentment, too. I resist for a moment more, but curiosity overcomes me. I open my eyes.

Darker beyond the curtains, dimmed artificial light, little noise. Night-time.

'Welcome back, stranger.'

'Hello, Sam.' I blink to stop my eyes closing again. 'How long have I been out?'

'Long enough.' Still beautiful. Even in a white coat and with her rust-coloured hair now tied back. A little tired, maybe. Tiny lines at the edges of her eyes.

'Are you working?'

'I just stopped by before I start the late shift. Want to tell me what happened?'

I close my eyes to piece the recollections together. 'Damsel in distress.'

'I might have known.'

'How bad is it?'

She glances down at the clipboard she must have scanned before I awoke, now laid across her lap. 'Not as bad as they initially feared. Concussion, for sure, but no signs of anything more severe. It's just how long you were out for that was worrying them.'

'Did you warn them I sleep like the dead?'

The slightest twitch of her lips. 'You still do that?'

I try to nod and regret it. Putting my hand to the side of my head, I touch layers of gauze.

She gives a rueful smile and stands up, returning the chair to its position against the wall. 'You'll have quite a headache for a couple of days. The nurse will bring you something for that in the morning. Rest is the best remedy for now.'

'Then why did you wake me?' Teasing. Almost.

She meets my gaze. That open, direct way she has of seeing right into you. Or, in my case, right through me.

'I was worried.' She blinks, surprised, as if she has just revealed more than she has intended. 'And,' turning away, 'I need to focus on my patients, not to be worrying about you.'

'Sam?' She turns back, holding the clipboard beneath her folded arms. Defensive. Her eyes are steady but wary. 'It's good to see you,' I offer, lamely.

I see the withdrawal in her eyes. A slight nod of the head. 'I'll see you in the morning.'

Friday

Chapter Three

London. 10th September 1976

I sleep most of the day, woken at each mealtime by the clatter of trolleys distributing food that reminds me of school; I have no appetite for any of it, but I force down what I can.

The summer sun streams in through huge plate-glass windows to my right, too bright for my eyes but comfortingly warming on the skin. I lie with my eyes closed but that just makes me more aware of the throbbing in my head.

I speculate when she might return. Perhaps at the end of her shift. Would that be eight hours? Ten? When I wake again, that time has come and gone. Maybe a double shift?

The day slips along and the sun tracks to my right. I try to stay awake, but the air is too warm, soporific. Electric fans whirr, their background hum restful, dulling the noise from the ward. I doze.

* * * * * * *

A pressure on my hand calls me back to consciousness. I stir, aching now from lying on my back for too long. I stretch my neck and roll onto my side, open my eyes. Smile.

'Hello.'

'I tried willing you to wake up, but it wasn't working. I must have lost my touch.' She smiles to herself, half light, half wistful.

My eyes aren't quite ready to stay open. I breathe in that surprisingly intimate memory. I used to love waking up to find Sam watching me sleep.

The hand she'd laid on mine moves away. I feel the loss and open my eyes. 'I didn't mean to say that out loud.'

She shakes her head. 'It was a long time ago.'

I seek safer ground. 'Did they say when I can get out of here?'

'They want to keep you for another night then they'll release you if someone can take you home.'

'There isn't anyone.'

'I said I'd do it.'

Why would she do that for me?

'My things are all at a hotel in Marylebone. I was supposed to check out.'

'I know, I called them. They've put everything to one side for you. I'll pick it up tomorrow.'

I frown but the tension it creates in my head isn't a good idea. 'How do you know?'

'There aren't that many archaeology conferences in London at this time of year. The university gave me the details.' A smile lightens her face. 'I see your charms are still working: Natalie on the organising team was most concerned when I explained why I was calling.'

'Which one's Natalie?'

'Based on her accent, she's from your neck of the woods.'

'Ah. From Kilnamanagh. I told her my namesake founded their abbey. She's wasted doing admin. Should be studying history.'

Another smile, masking our awkwardness. 'You think everyone should be studying history.'

'Well?' Advocacy comes as reflex after years of reprised arguments. But it's also safer ground for both of us. 'They should. What can be more important than knowing where we've come from?'

'How about living in the now?' There it is, that old flash of fire. 'Or,' casting around for alternatives, her hands mimicking the reaching of her mind, 'knowing how to heal people. Or being there for your family.'

She stands up so abruptly the chair begins to tip backwards. She turns to steady it but not before I catch the expression on her face. Suddenly, I realise she looks exhausted. Shit. What's that about? My stomach turns over.

'Sam.' I prop myself up to see her better. My tone tells her I've seen what she's hiding. She runs her hand over the top of her head, her back towards me for a moment.

When she faces me, her features are schooled into place. That control. Years of delivering bad news to patients and their loved ones. 'The police are coming to talk to you at nine. I'll come at ten, bring your clothes from the hotel.'

'Sam?' Trying to probe for more. Her eyes resist.

'We'll talk tomorrow.'

Saturday

Chapter Four

London. 11th September 1976

The day dawns grey and misty. I watch the sky lighten from charcoal to slate to smoke to dove. By the time a constable arrives to take my statement, the sun is high enough to be visible but remains shrouded in cloud, a dim and indistinct glow.

As I change into my jeans and shirt in the gents' bathroom, I think about Sam. Now I'm looking for signs, I find them: she's thinner than normal; her skin lacks colour; and the shadows under her eyes are about more than the daily demands of her work. Her hair hasn't been cut in a while and her fidgeting hands – ringless – betray a restless mind.

The reflection in the unframed mirror says I'm not looking much better. Forty-eight hours' beard growth would just about be acceptable on a dig, but I know it doesn't suit me. Thank goodness for Mum's blonde hair because there's no escaping my Celtic heritage in this ginger stubble. The head bandage has been replaced with gauze taped to my head, the hair around sticking up all over the place. Not that that's particularly unusual. And the man's fist has left one hell of a bruise blooming over my cheek bone.

Nothing that won't mend, I can hear Dad's voice in my head. Nature's man, a fifth-generation livestock farmer. And, who knows, perhaps further back than that. In all likelihood, Bren men would have been farming sheep in Wales long before Owen Bren followed Eithne Flanagan back to County Wicklow in 1829.

Maybe I should have been led by my namesake's example and followed Sam to London. Who knows where we would be now if I had? But we were so young. Too young. Would she have had her career if we'd got married? Would the British Library's stacks have brought me the satisfaction I find in being out at a dig site? I tell myself we would have made each other miserable, holding back our desires and goals for the sake of being together.

But nothing has ever come close to what I felt for her.

* * * * * * *

'Ready?'

God, she looks good. Loose, her hair falls in waves almost to her waist. Gone is the white doctor's coat, replaced with a yellow cotton dress, pulled in at the waist in a way that emphasises her curves in all the right places.

'Hmm,' I concede, stowing the toiletry bag in my holdall at the foot of the bed. She raises a hand and presses around the bruise with her little finger. 'How's it look?'

'You'll live, Henry Cooper. Come on, the car's out back.'

She pulls on a denim jacket as we head for a small yellow sports car parked on a side road. I pause at the bonnet as she unlocks the boot.

'What on earth is this?'

'It's a Triumph GT6 coupe, idiot. Don't they allow cars in Cambridge?'

'Not like that, it's far too sexy. The Bursar would have a heart attack.'

'Well, it's about time they injected some life into the place.'

'You seriously expect me to be able to get into something that small?'

She gives me an assessing look. 'Just fold your knees up under your chin,' she suggests. I like the laughter in her eyes, the colour it brings to her cheeks. The wind whips her hair forwards, and she raises a hand to hold it back. The movement brings back a memory, leaning over the rails of Clacton Pier, buffeted by a North Sea gale throwing spray over both of us, laughing and laughing.

'Are we going or not?' She stands with one hand on the open boot, one on her hip, watching me with that mind-reading intensity. She steps aside to allow me to deposit the bag in the boot – I note without comment that another overnight bag is already there – then she unlocks the passenger door and holds it open for me.

'I'm not an invalid,' I grumble, easing into the cramped space.

'No, but you are my patient,' she points out, slamming the door and coming around to the driver's side.

'Am I?' as I watch her settle behind the wheel.

She turns the ignition key, slots the gearstick into reverse. 'They wanted to keep you in for another twenty-four hours, but I said there was a family emergency,' turns to look over her shoulder as she pulls out of the parking space, 'so they agreed to release you into my care as long as I keep a close eye on you.'

'What family emergency?'

She idles the engine, foot on the brake.

'It's Dad.'

'What's he up to now?'

'He's dying.' She slams the car into gear, turns to stare, hard-eyed, out of the windscreen. 'Let me focus on getting us out of London and then I'll explain.'

Chapter Five

Cambridge. 11th September 1976

The clogged arteries of the north circular thin out as we head northwards and the streets of Victorian back-to-backs morph into 1930s suburban semis, which in turn give way to cropped fields and verdant hedgerows. The sun's rays push through the clouds, creating Jacob's ladders on the horizon.

The silence between us is oddly natural. Having delivered the news, I know she needs time to regroup, to settle her emotions before she can tell me more, so I ignore the sick feeling in my stomach and watch the familiar landscape disappear while the nippy little car eats up the miles. Think about Michael. Remember that first visit, that scrappy little thing she was then, all legs and freckles.

I catch her glance across at me and know she's looking for a way to open the conversation.

'You were wearing that same colour, the first time I saw you.' OK, maybe not the safest ground, but it's the first thing that comes to mind.

She frowns. 'I was?'

I touch my hand to my throat. 'Ribbon round your neck. I think it was supposed to be used to hold your hair back, but you had other ideas.'

'My hair had other ideas,' she parries.

'Strangest pair we ever had staying on the farm,' I tease.

'We've never been that conventional,' she concedes.

'Thankfully for me.' She looks away from me, staring at the road ahead. 'Sam,' I soften my tone, 'tell me.'

'He's got pancreatic cancer. The prognosis is weeks, a few months at most.' She holds up one hand as I start to open my mouth. 'Please don't say you're sorry. That's not what this is about.'

'What then?'

She gives me a sideways glance.

'How did your presentation go?' Deflecting? That's not like her.

'Lots of interest. In the techniques as much as the output.'

'What was your topic?'

'A dig in Anatolia in '73. One of the early Christian churches about to be removed for a new office block. I published a paper on it in February.'

'Three years later? You're still not good at getting the work written up then?'

I laugh, mainly to ease the tension. 'You know me. So much work to do, so little time. Blame my specialism. After all, there's a reason they call it rescue archaeology.'

She stops talking and I sit with the silence, knowing she will come back in her own time. I want to reach out, to make physical contact. In the past that would have eased things but it's rather more complicated now.

'I was all set to drive up to Cambridge to see you when they brought you into St Mary's,' she digresses. 'I'd just come on shift and saw the ambulance arrive. The damnedest thing, seeing you like that, lying on the stretcher, blood all over you.' She gives that characteristic gesture of hers when she's internalising something, running her hand flat over the top of her head, down to the back of her neck and pulling her hair to one side, over her shoulder. She sits there for a few moments, her fist resting sideways against her neck, her hair ponytailed in her hand. 'What the universe delivers,' she mutters, to herself more than me. She shakes her head, once, twice, like she's shaking herself out of her thoughts.

'You were coming to Cambridge?' I prompt.

'Yes.' She re-focuses, glances at me then back at the road ahead. 'It's the site. He's got all riled up again.' Frustrated.

'After all these years?'

'I know, I know. But it's this damn summer. The drought has been exposing crop marks all over the place and some bright spark from your place decided to fly over, taking aerial photographs. Now Dad's got it into his head they've found something new.'

'And have they?'

'Who knows? That's not the point.'

'What is the point?'

'He can't handle it,' exasperated. 'Physically, he's not in a state to be doing anything, but mentally he can't let it go. I haven't seen him this animated in years.'

'And?'

'And there aren't the resources to get it done fast enough. And who knows if there's anything there to be found or whether it's all just in his head.'

'Sam, where do I come into this?'

She breathes in deeply and exhales hard. 'Because I need you to go up there to finish it for him.'

* * * * * * *

I know that tone: it brooks no disagreement.

My practical mind runs through the implications. There are three weeks left in the long vac and I'm supposed to be writing lectures and preparing tutorial plans. Never mind the three funding submissions that are sitting on my desk for completion, at least one of which is already on an extended deadline.

And yet, there is that familiar feeling in my gut that I know so well.

'I know I'm asking a lot,' she admits. 'I know Michaelmas term is only weeks away and, knowing you, you've got loads of prep to do because you were far too busy over the summer.'

'Rescuing fourth century Roman remains before some Neanderthal lays tarmac over the top of them.'

'Digging up yet more shards of Samian-ware and the occasional tessera,' she baits me.

'Meaningfully enhancing our understanding of the decline and fall of the Roman Empire in Britain.'

She bursts out laughing at my indignant earnestness. 'I'm sorry. I really should know better than to wind up an academic.'

'I like to think I'm rather more than an academic,' I return, ever so slightly put out.

'Oh God, Eoghan, don't think I don't know how absurd this sounds. A world-renowned…'

'Let's not overdo it.'

'…peerless expert in the highly specialist field of rescue archaeology…'

'OK, OK,' I raise my hands in surrender, 'you've got me.'

'…getting involved with some tinpot little site of no historical significance or archaeological merit…'

'In some northern English backwater,' I contribute.

'…down a farm track in the arse end of nowhere,' she concludes. Then looks directly at me. 'But.'

'But this is Michael.'

'This is Dad.'

'And this is The Obsession.'

****

The sun breaks through properly as we hit the edge of Cambridge and skirt past the Botanical Gardens, heading for the Backs where the river meanders past the most central colleges. The meadows had been cut down several weeks before but the grass beneath is still parched to straw. It will take considerably more days' rain to return the city's common land and greens to their usual lushness.

Sam parks on the road behind King's College. She objects when I pick up both our bags from the car boot but knows better than to insist, even if I am walking wounded. My mother raised me to be a gentleman. At least, she tried.

'So, I assume you have a plan?' I open as we head towards the river.

'I called ahead. They've set me up in the matron's room. Apparently, she's away for another week and I'll be downstairs from your rooms, in case anything happens.'

'I thought you were supposed to be keeping an eye on your patient full time?' I query.

'That's close enough without raising eyebrows.' Raising hers, daring me to disagree. I shrug. Is she disappointed? She moves on. 'Let's drop your things in your room, grab lunch and talk things through.'

We navigate through a group of camera-laden tourists cluttering up the bridge and accumulating around the punt station. College is pleasantly quiet: the students won't be up until early October and many of my colleagues, particularly the married ones, are still away. Indeed, it's a rare pleasure to be here myself, not on a site somewhere.

'How come you don't have a project on the go at the moment?' she wonders.

'You still read minds, then?' I laugh. Or maybe she knows me too well. 'I had a short stint earlier in the summer, part of a large team in London.' We skirt the quad, enjoying the sight of one of the few remaining green lawns in Cambridge. There must be surreptitious night-time watering going on, given the hosepipe ban.

'The Roman one?'

'It's the site of some bank's new headquarters. They had three months to peel back the layers and see what they can find. I joined at the end of term.'

'Anything interesting?'

I indicate the corner staircase to my rooms and Sam leads the way. 'Second floor.' She keeps going up the stairs. 'Some rubbed-out remains of the old city walls, fragments of mosaic work. This is me.'

My rooms are at the far end of the short corridor, a white-painted four-panelled door with a rattly black Bakelite handle, loose from age and wear. A capital F marks out the room, my name handwritten in black ink by someone with a talent for careful copperplate on a card inserted in a brass frame screwed to the adjacent wall. Sam runs her index finger over it, a slight smile showing at the corner of her mouth.

'Dad said you made professor. Congratulations.'

I dig my keys out of my jacket pocket and unlock the door. 'Thanks. You'll have to forgive the mess,' immediately feeling the need to apologise as I push the door wide and invite her to enter ahead of me.

'The state of an academic's rooms is hardly going to come as a surprise to me, Eoghan,' she observes drily. 'I can't imagine you're any messier than Dad.'

To be fair, it could be worse. The large desk against the opposite wall is the typical pile of academic viscera, though temporarily without the usual accumulation of essays and dissertations waiting to be marked. One wall is fitted with shelves, floor to ceiling, and crammed with books in an organised array, including somewhere my own contributions to the canon.

The far end of the room is for tutorials. Two mismatched sofas ranged opposite each other, an armchair in between that I use to command some semblance of control and a few odd dining chairs scattered around in case the group should expand in size. Not that it has so far in the three years I've been here; archaeology doesn't attract large crowds.

The door to my bedroom is ajar but it looks like the housekeeper has been in to change the sheets so at least the bed is made. I drop Sam's bag by the front door and cross the room to deposit mine in the bedroom.

A small kitchenette – little more than cupboards, a fridge, a sink, a kettle and a toaster – is tucked in the corner. 'I'd offer you tea,' sniffing at the remains of a bottle of milk, 'but you might have to take it black.'

'I'll wait until there's something better on offer,' Sam decides as she roams around. 'These are nice rooms,' she reflects, and it makes me look at them with her eyes.

Three mullioned windows overlooking the court cast the bright midday sunlight into the room and bring a warmth to counteract the starkness of the white walls. The college furnished the rooms with just enough care to take the edge off: an orange rug in the sitting area, a couple of similarly toned cushions on the sofas and a scattering of prints showing the college in earlier times on the walls.

I know others make the effort to personalise their rooms, but I've never felt the need. Maybe I'm the proverbial rolling stone, wherever I lay my hat and all that. Likely it's the product of having been so many years in the field, living out of a rucksack. I don't accumulate the artefacts others surround themselves with. That's not me. I'm about the memories and experiences, not the things. All I have is two photographs that sit beside my bed: a black and white image of my parents, standing before the front door of our farmhouse; and a fading colour picture of the three of us – Michael, me and Sam, my arms around their shoulders, hers around my waist in the Master's garden at Michael's college.

I turn away, perhaps moving too quickly because I'm suddenly lightheaded and put out a hand to steady myself. Sam's there immediately, one hand on my arm, one on my shoulder, looking into my face.

'OK?'

I close my eyes and wait for the feeling to pass. 'It's nothing.'

'Do you want to sit down?'

'No, it's gone. I think maybe I should eat.'

Sam's hand discretely checks my pulse as she decides if she agrees with this self-assessment. She nods. 'OK, let's eat.'

* * * * * * *

A short walk through the city brings us to a small café on a side street, sufficiently tucked away to appeal to the locals more than the tourists. Sam orders sandwiches and coffee for both of us.

The air is warm and the café is quiet, only us at a table by the window and two older women over by the till. From the kitchen comes the clatter of plates and pots, and the tinny sound of pop music from a transistor radio. The shouts and laughter of children surface from the mingled noise of people outside.

Sam is watching me. 'I'm sorry I was so blunt earlier. When I told you about Dad.'

'For someone who's had quite a lot of practice delivering bad news, you certainly didn't sugar-coat the pill,' I admit.

'I'd been round and round in my head how to tell you. It came out badly.' Her hands are restless. 'I know how much he means to you.'

'Sam, he's your dad. I should be consoling you.'

'Yes. Still.'

'Still,' I agree. I sit back in my chair and think about Michael. My teacher. My mentor. My second father. Their old house not far from here, organised and orderly thanks to Sam, with Michael tucked in his chair in the corner of the lounge-diner, protected on two sides by a bookshelf and his rolltop desk, endless cups of tea always at hand.

And then from somewhere – maybe Sam's perfume? – I catch the scent of a late summer rose and, in my memory, I'm looking through the window at the back where tendrils from the neighbour's rampant rambling rose reached towards the open window. Looking out at the garden beyond where Sam was lying on her stomach on the lawn, propped up on her elbows, a book open flat on the ground before her, kicking alternating heels towards the backs of her legs. It was a childish action born of the memory of freedom and joy in earlier summers, but I noticed how that colt-like litheness she had when they first came to Glendalough had given way to new curves and felt the mental shift from amused brotherly tolerance to something else. The neighbour's tabby cat, wandering across the grass to rub its cheek against her legs, caused Sam to twist round to tickle its ears and, as she did so, she caught sight of me at the window and raised her hand to acknowledge me. Something in my expression made her stop halfway through the gesture and I saw in her face – her young, open, trusting face – a new knowing beyond her years. As if she knew me better than I knew myself.

The rattle of china as the waitress delivers our order calls me back to the present.

'You were miles away,' Sam notes.

And a lifetime ago. How is it possible to forget how much you loved someone? Are we such fickle creatures that love only exists when the person is present or front of mind? Or maybe it's always there, waiting to be recalled, waiting for a moment of unawareness to remind us of our true selves. I present many faces to the world. Only two things ever make me feel whole: when I lose myself in a dig and loving this woman. 'Sam…'

'I remember the first time we came to your farm.'

'You were such a scrap of a thing,' I re-join. Then recall: 'And he was so focused. I'd never known anyone like him.'

'That's how I want to think about Dad. That single-mindedness. Before this thing took hold of him.'

Does she mean the cancer? Or The Obsession?

'Is there nothing they can do?'

She shakes her head, her eyes on where she is absentmindedly stirring her coffee. 'It's gone too far for treatment or an operation.' She rests her chin on her hand. 'Maybe that's a blessing. I'm not sure he's got the appetite to fight it anyway. It would be too much of a distraction.'

'From the site?' She nods. 'Tell me.'

She glances out of the window as she gathers her thoughts. I can see the medic's mind at work. Sifting through the facts, isolating the salient points then gathering them together in a way she wants to be accessible to her listener. It infuriates the historian in me, always wanting as much data as possible to assess situations for myself.

'The university and local archaeological group are on site for the summer, so up until two weeks ago he was down there most days. Driving them all nuts, no doubt,' a ghost of a smile rises and dies in a moment. 'The aerial photographs came in mid-July from Adam Richards,' she glances at me to check my colleague's name registers with me. 'They seemed to change everything, like he'd found the missing link. Now he keeps insisting they're looking in the wrong place. But Ernest Montague is leading the dig and he's having none of it. They're turning up plenty of finds around the manor house and the main street. No earth-shattering insights but enough material to keep them all smiling.'

'Where does he think they should be looking?'

'The lower village, beyond the church.'

'Why?'

She shrugs. 'I don't know. He says there's a building there that they haven't seen. He's grasping at straws, looking for signs of something.' She stops, not wanting to acknowledge what we both know this is. I say it for her.

'Or someone.' Her eyes fire with frustration, not at my suggestion but at the tenacity of this long fixation. 'The missing lady. The one he believes has been wiped from the records.'

Chapter Six

Cambridge. 11th September 1976

She's trying to hide it from me, but her frustration is simmering as we walk back to college.

'Sam, you can't fight it. Not now.'

The noise of disgust in the back of her throat is expressive. 'This damn obsession. How much could he have done with his career if he hadn't got side-tracked with this?'

I glance at her. 'That's not what this is about.'

'Isn't it?' Sullen almost. No, stubborn. Because she knows the truth and knows too that I won't let her avoid it.

'You're angry but it's with the cancer. The Obsession is just an easier target because you know you can't do anything about the cancer.'

She almost growls in response, her hands tensing as if she wants to throttle me. 'Just once, can't you sympathise instead? God, how can a man have so much insight into dead people but no empathy for the living?'

I almost laugh out loud at that. Thankfully, I check myself in time; humour is hardly helpful right now. I push my hands into my pockets to resist a sudden temptation to put my arm around her.

'I can't tell you how hard it is to be a doctor and know there's nothing in all my knowledge and experience that is of use to him now.' Her voice is low, her eyes fixed, her arms wrapped around her waist. I consider for long seconds before responding.

'That's not quite true, is it?' She frowns at me. 'Maybe you've reached the limits of your medical knowledge, but you've always been about more than the physical form, haven't you? Maybe that's what he needs more at this point.'

That brings her up short. I stop walking too and turn back to face her.

For an instant, she looks surprisingly fragile. This woman who is stronger than any I have known. Intelligent. Single-minded. Compassionate. The one everyone else turns to when they need help. I wonder who's there for her now when she's in need.

'I didn't think you believed in any of that.'

'I don't.' I stop myself because the least I can do is give her my honesty. 'At least,' I admit, 'I don't think I do.'

I shrug and start walking again as I cast around for a way to explain. She falls in beside me. 'I guess being raised Catholic made me more open to such ideas than the rationalist in me would like to admit. Sometimes when I'm on a dig, when I'm really focused on what I'm doing, I can sense the people I'm investigating. Not in the abstract, not generically. It's very specific: a sense of individuals, personalities, motivations, emotions even. But what is that? Is it just me putting together fragments of what I know about the era with what I know about human nature? Or is it more, like tapping into an echo of that past?'

Sam's quiet. And as we turn the corner on the cobbled street and into a shaft of sunlight pushing between the warm sandstone buildings, the city is hushed too. The body of the ancient university, wrapping around us, clothed in these centuries-old stones, breathes softly.

'I've never heard you talk this way,' she considers.

'I've never said any of that to anyone.'

'I've seen too much not to believe in life after death,' she shares. 'So many of my colleagues go the other way: they insist on believing only what's in front of them. But I've seen people at the point of death and, to me, it's almost palpable, the moment when consciousness departs from the body. And I've talked to people who've come back after their heart has stopped – and to all intents and purposes they *were* dead – and every one of them talks about something that exists on the other side.'

I nod to the porter as we re-enter college and head towards my staircase.

'Have you talked to Michael about it?'

She shakes her head. 'I can't get him to talk about anything but the site.' She pushes the heel of her hands into her eyes to force back tears.

I stand aside to let Sam precede me up the stairs and along the corridor, then pause as I push the key into the lock and look down at her. 'So, you think you have to help him find peace by getting answers?' I suggest.

Up close, I can see deep weariness in the shadows under her eyes, tension in the frown lines between her brows. Her shoulders sag as she stops resisting. 'Yes. It's why I decided it was time to come to find you.'

That gives me pause. 'When did you find out about the cancer?'

She purses her lips before she responds: 'In April.' Five months. And she's only telling me now. She lays her hand flat on my chest; she means to comfort me, but it has quite a different effect. 'I'm sorry, Eoghan, he didn't want you to know.'

'What, until later?' The bottom drops out of my stomach.

'At all.'

She turns the handle to open the door and reaches past me to grab her bag. 'I need to sleep,' she avoids, unable to look at me. 'I came straight off the night shift. Let's meet later for dinner.'

* * * * * * *

I close the door to my rooms behind me and stand for a while with one hand on the jamb, lost.

This man means so much to me. From the moment I was introduced to him, standing in the dark, cool, stone-flagged hallway at home, briefcase in one hand, old-fashioned suitcase in the other and a gangly teenage daughter hovering in the sunlight behind, I was drawn to him. There is an energy to him that comes from his singular focus on his subject, but he's also a man who has stepped out of time.

Occasionally perplexed to find himself fulfilling societal roles – professor, tutor, father – his reality centres only on delving into others' realities, piecing together the fragments they leave behind, the piecemeal footprint of their existence that, threaded together, recreates that life again.

The empty feeling in my stomach turns to nausea and propels me across the room in search of water. I down the glass quickly and refill it. Sweat breaks out on my skin and I feel an inexplicable chill though I know the room is warm because the early afternoon sun is streaming in through the windows.

I move the cushions to one end of the sofa and lie on my side facing the windows, letting the sunlight warm me. Specks of dust in the air catch the sunlight and spark gold, then fall and fade. My head feels heavy, pressure still where the gauze covers the gash in my scalp. I fold my arms across my chest and stare at where the leaded windowpanes frame wispy white clouds against an azure sky.

Chapter Seven

Cardiff Castle. September 1318

It is so cold in the dark. The air has the bite of winter, dank, clammy and heavy, though it is not yet Michaelmas. Moisture runs down the wall and seeps through her clothes where her back rests against the stones.

The dampness fills the air with its own mouldy smell, mingling with the earthen floor to become the smell of when they bury someone in the churchyard at home.

The darkness is deep, the cell invisible in night's blackness, unable to see much beyond her own breath misting before her face. But she feels a bitter wind coming in off the sea and blasting through unseen gaps in the high walls. She smells salt in the air, can almost taste it on her tongue, dry and swollen from lack of food.

Her small body aches from the cold, from two days' hard ride, from long hours in a huddled position on the floor. She shivers and tries to draw her arms closer around her raised knees but her muscles, aching with cold, protest with pain and tears sting her eyes.

She has tried not to sleep but how could she not? There is no life left in her. But it fills her with remorse: elsewhere in the castle, her father is awaiting the sun's rise on his last day on this earth.

She lifts her head to seek her mother, but she is little more than a denser darkness on the other side of the void. They have not moved either, Mama and Matilde, kneeling at the prie dieu, the only furniture in the room.

Twisting her arm behind, she lays her hand flat against the stones where the water drips, then touches it against her face, her parched lips. Cold as ice.

She closes her eyes because it makes no difference to the darkness, but memories play across her mind.

Papa in the Great Hall, forced to his knees below the dais, Gruffydd trying to resist, too proud but too weak, both men thin and aged from two years' imprisonment. Mama standing rigidly erect, flanked by her other five sons. The stifling room, crammed with bodies from wall to wall trying to glimpse this traitor – their hero – brought from the Tower for trial.

Hugh Despenser, the new lord of Glamorgan, sitting back in his throne-like chair, watching Sir William Fleminge direct events on his behalf, tracing the detailed carving on the armrest with his finger. The brilliant colours of his dress, of the covering on the table before him, of the tapestry strung up behind him. The contrast with the hordes standing below, all in workaday clothes.

Reading out the accusations – nay, crimes, with the accused already deemed guilty. The murmurings of dissent beginning softly at first, the growing hubbub with more joining in. The first voice to cry out loud in defence, then the next and the next.

Wasn't he just defending his family, his people? Trying to protect them from the brutality of Payn de Turbeville? Didn't they know we were starving? Two years of rain, two years of blighted crops. They had no food, yet this English lord sought to take what little they had while women and children died and men scavenged on dead dogs to survive. Llywelyn Bren had risen up for them, challenging the injustice of de Turbeville's tyranny, defending his dependants as any true lord should. How can he be punished for that?

Pride – in her father and the Welshmen ready to speak for him – opposing the sickening dread within her and a spark of hope arising. But soon snuffed out by a shout from the chamberlain, Despenser's men drawing their swords high, menacing over the gathering. The protest dying and the air falling still and silent.

And then the sentence. The chamberlain standing over the two kneeling men, speaking over their heads to those beyond. Execution. All the air beaten out of her body, bile filling her throat and a chill skittering across her skin. No! The voice inside her crying out as blood beats in her head, even as she tries to stand as rigidly as her mother, unflinching, betraying no emotion.

All the time, Despenser sitting in silence. There is darkness in this man, no hint of doubt or compassion in his face. Emptiness too. Like all the power in the realm will not be enough for him.

And then her father moving to his feet, rising awkwardly with his manacled wrists and ankles. Sir William falling back nervously and armed men moving forward, but he only squares his shoulders and addresses himself to the man on the dais. Acknowledges his crime, embraces the sentence. And asks that this be visited on he and he alone as the one responsible for the uprising.

The Hall hushing. Everyone waiting.

Until the light changes. Suddenly, the sun breaks through the heavy rain clouds, lifting the gloom, and its rays, piercing the high windows, fall in long shafts of light on Gruffydd, kneeling beside his father, until his red hair blazes like flame. Seeing it, Llywelyn silently places his hands on his eldest son's head and closes his eyes in prayer and blessing.

Shock and faith respond with audible intakes of breath; surely this is a sign from God? Watching the blood drain from the chamberlain's face, instinctively crossing himself and looking doubtfully towards the dais.

Despenser rising, standing for a long moment, and taking his time to look slowly from one side of the room to the other, quelling the masses with his will, with his arrogance, with his hold over their lives.

He sentences Gruffydd to imprisonment in Cardiff Castle for an indeterminate term and their mother with him as surety for the acquiescence of the rest of the family; the rest are to be separated, scattered across England, forced into households with no status and no protection.

And Llywelyn Bren, for his betrayal of their king, for his treachery in raising rebellion in the crown's Welsh lands, faces the ultimate punishment: execution by drawing, hanging and quartering. If he wants to take this punishment on himself, there will be no sword to end his life quickly, there will be no mercy.

A gull screeches outside and her awareness snaps back to her body, icy and stiff in this dungeon.

'Come, pray with us, Christiane.'

Now she can see her mother's form across the other side of the room, her face upturned to a plain wooden cross, poorly carved and uneven, nailed on the wall above, and Matilde's head bent over her interlaced fingers.

Matilde shuffles across on her knees and Christiane squeezes in between her mother and her nurse, pressing her palms together and hoping for prayer to come.

'You must be brave today, Christiane.' Her mother's voice is low and soft, but her intent is like steel as she holds her daughter's chin and looks into her young face. 'Today, you must show the world what it means to be the daughter of Llywelyn Bren. We will show no tears. We will show no fear. If you cannot face what you see, think yourself back at home. Imagine yourself hidden away in a corner as usual or sitting beside the fire, one of the dogs at your feet. Can you do that?'

She nods. 'What will happen to me after today?'

Her mother is silent for a moment. 'I know not,' she confesses, covering her uncertainty by kissing her daughter's forehead.

The sound of the lock being turned draws their attention towards the door. A guard opens it, bearing a torch, and stands aside to allow the chamberlain to enter.

'The sun rises.' The man's voice is harsh, and the flickering flame shows malice in his face. 'It is time.'

Christiane and Mathilde look to Lleucu for guidance. She crosses herself and pushes against the prie dieu to rise up from her knees but, stiff from hours of prayer, she stumbles. The guard comes forward to aid her. 'Lady Senghennydd…'

'Not anymore, fool,' the chamberlain chastises. 'This is the wife of a convicted traitor. She is our prisoner, without a home and without a name. And soon to be without a husband.'

Lleucu appreciates the guard's support and draws herself up.

'William Fleminge,' she stands before the chamberlain, looking up into his face, a head shorter than he but full of force and command, 'you will come to regret what you do this day, for turning against those you should serve in favour of a master who buys your obedience.'

Even in the dim light, Christiane can see his face drain of colour. 'I do not fear your curses, harridan!' he spits, though the tremor in his voice belies his words. 'Come!' He turns on his heel and strides across the room.

'I will not have the child witness this.' Lleucu's words halt him at the door. 'She must remain here.'

He barely glances at Christiane. 'She will watch,' he negates. 'She will see what happens to traitors in these lands. As will all who think to challenge my lord.' He scurries from the room before she can counter him.

Lleucu's body is rigid. Christiane senses the anger and grief and despair, and how she fights to bring them under control. She hardly moves and yet Christiane knows the moment she has readied herself. Matilde must sense it too because she places her hands on Christiane's shoulders and guides her as they leave the cell.

The Great Hall is almost empty as they enter from the spiral staircase in the corner. Through the high windows the sky is full of heavy clouds, blocking out the sun.

The few servants who are still about their business stare as they emerge. Matilde pulls Christiane close and protectively sweeps the hem of her cloak around the child, as if she would hide her charge away.

Sir William hurries them across the tiled floor towards the massive oak doors, flanked by two guards.

Christiane becomes aware of a huge noise outside, muffled by the solid timber and iron. The whole world slows and intensifies; she can hear her heart's beat thudding in her ears and the sound of her own breath, in, out, the sting in her skin where the heat of the room counters the biting cold from below.

The guards pull open the doors and the noise rips the air, tearing over her into the silent room behind and pounding against her head. It is the baying of hounds before the hunt but – her blood runs cold – those are human voices, not animals, crying for the chase, for the kill. A multitude of voices, women as well as men, chanting, shouting, screaming. Incomprehensible, unintelligible, base.

She stumbles against Lleucu as the guards push them down the long flight of steps and into the mêlée in the inner bailey. Her mother turns to look but she no longer truly sees her daughter; she has turned inward, and her eyes betray no sign of recognition.

Christiane looks to Matilde for reassurance but one of the guards is pulling the nurse away even as the other pushes Christiane forward.

Blindly, she follows through the throng, hands snatching at her clothes, her hands, her hair. They are crushed so closely about her she can't even see the sky, only feels her feet slipping in the mud they have churned up. Her leg catches as they push her up rough-hewn wooden steps and blood runs down as she starts to ascend.

The platform brings her out above their heads, and she looks back across the hordes towards the keep. Their path through has already been swallowed up as spectators push for a better view.

'Courage, Christiane,' Lleucu reminds her, her eyes fixed on the distant castle wall where the gate is opening.

Above the cacophony, horses' hooves ring out on cobbles and there is an instant hush. Then they catch the shouts of those following the cart and all take up the cry until it fills her ears.

Fingers of fear reach out from her heart and creep like ice through her veins. Her lungs tighten and her breath shortens, her throat closing with emotion. She has seen dead bodies before but never watched a man be killed. Is it like watching an animal be slaughtered? Can she pretend this is not her father, her beloved, adored, honourable father, and think of him as just a man, any man?

The crowd parts where the horses pull alongside. She cannot see the hurdle he was attached to as they drew his tethered body through the town, but she sees the guards bend down to untie him and raise him up.

His face is almost unrecognisable, covered in swellings and cuts and blood and mud. His beard has been removed, roughly hacked away, and it makes him look like a washed-out shade of himself. His eyes are unfocused, like he seeks to remove himself from this world before his body gives in, a body so beaten and broken that it takes five men to man-handle him onto the platform, where he lies in a heap, unable to raise himself up.

Sir William steps forward and she sees sickness in his face: the situation is out of control and this execution risks turning into a riot.

'Llywelyn Bren, you have been convicted of treason against the Crown.' His voice shakes and carries no distance. The mob demands more and he tries to raise it. 'Treason will always be met with the most severe punishment,' he opines tremulously, and the noise resolves into a constant chant. Death. Death. Death. The chamberlain pales and steps back. 'God have mercy,' he mutters and signals for the executioner to proceed.

She stares across the other side of the platform to where her brothers are lined up, surrounded by men in Gloucester's colours, armed with pikes and staffs, ready to quell any sign of rebellion. Their hands are bound but their heads are unbent, and, to a man, they stare, unflinchingly, towards their father as the rope is slung around his neck.

The sky darkens and a colder wind whips against her face. *Don't look*, says the voice in her mind. *What you see can never be unseen.* She tries to picture in her mind their Hall at home in Senghennydd. The fire ablaze in the hearth. Light and warm and safe. The dogs scrapping in the corner. The servants setting out supper. But the here-and-now intrudes, the noise is too strong.

She turns her head to stare out across the watchers, anywhere to avoid looking towards her father, even as she catches the motion of him being dragged across to the gallows and yanked upwards.

As she stares, she glimpses faces that are looking at her, not watching her father's body hanging in the air. Welshmen and women, appalled by this injustice but here to stand in respect at the passing of their loved lord. Ashen-faced, standing straight and silent among the noise and hatred.

Their solidarity chokes her throat and tears form with heated, hated prickles at the back of her eyes. She tries to force them back but to no avail. Then the wind blasts into her face as the clouds break. Heaven weeps, and she turns her face up to the sky to let the heavy rain fall on her face, filling her eyes until any tears become indistinguishable.

She looks down and sees an old woman watching her, her face carved with malice. She shouts at Christiane, but the wind whips her words away even as it blows Christiane's hair across her face. Waves of malevolence come off this woman, but she cannot tear her eyes away and, in a flash, experiences the emptiness of the world without her father. A widow hollowed out with grief and loss, constrained for years in this castle where she saw her husband torn apart. Gruffydd eaten away with pent-up hatred, bent to the will of this English lord. Brothers lost and alone in households where they are treated with disdain and contempt.

And for her? An empty unknown stretches before her, a black and unlit path, not knowing if she will ever again feel love and surety and peace.

The thought of losing him overwhelms her, this powerful and present influence in her life, her security, her moral guide, his strength and physical presence gone, cast adrift without his assuredness in knowing what is right.

No! She cannot let them see her weakness. These ignorant animals. All humanity and fellow-feeling driven out of them by these brutal Englishmen. They are not worth her tears. She will not bring pain and shame on her family by giving in to them.

The anger drives her blood and stops the tears, fires heat in her heart even as her limbs tighten and go rigid. She sees herself from the outside now, the rain streaming down her face, matting her hair to her head, running inside her clothes and across her skin. Her heart is thumping hard in her chest and pulses at her neck and in her wrists. Her nails dig into the flesh of her palms, her fingers tight with strain.

And her eyes stare, her unblinking focus on the old woman. The lines of her face, the movement of her mouth as she chants and chants and chants, her hands beating that rhythm, her feet stamping. A thumping taken up by the rest. Thud. Thud. Thud. Death. Death. Death.

The world falls away until it is just her and the woman, darkness all around them both, binding them together, isolating the two of them in this long moment of murder. Blood pounds in her temple, its noise filling her ears, the taste of it bitter and metallic in her mouth.

The woman's eyes turn towards the middle of the platform as her mouth becomes an open scream of elation. And the baying pierces Christiane's isolation, an extended screech filling her ears. Until it is replaced with the scream of another voice, a beloved voice that calls her eyes to him against her will.

He has been cut down and lies again in the middle of the stage, supported behind by one of the guards who tries to raise him up for all to see. The executioner is on his knees before him, his hand wrapped around the hilt of a knife, black-red and slick with blood that runs down his arms. He hacks with the knife and her father cries out again, weak now, his eyes turned to heaven, his head falling back.

The executioner grasps Llywelyn's entrails with both hands, slippery with blood, struggling to hold them, and pushes to his feet, holding the intestines high to show them to the crowd, then flings them into the burning brazier. Sickness bursts through Christiane's body and she tries to hold it in as the noise erupts again, feels it burn in her nose, her throat, her gut.

The woman turns, her gaze locks with Christiane's and she screeches her delight, her glee, her hatred.

A rage like none she has ever known drives through Christiane. Redness fills her eyes, her ears, her head. Impotent anger floods through her, demanding to be let out, to fight, to hurt, to kill. A scream builds and builds in her chest but has nowhere to go and it scythes through her heart, her mind, her soul.

In her head it mingles with her father's final scream as they cut out his heart. And something breaks within her. For a moment more, she feels the sting of the rain driving in her face, the lash of the icy wind. Then waves of relief as the nails digging in her palms release, the rage lets go of her limbs and the world darkens around her. Until all that remains is the scream, echoing in her ears.

Chapter Eight

Cambridge. 11th September 1976

The scream tears through the air and forces me to my feet, every cell in my body driven by an instinctive need to protect, to defend. I'm standing before I even know I'm awake, my head thick and heavy, my eyes struggling to focus. Immediately, I'm overcome by nausea, bitterness rising rapidly in my throat. As I make it to the door, Sam appears on the other side, but I push past her to the bathroom beyond. I just make it to the toilet before I start vomiting violently.

It goes on until I'm retching with nothing coming up, my throat and nose burning with acid from my stomach. I hock and spit to clear my airways and slide across to prop my back up against the bath, my body drenched in sweat.

Sam runs a flannel under the tap and hands to it me, placing her palm against my forehead. 'God, you're freezing!'

As she says it, I start to shake uncontrollably, and my joints and muscles are stiff and achy as if from being locked in place. 'Sam,' my teeth chattering, 'I feel like hell.' I struggle to get the words out and I think I'm slurring.

She checks my pulse, which I can tell her is slow and thready, and looks into my eyes.

'We need to get you warm,' she decides. She disappears into my rooms and comes back with blankets from my bed and extra clothes. 'We can't go in there, it's absolutely freezing. Here, put these on,' she hands me the pullovers and coat, but my hands won't work, and she helps me into them like a child before wrapping the blankets around me. Then she sits down on the floor next to me and pulls me against her, rubbing her hands hard on my arms and legs to get the blood moving.

Slowly, my body warms, my skin prickling painfully. My head is tucked against Sam's shoulder, one arm around my neck; my shallow breathing is out of kilter with hers, the easy rise and fall of her chest. I close my eyes and focus on the warmth seeping through me.

Eventually, after long minutes, she speaks. 'What happened, Eoghan?' Her voice has that soft, coaxing tone she uses with patients. 'It's 68 degrees outside but your room is like an ice box.'

I keep my eyes closed, seeing again those impossible images.

'I think I was dreaming.'

I can almost feel her frown. 'About what?'

'The execution of Llywelyn Bren.'

'Who?'

'Llywelyn Bren. He was a medieval Welsh lord, executed for treason in 1318.'

'Bren? Like you?'

'Yes. I remember Dad telling us the stories, how he led a rebellion after years of harvest failures and famine left the people starving.'

She shakes her head in confusion. 'What does that have to do with your room being freezing?' I can't answer that. All I know is that it feels the same as that girl felt in the castle dungeon. Sam pauses for a moment. 'Let me check your room. We should get you into bed.'

'Best offer I've had all week,' I joke feebly as she leaves the bathroom. She's back a moment later, a baffled expression on her face. 'It's fine, the temperature is completely normal.' She shakes her head. 'If I hadn't seen it for myself… Christ, Eoghan, my breath froze in front of me!' She leans down to help me to my feet and supports me through to the bedroom; I lie down on the bed, huddled in all the blankets.

'Sam, I'm still cold. Come under here with me, will you?'

She stands with her hands on her hips, a slight smile on her lips. 'You think that old ploy will work with me?' she jibes. 'I'll make you some tea.'

'Make it coffee,' I advise to her retreating back. 'No milk, remember?'

The sounds of her pottering around my room are comfortingly mundane after those shocking scenes. When she brings in two mugs, she settles down beside me on the bed.

'It's going to sound mad,' I reflect, 'but it's like I was actually there. Not just dreaming it, experiencing it.'

'Was it cold in the dream?'

I nod. 'There were three women in prison, awaiting the execution. Well, two women and a child. Christiane. It was so cold. Are you thinking this was psychosomatic?'

'Perhaps,' she concurs. Of course, it doesn't explain the temperature in the room; the thought hangs unspoken between us. 'Who were the women?'

'The wife and daughter of Llywelyn Bren. And the child's nurse. Who I think had been the mother's nurse before that.' Where did *that* come from? 'Eleven years old and they made her watch her father being hanged and disembowelled. She was so young. Small for her age, slight of frame like her mother. That pale Celtic skin and flame red hair.'

Sam stills, and I can feel tension grip her body. 'That's a strange amount of detail to have from a dream,' she analyses distantly.

'I guess,' slightly offhand because there's so much more that I'm not admitting to her.

'Do you know much about this Bren ancestor?'

'Not much from Dad's stories,' I offer, slightly evasive.

Because the truth is I feel like I know everything. As if all that girl's knowledge is now mine. At least, all her knowing up to that point in her life. I can see their family home, the places she likes to hide from her brothers, the books she likes to read. Hell, I even know the names of their dogs and horses and servants! I was accessing her world as she saw and knew it, but I was still an observer, standing outside of her.

I realise Sam is waiting. 'He was lord of two manors near Caerphilly. Two years' harvests were destroyed by almost constant rain. The uprising came in 1316. Although actually he started that because he thought Edward II was going to have him executed after he had a disagreement with Edward's man in Glamorgan.'

'Eoghan, you're not making much sense,' Sam struggles. I shrug helplessly. I'm disorientated, finding it hard to reconnect with the present and struggling to put thoughts together, which is not like me.

'Perhaps Michael can explain it better. He's sure to know,' I suggest.

'That'll have to wait, then,' she pulls her legs up against her chest, defensively. 'I can't take you up there now.'

'What?'

'This has to be related to your head injury,' Sam gestures towards my bandage. 'It says to me you're still suffering from concussion, so you have to rest. Travel is out of the question.'

Denial – and an icy, fear-driven rage like nothing I've ever known – shoots through me. 'Like fuck it is!'

My reaction is so violent that Sam flinches. The shock registers on her face. 'Eoghan,' hesitant now.

It's gone as fast as it came. The rushing noise in my ears drops away and all that's left is adrenalin coursing through my veins, my heart rate elevated. 'What the hell…?' I rub my hand over my eyes. 'I'm sorry, Sam, that wasn't me. I…' How do I explain without sounding insane? 'I have to go, Sam. I don't know why. Whatever this is, it's tied up with Michael. And the site.'

A strangled sound of disgust – despair? – catches in Sam's throat and she pushes off the bed and strides out of the room. I hear a loud, dull thud, like she's hit or thrown something.

I haul myself out of bed, but my head is weak, and I stay sitting on the side until she returns to the doorway.

'Please.' She's schooled her features to disguise the depth of her feelings. 'Please don't let this take you over as well.'

'I get it, Sam.'

'Do you?' she challenges, coming to stand in front of me. 'Really? Do you know how it's felt all these years to see The Obsession grow and grow in him until he's unable to think or talk about anything else? Do you know how it hurts to see someone you love so much lose touch with reality? How frustrating it is to try to hold onto them and to know that nothing you do will stop them slipping away?' She's staring at her two hands, palms turned up, like she's watching sand slide through her fingers. 'What have I started?' she asks herself, closing her eyes and running one hand through her hair.

I reach out and, taking her other hand, gently pull her to me until she's standing between my knees. Her hands naturally come to my shoulders as my arms go around her waist and I hold her close. Gradually, the resistance eases out of her, and I feel her cheek come to rest on my head, her fingers in my hair. I close my eyes and enjoy the warmth and closeness of her, her familiar scent and shape. Gone so long but still the same.

Eventually, she eases back from me, balance restored. 'You seem to have warmed up now,' she observes with a smile.

'I'm starving,' I observe as my stomach grumbles. 'What time is it?'

She checks her watch. 'Almost nine.'

'What?'

'You were asleep for hours. That's why I came to find you.'

I shake my head. 'I had no idea. I thought I was only out for a matter of minutes.'

'Let's go down to Hall,' she suggests. 'We should be in time.'

The staff are clearing away plates as we enter but they manage to find us two portions of coq au vin.

'Can I suggest we find a safer subject while we're eating?' looking at her across the refectory table. 'Tell me what's going on in your life. How's Paul?' I'm bemused when she bursts out laughing.

'That's a safer subject?' she queries. 'I know you've noticed I'm not wearing my wedding ring.' She sobers quickly. 'Paul's gone.'

'Gone?'

'We separated eight months ago. Dad didn't tell you?'

'We haven't spoken in a while.'

She shrugs at the expression on my face. 'It hadn't been right between us for years. It just took a long time for both of us to agree on that.'

'Was anyone else involved?'

'No, nothing like that. Yes,' holding up a hand to forestall me, 'I know you would like to have a reason to think badly of him. Don't think I'm not aware of what Dad thought of him.'

'He never said...' I start to deny.

'He didn't have to. I read both of you like a book.' Unfortunately, that's true. Which means she also knows how resentful I am that she moved on so quickly after me. For a moment, that long-harboured resentment resurfaces, but I suppress it before it can take hold; I've been to that empty place before, and I don't relish going there again.

'Where are you living?' That's it, try small-talk.

'A flat near the hospital. At least that makes work easier. The house sold within days of us putting it on the market and we haven't seen each other since. It's remarkable,' she mulls, 'how easy it is to walk away from ten years of marriage.'

'Ten years?' That shocks me. 'Is that how long it's been?' A decade since we split up. She'll know that's what I'm thinking.

'Do you even know what year it is?' she deflects. 'Or are you becoming as disconnected as all those other ancient academics?'

'There's something about focusing on the past that makes you lose track of time.' I can see that makes her think about Michael, but she pushes the thought away.

'And you? Is there anyone special in your life?' Another woman might feign nonchalance; Sam just looks me directly in the face. It has the effect of demanding equal directness from me, all the usual self-defensive nonsense about not having enough room in my life instantly dissipating.

'There have been women. Nothing lasts.'

'Because you don't want it to.' It's a statement, not a question.

'I still don't know how to make it work. Being away so much.' Long-distance relationships fail. We both know that.

'And that hasn't changed since you came to Cambridge?'

'I'm still away a lot outside of term. There's always some dig or other that needs help.' I hesitate to ask the next question, but I need to know. 'What condition is Michael in?'

I can feel the daughter's distress in her warring with the doctor's dispassionate distance. 'He was OK for the first months. Focusing on work helps. Much as I hate it, I know it keeps him going. But he's weakening now. I can see it, however much he tries to hide it from me.'

'Why didn't he want me to know?'

'He didn't say.'

'Sam.' She'll have a view, even so.

She folds her hands in her lap. 'I don't think he could bear to have you remember him this way. You've hero-worshipped him from the day you met. And he loved you like a son from that first summer.' It's almost an accusation.

'Sam, he loves you more than anyone,' I strive to reassure her.

'I know that,' she affirms. 'I think Marilyn leaving the way she did, the only thing he could do with that love was channel it towards me.' I've never got used to her talking about her mother this way. But then, she never knew the mother who left before Sam was even walking. 'But the affinity between the two of you was so much more. Believe me,' she reassures, 'I don't have a problem with that. Though, God knows, I did wonder once or twice if we were together just because I'm his daughter.'

'You're kidding, right?' The thought riles me more than it should.

'Maybe. Anyway,' dismissing the subject, 'that's ancient history.' She looks at me. 'You need to prepare yourself. It'll be a shock when you see him.'

'I'll cope,' I dismiss, still aggrieved.

'No,' she reaches across the table and puts her hand on mine. 'I mean it. I know how you feel about him. I always have. And I know I've landed this on you with no notice and no time to prepare. And you're dealing with your own issues. I'm sorry to do that to you. But we're at the end of the road and time is against us. We just have to do what we can.'

'What's happening with the site?'

'I'll let him tell you about that.'

'What about you? Are you staying when we get there?'

'No, I have to get back.'

'Sam…' I want to tell her how wrong she was with that comment about us but can't find the words. I know she can interpret the tone of my voice, that she understands what can't be spoken.

'Don't, Eoghan,' she warns. 'This isn't about us. It's just about him. Pure and simple.'

But we both know it's never that simple.

Sunday

Chapter Nine

York. 12th September 1976

It's hot on the long drive to Yorkshire, even with the windows rolled down. We make superficial conversation, but there's an unspoken tension hidden behind the words that, in my current mood, I find exhausting.

We stop to refuel on the north side of the Humber Bridge. After that, Sam is silent, so I close my eyes and let my mind drift, welcoming a thought-less void.

When the external noises change to the urban buzz of York's narrow streets, I open them again and ease my stiff limbs, as much as I can in the cramped sports car. Sam's knuckles stand out where she's gripping the steering wheel too hard, and by the time we pull up at Michael's flat, her face looks pale with strain.

I stretch properly when I climb out and turn to make a joke about it to Sam, but her expression stops me; I can see how much this is weighing on her. I pull my bag from the boot and follow her across the road.

This red-brick eighteenth century house, together with several of its neighbours, is owned by the university, which converted it into flats for unmarried dons. Though he's only lived here for the last thirteen of his sixty-four years, it's the place where I feel Michael is most at home. He was never cut out for the domestic life, any more than I am, but he's carried guilt about not being able to give Sam what he considered to be a normal upbringing. Not that normal would have worked for Sam either. So, whenever I think of him, I like to imagine him here, surrounded by his books and papers. It's always like stepping into a time warp, which remains endlessly reassuring to me.

Sam lets us in the front door, and we walk up the narrow, creaky staircase to the first floor flat. The door is on the latch, which bothers Sam, but Michael still lives in a different era and locking doors will never come naturally to him.

As always, it's the smell I notice first, musty with paper, paper everywhere – books and lecture notes, manuscripts and research notes, essays, correspondence, even newspapers.

Maybe it's the smell, maybe the décor, maybe the age but there's a lovely, settled atmosphere in this place. The dark-stained floorboards are polished to a shine by years of use, and the collection of Arabian rugs scattered under chairs, desk and dining table are worn in a way that has softened their garish colours to muted harmonies. The bookshelves that project across from the main wall naturally divide the front-to-back, double-aspect room into two usable spaces, a study-cum-sitting room at the front, a dining room and kitchenette at the back with an adjoining bedroom and bathroom on the short line of the 'L' shape. As with my rooms, it's assumed professors and lecturers will eat in the dining hall, so kitchen facilities are minimal.

It feels just as it has always felt. And to me that's like coming home, for a delicious, fleeting moment. But Sam was right: nothing could prepare me for the change in Michael.

He's sitting in his usual corner chair, barricaded by bookshelves chaotically filled with a career's collection. As ever, there are teacups everywhere: three crowded together on the precarious round table beside his chair, two atop paper piles on his desk by the window, more lining the mantlepiece over the ugly gas unit they've wedged into the old fireplace.

Even seated, I can see how much he has shrunk. He must be half the weight he was when I last saw him three years ago, his eye sockets are hollowed and the flesh hangs off his cheekbones with nothing else to keep it up. His always clean-shaven chin is dark with stubble while his hair, though still thick, has turned almost entirely silver. The collar of his shirt hangs loose around his neck, even with a tie still in place, and blue veins on his hands stand in stark relief against paper-thin, almost translucent skin.

Sam uses her greeting to give me time to adjust. 'Hello, Dad,' she crosses the room and bends down to kiss his cheek, before crouching to straighten the plaid rug that's sliding off his knees and gather up the papers that he's let slip to the floor. 'We made good time on the road. I brought some things for us to have for lunch.'

The brown eyes take a couple of moments to adjust, recognise and register. 'I thought you were coming on Sunday.' The voice is gravelly, rusty almost.

'Yes, Dad. That's today. I'll put the kettle on, shall I?' She glances over her shoulder at me. 'I brought someone to see you.'

I step into the light from the window and catch the swift succession of emotions that chase across his face. 'Eoghan! Oh, my boy!' It's sheer joy that automatically makes him rise out of his chair. Then dismay as his wasted body fails him and he falls back into the seat. Followed by shame and, for just a flicker, anger – whether at the cancer or at Sam for breaking her promise in bringing me here I can't guess. And then, worst of all, despair. Sinking back into his chair and covering his eyes with one hand so that I almost miss his broken defence: 'I didn't want you to see me like this'.

All those emotions are mirrored inside me. But this is not the time to face them, so I reach for the only prop we can rely on.

'Sam says they've found something new at the site,' I offer by way of explanation. 'Michael, I'm here to lend my services.'

And in an instant, he's transformed into the old Michael again, the same fire and passion lighting him up from within.

'Yes! Yes, my boy. Come, come.' He forces himself to his feet, grabbing at two canes to support himself over to his desk. I pull out the chair for him and he immediately starts rifling through papers. 'Where is it? Where is it?' to himself. As I grab a chair from the dining table, Sam comes back in with a tray. Her eyes are bright with unshed tears and she avoids my gaze, wanting to hold them back, but briefly squeezes my forearm as she passes, then collects up all the discarded crockery and takes them through to the kitchen.

Sitting alongside Michael at the desk, I start to assess the mess of papers. Mostly it's facsimiles from county and ecclesiastical records, some maps, some dense pages of unreadable but elegant script that must be in medieval Latin or French. I catch sight of the corner of a photograph and dislodge a file to find it's one of a handful of black-and-white aerial pictures spilling out of a brown envelope.

'That's it, that's it!' Michael almost snatches the package from me in his eagerness and tips all its contents on top of the pile of papers, scattering them around. 'Look!' He pulls one to the top and points to the area in the bottom left-hand corner, which appears to be a small copse in the middle of a rough pasture. Sam comes to stand behind us, one hand on her father's shoulder. 'And here,' pulling out another photograph, 'and here,' on a third.

I have no idea what he intends me to see, but then I've never taken more than a superficial interest in this site.

'Don't you see?' He seems genuinely perplexed by my lack of understanding. 'It's another building. All this time, we've been looking in the wrong place.'

Sam comes to my rescue. 'Dad, why don't you take Eoghan through it from the beginning? Give him the context so he understands it properly.'

'Yes!' He starts to rise again then checks himself, smiles almost ruefully at realising again his own physical constraints. 'Samantha, would you mind fetching the site plans. They're on the dining table.' He pats the hand on his shoulder tenderly. 'And,' with a hopeful look, 'did you say something about tea?'

There's relief in her eyes. Much as she hates it, The Obsession is what's keeping him alive.

* * * * * * *

'Threfield was already established as a community by the time of Domesday, and it's one of a number of manors that were transferred to William de Percy by the Earl of Chester, under

William the Conqueror.' Michael draws his finger around the perimeter on the map, encompassing what would be a small manor with a village at the base, boundaried by a river and stretching back up an escarpment into fields, with woodland beyond.

'William became the first feudal baron of a manor called Topcliffe in Yorkshire, and the village's name was extended to Threfield Percy to reflect the change of ownership. Little changed in the first two centuries. The family progressed nicely and the manor's population gradually grew. Like many others, in the thirteenth century it benefitted from rising prices, with increasing demand from the growing towns for their agricultural produce, and most of the peasants would have been able to earn money by selling their surplus at the markets as well as sustaining their own families, which meant the lords reaped increased profits too.'

It's like being back in the lecture theatre. Sam, who has clearly heard this many times before, disappears back into the kitchen and I'm hopeful the clatter of crockery and cutlery suggests she's working on lunch as well as a brew.

'The period that interests me is when the ownership changes. In 1309, Henry de Percy, by this time the seventh feudal baron of Topcliffe, buys Alnwick Castle from Antony Bek, Bishop of Durham.'

'Oh,' insight dawns, 'they're *those* Percys. The Dukes of Northumberland.'

'Not at this stage,' Michael corrects me, 'but, yes, the direct line goes down to when they become dukes in the sixteenth century. What's relevant here is that Henry shifts the family's focus from Yorkshire to Northumberland and cedes day-to-day management of parts of the original estates to minor members of the family. In this case, Threfield Percy comes to Geoffrey Goscelin, who was married to Amicia de Percy,' he pulls out a family tree and shows me the lineage, 'the only child of Henry's youngest brother. Geoffrey is from a Flemish family and appears to have encountered the family through trading links, presumably for wool for their cloth-making industry.'

'A merchant marrying the niece of a Percy? Sounds a little unbalanced,' I suggest, 'in societal terms.'

'Not necessarily.' Michael's quick to leap to Goscelin's defence. 'Bear in mind the Percy family is still up-and-coming. Henry has made a name for himself – and some money – in Edward I's Scottish wars but he's still a minor baron, not one of the great earls. Amicia has a good name but doesn't bring much of a dowry to the marriage and Goscelin has some personal wealth.'

'OK, so the village is thriving and has a new lord,' I summarise.

'Yes. And yet, within fifty years it's all but gone.'

'That makes no sense,' I observe. 'Established communities don't disappear that fast.'

'Exactly. And yet,' pulling the photostat of another document out to show me, 'by 1360 the population is down to two households. The fields are still being farmed but almost all the tofts and crofts are abandoned and so is the manor house. The diocese refuses to fund repairs to the bell tower in 1343 and after 1355 has services covered by the priest at the neighbouring parish of Wharram. In fact, church services cease altogether within another ten years.'

'So, what are you saying? That the Black Death wiped them out?'

'I can't see what else would make sense. But there's a growing consensus among the DMV community that the plague's impact was less than many assumed.'

Deserted Medieval Villages. Of which there are dozens in Yorkshire alone. Why does this one have such a hold over Michael?

'Didn't it wipe out half the population?'

'In places like London, yes. Less in most rural communities. Largely it accelerated other trends, like the migration to towns. Of course, that was compounded by prices collapsing because there were fewer people needing to be fed and by the increased cost of labour. Both factors led more lords to go over to wool production, needing less labour but creating a downward spiral in demand and supply. But these trends take decades to play through, and most other villages only become deserted a hundred and fifty to two hundred years later.'

I sit back in my chair. 'OK. So, something happened.'

Michael nods, approving because I've drawn the same conclusion as he. 'A catastrophic event that caused whoever was living here to desert their homes almost overnight.'

'What?'

He shrugs. 'I don't know. It's where the records fail me. I assume key records were destroyed, but how and when isn't apparent. And even if some had been destroyed, I'd expect others to give me something to work with. But there's nothing.'

I sit back in the chair and fold my arms. 'And how does The Woman fit into this?'

If I thought he looked ill before, I am shocked by the effect my mention of her has on him. What little blood there is in his face drains away. He closes his eyes, as if to tackle some inward pain, and the lines on his face deepen and harden. Some emotion flickers across that much-loved face; if I didn't know better, I'd say it was guilt.

He takes a deep breath. 'It tortures me,' he whispers, the confession wracking his body until he shakes. 'I can't help her. I have to help her, but I can't. I can't find her. I don't understand. I don't know what I have to do.' The words are full of despair and his eyes are haunted with failure. He puts a hand on mine and it's cold, lifeless almost.

'Michael,' I prompt. He blinks and, in an instant, changes again; colour infuses his cheeks and his eyes clear. He reaches for the photographs and starts tidying up the papers.

'I have to do something,' he insists, his voice weak but resolute. 'I have to know what happened.'

All the love I have for this man wells up within me. He has been a central part of my life for more than twenty years. He has pushed me and challenged me, encouraged me and supported me. However irrational this is – whatever *this* is – it is now my burden as well as his. In whatever time is left to us.

'Then tell me everything I need to know. Tell me where I need to dig and what I'm looking for. I'll be your eyes and ears – and hands – on the site. And if there are answers to be found, I'll find them for you.'

He looks at me then and there are tears of relief in his eyes. He's no longer alone.

* * * * * * *

We talk for hours as he meticulously walks me through the detail of what he's found over the years. I'm astonished by how much material he's uncovered and find another level of respect for his abilities as a historian. Sam maintains an endless supply of tea as well as providing lunch, and sits in the corner chair, watching the two of us at work. And, I suspect, enjoys seeing Michael animated and alive, absorbed by his work; she's storing up memories of her father as she most knew him. Just like when I stayed with them in the holidays and she would sit with him in the evenings and at weekends, endlessly reading books about science or medicine or philosophy or even spirituality while he worked on his lectures and marked students' essays or graded exam papers.

He tried to give her a normal upbringing in that semi-detached house in Cambridge's suburbs, but it doesn't matter what environment you put an academic in, they soon revert to type. Sam adored him and made up for his lack of domestic skills with her own natural independence, taking on management of the house and their lives from a remarkably early age.

I watch her as she stares out of the window, looking over the wall opposite towards the gardens surrounding the Museum of York. She no longer tucks her legs under her in the chair, the way she did through her teens and into her twenties, but the presence she exudes is the same: there's a powerful centredness at the heart of her and a focus that's, somehow, timeless and boundless. I've always felt it in everything she does: in how she brings ease to those in pain and peace to those who grieve; how she encourages and uplifts those who are drawn to her for guidance; how she offers acceptance and understanding to those whose decisions diverge from her own. Even when it hurts her own heart.

Her eyes meet mine and hold my gaze. And it's like experiencing again everything that has passed between us in the years we've known each other. And more. We've been apart longer than we were together and there's no doubt we've both changed over the last decade but there's still a strong sense of connection. I know this woman – and she knows me – in ways that can't be explained.

'Dad,' Sam's still holding my gaze as she catches Michael's attention. 'What can you tell us about Llywelyn Bren?'

Chapter Ten

York. 12th September 1976

I frown. Her eyes are steady as she looks as me very deliberately, her intent apparent but, to me, unfathomable.

'Hmm? Bren, you say?' Michael turns in his chair to look at his daughter and, finally, she moves her gaze across to him.

'Yes. Something about a rebellion in the early fourteenth century?'

It takes Michael a long moment of concentration to switch his focus away from Threfield Percy. I can see him trawling his memory, working through his answer, piecing the elements together that will enable our greatest understanding, with just enough detail to bring it to life. Of course, that's where Sam gets it from.

'He's best known for the rebellion he led in 1316. In 1314, Gilbert de Clare, earl of Gloucester, was lord of Glamorgan in South Wales, which would have encompassed Bren's lands around Cardiff and Caerphilly. Gloucester was the son of Joan of Acre, so nephew to Edward I and cousin to Edward II. His father died when he was four years old and, under the terms of the marriage, Joan held the earldom until she died in 1307. Gilbert was invested as earl a few months later, even though he was only sixteen. Early on, he was drawn into the Scottish wars and was killed at Bannockburn.

'He was twenty-two when he died and, though he'd been married to Maud de Burgh for several years, they hadn't produced an heir, but she claimed to be pregnant for an improbable length of time after his death. His lands were taken into royal possession while the question of who should inherit was being addressed and Edward appointed first Bartholomew de Badlesmere and then Payn de Turberville as royal custodian in Glamorgan.

'Those were turbulent years in the region. Thousands of Glamorgan men had died with Gloucester against Robert the Bruce, which heightened tensions between the Normans and the native

Welsh. De Badlesmere contained the violence, but de Turberville persecuted the populace at a time when the Great Famine had gripped all of Europe.

'You see, it had rained almost constantly from the summer of 1314 through to 1316. The temperature was also very cool, leading to widespread crop failures. This meant not only a lack of grain for bread but also a dearth of straw and hay for animal feed. Plus, without sufficient sunshine, the sea salt couldn't be effectively evaporated from the brine so the only means of preserving meat became scarce and very expensive, further inflating food prices.

'Of course, the peasant classes suffered most because their subsistence farming methods offered little margin for failure. They had no choice but to eat the seed grain and to slaughter the livestock that would have been kept for production. There are reports of elders refusing food so the younger generation could eat and stories – hopefully apocryphal – of instances of cannibalism. Estimates suggest between five and twenty-five per cent. of the population died during the famine or as a result of its effects.

'Against this backdrop, de Turberville pursued a regime of increasing taxation, extracting food for his table from those who could least spare it.

'Llywelyn Bren was never going to stand for this. He came from a family known for its rebellious nature, but he's also described as a man of considerable honour and education, and Gloucester appears to have trusted him as a close adviser. He clashed with de Turberville, who then removed Bren's lands and distributed them amongst his own friends and family. Bren is said to have threatened de Turberville, at which point he's accused of treason.

'Bren appealed to Edward II, who called him to Westminster but then refused to see him and ordered him to appear before Parliament in Lincoln to answer the charge of treason. Edward promised that, if the charges were found to be true, Bren would hang.

'Believing his life to be in danger, Bren returned to Wales and prepared to defend himself and his lands.

'The revolt began in January 1316 with a surprise attack on Caerphilly Castle. He succeeded in taking the outer ward and captured the constable but couldn't penetrate the inner defences, so he burned the town and started a siege. Unsurprisingly given the conditions in the country, the revolt spread quickly through other fortified towns in Glamorgan and Gwent.

'Edward came down hard, fearing contagion across the rest of the principality. He ordered the earl of Hereford to put down the revolt and he gathered huge forces supported by the Marcher lords and the earl of Lancaster. In March, they advanced from Cardiff and broke the siege of Caerphilly after six weeks.

'Bren surrendered unconditionally to Hereford and was sent first to Brecon and then to the Tower. Interestingly, both Hereford and Roger Mortimer interceded on his behalf with the king, appealing for pardons for many of Bren's men.

'Bren and his family were held in the Tower for a year or so but, at some point, his wife and five of his six sons were released, though Llywelyn and his eldest son, Gruffydd, continued to be held.

'In November 1317, Edward finally resolved the question of Gloucester's inheritance and split his lands between de Clare's three sisters, all of whom had been married off to Edward's favourites. Glamorgan came to Eleanor, wife of Hugh Despenser the Younger.'

At the mention of his name, I recall that empty darkness and feel a chill run across my skin. It triggers again the biting cold and blackness of that prison room, the dampness running down the walls, the cloying smell of the compacted earthen floor. I shake myself before other memories can crowd in. Looking up, I find Sam watching me, but Michael hasn't noticed.

'Sometime in 1318 – certainly before the end of October – Despenser has Bren brought to Cardiff Castle, apparently not at Edward's behest.'

'It was September. Not yet Michaelmas.' The words come from me but don't feel as if they are mine.

Michael looks questioningly at me, but I don't offer an explanation. He lets it go. 'Despenser had him hanged, drawn and quartered, a punishment that hadn't yet been formally adopted for high treason. No one knows why Despenser took it upon himself to execute Bren at this point and in this way.'

I look directly at Sam. The knowing is too strong within me not to be spoken. 'He wanted to showcase his authority in his new lands. To demonstrate his power. To parade a sovereignty on a par with the king's.'

'That sounds a logical supposition,' Michael allows, 'though we don't have the evidence. He certainly came to regret it later: it was one of the main accusations at his own trial that Bren's execution had been illegal. Though someone else took the fall for that.'

'Sir William Fleminge.' The thin-faced, cowardly chamberlain.

Michael looks surprised. 'Yes. How did you know?'

'What happened to the family, Dad?' Sam's voice is quiet but insistent.

'The records are a little sketchy there. Certainly, Bren's wife and eldest son were held in Cardiff Castle for some time after, but it looks like she died many years later. The other sons may have been dispersed initially but they were all in the service of Hereford by the Battle of Boroughbridge in 1322 where the earl died. Two of the sons were involved in the capture of Hugh Despenser in 1326, so they had their revenge in time, and their lands were restored to them after Edward was deposed by Queen Isabella in favour of their son, Edward III.'

Sam is still staring at me, willing me to ask the question. But it's too raw. I want to know but something is holding me back. So, she asks it for me. 'What about the girl, Dad? What about his daughter?'

Michael shakes his head. 'I'm not aware of a daughter.'

A powerful emotion shoots through my body again. Not the icy rage I felt last night, but something just as strong, just as real. It's compulsive and demanding, pushing its way into me, into my time and space.

My muscles go rigid as I fight to keep control of my body. Fearing I'm losing my grip, I try to focus on Sam, try to see beyond the blood rushing in my head.

'Eoghan,' her voice is low, almost a whisper. 'You have to tell him. He needs to know.'

'She was born on the day the old king died.' The words come through me, not from me.

Michael is looking from one of us to the other, confusion etched in his face. 'Who was?'

'Christiane Bren. Llywelyn Bren's daughter.'

'Who?'

'She was their seventh child, born seven years after their sixth son.' All this knowledge is rising within me, and I could not keep it down if I wanted to.

'Born on the day the old king died?' Michael is struggling to follow.

'What date would that be?' Sam prompts, looking fixedly at me now.

I shake my head. 'She didn't know.'

Sam baulks. 'She doesn't know what date she was born on?'

'They often didn't,' Michael interjects, bemused by what's going on between us. 'The calendar was marked by holidays and saints' days. They might be named after the saint's day they were born on, which helped them mark their birth date. Years were largely meaningless to the masses; when your life is shaped by the seasons, you don't really need to know your age. But,' he looks across at me, 'if you mean it was when Edward I died, that would be the seventh of July 1307.'

'Her mother was Welsh too. Lleucu,' I recall. 'She lost three pregnancies between the youngest son, Roger, and Christiane. She was a slight woman and had carried her earlier pregnancies well, but they had taken a toll on her body. Those deaths caused her considerable distress, but she found solace in her faith. When she found she was carrying again, she told Llywelyn she had promised this seventh son to God and wanted him, at the right time, to join the monastery at Glastonbury where her own cousin resided.'

Sam's frowning at the new insights I'm relaying.

'The baby was strong and Lleucu had so much difficulty in childbirth that the nurses feared she wouldn't recover from the quantity of blood she lost. But she was a fierce woman and would not leave her child.

'She never expected to have a daughter and she could not bring herself to fulfil her promise to commit the child to the Church.

'Llywelyn was distraught at the thought of losing his beloved wife and made his own vow not to endanger her life again with another child. Christiane believes that was very difficult for both of them because there was more love between her parents than was typical with a lord and his lady. And she knows her father sometimes seeks solace elsewhere because she has at least two half-brothers who are spoken of by the villagers, if not by the family. They're well provided for, but Llywelyn will not bring them into the household for Lleucu's sake.'

'What is this?' Michael's bewildered. 'Where is all this coming from?'

'Matilde, Christiane's nurse. She was also nurse to Lleucu and loved to tell the little girl the stories.'

Sam smiles. 'That's not what he means, Eoghan.'

Her laugh jolts me back into the present, and it's only then that I realise I was lost in the past, seeing in my mind their home at Senghennydd and hearing Matilde tell Christiane stories as she brushed her long hair, glowing richly in the light from the fire in her mother's chamber.

I look across at Michael. He's frowning heavily but he's also caught up, half leaning forward in his chair, a strange eagerness in his eyes.

I shake my head to attempt to clear it. 'I had a surreal experience yesterday.' I glance at Sam who nods her reassurance. 'It was like a dream, but more, like a memory that I was living again. But not a memory because it wasn't me. I was witnessing real events or, rather, someone's experience of real events.'

'What events?'

'The execution of Llywelyn Bren at Cardiff Castle in 1318.'

Michael's expression is quizzical. 'I've heard of something like this before. Historians who get so consumed by their subject they start dreaming in that era.'

'But this isn't my era, is it?' I challenge. 'It's yours. I know comparatively little about it.'

'What do you think it is, then?'

Sam lets out a huff of frustration. 'You're not asking the right question!'

We both stare at her. 'What is the right question, Samantha?' Michael responds cautiously, unused to passionate outbursts from his calm and controlled daughter.

'Who is she?' Sam exclaims. 'Who is Christiane?'

Michael turns towards her. 'Who is she, Samantha?'

I hold my breath, watching Sam, feeling a fierceness almost sparking off her. She leans across and takes his hands in both of hers, staring into his face. 'Don't you see, Dad?' Her voice is gentle but filled with determination. 'She's who you've been looking for. Christiane's The Woman.'

Chapter Eleven

York. 12th September 1976

There is conflict written all over Michael's face. Maybe he's wanted this for too long. Maybe he's afraid he will never know. But now he's faced with an answer he both wants to believe and fears to.

'What makes you say that?' His voice shakes, and I'm shocked to see his physical weakness re-emerge, having abated over the last few hours. Now, he looks older, thinner, feebler. It hurts to see him this way.

And I can see the doubt flood through Sam. I don't know how she's made this leap from my dream to this conclusion and it's not like her to be anything other than empirical and analytical.

Suddenly, I feel an overwhelming impulse to stand up and step away, and I push my chair back so abruptly that they both look up, startled. I cross to the far end of the room to stare down into the garden. I don't want to know Sam's answer, don't want to know if she has a theory about what this is. Last night's experience is too raw. And confusing. It makes no rational sense. I know I've always been about more than the rational in my work, but this is beyond anything.

My head is pounding, a headache I haven't even noticed coming on. In some ways, I feel like I'm not quite here, like I'm slightly disconnected from this time. Maybe it's because I feel drawn to that other time. I can't help but wonder what happened to Christiane.

Their voices continue behind me in quiet murmurs. I tune into the noises beyond the open window: the blackbirds arguing in the garden; vague chatter and the tinkle of china cups where a group are having afternoon tea under a fruit-laden apple tree further down the terrace; the more distant shouts of young children, presumably running around the Museum Gardens. The air is warm and soft, a gentle breeze swaying the feathery fronds of a congested pampas grass that is becoming too big for its corner of the garden.

Resting my forehead against the glass, its coolness soothes me. I listen to the sound of my breathing and feel the rise and fall of my chest until my mind quietens.

In my mind's eye, I see Christiane, not as the child she was in my dream but as a grown woman. A beautiful woman. I can't see all of her – she's surrounded by darkness and shadows – but her face is as clear as if she were standing inches away from me: flaming hair frames pale skin and eyes the colour of newly unfurled leaves in spring.

At the corner of my eye, something moves. I try to follow it with my gaze, but it's just beyond the edge of my vision…something reaching out to me.

I jump as Sam touches my shoulder and turn around. Michael pulls a handkerchief from his trouser pocket and wipes a tear from his cheek.

'I have to hit the road now if I'm going to get back to London tonight.' Her eyelashes are wet too.

'That's a long drive for you,' I observe, absently.

She pushes away my concern. 'Dad has a nurse coming in at six to check on him and they'll bring him supper at eight.' She glances across to Michael as he settles in his armchair by the fireplace and pulls a rug across his knees. 'He's pretty tired. Why don't you head over to your room at the pub? Come back tomorrow morning before you head to the dig site.' She hands me a set of keys. 'Those are for Dad's Volvo, it's the brown car out front. And a spare key for the flat.'

I nod. 'OK. I'll walk you down to the car.'

She searches my face. 'How are you feeling?'

'I'm fine,' I dismiss.

'Any headaches? Nausea?'

'Sam, I'm fine,' I insist.

She glances over at Michael. 'As a doctor, I know I shouldn't be asking you to do this,' she assesses. 'After what you've been through in the last few days, I should be prescribing rest and no stress.'

'But as a daughter...' I imply for her.

She turns towards the window so Michael can't hear her. 'I don't know how much time he has, Eoghan. I can ease his pain and make him comfortable, but you... Any peace of mind you can give him...'

She can't continue. Her pain is a tightness in my chest; I want so much to hold her, but there's a tension in her that's keeping me at arm's length.

'I'm not making you any promises,' I warn, as gently as I can. 'I don't know what I'm going to find when I get there.' Her eyes are bleak, and I feel how important this is to her as well as to him. 'I'll do everything I can,' I finish. 'That's all I can promise.' She nods and turns to take her leave of Michael.

As we head out to the car, she hands me a scrap of paper. 'I assume you'll come by each evening to update him on the day's progress. This is my number in London. I switch to the early shift tomorrow, so I'll be at the flat any time after six o'clock. If there's anything to report, will you call me? You can use Dad's telephone to avoid paying at the pub.' I nod and open the car door for her. 'Thank you for doing this, Eoghan.'

'Please,' I remind her, 'don't expect too much. If he hasn't found answers after all these years, there's only a slim chance that I will.'

'I know,' she recognises, climbing into the driver's seat and firing up the engine.

'Sam,' I crouch down and she winds down her window. 'What did you tell Michael? About why you think Christiane is The Woman?' She purses her lips, like she's resisting telling me. 'Please,' I ask. 'What made you say that?'

She lets in the clutch and puts the car in gear. For a moment, I think she's going to drive off without answering. Then she turns to look at me directly; I can't fathom the expression in her eyes. 'It was when you described the child in your dream that I knew. Because I've seen her. I've seen her at the site.'

* * * * * * *

She drives away before I can say anything, accelerating so hard the tyres throw up stones and dust. I stare after her. What the hell?

'Do you think there's anything in what she says about this Christiane?' I'm barely through the door when Michael fires the question at me. Scepticism and eagerness war within him.

'What does she mean she's seen her?' Throwing my own question back at him, I turn the desk chair round so I can face him, leaning forward and resting my elbows on my knees. 'She drove off without explaining.'

'Like a ghost, maybe? Not that I believe in them.'

'But Sam does.'

That raises a disapproving grunt.

'I need to look into this Christiane Bren,' Michael muses. 'Ask my colleagues at University College in Cardiff.'

'It seems a stretch,' I muse. 'From my dream to The Woman.'

He looks at me, ruefully. 'Eoghan, I'm at a dead end, literally and metaphorically,' with the shade of an ironic laugh. 'I've exhausted every avenue in my experience. And you know full well, if I could have avoided resorting to archaeology for answers, I would.'

It's my turn to laugh. 'Nice to know you still think so little of my chosen field.'

'You don't take it personally,' he shrugs. 'Any more than I did when you rejected mine in favour of archaeology.'

'That's not how it was!' I object. 'I have huge respect for what you do.'

He relinquishes the point with an indulgent smile. 'From the moment I took you onto the dig at Glendalough Abbey, you had the bug. Anyone could see it. And you're doing amazing work. I keep up with your papers. When you eventually get around to publishing them,' lightly chiding. 'What's the story behind the bruise?' He nods towards my face. 'I didn't want to ask in front of Samantha in case it's about a woman.'

I touch it self-consciously. It's turning that unpleasant yellow colour, but the swelling has gone down, and it looks better than it did. 'It is, but not in the way you're thinking. A man was threatening a woman and I got in the middle of it.'

He absorbs the information without comment, leans back in his chair and folds his hands across his stomach. Looks at me with that penetrating, thoughtful gaze of his, the one Sam's inherited. 'I didn't realise you and Samantha were still in touch.'

'We're not. She was there when they brought me into the hospital.'

'It's coincidence that brought you here?'

'Not exactly. Sam was coming to find me anyway.' I won't lie to him. 'I know you told her not to tell me about the illness, but I'm glad she did.'

He nods. 'I've missed you, lad.' He says it so simply, without regret or recrimination. I'm shocked. The Michael I know never shows his affection; he comes from that generation. 'I know,' he reads the surprise in my face. 'One finds honesty when confronted by one's mortality.'

I want so much to tell him how sorry I am about the cancer, to apologise for not being around for the last three years, to express what he means to me. But it's too much. I'm not ready to say these things. The news is too recent, and I can't yet accept that I'm losing him.

'Tell me about Christiane Bren.'

'Michael...'

'I know, it's all so far-fetched. Absurd, really.' He leans forward in his chair and there's a light in his eyes. 'Indulge me.'

I stand up again, that familiar restlessness coming over me. In my mind, I see her again in that subterranean cell at Cardiff Castle.

'She's small for her age, I think. She has her mother's slight frame, but her brothers are all big like their father. She has the Celtic colouring and immense pride in that heritage. Daughter of Llywelyn Bren, son of Gruffydd, son of Rhys, lord of Senghennydd and Meisgyn.' I can hear her saying that, a childhood chant she repeats over and over.

'Her mother is Welsh too, but her nurse is French, and an English monk tutored her brothers and now teaches her. Llywelyn himself taught Lleucu to read when they married and insisted all his children be educated, including his daughter.

'She adores her father. He and her brothers are very protective of her, being the youngest and the only girl, but Lleucu ensures she's not indulged. Llywelyn has a powerful belief in the duty that comes with privilege, a responsibility to protect the people of his manors, to help them flourish, to support them when they struggle, to maintain order for the good of all. He stands for justice and fairness, and he teaches all his children that with power and position comes the need to understand how these principles are upheld and, if necessary, enforced. He feels too the weight of his lineage, coming from a long line of respected and trusted nobles who supported the kings and princes of Wales for centuries. Winter nights are filled with the re-telling of those ancient tales.

'When Llywelyn is away, Lleucu manages the manors and maintains the order her husband has established. It's from Lleucu that Christiane gets her deep interest in people.

'Theirs is a farming community – they rely on sheep and cattle more than crops – but Llywelyn owes allegiance in the form of fighting men when required, and her brothers and the men of the manor regularly train to fight. More than once in Christiane's life they've gone to war in support of their Glamorgan overlord. When

Llywelyn rebelled, they all believed they were fighting for justice for their families. And they felt his imprisonment and execution as the deepest betrayal.'

On the edge of my emotions, I can feel her childlike grief at losing her beloved father, a hollowed-out confusion matched by a righteous indignation at the injustice of it. But it's amplified as it comes across the centuries to me until it becomes powerful and vast, too much to look at directly. Emotions bigger than anything I've known. I come to a halt at the chair and grip the back to stop myself shaking. I try to focus on Michael, but my vision is blurring at the edges. I hear him say my name, but it comes from a distance, and it's only when I feel his hand on my arm that I can concentrate enough to move to sit down. I feel light-headed and lean forward to put my head between my knees until it passes.

Michael's frowning. 'What was that?'

'You asked me to tell you about her.' I can hear the stubbornness in my voice, almost combative.

'I thought you were going to tell me where she was born, when she died,' he protests. 'I didn't expect that.'

'I know what she knew about herself at that age.' And what she knew about everyone around her, but I can't admit that to Michael, it's too absurd. And more than that: I feel what she feels. But intensified, multiplied somehow.

He shakes his head, unable to take it in, and sinks back into his chair. He's filled his life with facts, with data, with documents. He can't cope with this, not on top of everything else. He needs something to ground him.

'OK, Michael,' I force myself back to reality. 'Let's start with what we know. She was born in 1307 at the Welsh manor of Senghennydd. She was at the execution of Llywelyn Bren in 1318 in Cardiff. Let's see where the facts lead us.'

He seems relieved, and suddenly very weary. 'I'll write some letters. See if we can find a paper trail to follow.'

I force myself to my feet. 'And I'll drop by in the morning before I head to the site.'

Michael nods absently, his face colourless and tired again. 'Tomorrow…' he murmurs and closes his eyes.

I quietly shut the door behind me.

* * * * * * *

The Red Lion is a much-needed injection of normality, light, warm and welcoming. I take a corner table in the snug with a roast dinner and a pint, allowing the comforting atmosphere to wash over and through me. The air is still and soft, holding the heat of the day; it slows my mind and relaxes my body.

As the sun goes down and the bar quietens, I sit with my thoughts about the last two days.

I feel disorientated and partially disconnected from my existing reality; I've stepped into something unknown.

But it's also calling me. I've known digs to speak to me before, but this is different. I'm drawn to it and to Christiane. Instinctively I know that Sam is right, that Christiane is The Woman.

And I also know she's right to fear that this obsession won't stop with Michael.

Chapter Twelve

Kirkham Priory, Yorkshire. November 1318

The snow is coming down thick and fast, and in the failing light they ride nose-to-tail to keep to the trail. Christiane's body is stiff with cold and the long hours of riding on the back of the page's horse, careful treading from the moment they left York on the mud-churned roads. The sky was grey and heavy from the outset, prescient of the snowstorm that now surrounds them. Her eyes ache from staring into the blizzard and her fingers are frozen in place.

Almost seven weeks have passed since the execution. The Brens continued to be held at Cardiff Castle, though she saw little of her brothers in that time. One by one, they were sent away, divided among the households of Despenser's supporters, separated to prevent further rebellion, until only Gruffydd remained, isolated in the underground cells. On the night of her husband's death, they moved Lleucu to a room in the Black Tower, more comfortable but a prison, nonetheless.

Yet they seemed not to care about Christiane, and during the day she was allowed to roam freely around the castle, wraith-like with nowhere to go and no one to direct her. She ate in the Hall with everyone else, wandered through the kitchens and yards and stables, evaded the guards in the outer bailey and avoided anyone in Despenser's household, most of whom mercifully moved on to Westminster after ten days to re-join the court, though the despised chamberlain remained. The chapel became her haven, her place to hide from curious and hostile eyes that stared at her, from stable boys who plucked at her skirts and taunted her, from kitchen servants who pushed her roughly out of the way; yet she was as content as she imagined she could be in the circumstances.

Until the visitors arrived a se'nnight since. She was in the outer bailey watching the blacksmith shoe a horse as they rode through the southern gate. There had been heavy rains overnight and the horses' legs were caked with mud up to the hock; it seemed they had already ridden many miles that day, though it was not yet noon.

Three riders: a well-dressed man of middle age and middling height accompanied by a young page; and a boy who was clearly his son to judge by his similarly stocky build, though his thick hair was black where the man's was dark blond and greying, and his complexion was ruddy where the other's was weathered and darker than most, as if he had travelled many times to warmer climes.

The castle received travellers of varying sorts most days, but these drew her attention; with nothing else to distract her, she followed as they dismounted to send their horses into the stables and were directed through the inner bailey gate towards the Great Hall.

The boy, who appeared to be much about her age or maybe slightly older, seemed sullen. No, more than that: anger was bubbling just below the surface, evident in his clenched jaw. He refused to respond to his father's admonishment to hurry, dragging his feet. The older man unstrapped his sword at the door to the Hall, then waited for the boy, showing remarkable patience.

As they approached the dais, Sir William Fleminge appeared from the adjoining private apartments and came forward to greet them. From where she hung back in the shadows, Christiane saw the chamberlain show a little respect, but only a little, so this was a man of some importance but not of very high standing.

The boy too held himself a little way off, as if to communicate his disgust for the discussion. His eyes drifted around the room and when they came to rest of her it was with a hard, assessing look, disrespectful and calculated to make her feel diminished. Unbowed, she returned his stare until the older man turned to call the boy forward and introduced him to Sir William.

To her surprise, the chamberlain suddenly pointed in her direction and the man and boy turned towards her. She shrank into the shadows but too late: Sir William was already imperiously beckoning her forward.

Though reluctant to obey his command – it was the first interaction she had had with him since he stood before the beaten and mutilated body of her father – she would not be cowed. She was her mother's daughter, after all.

'Christiane Bren,' the man could barely raise his head as she approached, let alone meet her steady gaze, 'this is Geoffrey Goscelin and his son, Ralf.' She acknowledged the older man with a graceful bow and saw some kindness in his eyes when he courteously responded. She met the boy's eyes with calm curiosity and received a lip-curling look as retort. 'It has been decided that you will go to live with them in Yorkshire.'

'No!' The instinctive plea of denial was out of her mouth before she could stop it and she saw a flare of triumph in the boy's face at her evident discomfort. 'You cannot mean me to leave Mama too!'

'That is exactly what I intend,' the chamberlain confirmed. 'You are the daughter of a traitor, girl. You are fortunate that anyone is prepared to house you!' It had required much effort on his part to finalise the arrangements for each of Bren's children and he was weary of this drawn-out process with which he had been tasked. As offspring of a traitor, no one would have been surprised if they had just been thrown out on the street; his lord must greatly fear this family's continuing influence in Wales to have put him to the trouble of placing each with such care.

'Do not fear,' Geoffrey Goscelin added, and she unexpectedly saw concern in his eyes. 'You will be welcome in our household.'

Christiane held her tongue, refusing to give voice to the anxiety welling up within her. The chamberlain took it as acquiescence.

'You will leave at first light tomorrow. You have tonight to pack your things and say your farewells.' He must have read the dismay in her face. 'Think yourself lucky you are being allowed that,' he warned before he turned on his heel and strode away.

He was right: it was more consideration than had been extended to her brothers.

* * * * * * *

The parting from her mother was strained. Grief for her husband and each successive parting from a child had hardened within her, making her unnaturally distant. Unsure that her imminent removal was even understood, Christiane gave her mother the parting blessing that she might herself expect to receive; as she did, certainty settled within her that they would not meet again.

Matilde wrapped her young charge in her arms one last time, but she too was consumed by Lleucu's needs and released Christiane to her uncertain future with little more than a resigned sigh.

They mounted the horses just as dawn's hues softened the darkness, three horses, with Christiane behind the page, plus two sumpter horses carrying most of her meagre possessions.

They made slow progress, their winding journey dictated by which roads had not yet been washed out by the early winter weather. At each major town, they halted longer to allow Geoffrey to complete business with the merchants there, and Christiane came to understand he traded in cloth and wool, a useful interchange between the English producers and the weavers of his native Flanders. The sumpter horses' loads became heavier at each stop.

Geoffrey intended to reach Threfield Percy by dark, but the snow is thicker north of York, hampering their journey, and the storm worsens the further they go.

He reins in and signals to the others to stop while he reviews their position. In this weather, everything is distorted, and it takes him a moment to discern well-known landmarks.

He glances back at his son and the girl. Had he been riding alone, he might have been inclined to push for home, sure of his path with ways familiar from his frequent trips to the major cities and ports of this country. The boy looks as morose as usual, glowering resentment whenever he looks his way, though Geoffrey has some sympathy for his justification on this occasion.

The girl hasn't complained once since they left Cardiff. Appalled to hear her tale from the chamberlain, he can't imagine what inward turmoil is masked by her calm exterior.

He thinks for a long moment. They are rapidly losing the daylight and all of them are chilled to the bone. Moreover, an evening's conversation with the prior appeals rather more than the confrontation with Amicia that lies ahead. That decides it: they will complete the journey tomorrow and seek a night's shelter at Kirkham Priory.

* * * * * * *

A small fire has been lit in the guest quarters and the almoner ushers them in front of it to wait while he sends a boy to alert the prior to their visitors.

'They're at Vespers currently,' he warns. 'I'll have beds prepared while you wait. We'll have to put the young lady in with the Prioress de Lacy. She's visiting from Molseby Priory.'

Geoffrey takes a seat by the fire, signing to Christiane and Ralf to join him. The page, David, follows the almoner and presently brings them wine and ale, and some bread, cheese and apples. In the quiet room, the wind carries to them the distant chants of the canons' evening worship.

A tall, lean man arrives shortly after the service finishes. There is that in his stature and upright bearing which commands respect, and all the guests rise as he approaches.

'Prior Robert,' Geoffrey greets him with a bow. 'We appreciate your hospitality for a night. The snow has made it impossible to complete our journey this day.'

'You are always welcome, my friend,' the prior hails him warmly. 'It is some while since we had the opportunity to discuss your latest travels. Perhaps you might join me in my lodgings after Compline?'

'With pleasure. You remember my son, Ralf, and page, David FitzAlan?' He greets the boys with a nod, some wariness crossing his brow as his eyes fall on Ralf. 'And this is Christiane Bren, who is joining our household. Christiane, this is Prior Robert de Veteri Burgo.'

'Thank you for giving us shelter, Prior Robert.' As she looks into his face, she muses, almost without thinking, 'I'm sorry you are missing your home. It must be harder for you when our winter descends like this.'

He starts with surprise and looks at her more closely. 'What makes you say that, my child?'

Christiane considers for a moment. 'I sense it in you, how you carry your homeland in heart. It makes me see different shores, where the soil is a rich, russet red and the sky and sea are a brilliant blue and the air dances with the warmth of the sun.'

'Catalonia…' he breathes, entranced. 'Land of my fathers. I was thinking about it only this morning when the snow started to fall so thickly. But,' collecting himself, 'God called me here to bring light to this dark country, my lady,' with a tender smile in his eyes 'and I am pleased at least to have the honour of being of service to you tonight.'

'She's no lady!' Ralf thrusts himself in front of Christiane with a vehemence and anger that makes her step back from him. 'She's a traitor and a penniless beggar.'

'Ralf, no!' Geoffrey is appalled. 'You will not speak of Christiane in that way.'

'It's naught but the truth,' Ralf protests, shrinking back as if surprised by the vehemence of his father's denial and glaring at Christiane.

'Her father's actions do not make her a traitor,' Geoffrey argues.

'Am I though penniless?' Christiane looks straight at the older man, her eyes clear and questioning.

'What do you think, fool?' Ralf scorns. 'All your father's lands were confiscated two years ago when he betrayed our king!'

'He was protecting our people,' Christiane defends, fear and pride rising within her.

'Stop this, both of you!' Geoffrey demands. 'Show our host proper respect by not carrying on in this way before him.'

The prior is watching them curiously, taking in the reactions and emotions of each. 'Visiting the iniquity of the fathers upon the children',' he murmurs to himself.

Christiane gives him a curious look. 'I trust to God's judgement more than man's whether my father's actions constituted a sin,' she states, simply and without rancour.

'You are a most interesting child,' the prior returns with a slightly discomfited laugh. 'If Geoffrey doesn't object, I invite you to join us later. There is someone you must meet.'

* * * * * * *

Christiane loves the prior's house the moment they step over the threshold, reminded as she is of home.

Compline is over and the canons are retiring to their dormitories as Geoffrey leads Christiane around the cloister. She is surprised to find there are so few of them, quite out of proportion with the size of the monastery they inhabit.

The prior's principal room is comfortably furnished and richly decorated with tapestries illustrating Biblical stories; it serves as his office for conducting priory business, his sitting room for quiet contemplation and his library for a surprising number of books. She suspects he spends rather more time in here than might be expected of one in his role, but she can understand why.

Prior Robert draws them close to the fire to counter the external chill invading through the gaps around the windows and door, but he soon takes in Christiane's frequent glances at his library and invites her to peruse it while he and Geoffrey converse. The smile that shines from her face and the way she runs joyfully over to the shelves brings an unexpected warmth to his heart.

'I must apologise for my son's behaviour earlier, Prior Robert,' Geoffrey opens, accepting a cup of wine from his host.

The prior nods an acknowledgement. 'He is a strong-willed boy…' he offers half-heartedly.

'He's hot-headed and stubborn.' Geoffrey has few illusions about his son's nature. 'And has far too much of his mother's veneration for position for my liking.'

'Your guidance and discipline are the strongest tools in your armoury against such influences,' the prior hints.

'Which you know are not my greatest strength,' he responds, ruefully.

The prior nods. 'Yours is an accommodating spirit, Geoffrey, but the responsibility is yours, nevertheless. "He who spares the rod hates his son but he who loves him disciplines him urgently." Besides,' lowering his voice slightly to avoid Christiane overhearing them, 'my friend, I fear that if you don't you will face worse ahead. I have seen anger such as that before. It festers like an unhealed wound unless addressed.'

'I hope he will not take his temper out on the girl,' Geoffrey worries, reluctant to accept his friend's warning. 'She has had much to endure already, for one so young.'

'I rather suspect he will find her more than his match,' Prior Robert smiles into his wine. 'Presumably, his mother is unlikely to help?' A sorrowful shake of the head confirms his thought. 'How is Amicia's health?'

'She largely keeps to herself now. I give her everything I can afford to make her comfortable, but life is a perpetual disappointment to her.' He gives a helpless shrug.

'How will she take to the girl?'

'Are you sure you want to listen to this? Eavesdroppers rarely hear well of themselves,' a voice warns from close by Christiane's ear. She tears her attention away from the conversation and turns quickly to find a tall, slender lady looking at her teasingly with a raised eyebrow. Her attire reflects the simple lines required of a nun, but her cope, wimple and veil are of exquisite quality, and her eyes draw Christiane's attention, such a clear, rich blue, so calm and still, like the deepest lake reflecting back the glories of the heavens above.

'It was not intended, my lady,' she protests. The woman smiles.

'I am Alice de Lacy, Prioress of Molseby Priory. You must be Christiane Bren?' she concluded. The girl's face shows surprise at being recognised. 'Prior Robert suggested I might like to meet you tonight.' She extends her arm to invite the girl to join her on the bench facing the prior's desk. 'Christiane is an unusual name?'

'My mother wanted to name her last child Christian. When I born a girl, she had to adapt, and my nursemaid suggested a compromise.'

Lady Alice laughs, a pleasant, almost musical sound that draws upward-leaning lines on her smooth face. 'You were a surprise to your mother?' Christiane nods. 'And I'll warrant you've been surprising her ever since,' she evaluates, tilting her head to one side. 'What brings you to our tumultuous lands, my child? Your accent is not from these parts.'

'I am Welsh by birth,' she affirms. 'I am to join the Goscelin household.'

'So Prior Robert informed me, though not how this came about.'

'My father led the siege of Caerphilly Castle almost three years since. They call it rebellion but, in truth, he was only trying to defend his home, his family and his people. For nigh on a year, Papa, Mama, my brothers and I were all held in the Tower, then they sent most of us back to Wales and we didn't see Papa and Gruffydd until they were brought before my Lord Despenser and he pronounced judgement on them. Judgement he had no right to make!' Her eyes glitter with anger. 'He presented himself as the executor of the king's justice but there were no thoughts for the king in him that day, only for his own power and position and dominion over the Welsh people. I have never seen a man with such poison in his heart and soul, my lady.'

'You would do well to curb the thoughts you express on the subject of Hugh Despenser,' Lady Alice advises softly, surprised by her vehemence. 'I am no supporter of him myself, nor yet his father, but their star rises, and so I temper my words and keep my thoughts within.' She frowns. 'Our king has had favourites before and allowed himself to be led by those who are not fit to guide his hand.'

Christiane's open gaze suggests she is considering the advice.

The prioress frames her next question carefully. 'Do I take it you see more than others do when you look at people?'

The girl ponders that. 'I cannot know what others see, my lady. Only what I see.'

Lady Alice smiles. 'You have a logical bent to match your passionate side, I see,' she remarks. 'May I ask, what do you see when you look at me?'

Christiane contemplates her. 'Your light is very bright, my lady, white and silver, with a touch of blue. It is a colour I have rarely seen in people. It speaks to a strong intention, a clear focus and dedication, particularly to God but also to helping those in pain. You are sensitive to people, their moods and minds and hearts, and many are drawn to you and to the understanding and compassion you offer.'

'Christiane, you have remarkable insight,' she concedes, 'particularly for one so young. I have heard before of those who can read the spirits of others. Is this something you gained from your mother?'

She shakes her head. 'I never heard it spoken in our household. Matilde, my nurse, had known an old woman when she was growing up in France who saw similarly. She encouraged me to practise and hone it, but she also told me to keep it hidden, if I could.'

'You must beware of how you use it in your new home,' the prioress affirms. 'They are superstitious people in this country, God-fearing but ill-educated, though Prior Robert has long made it his mission to address that.'

'Is it usual for prioresses to travel in this part of the country, my lady?' Christiane asks. 'It would not be expected where I am from.'

'No, my child, though as members of Augustinian monasteries the prior and I have a responsibility to support the communities of which we are part, through healing or education or provisions. I am here because the prior has asked me to consult on some cases the infirmarian is handling. As you have already observed, I have some skill in healing, particularly in women's matters, and there is a patient in the village with a persistent problem.'

'Are you able to cure her?'

'Sadly, no, but I can reduce her pain and I think ease her mind too.'

'Her mind?'

'She frets about how her family will cope without her. It's important that she finds what joy she can in the time that's left to her.'

'She is dying?' A nod of confirmation. 'Can there be joy in such a difficult time?'

'Always, my child,' she assures. 'And if not joy, then peace. Know you not that peace can be found in even the darkest moments?' Christiane glowers her response. 'Do you think, for instance, that you could be happy in a convent?'

'Never, my lady!' The reply, all instinct, comes almost unbidden from her lips.

'Indeed,' Lady Alice smiles. 'I thought much as you do when my family first suggested it after I was widowed. And though I submitted, inside I railed against my situation for weeks, nay months. But, in time, I came to value certain aspects of my life: the services that give structure to my day, the opportunities for reading and contemplation. I found the voice inside me that is my daily guide and learned the power and purity of gratitude.'

'I know that voice,' Christiane turns the thought over in her mind. 'When I'm very still and quiet, I hear its words. It feels like love.'

'It is love. The love of God for you, his child. The love of the Spirit and all that is, and all that is to come.' She appears to be thinking hard for a moment. 'You do not feel any calling to the Church, child?'

'None!' she denies vehemently.

Lady Alice smiles. 'There is an energy and a strength in you…' she considers, half to herself. 'I am glad for I think you shall need it.'

'Because I am wholly dependent upon a family I do not know, who have no reason to have my best interests in their hearts?'

The prioress looks across at the two men deep in conversation by the fire, her lips pursed. 'Christiane, has no one informed you of what's intended for you?' A shake of the head brings a frown to Lady Alice's brow. 'Dear child, you are to be betrothed to the son. They intend you to be Ralf Goscelin's wife.'

Monday

Chapter Thirteen

York. 13th September 1976

'Michael, I'm about to head out to the site.' I call out as I run up the stairs and push open the flat door.

'I'm coming with you.' He's standing in the middle of the small room, resting heavily on his cane but otherwise looking somewhat stronger than last night.

'Is that…'

'Don't even think about contradicting me,' he interrupts, and I see he's ready for a fight. But I don't want to give him one.

'I'll clear the passenger seat,' I concede.

'And we need to stop at the post box,' waving three envelopes at me. 'I've written to the faculty in Cardiff, the curator of the city museum and the Glamorgan archives. Let's see what they can find on Christiane.'

* * * * * * *

We head out of York, and he directs me onto the road to the market town of Malton, heading north. It's a glorious late summer's day, with a chill in the air as it's only just gone eight o'clock but a sky that is a clear, sharp blue; the sun promises to have some warmth by late morning. Even more promisingly, there's an energy in Michael, vibrating like a violin string.

'Remind me how you came to know about this site?' It's obvious what's lifted him, so I might as well encourage it.

'The university started mapping Yorkshire's deserted villages in the late fifties. I was at Cambridge at the time, but they wanted extra resources and asked if I would do some fieldwalking for them during the Easter vacation.' He stares out of the side window, remembering. 'I was drawn to the site the moment I saw it. It's quite an inaccessible place…'

'Don't give me any specifics,' I interrupt. 'Let me form an impression when I see it.' He glances at me, quizzically. 'I find it helps me when I'm first there to have a clear mind with as few preconceptions as possible.'

'It's like the place is speaking to you.'

'Yes!' His insight surprises me.

'I felt that way the first time I came here. The moment I walked through the village boundary I got goosebumps all across my skin, and the further I walked, the more that feeling intensified. My hands went cold, though it was a warm day, and the hair on the back of my neck stood on end.' He seems to drift away from me, his mind back in his memories. 'I remember the wind whipping up as clouds skittered across the sun and the whole valley became overshadowed. Suddenly, it was like I was looking at this place with eyes other than my own, like I had stepped out of time.

'And my throat closed,' his hand rises to his neck, 'like I was being choked, not by a hand but by emotions: despair and helplessness and failure.' He shakes his head as if to cast off the experience and looks across at me. 'My colleague was walking ahead, oblivious to what was happening to me, unaware that I'd stopped, that I could barely breathe. The feeling disappeared almost as quickly as it started. But by then, I was in its grip. Whatever "it" is.' He shrugs, a little embarrassed, maybe. This isn't the reserved, dusty historian we're both used to. 'When we returned, I had to know more. I was compelled to find out everything I could about the site and its history and the people who lived here.'

'When did they start digging?'

'Three years ago.'

'Why not before?'

'The DMV project team said the site was of no significant archaeological merit; they've focused their efforts on other locations. But I couldn't let it go. I pulled all the documents I could lay my hands on to piece together the history I showed you yesterday. And that's when I started to realise there were gaps. That she was missing.'

I hesitate to ask but Sam's parting remark yesterday has thrown me. 'Have you ever seen her?'

He shakes his head, and it feels...regretful? No, something worse. Unworthy.

'I felt something...a presence, maybe...that first time. I've hoped for more each time I've come back but whatever – whoever – it is, they evade me.'

He's silent for long moments as we drive up onto the ridge of limestone that forms a raised line before it descends towards Malton.

'She's the reason I came to York. When the university decided to establish the department and offered a seat to me, it gave me a reason to be close to the site and here as often as I wanted.'

'I always wondered why you left Cambridge,' I admit. 'I thought you were settled there.'

'As did I. But everything was drawing me here. And you two didn't need me around: Samantha was studying in London, you were starting your PhD, and both of you were spending your weekends and holidays together.'

I want to ask about Sam, but it can wait until later.

'That's Kirkham Priory,' he points away to my right and through breaks in the hedgerows I catch a glimpse of the ruins, down below in the valley. 'They chose a beautiful spot by the River Derwent for the monks.'

'Augustinians?

'Yes.' Surprised by my knowledge. 'It was founded in the 1120s by Walter l'Espec, Lord of Helmsley, who also endowed Rievaulx Abbey. It was never a particularly wealthy priory; records show it was heavily in debt by the end of the thirteenth century and supported only sixteen canons by the time of the dissolution.'

'How far to the site?'

'We're close. Kirkham sits on the southern side of a big "C" shaped bend in the River Derwent; Threfield Percy sits on the northern side across the river. Maybe two miles between them as the crow flies.'

The leaves of the horse chestnuts lining the road have already started to turn brown, earlier than normal thanks to the long dry summer. The sun plays through them from my right; it will shortly burn off the slight mist in the valley below.

'I hope the weather holds,' Michael frets. 'The forecast for the next couple of weeks is patchy at best.' He sinks back in his seat and gazes with a melancholic stare out of the window; he's thinking that the weather could get in the way of the dig.

We turn east off the main road and down a single-track lane. A few houses and a pub cluster together as a small hamlet – Marston – just past the junction and then we're into open countryside, high banks and hedges hemming in the road and closing off the view.

'There!' Sitting forward in his seat, Michael points at an unmarked turning between an overgrown hawthorn hedge, the track barred by a rusting five-bar gate. I swing the car in and get out to open the gate.

I pause, feeling a strange prickle on my skin. A breeze sweeps down from the ridge and sets the trees whispering. It blows my hair in my eyes and, as I lift my hand to push it out of the way, I feel as if someone is standing right in front of me, staring me in the face. A shiver runs through me.

'Whose land is this?' I check as I climb back behind the wheel.

'A local farmer's. His house is a little further along the lane. His wife has never been too keen on us digging the site but he doesn't farm the land so there was little reason for him to refuse. They're a superstitious bunch around here.'

'Superstitious?'

'Old tales,' he dismisses.

'What sort of thing?' I probe.

'Pull up here,' he orders, ignoring me. The farm track has brought us between two open fields, just stubble after the harvest. At the other side, there are half a dozen cars parked in a disorganised fashion in front of another boundary hedge.

Michael waves me away as I move to help him out of the car, so I grab my coat and rucksack from the back seat and follow him towards a low bridge, almost obscured by the hedge.

It's quiet, just the distant drone of a small plane and the chitter-chatter of birds. The hedge, it turns out, borders the two banks of a small stream, about eight feet below it. It looks to have been a much wider river at some point, but the trees have allowed the soil to encroach, and weeds are choking the flow from either side. Now, it's just a shallow trickle, clear but slow moving, no more than six inches deep.

'It's a tributary of the Derwent,' Michael outlines, leaning heavily on his cane as he crosses the bridge, which is little more than three railway sleepers bound together with a makeshift wooden handrail on each side. 'They dammed it downstream to create a fishpond for the village.' He points ahead with his cane. 'There's the village boundary.'

There's a track running west, curving away from the stream towards a standing stone.

'Where did the track lead?' I nod to my right where I can see it run parallel to the hedge until it peters out maybe three hundred yards away.

'Back up to the Malton road. It was never a thoroughfare; it ends at the site so hasn't been used except for farm access.'

We turn left and walk up a slight incline. The standing stone is a solid block of sandstone, five-foot high, which means there's probably half that again sunk below ground, pockmarked with the stones or chisels that were used to carved it into a rough obelisk. Grass grows around the base and a dense hedge runs away to the right, curving upwards along the line of the escarpment.

I pause at the stone, resting my hand on the rough-hewn surface, weathered and painted with patches of yellow and white lichen. I love the peace that comes to me from something so old and established, a feeling of continuity that says all is well.

'If it's just a dead-end, why do you think there was a village here at all?'

'There's some typographical rationale,' Michael evaluates. 'It's sheltered in the valley, far enough away from the main river to avoid flooding but with good soil. There's a ridge of higher ground that may have been woodland originally but was cleared for the manor buildings and the majority of the tofts and crofts. But it looks like the church was the first structure here, so it's possible it had some religious connotations initially. The stone could be Saxon.'

'It feels older,' I surmise. 'Maybe the Britons had a sacred site first, because of the water.'

'We've not found anything older than Saxon here,' he disputes. But he knows better than to disagree with my instincts.

As we step past the stone, a large cloud covers the sun and the light levels drop dramatically. At the same moment, the gentle breeze turns into sharp gusts of wind, buffeting both of us so hard that I turn my back to shelter from it. It's instantly cold, an inexplicable drop in temperature of several degrees. And now there's no birdsong in the air, just an abrupt and unnatural silence.

Michael turns to me and I can see tense excitement in his face, holding his breath. We wait, feeling the atmosphere, almost like a crackle of electricity in the air. His hand goes to his throat, blue veins standing out against the pale, almost translucent skin, and I see his arm tremble.

'Do you feel it?' he whispers, his eyes darting around as if to divine the source of this atmospheric shift.

I don't answer because that feeling of a presence is back again: an invisible force, a pressure in the air in front of my face. I attempt to see it, though I know there's nothing there.

Michael grabs my forearm with surprising force. 'Do you feel it?' he demands. I nod dumbly, and there's indescribable relief in his face. 'Thank God,' he breathes. 'It's not just me.'

And for a moment I glimpse the loneliness of this obsession that has held him in its grip for so long.

* * * * * * *

A bell is ringing for the morning meeting as we approach the site. They've set up headquarters beyond the standing stone, two large six-berth tents with their backs to the rising escarpment, their rolled-up entrances revealing a series of folding-leg tables and canvas camping chairs inside.

A trestle table has been set up out front as the hub of the campaign, covered with papers in plastic envelopes, plastic boxes stacked to await new finds and all kinds of paraphernalia, from balls of string, wooden pegs and winding tape measures to tags and pens, clipboards and graph paper.

The group of – I count them – twenty-three workers are loosely gathered with their backs to us, some standing at the rear, some seated at more trestle tables that have been set up as a refectory area, a few lounging on the grass. It's mainly men but there are a handful of women in the group; most are young, many are university students at a guess. They're drinking mugs of tea or coffee from thermos flasks that are being handed around; a makeshift kitchen area has been established just beyond the group, with a smaller tent presumably for provisions, a couple of Calor gas bottles and a camping stove.

There are two older men in command, standing behind the trestle table to address their troops. I recognise Ernest Montague from York's archaeology department. He's a craggy, bearded man, broad of shoulder, once muscular but now carrying a paunch. His face is what mine will look like in twenty years: weather-beaten and heavily lined from being outside so much. Though he's not that tanned, so it looks like he now spends more time in the lecture rooms than in the field.

He catches sight of us as we merge into the back of the gathering and he's not happy that we're here.

Finishing the briefing, he hands his clipboard over to the other man to allocate work for the day. My arrival has set a couple of the young women whispering together and sending interested looks my way. I can't help but notice, but I shrug it off; that happens a lot.

'Michael,' Montague shakes his hand with a semblance of warmth but also an underlying wariness. 'I wasn't expecting to see you.'

'I've brought you some extra help, Ernest.' Michael has sensed the wariness too and seems frustrated by it.

'So I see. Eoghan Bren, right?' shaking my hand, and with an obvious frown at the bruise on my face, though he's too formal to mention it. 'I've seen a couple of your presentations at conferences.'

'And?' We might as well get this out of the way.

'Your work is good,' he begrudges. 'But I'd prefer a bit less supposition.'

I nod, not because I accept his view but because I'm very used to this response. How can I explain that what they see as supposition is just a knowing I have that I can't validate and can't explain?

'Actually, Michael, I think we've got enough bodies on site already,' he posits.

'I meant what I said on the phone.' Michael stands his ground. 'We need to investigate the other building.' Leaning on his stick with one hand, he points left beyond the semi-derelict church.

Montague gives a sigh of annoyance. 'That's not going to be an effective use of resources. We're already digging the critical parts of the site, and we've only got a matter of days left before we start winding down the trenches.'

'Then I'm sure you won't mind if Eoghan takes charge of investigating that area?'

This is not what he would want, any more than I would in his shoes. To him, I'm a challenge to his authority and a potential diversion of his resources, which could undermine what he's already mapped out in his mind.

'But I'm site director,' he complains. 'Either I'm in charge or I'm not. I could have been digging anywhere this summer,' he defends, dramatically throwing his arms up in the air. 'I only did this as a favour to you.'

'And I'm paying for the dig.' Michael's voice is quiet, low and absolutely firm. 'I've given you a lot of leeway, Ernest. I'd appreciate it if you showed me the same courtesy in this.'

Montague's bluster fails him, and his face goes rigid with anger before he storms off.

'You're paying for the dig?' That's news to me and I turn in surprise to question Michael. But his face has gone pale again and I realise he's verging on collapse.

Putting my arm around him, I propel him into the main tent. Two of the students are there, laying out boxes to store any new finds, and I send one of them for some hot, sweet tea.

Michael sinks into a camping chair and gratefully accepts the mug, wrapping his hands around it as if for warmth, although the air is already stifling in here. I crouch in front of him, watching closely as the colour gradually seeps back into his face.

'You gave me a scare,' I tell him, but he shakes off my concern.

'He's a stubborn old goat is Ernest,' he smiles to reassure me. 'Good at what he does but pig-headed. I pushed for him to put people on the other building, but he kept resisting. I knew I had to come here to force the issue.'

'You've been paying for the dig?' I press.

He nods. 'Since it started.' He sees the protest in my face. 'It was the only way to do it. The university was never going to commit the money. And I need answers.'

'Does Sam know?'

'No. And she doesn't need to. She'd only worry.' That belligerent look is back. 'Now stop fretting and get out there to look around,' he commands. I smile; it's no great hardship to give in to that demand. 'I'll stay here, maybe have a look through the finds.' His eyes are already straying towards the boxes on the table.

Montague is hovering outside the tent.

'I came back to apologise,' the roughness in his voice giving away how difficult that is for him. 'It's his project, after all. And, well, I hadn't realised how unwell he's become. I should have been more understanding.'

'Why don't you go in and have a word?' I propose. He nods. 'And, if it's alright with you,' I defer to him to restore some of his pride, 'I'll take a look around to familiarise myself with the site. Then we can have a chat about how we might tackle it.'

I hardly notice how Montague responds. The familiar excitement in the pit of my stomach is building, that sensation I get when a site starts talking to me.

It's time to find some answers.

Chapter Fourteen

Yorkshire. 13th September 1976

Ahead, there's a clear wide path – presumably once an even broader thoroughfare – marked by hardened mud and parched grass. No sign of tyre treads in the dirt, so it's probably just dog walkers, hikers and riders maintaining the track now.

It makes me realise that the gap by the standing stone is too narrow to have allowed carts to pass through and I glance back at the entrance, wondering. Yes, the part of the hedge closest to the stone is different from the main boundary. And I can make out a second stone, hidden by the hedge, wide enough to have acted as the pillar for a gate. It could be modern, but at this distance the two stones look similar. A gate? Could it have been contemporary with the village? If so, that's unusual; I can't think of another instance in my experience. Towns, yes, but a gated village? Why?

Moving on, the path splits in two, following the natural line along the floor of the valley and scaling the hillside away to my right. The latter rises to a plateau, maybe thirty feet above, which I know extends out into the modern farm fields. The village followed the profile of the ridge and terrace, two lines of buildings facing each other across those different levels.

At the far end of the lower path, the church is still quite recognisable, though roofless and glassless, a small, unimpressive building.

It's tempting to start my investigation there, to head straight for the area that interests Michael. But I temper my impatience; I know I will do better to gain an impression of the whole site first, which means starting on the upper level.

Climbing the slope allows me to assess the position of the village: the gate is at the eastern end, the church to the west, the manor house complex ahead is the northern-most point and most of the peasant houses run along the ridge from north-east to south-west.

Beyond the northern boundary are the fields the villagers cultivated, including the lord's demesne land, and the south-western end is marked by woodland.

As the land levels out, the track continues towards the manor house while another branches off to my left. The cottages lined up here, laid out across nine plots according to Michael's plans, with a second trackway behind for moving the livestock and for access to the tofts at the rear of their crofts where each family grew their own vegetables and maybe fruit trees. The area is covered with grass now, but the line that would have separated their land from the communal farmland is still hedgerow at the southern edge of the farmer's fields.

Earthworks for the nearest cottages show up where the grass has subsumed stone foundations, raised ridges burnt brown by the sun. Even from here, the perimeter of each property is still defined: ditches, now filled, where the soil levels sink down and the grass grows green.

The archaeological activity is focused ahead of me. The first team is working on a villager's cottage, one of two on a different alignment, facing towards the manor house, and of a larger scale than those I've just walked past. They've removed the turf and topsoil to expose substantial foundations: the strong, clear lines of a medieval longhouse. Even the sandstone threshold is still in place in the eastern wall. There are eight working on the site, following down below the walls for signs of structural changes over time. Others are recording what's been uncovered in detailed drawings, using pegged-out gridlines and height markers set at intervals across the site.

To my right is the manor house and its associated buildings. The bottom few courses of a dry-stone wall mark some kind of enclosure; it rises higher in places, perhaps four-feet high originally. A substantial gap marks the entrance. The track is drier and dustier on the more sharply draining ridge.

The wall follows the same route until it meets a hedge marking the start of the next field. That would have given them quite an extensive kitchen garden, perhaps even an orchard.

This is a large site and teams are spread out across several locations. Foundations are evident everywhere.

The other older man catches sight of me and raises a hand of greeting. 'Martin Meadows,' he introduces himself. 'I lead the local archaeology group and Professor Montague asked for some support. Of course, most of these kids,' gesturing at those diligently scraping away at the dry soil, 'know a lot more than I do.'

I acknowledge his contribution, knowing how much I've relied on passionate locals in the past when I've needed to make rapid progress.

He blushes. 'Strictly amateur hour, here. But I do have the advantage of having worked on the site since we started.'

'Give me the broad layout?' I invite him.

He turns back towards the entrance, his hand sweeping across the main areas in turn. 'Immediately behind the wall are the kitchens, separated from the main buildings. There's a dovecote over there, the bakehouse and brewhouse are on the far corner, adjoining the buttery and pantry for easy access to the food stores. That connects directly into the Great Hall; it sits on an east-west axis, presumably with the dais at the eastern end. Behind, there's a decent size solar block, three separate areas, best we can tell. Stables in the corner,' pointing back towards where the drystone wall disappears into the hedge, 'and a very substantial barn at the far end, probably for grain, though its layout is not dissimilar to ones used for sheep in other parts of the Wolds, so who knows?'

I nod, feeling the picture take shape in my mind. 'Single storey buildings?'

He grins and it's a smile of pure delight. 'Possibly not, based on what we found yesterday.'

He leads the way towards the manor's main private living quarters. 'Tim and Lucy started uncovering this late last night so we're hoping to get a clearer picture in the next day or so,' he nods towards the two students in one corner of the solar area immediately behind the dais. 'We've been looking for the base of the foundations, assuming they were similar to the villagers' houses, but we've not yet found the bottom.' He shows me where they've dug a square exploratory shaft, now as deep as Tim's arm can reach with him lying flat on the ground. 'It's going much lower than the line of the foundations for any of the other buildings.'

'You think it's a sunken undercroft,' I surmise.

Martin hesitates but his excitement is clear. 'I know it's too early to say,' he caveats. 'But it might explain why the foundations are only sufficient for a single-storey building above ground when we would have expected a solar of this date to have two floors.'

'And it would have been an economic use of the site,' I suggest. 'Digging out the chalk to use for the building and then using the pit as basement storage. But how is it you're only hitting this now? Hasn't most of the work always been focused on this area?'

'It's been slow going all the way because there's rubble at every level, in the Hall as well as in the solar. It's as if they just shut the place down and walked away. They didn't even bother to strip out the sandstone blocks they faced the building with.'

I look at the layout, considering. 'There's probably an outside entrance somewhere if you want to chase that down?' I glance around. 'Maybe that corner, where the solar juts out from the Hall. You see how the land falls away slightly? It could be that the path sloped down to the lower level for access.'

He walks over to inspect the area. 'I hadn't even considered why the ground is lower.'

'Do you know,' I contemplate, 'this could be the best chance you have of understanding what happened at the end of the building's life. It'll be interesting to see what finds come up amongst the rubble.'

'Let's not go leaping to any conclusions until we've got the evidence, shall we?' Montague interrupts, coming up behind us.

Martin circumspectly moves away, back to supervise the diggers.

'Martin's just giving me some context,' I explain, ignoring his jibe. 'Before I head over to look at the anomaly.'

'I think I'm better placed to do that. I'll give you a precis as we walk down,' Montague dictates. I let him lead the way.

'This is our third season, six weeks' digging each year over July and August, usually, though we've extended this year. So far, we've chased out the foundations of most of the major buildings in the manor house complex, confirmed as far as possible the rough site drawings that Michael had done on the earthworks, and dug out the Hall, the kitchens and the adjoining storage areas, and the parsonage down by the church. We've also been round the village boundaries and cut cross-sections at various points for dating evidence. Some of Martin's local group have been walking the fields each spring to see what the previous year's ploughing has turned up.'

He pauses alongside the row of houses on the edge of the plateau, from where we can survey much of the site. 'There are ten houses along here, three facing them on the terrace below and the parsonage between them and the church. There are a couple of oddities: a small house by itself by the entrance, behind where the main tent is pitched; and two larger long-houses facing towards the manor house.

'Plot 9 is interesting for having two long-houses on it. It would be sensible to excavate to see if we're dealing with different periods of construction or occupation, perhaps with an original building being downgraded to livestock use when a new house was completed. But,' complaining, 'Michael won't countenance putting resource there. He's only interested in the principal high-status buildings, though he won't explain to me why.'

'What are the key questions you're looking to answer?'

He looks aslant at me, as if he suspects me of trying to trip him up. 'Michael's always been clear: his interest is in the manor buildings and, at a push, the parsonage and church. He wants a date of last occupation and a reason for why the village was deserted. But that's it. I ask you, how are we adding anything to the collective understanding of deserted villages? What merit or value is there in digging out yet another manor house, and a mediocre one at best?' This academic is clearly frustrated by having his opinions disregarded. 'It's why I put a team on one of the long-houses; I want to get something worth writing up if I can.'

'How much longer are you planning to be on site this year?'

'This is our last week. We've already stayed longer than usual at Michael's insistence, but we can't drag it out further. We'll lose many of the diggers shortly for the start of term, myself included. One or two might stay, especially the post-grads or the locals, if you're lucky.'

'Where's everyone staying? They can't all fit in those tents by the entrance,' I surmise.

He looks a bit embarrassed. 'Michael pays for everyone to stay at B&Bs or the pub in the village, those who don't have cars to get back home at night. It's the only way I could get enough people on site,' he defends without my even reacting, 'to promise salaries, food and lodging to anyone who would join the dig.'

'Salaries? Even the students?' This is not normal.

'It was necessary,' he argues angrily. 'How else do you think I'd get them to a Godforsaken little site for six weeks over the summer? I've given up my own summer holiday for this!'

I raise my hands in surrender. 'It's your dig, Montague,' I concede. 'And Michael's money.' I return my focus to the site briefing. 'What do we know about the village's history?'

'Most of the finds are twelfth and thirteenth century. The pottery is the common domestic sort of the region, made in the Vale of Pickering, which gives it a long dating period anywhere within 200 years. There are some more valuable pieces, some glazed maiolica on the manor site.'

'What else are the finds telling us?'

'Interestingly, there's evidence for a large number of horses, which they must have been using instead of oxen to plough the lighter chalk soil; that's quite common in the Wolds. The fields have turned up Roman and Saxon material as well as medieval, and there are Saxon postholes in the parsonage site so we can assume there was fairly continuous occupation. The further we go down in the long-house, the more it looks like there was constant rebuilding and changes in the alignment of buildings over time.'

'And what do you surmise about when the site stopped being used?'

'There's nothing datable beyond the mid-fourteenth century.'

'And?'

'That's it. We've found nothing to tell us why that should be the case.' His tone is almost aggressively defensive, and I'm about to push him further when we're interrupted by a student running down the path, slipping slightly on the scree that litters the chalk surface.

'Professor,' catching his breath, 'Mr Meadows has asked if you can assist at the solar, please, sir.' Montague looks to be on the verge of refusing. I take it he doesn't like the idea of me wandering about his site unsupervised. 'He says they need some guidance on how to proceed.'

With his ego suitably engaged, Montague smiles broadly. 'I'm coming,' he affirms, then turns back to me. 'I'll meet you back in the main tent, Bren. You can tell me if you find anything. Not that I think you're going to,' he throws out as he turns away.

* * * * * * *

I feel relief wash through me as he goes and silently thank Martin for concocting a distraction. Now I can be alone with my thoughts for a while.

Turning the corner, I walk the path along the terrace. The sun is hotter down here and the slope to the right serves as a windbreak. It looks like it's never been used, except maybe for grazing livestock.

To my left I can discern the outline of the lower village houses and, after a slight gap, the parsonage. Where the parsonage has been dug out previously and then re-covered to protect the chalkstone, the ground is still quite exposed, but the grass is encroaching once more.

Walking along the path, the babbling stream comes back into my awareness. The hedge traces the line of the valley off into the distance, the river making a natural boundary.

I decide to take a quick scoping of the church. The walls are built of sandstone blocks, beautifully faced and well laid. The window mullions are Gothic, with pointed arches, and look to have been adapted at some point, perhaps from the original Norman style. The tower at the west end is oddly built, half in and half out of the building, but the upper part and outward-facing side have slumped inwards where a deep crack has riven the mortar.

There's a doorway on the north side, closest to the street, which most of the parishioners would presumably have used. I step inside to look around.

A few tiles remain in situ on the floor between the north and east walls, but the rest of the space is overgrown with weeds and grass. Any wall plaster has disintegrated as the roof and rafters are long gone.

It's possible to discern some phases of development with the stonework exposed. It would need an architectural historian's expertise to piece it together properly, but it's very obvious where a second door has been cut into the original stones on the western wall.

I cross the aisle, treading carefully where an old grave slab has subsided at one end so that the opposite side juts upwards.

As I do so, a slight breeze lifts my hair, and it's like someone's fingers are running over my scalp. I turn quickly, looking behind even though I know there's no one there. I shake myself; I'm becoming too fanciful, even for me.

Reaching the western doorway, I find it's surprisingly detailed in the carving, with pins for substantial hinges still set into the blocks and a heavy iron hasp for a lock on the opposite side.

From where I stand, there are now two features of interest. First, a wide, roughly circular area of reeds growing thickly where there's a drop in the valley floor; presumably this is the fishpond Michael mentioned, created in a lower lying area as it would have been straightforward to divert water from the river.

Second, a large mound rising up between me and the woodland, about thirty feet from the church, long overgrown and currently covered in a high bank of nettles.

Excitement rises now I can focus on the area I get to excavate. This is where Michael wants us to be. This is what's caught his imagination and fired him up in a way that's so at odds with the disease ravaging his body.

The world holds its breath with me. The breeze up on the plateau has dropped here; there's not even a wind rustling in the trees. There's a buzz in the atmosphere, like static before a storm.

I run my eyes across the ground, trying to overlay what I've seen in the aerial photographs. They're not strong lines but they are lines, nonetheless, arcing away from the church and towards that mound. And, if I remember rightly, starting not far from this door.

Something – I can't say what, it's just that instinct that comes over me at times, an insight that drops into my mind and becomes an instantaneous, inexplicable knowing – something makes me take my boots and socks off so that I'm connected to the earth, torched grass against my soles. I stand still for several moments, adjusting, then take two tentative steps forwards; I shift further to the left and, immediately, know I'm standing on top of what's buried underneath. It's like the earth and whatever is beneath are giving off two different energy signatures that I can sense through my skin.

The desire to prove it to myself is overwhelming. I drop my rucksack on the ground and pull out a trowel, hoping it's not too far down to make an exploratory search fruitless. The ground is baked dry at the surface, and I dig hard to remove the top turf; thereafter, it's just persistence to scratch through layer after layer of soil. In moments, I'm sweating, my shirt sticking to my back.

Maybe four inches down, I strike something. It's such a satisfying moment, the simultaneous sound and vibration of metal hitting a substance other than soil. It takes several more minutes to clear enough away to be able to see as well as feel. I rub away the soil with my fingers and feel the silk-like smoothness of glazing on a floor tile.

But in that instant, I know it's not from the inside of a building, which is where it should belong. It's from a path. It's like I can see it in my mind. Glazed square tiles in a soft, sage green, exquisitely laid in a careful curve, bordered with a patterned tile on each edge fired with yellow fleur-de-lis against the green, right up to the door of the church.

And at the other end? I turn my head towards the mound as I try to see the rest of the path in my mind. But there's just darkness. Not blankness…darkness. Impenetrable. Ominous. Heavy.

Suddenly, waterfowl cry as they take off from inside the nearby reeds, rattling them together with an empty, dead noise; harsh calling cuts the air as they ascend and turn towards the south-west.

Standing up, there's an inexplicable tension in my body, different from what I would expect to feel at this moment. My thrill of anticipation is gone. I feel reticence, wariness even, and an uncertainty that is wholly unfamiliar to me. I'm on the verge of something new and unknown.

I'm both drawn to and repelled by whatever is beneath that mound of earth. It extends some distance towards the woods, blending into the background where self-sown plants connect it to the woodland. A path from the trees skirts round the far edge to join the main village road: the dog walkers' way of reaching the terrace and plateau. I come to a halt before I reach its edge but feel unable to go any further.

It's darker here. Neither the wood nor the church casts shade on the site, and yet the light is distinctly less and the air is colder. In spite of myself, I shiver.

My mind wills me to move forwards, but I can't; my limbs are heavy and immobile, and my muscles are rigid. Slowly at first, and then building and building, I feel a spiral of energy whirling around and within me, turning like a tornado, a sweeping, uncontrollable force. A wind-like noise rises and rises around me, becoming the sound of a sharp, piercing whine – a high-pitched scream.

And a wall of energy slams against me, hard against my chest, driving the breath from my body. I stagger backwards, away from the mound, feeling as if I've been hit by a truck.

But my limbs are now free and I step further back, almost as far as the church, until I feel the energy let go, then I lean forward with my hands on my knees, breathing hard, blood thumping in my head.

As quickly as it came, that powerful force has gone, leaving me shaken and immediately doubting the reality of what I just experienced.

And as the warmth of the sun starts to seep back into my skin, I can smell a strange perfume in the air. I catch just the slightest whiff of it, so slight that it's there and then it's not. I look around, but there's nothing here that could have caused it, no late-flowering plant, no breeze to carry someone's scent to me.

Besides, it's a scent I've smelled before, when I was working on a project in the Middle East, and it has no place here. It's oud, the oil they use in perfume, with its distinctive pungent, woody, musky smell.

Something – some inner suspicion – comes over me. And I can't help but speak out loud.

'Christiane?'

I feel foolish even as her name passes my lips. But in the same instant, there's a tingle across my skin. Like someone touched my cheek. I feel absurd, but the knowing is absolute. She's here.

Chapter Fifteen

Threfield Percy. November 1318

They hear the church bell toll as their horses cautiously tread the downward slope from the New Malton road towards Threfield Percy. The final miles from Kirkham have been very slow, wading through thick snowdrifts in places and fording the swollen river with some trepidation. Even now the sky remains heavy and tinged with yellow, promising yet more snowfall.

'That's the noon bell,' Geoffrey explains as they approach a gate and he helps her down from her mount. 'My lady wife likes to maintain a rigorous structure to the village's day; the bell rings at noon to call everyone to dinner, whether they eat in the Hall or in their own cottages.'

He pauses thoughtfully. 'Christiane, you will find we have some peculiar ways here. You will get used to them, in time.'

The girl nods. He is finding she receives and absorbs whatever he tells her in an outwardly accepting manner, yet he senses in her an inward contemplation, and he witnessed her intelligence in conversation with Prior Robert and Lady Alice the previous evening. It was his first opportunity to converse with her in Ralf's absence, and she pleasantly surprised him with her considered engagement in the discussion.

When he accepted the suggestion, conveyed to him by Lord Percy's steward, of the betrothal between Ralf and Christiane, he had little considered what it would mean for the girl. In truth, he himself was being given minimal choice in the matter: the relevant discussions had already occurred in rooms to which he did not have access, whatever Amicia's status as a member of the Percy family. Henry Percy had been advancing his position as long as Geoffrey had known him, and his own principal consideration was to maintain good relations with the family; compliance with this request was materially beneficial in that regard, though his wife will see it otherwise.

Grabbing his staff, he bangs it against the heavy wooden gate that bars their way into the village until he sees movement from the cottage by the boundary wall.

''Tis I, Walter,' he calls as the gatekeeper struggles forward. 'Take your time, no need to rush.' As the man approaches, Christiane can see how his spine is curved out of shape, causing his hips and legs to twist awkwardly, making his progress slow.

He reaches for a hefty key attached to his waist to unlock a solid iron bar that fixes the gate to the stone pillar. With joints and knuckles swollen and red, he struggles to force the key into the lock, dropping it twice before he succeeds.

'We did not know when to expect you, my lord,' Walter apologises as Geoffrey puts his shoulder to the gate to help him move it against a drift of snow, 'or I would have been out to clear the snow this morning. I feared more was to come this afternoon so thought to avoid having to do the clearing twice.'

'Most wise, Walter,' Geoffrey reassures him.

Walter freezes as Geoffrey steps forward and he catches his first glimpse of Christiane. 'A stranger, my lord?' he asks, at once afraid to challenge his master and fearful not to.

Geoffrey beckons Christiane forward. 'Not so, Walter. This is Christiane, who is to be betrothed to Ralf. Though keep that news to yourself for now.'

'Betrothed?' The gatekeeper glances towards his lord's son, whose scowling face he quickly turns away from. 'Then I am most glad to meet you, my lady,' bowing to Christiane. 'You are welcome to Threfield Percy.' Confusion crosses his face for a moment. 'But, my lord…'

'Do not worry yourself, Walter. My lady wife is expecting her.'

Relief follows.

'Do your hands trouble you in this cold weather, Walter?' Christiane asks.

'Aye, my lady.' He looks down at his gnarled fingers, almost embarrassed by them. 'Always when the days are wet and chill.'

'I have some ointment in my baggage that my mother's maid prepares for her. You may find it soothes the stiffness, if you wish to try it?'

A strange look crosses Walter's face as his eyes flick nervously from the girl to Geoffrey for guidance. 'You cannot mean…' he stumbles, and it's shock she hears in his voice.

'No, no,' Geoffrey intervenes. 'Calm yourself, Walter. There is nothing dangerous in this,' putting his hand on the girl's shoulder to reassure her at the same time. 'I wonder if Margery might inform my wife that we have returned? We will visit her once we have dined.'

'I shall ask her right away, my lord.' Walter bows himself out of the way as they lead the horses through.

'Did I do wrong in offering Walter the salve?' Christiane queries softly, frowning as she watches Walter secure the gate behind them and ignoring Ralf's evident pleasure at her discomfort.

'No, child, it was a kind thought,' Geoffrey sighs. 'My wife has laid down some strict rules about what treatments she does and does not deem acceptable for the villagers to use. The people here have grown a little suspicious, that's all.' The girl frowns but lets it lie.

Peculiar ways, indeed, he reflects as they lead the horses up the slope. But she will come to understand soon enough.

* * * * * * *

The bell has stopped tolling and quiet settles over the valley, with what few sounds there are being muffled by the snow. Some villagers pass them, hurrying to their homes. Geoffrey nods in greeting but doesn't stop to talk, keen to get out of the cold and wet. They acknowledge him respectfully enough, but as their gazes fall on Christiane, their responses range from wariness to outright hostility. One of the children even hides behind his father's legs until he is released to run home ahead of them.

A high wall around the manor conceals Christiane's new home from her until they come to another heavy gate, though this one is neither locked nor attended. It opens onto a large yard with the Great Hall to the right, stables to the left and a smithy's forge in the far corner, fired up for work and glowing warmly in the winter light.

Geoffrey sends Ralf in search of the steward and orders David to stable the horses.

'This way, Christiane,' leading her towards the Hall, unfastening his scabbard as he goes. Pushing the door inwards, he leaves his blade with others by the entrance. 'Welcome to your new home.'

He stands for a moment to let her take it in. He has often felt embarrassed by this meagre manor of which he unexpectedly found himself the lord, but at least the Great Hall is a pleasing sight. Some sixty feet long and double height thanks to the cruck frame built over the walls – with oaks grander than anything that now grows in the nearby woodland – this must have been created by someone whose income far exceeded what is generated from Threfield Percy alone. And though it is now over a century old, the stonework remains sound and the windows, at some point enlarged and glazed, bring a good amount of light in on a brighter day than this. Had he the resources, he would modernise a little, perhaps replacing the central fire before the dais with a hearth and chimney to one side so that they might not have to put up with so much smoke in the air. The tiled floor looks well but has become quite uneven in places and could do with re-laying. And it would be pleasant to add some decoration perhaps to the glass or the walls; the painted plasterwork is now quite faded and whatever design had once been captured has long since diminished into obscurity.

How must it look to the girl, having enjoyed some comfort in her early years, if not during her more recent sojourn at the Tower?

The Hall is starting to fill with people come for their meal. The dozen or so who are already seated at the benches rise and bow as he enters, and he motions to them to resume their seats and continue their meal. As many again are milling around, bringing bread trenchers and ale from the kitchens and buttery. A large fire is putting out a good heat, though the smoke is already accumulating in the rafters in spite of the vents in the roof.

He calls one of the servers across as she heads back towards the kitchen and orders food for the top table. 'Come, Christiane,' he encourages. 'I'll show you the solar and then we'll eat.'

The room immediately behind the Hall was all that had stood as a solar when he came here with his bride fifteen years ago; room enough for their bed, a chest for their clothes, a chair for him and stools for her and any guests. That would not suffice for Amicia, though, being used to more substantial accommodation; soon she progressed improvements, adding a chamber for each of them, and a room beyond his chamber that might serve for guests but which, since these were so rare, now served as additional storage for his more precious trade items. She had reworked the principal room into what had then seemed a sumptuous private space for them, but he saw how, in the years since, it had regressed to being purely functional: a table for business, a chair where more often than not he sat alone by the fire, few signs of adornment or distraction or entertainment. How long was it since there had been the sound of laughter or music or female voices in this room? How long since anything has been discussed here but trade and investment and profit?

He watches Christiane take in the room, dark after the brightness of the Hall with only two small windows looking out towards the gardens and neither fire nor candles yet lit. Even the walls are bare.

He arrived here a lifetime ago with so much hope in his heart. How has it come to this?

He shakes off his melancholy; he is little given to self-reflection, knowing from experience that he finds much to displease himself there.

'Your chamber is through there,' he indicates a small door in the far wall, 'and mine is beyond,' pointing opposite. 'Your room has not been much used in recent years, but I asked them to freshen it in preparation for your arrival.' She nods and crosses to look in, assessing the room briefly. 'If it lacks anything, we can address that in time.'

'You have a very pleasant home, my lord.'

'You are generous in your assessment, Christiane,' he allows. 'But I hope you will in time find some ease here.'

'When shall you inform the household of the betrothal?' She meets his eyes directly and he tries to discern whether the thought brings her comfort or concern, but her expression, though open and guileless, yet gives him no insight.

'Maybe tomorrow. We must visit my lady wife first.'

'She does not live in the manor house?'

He shakes his head, and she sees how discomfited he is. 'Amicia requires her own accommodation, Christiane. Her ailments...' his voiced trails away, unable to make the usual excuses for her. 'It's best you see for yourself,' he finishes roughly, 'after we eat.'

* * * * * * *

They have set places for them at the table on the dais, and Ralf joins them as the kitchen servants bring bread and meats and wine. At Geoffrey's behest, Christiane takes the seat to his left while Ralf sits to the right; murmurings stir amongst those at the table below looking on. A servant comes forward with the bowl and ewer for them to wash their hands.

As they eat, a man enters the Hall and approaches the dais, brushing off his cloak.

'God be with you, Master Steward,' Geoffrey greets him.

'Welcome, my lord. The snow is falling again and coming thickly now,' he responds. 'It is well you returned when you did.'

'Thank you, my friend.' Geoffrey's voice holds warmth for this man, and he beckons him to join them on the dais so that they might speak more privately. Christiane watches the man approach. His face is as dark and lined as Geoffrey's beneath his greying beard, and though he is maybe ten years the younger, his visage seems to be etched more deeply with signs of pain and struggle. His body looks to have once been strong and lithe, but his walk is slow and as he nears Christiane can see the paralysis that has seized his left side, drawing his face down in a perpetual grimace and leaving his arm useless. It is with some effort that he forces his left leg forward in an awkward but functional movement. Geoffrey directs a chair be drawn up behind so that he will not have to stand while they talk.

'We fared well in Nottingham this time; some choice pieces that should do well either here or in Flanders.' He hands him a key from his pouch. 'Would you see them safely stowed in the lower chamber?' The man nods. Geoffrey turns towards the girl. 'Christiane, this is Richard Prudhomme, my steward and my oldest, most trusted friend. He has long served with me, first as we plied the trading routes of Europe and now as my overseer here in England. Richard, this is Christiane Bren.' He drops his voice to ensure he is not overheard. 'We will undertake the betrothal before Ralf departs for the north. You may inform the people tomorrow after I have been to speak to my lady wife, and we must arrange a celebration feast for the village.'

Christiane feels the man studying her for a long moment and cannot help but observe his expression when he glances at Ralf; though he seeks to conceal it quickly, there was disquiet evident in his look.

'I offer my congratulations, my lord,' bowing his head towards Geoffrey and then towards Christiane. 'You are welcome, my lady. I hope you will find your chamber has been prepared to your liking.'

'Thank you, good sir,' she responds. 'It seems well set.'

'We brought most of Christiane's belongings with us, but some will follow by cart in time, when the weather permits.'

'Is there anything you will require until then, my lady?'

'I have but few clothes.'

'I believe my lady left some of her older items in the chests in your room,' Richard offers. 'I shall have the women clean and air them then you can see if any suits your needs.'

'Is there anyone who might help me, Master Prudhomme?' Christiane asks.

'A handmaid, my lady? There is no one trained. But if you would be willing to instruct a young girl, I believe the cook's daughter might serve your purposes.'

'Thank you, Richard,' Geoffrey concludes. 'Let us meet after supper to go over the latest business. I would welcome your thoughts on what we brought back.'

Richard rises and leaves the dais, taking up a position by the wall from where he surveys all the activity and people.

'Does Master Prudhomme not eat with the rest of the household, my lord?' Christiane asks, looking around as she eats.

Geoffrey glances at his friend, his face mirroring her concern. 'I'm afraid my lady wife maintains some…' he seems to be reaching for the right word, 'odd traditions. She likes the steward to stand over the service at dinner, on ordinary days as well as feast days.'

'Which he does even when she is not present to witness it?'

Geoffrey laughs. 'You are very blunt, Christiane. And practically minded!' He sobers quickly. 'Sadly,' he warns softly, 'there are some who would be quick to alert her should any of her instructions be undermined. I find it best not to challenge what does little harm.'

'I hope Master Prudhomme's food is kept warm for him,' watching Richard at his post.

'I'm sure the kitchen servants take care of him. Let sleeping dogs lie, Christiane,' he advises, giving his attention to his food.

'My lord?' Christiane ventures. He turns to look at her again. 'Your son is intending to leave us soon?'

'Ralf is part of Lord Percy's household,' Geoffrey clarifies. 'He became a page at the age of seven. Lord Percy is my wife's cousin, and he has favoured us with taking on Ralf's education.'

'I'm training to become a knight,' Ralf inserts, pride and belligerence warring in his tone. 'I beat all the other boys in swordsmanship and archery, and we have been promised our first lessons in jousting next spring. I shall earn my knighthood in battle and prove my courage and strength to the world!'

'My brothers trained with the previous Lord Glamorgan,' Christiane engages, 'and have fought in both Scotland and Ireland for the king's armies…' Geoffrey hears her voice tail off as she recalls the rebellion and more recent battles, but she gathers herself quickly to respond warmly to Ralf. 'I'm sure you will bring much honour to your father and your name.'

The look he gives her is scornful. 'I will raise my status far beyond that,' he brags. 'I shall win fame and fortune and be awarded lands so valuable and extensive that this manor shall be but a drop in the sea of my wealth.'

'You do not intend to support your father in his business?' Christiane queries.

'A mere merchant?' Ralf mocks. 'My mother would never tolerate it!'

Christiane glances at Geoffrey, expecting some reaction to Ralf's disrespect, but he must be inured to such insults for the comment seems barely to register with him.

'I have an older son,' Geoffrey elaborates, 'living with my sister and her husband in Ghent. He is being trained to take over the business when he's older.'

'You were married before, my lord?'

He nods. 'Many years ago, in my home in Flanders. Gelda died in giving birth to Hughes. Fortunately, my sister was able to take him in so that I might continue to travel and trade, and he has grown up happily with his cousins. When I married Amicia and came to live in England, my brother-in-law took charge of the Ghent operations for me so I might expand here and build our trade networks. One day, Hughes will lead it instead of me, and Ralf will receive his fair share as well as inherit this manor.'

'As long as I have enough money for my armour and destriers and squires,' Ralf demands.

Geoffrey sighs. 'Then we had better hope that your mother does not spend it all first,' he mutters. He collects himself and, draining his wine, stands abruptly. 'Ralf, you stay here.' He draws a heavy breath. 'Come, Christiane. It is time you met my wife.'

Chapter Sixteen

Threfield Percy. November 1318

She feels Geoffrey's tension as they tread through the snow drifts, cloaks drawn tightly against the thickly falling flakes. As he leads them back down the hill and turns right towards the church, his silence speaks his internal preoccupation, inattentive to the similarly mute hooded figure by his side.

Against the snow flurries, Christiane can just make out a row of houses and a church as they pass, trying to keep pace with Geoffrey; he has braced himself for this encounter and is keen to avoid having time to reconsider.

There's a shift in the air – as if it has become thicker and harder to draw in as breath – as they move towards an ugly circular building squatting on the edge of the forest. The land it stands on has been scratched out from the woodland, a nasty scar on the earth where trees have been felled but stumps remain as pained reminders of what has been taken. Above, rooks stand sentry in the branches of bare trees, ominously silent, eyes intent on this strange pair.

There has been some attempt to create a beautiful building: the stone is masterfully dressed, and each block carefully abuts the next to create the illusion of smooth roundness in the walls; there are also detailed carvings in the posts and lintel of the doorframe. Yet nothing can lighten the heaviness of the structure, the thickness of the walls and weight of the timbered frame above being out of all proportion to its size; it has clearly been built principally for protection.

Two circular windows in the upper level face towards the village, resembling nothing so much as a crouching predator watching its prey. There are no windows in the lower part, only a heavy door secured with a substantial lock.

A path from the door has been cleared of snow, but it takes the route to the church, not to join the lane which Christiane and

Geoffrey now tread. Footprints created when the kitchen staff brought dinner are being rapidly erased by the new snowfall.

What daylight there is cannot penetrate these gloomy reaches. At Geoffrey's loud rap at the door, the rooks rise in a cacophony from the skeletal trees. Christiane is surprised to see Geoffrey cross himself.

There are long moments of shivering in the cold before they hear the scrape of a key being turned in the lock. At last, the door swings inwards and they are admitted into the bowels of the building.

The room should have been dark with no windows to admit the day, but it is ablaze with light; a multitude of candles are lit in sconces all around the room and huge logs flame in a large stone fireplace. The fire laid is too big for this relatively modest room and the heat is almost unbearable, the more so after the external chill.

A large and high bed dominates the space, thickly layered, dressed with an exquisitely embroidered coverlet and partly enclosed by hangings and a canopy of a heavy scarlet damask, the golden thread of the decoration catching the flickering flames. All around the room, chests of many different sizes stand against the circular wall, all locked. At the foot of the bed, Christiane is shocked to see a Turkey carpet laid out across wooden floorboards. A long curtain conceals a garde robe. The opulence of this room stands in stark contrast to the paucity of decoration in the Great Hall and solar; in truth, it seems more in keeping with how her father described the lodgings of the king and queen.

As they shed their mantles, the door is shut behind them and the lock secured once again.

'Thank you for making us wait in the cold, Father.' Geoffrey's nervousness flares into frustration as the priest turns to face them.

The man hangs his head, which has the effect of bringing his naturally hunched shoulders even lower, as if his own body were unable to stand the weight of even such a meagre frame; the black robes he wears hang on him, giving the impression they had been first cut for someone else, and the wrists, sticking out of too-short sleeves, are naught but skin and bone.

'Forgive me, my lord,' he defends, unable to look up. 'My lady would not countenance my moving until I had finished the passage to which she wanted to listen.'

Geoffrey sighs: she is going to be difficult. 'Never mind now,' he concedes. 'I have brought the girl to see her.'

The priest nods, somehow still without raising his head, and holds his hand out to encourage them to precede him up a wooden staircase that rises with the curve of the wall.

As they emerge onto the upper floor, it becomes evident the ornamentation continues there in even grander style. A series of carpets cover this wooden floor too, so densely laid that they overlap each other in places, and large tapestries woven with bright silks display Biblical scenes across the walls. Around the room are arrayed a plethora of distractions, entertainments and ornaments, all lit by an inordinate number of candles in elaborate holders and sconces. A draughts board and a large, illuminated manuscript lie on an ornately carved table, besides which stands an equally detailed prie dieu beneath an intimidatingly large ebony and silver cross on the wall. More books are visible in one of three large chests. On the closed lid of another sit three ivory caskets, inlaid with silver, and a fourth is open on the table, where Christiane can make out a large ruby brooch sitting on top of other items that glisten with pearls and diverse gems. A lute and a harp are propped up against the end chest.

The plasterwork of the walls is painted vermilion, with geometric shapes in emerald green on the wainscot, picked out with gold tracery that shines in the candlelight. The ceiling is dark blue like the night sky, with stars depicted in gold and silver.

To the east, the ocular windows are set back in the thick wall and hinged to allow them to open inwards. On the western side, three narrow, arched and leaded windows give a church-like feel, but their dense and painted glass serves only to stain the air with their jewel-like colours, thick enough to prevent light from invading the room.

Before the chimney breast, a lady sits in a gilded chair with her back towards them, staring into another large fire. The air is thick with heat and sweat runs down Geoffrey's brow.

'Good day, dear lady,' he starts. 'I trust I find you still in better health, as when I departed?'

She turns her head slightly to the right as he speaks, enough for her to see the three forms in her peripheral vision, but she does not respond to his greeting. Her face seems set with hardness, her body stiff with resentment. Geoffrey draws a breath to stem the anger he feels rising to defend himself against hers and crosses to stand before her.

'Good day, my lady wife. We are returned.' She lifts her chin to look at him directly then deliberately turns her face away.

'You will speak to me, Amicia,' he insists, keeping his voice steady and calm, though his tense hands betray his frustration.

'You speak to me only when you choose, not when you should. Must I, then, be compelled to speak also only at *your* pleasure?' Her voice, thin and high, is as hard as her expression.

Geoffrey clasps his arms behind his back, disadvantaged by his own wrongdoing. 'I had not the time to inform you myself about the betrothal before I departed,' he concedes. 'For that, I ask your forgiveness.'

'Inform me?' As she turns her angry eyes towards him, her bony fingers hook around the carved arms of the chair, like eagle's talons. The air almost crackles with her fury. 'Have I not the right to be consulted? My own son's betrothal and you think only to inform me? And deign to do that in a missive sent back to me when you are already departed to collect the slattern who is to be his wife! Are you so afraid of me, husband?' she spits.

'Amicia, she is standing behind you. Kindly curb your tongue.'

'I care not what she hears!' she cries, her rage bursting out of control and driving her to rise from her seat. 'As I have not given my approval for this match, she,' pointing an accusing finger at Christiane, 'is nothing to me.'

'Wife, you must understand...' Geoffrey puts out a hand to calm her, but she slaps it away.

'No!' she contradicts fervently. 'It is you who must understand. I am a Percy. My son is a Percy.'

'Our son bears my name, not Percy's,' Geoffrey counters, taking a step back from her and folding his arms. 'And, believe me, when Henry's steward presented me with the proposition, it was made very clear that this was not a request.' He glances at Christiane briefly as he speaks but there is little he can do to shield the girl from this.

'I don't believe you!' she flings back. 'Henry would not so dishonour me as to ally my son with the child of a traitor.'

'My father was no traitor...' The words, all instinctual denial, are out of Christiane's mouth before she's even aware, and Geoffrey's despairing glance immediately confirms her error.

Amicia moves so fast Christiane barely has time to step back towards the shelter of the wall. Her long nails dig into Christiane's cheek as she grabs her chin and screams in her face, 'How dare you contradict me! How dare you even speak in my presence! Worthless girl!'

'Nay, my lady. My father was a lord too.' Geoffrey can't believe how Christiane is standing up to his wife, speaking so clearly, almost calmly in the face of such uncontrolled spite. The priest stands within touching distance, but his hands are covering his mouth in shock; he would never dare chastise her.

Inflamed as much by Christiane's courage as by her words, Amicia grabs the long red plait that hangs over Christiane's shoulder and roughly pulls it, forcing her head backwards. 'Spawn of a traitor and a whore! Even your hair is an abomination to God, a sign you were conceived during your mother's flow and are forever tainted!'

'Enough, woman!' Geoffrey's shout of anger stuns Amicia, for her hands fall away and the blood drains from her face. 'You will not harm the child!'

Moments later, she seems to crumple, her hand coming to her forehead as if experiencing excruciating pain, her legs starting to give way. It is done so naturally that Christiane cannot say whether it is real or feigned, and yet she falls so slowly, allowing a surfeit of time for both men to take in the sudden collapse and cross the space to catch her before she drops.

Between them, they support her back to the fire and Geoffrey eases her into her chair, kneeling beside her to look into her face, though she tries to cover it by resting her forehead in one hand.

'Do not shout any more, husband, I beg you,' she whispers. 'You know how it pains me.'

'Bring wine, Father,' Geoffrey sighs to the priest, who pours from an engraved pewter jug into a similarly opulent goblet.

'Sit, Christiane,' Geoffrey exhorts her, nodding towards a stool by the wall, out of Amicia's eyeline. 'Here, my love,' he speaks softly as he hands her the wine to drink, then stands awkwardly while she calms, staring through one of the east windows, hands clasped behind his back.

For long moments, silence settles in the room until only the crackle of the fire is heard. Eventually, Amicia raises her head and Christiane sees lines of tears on her cheeks. 'Is it not enough that his father would permit such disparagement in my own marriage? Must the son also insult me by marrying my only child to such a one?'

Geoffrey draws a deep breath before he turns back to face her. 'Amicia, you must know how my hands were tied in this. How important it is that we keep on the right side of the family.' He waits for her response and takes silence as acknowledgement. 'In truth, I think this was not something Percy himself relished being asked; Despenser put him in a difficult position. For him, this was perhaps the best answer he could find.'

'Maybe if you weren't so inclined to harmony yourself, you might have used this to bargain for an improved position,' she chastises.

'I am not the fool you take me for, Amicia,' he responds, wryly. 'He has given me the first right in bidding to buy forward the fleeces from all Percy lands when next the contract arises.'

That causes her to raise her head in surprise. 'From Northumberland as well as from Yorkshire?'

He nods. 'As Percy prospers, so shall we,' he almost smiles.

'I wonder what Despenser intends in marrying off the child,' Amicia mulls.

'I don't believe any but the king and his father truly knows what is in Despenser's mind,' he shrugs, his eyes on Christiane. 'Though, in his place, I would be concerned about the residual anger in Glamorgan. Despenser may have executed him as a traitor – illegally some would say – but Bren is a hero to many in Wales. Percy certainly saw value in doing this favour for Despenser,' he glances back at his wife. 'Your cousin plays the factions at court well. And,' he admits reluctantly, knowing there is no hiding this from her, 'he has also committed to pursue some sort of dowry for the girl. The brothers were given nothing when placed in households, but the mother is to receive a pension when she is ultimately housed, so it is possible Despenser might entertain something for Christiane as well.'

As he expects, Amicia's eyes flare with interest at the news. 'The girl shall have no need of that; I will take charge of it when it comes.'

He sighs; always it is the money with Amicia. 'I would ask you, then, to take some responsibility for the girl. She should be properly overseen as she grows.'

That proposition is evidently less appealing. 'How can you ask this of me?' she whines, resting her head on her hand again for effect. 'I, who am so unwell and in need of tending myself?'

'Maybe I can be of service to you, my lady,' Christiane speaks up. 'I can do whatever you need.'

'You, child?' As she cranes her neck to stare at the girl by the wall, there is scorn in her face, but also, for the first time, some curiosity. 'What could you ever do for me?'

'Whatever may please, my lady. I can fetch and carry for you. Sit with you should you desire company. Read to you. Sing and play if that is your preference.'

Amicia's eyes narrow. 'You read. Do you also write?' Christiane nods. 'Can you sew? And embroider?' Another nod. A long moment of consideration passes. 'There are some menial tasks I might sooner trust to you than to the clumsy fools of the village,' she concedes. 'And if you show promise, I shall allow you to dress me. Let's hope you can do better than that stupid kitchen girl.'

The girl stands and approaches the side of the lady's chair.

'May I know what ails you, my lady?' she asks softly, one hand coming to rest on the woman's fingers with their distorted knuckles. 'I see how much pain you bear.'

'See, child?' Amicia frowns at where their hands touch, as if something passes between them where they are joined. Her voice drops to a murmur as she looks into her face. 'What do you see?'

'Your eyes show me the burden you bear, my lady. Your light is dimmed by your suffering.'

'You are an odd creature,' Amicia muses. 'Christiane? That is your name?' She nods. 'It has been God's will these many years, Christiane, that I withdraw from the world. Noise is abhorrent to me, and light so pierces my eyes that the day is torture.'

'I would do what I can to ease your pain, if you would let me.' The girl looks straight into her eyes, her gaze steady and true.

Amicia shakes her head, as if to pull herself out of a reverie. 'Perhaps, child,' raising her hand to dismiss the girl, who steps back out of her sight. Amicia stretches the fingers of the hand she had touched, a frown on her brow.

Geoffrey's eyes flick between the two, unable to fathom what has just been exchanged between them but daring to hope that the situation might yet turn out well.

'Ralf starts his return journey to Lord Percy before the end of the week,' he reminds Amicia. 'We must make arrangements for the betrothal to take place the day after tomorrow.'

Amicia's face hardens again. 'If we must obey, we must obey,' she forces. 'Who will stand for Christiane in the agreement?'

Geoffrey pauses. 'I hadn't thought. There is no one…'

'She can hardly do it for herself,' Amicia mocks.

'Maybe the prior?' he wonders.

'If I may,' Christiane suggests, 'I thought perhaps the Lady de Lacy…' Geoffrey starts with surprise. 'She seemed interested in me and appeared willing when I raised the point.'

'When did you do that?' Geoffrey can hardly credit the foresight of this young girl.

'As we parted this morning, my lord.'

He laughs in disbelief. 'It is as well you gave more thought to it than I, Christiane. And,' he turned to Amicia, 'the prior did suggest that she might visit you to see if she can offer any healing.'

'I'll have no wise woman here!' Amicia cries, fear filling her face.

'Be calm, wife; she is the prioress at Molseby, west of here. Prior Robert speaks warmly of her abilities. You can hardly object to that from a good Christian nun, I'm sure?' Amicia sinks back into her chair, though worry still mars her expression. 'Will you come to the Hall for the ceremony?' hoping against hope.

'No. We shall do it here,' she commands. 'Bring the steward and the reeve to witness, we need no other. Father Peter, I'll mark it in the book myself. De Lacy, you say? Is she kin to the Countess of Lincoln?'

'I did not stop to ask,' Geoffrey confesses.

'Such matters are essential, husband! She may count the Earl of Lancaster as family.' Amicia deliberates for a moment. 'I must think about what clothes I shall wear if she is to attend. Christiane,' she beckons the girl back to her side, 'you shall return early tomorrow morning and help me sort through my attire.'

Geoffrey smiles to himself. Never a thought for what the girl should wear to her own betrothal.

'I have asked Richard to arrange a feast for the tenants and household,' he adds.

'Certainly not!' Amicia rebukes him. 'That would be an unnecessary waste of food and money we can scarce afford. It's not as if this is a match of which we may be proud. The kitchens can prepare something particular for the prioress as our special guest, but the rest can partake as usual.'

'We cannot let the betrothal of our only son pass unmarked,' Geoffrey vows. 'Nor would it be fair to Christiane; she must make her life here and the people must see her welcomed into the family or they will not accept her.' He holds up a hand to forestall her objection. 'The climate of fear you engender, Amicia, will work against her.'

She sits back stiffly in her chair, pursing her lips and drumming her fingers on the arm.

'Did you bring me no gift from your travels, husband?' So changeable; an icy northern gale one moment, a warm and cozening western wind the next.

'Have I ever failed you, sweetheart?' he smiles, falling in with her sudden change of subject and reaching into the pouch hanging from his waist. 'I met a man travelling from the Moorish lands. He says none but the highest in their lands might possess a scent such as this. One to add to your collection.'

She struggles with the small stopper on the bottle and holds it out to him. 'Open it for me!'

'Nay, my hands are too awkward. Christiane?' holding the fragile vial out to the girl who deftly unstoppers it.

Amicia holds out an arm, commanding, 'Put some on my hand.' The girl tips the oily liquid onto one finger and rubs it across her almost translucent skin. 'It was expensive?'

'The merchant was taking it to the court at York in the hope of finding someone able to pay the right price.'

She breathes in the heavy scent. 'Then I have what many noble ladies want to possess! There is a chest of perfumes downstairs, girl,' directing Christiane. 'You may put it with those.'

Geoffrey sighs in relief. The worst is over, and they might depart. 'We will take our leave of you, good lady,' heading towards the stair.

'You have not said what you think of my new dress, my lord,' she calls as she stands to forestall him, reluctant that they should leave.

'It suits you well, wife,' he complements her, though it seems more low-cut than he might deem appropriate should she be inclined to appear in public.

She smiles, running her hands over the fabric. 'It is of the latest fashion Queen Isabella is wearing, they say. And I had the furrier from York send ermine to trim my mantle. I shall be sure to look well when we are next called to court.'

'None could compare.' He forces a smile and, bending down, kisses her brow. It is with no small relief that he leads Christiane back down the stairs.

As the priest relocks the door behind them, they pause to take in the snowy landscape and to adjust their eyes from the brilliant internal brightness to the fading wintry gloom.

'She uses far too many candles,' he condemns, almost to himself. 'But I cannot chastise her for it, for surely I would go mad shut away in such a place.'

Christiane glances up at him curiously. 'When mean you to go to court, my lord?'

He draws a heavy a breath and, pulling his mantle close, starts to walk back along the lane. 'Never, Christiane. At least, Amicia shan't. She rarely leaves that place now, save to enter the church for prayers.'

'What is her malady, sir?'

'It is hard to give a name to, child. For certain, none of the physicians has been able to do so.' He trudges through the snow, feeling the weight of his years. 'The best I can tell, it started when she was with child. For months before Ralf was born, she took to her bed, showing barely any interest in anything, foregoing all but the blandest of foods, caring not whether it was night or day. When she did ultimately return to the world, it seemed the sun had become intolerable to her. Now, if she dares emerge into the day, it is only with thick coverings shrouding her from head to foot. She says any touch of sunlight causes a redness and pustules on her skin. It terrifies the children of the village; the stories they've woven around her are grotesque.

'She has moments,' he deliberates, 'when I think she retreats into her childish hopes for a life of excitement and opulence. It is then that she forgets the ailments and fear that confine her to that room. Maybe it is her way of coping.'

'What fear restrains her?' Christiane responds.

'She will not tell me. That came upon her later. It is the reason for the gate and the locks on the doors, and for her nervousness whenever the villagers go to the markets.' The wind picks up as they approach the higher part of the village. 'I fear,' he murmurs, 'her temper has suffered through her retreat from the world. She has a sharp mind but insufficient distraction. It is as if her mind has turned against her and, filling her with fears, has turned her against the world. Her mood is like quicksilver, changing from delight to rage in a moment. She takes slight at the smallest things and constantly sees threats were there is none. I hardly know now what is true and what is her imaginings.'

'That must be very difficult for you as well, my lord.'

Surprised at her sympathy, he looks across at the girl; her innocent face shows only interest and concern. 'Christiane, you are a strange one.' He contemplates her for a long moment. 'It's almost as if...' he laughs, half genuine, half bemused, '...as if you could see into a man's soul.'

They fall into silence as they walk up the hill and head towards the Hall, only the cawing of the rooks breaking the stillness.

'Well, Christiane,' he asks as he pushes the door open for her, 'what think you of your new home?'

The girl's guileless smile warms his heart as she passes before him without a word.

And what, he wonders, am I to think of you?

Chapter Seventeen

Threfield Percy. 13th September 1976

I feel strangely dislocated as I walk back along the path, half in my world, half in hers.

This connection to the past is stronger than anything I've experienced before. It both thrills me and scares me because I'm not in control.

Ernest Montague is coming back down the lane. Frustration floods through me: I know he'll hope to intercept and influence me before I speak to Michael. I'm not having it, this is Michael's dig, Michael's drive for answers, and I feel fierce loyalty towards him.

'What did you make of it?' he starts.

'Let's take this inside,' I cut across him, not breaking my stride. 'You and Michael can hear it at the same time.' My tone brooks no opposition.

I push through the flap of the tent and Michael looks up, startled. I face him, arms folded. Montague dispatches the two students to the main site, so we have the tent to ourselves, then stands by the entrance, his body language mirroring mine.

'The lines in the photograph aren't a building,' I address Michael directly. Montague's smirk grates. 'But there's a substantial, high-status building underneath the nettle-covered mound by the wood.' Hope surges in Michael's eyes.

'Don't be ridiculous,' Montague scoffs. 'That's just a midden. That's why the nettles grow so profusely there.'

I suppress my desire to argue: if I tackle him directly, I know I'm going to get riled up and he's going to look like a fool, and I still need his co-operation. 'The lines you saw in the photograph are a path laid between the building and the church; a path to a door that I think was added to the church's west wall during the period that you're interested in. That's a guess but an expert should validate it. The path is very unusual: it's laid with the kind of high-quality glazed tiles you'd normally expect inside the solar. They're better quality even than those inside the church. And it takes you directly to where the mound now sits.'

'And based on that you're identifying a high-status building?' Montague's tone drips sarcasm.

'The size and shape of it might lead you to conclude that it's a midden,' I concede, 'but that path would never have been built for the village rubbish pit. And a growth of nettles that dense and prolific,' I pause to look back at Michael, 'could equally suggest extensive burning. Meaning the building was destroyed by fire.'

Montague throws his hands up. 'How on earth can you make such a leap?' he demands. 'Where's your evidence, man?'

How do I know? I can't say, but I do.

One look from Michael tells me I don't need to convince him. 'How will you approach it?' he asks me, a little breathless.

'Treat it as I would a rescue dig,' I tell him. 'We want fast results. Clear the area, be prepared to move quickly through rubble and debris when we find it and get to the heart of whatever is there.'

'This isn't a rescue dig,' Montague disputes. 'We're not under time pressure…' He looks at Michael and understands what I'm proposing. 'I mean…' he stumbles, then closes his mouth, embarrassed. The unspoken words hang heavily in the air.

Michael looks at his colleague; the irony is the sympathy is coming from him, not for him.

'What do you need?' Michael turns back to me. Montague sinks into a chair, defeated.

'First, some strong labour to do the initial clearing, maybe a day's work.'

'The farmer has some casual labourers working for him who might spare a day if we pay them,' Montague offers, a gesture of conciliation. 'I'll talk to him this afternoon.'

'After that, I'll need three or four of the diggers, the more experienced the better. I need people who know what they're looking out for, given the pace we'll be going at.'

'Hang on a second!' Montague protests. 'We've just uncovered what looks like a sunken undercroft that needs to be explored, and we're a substantial way into the dig on house number two. On top of which,' he implores Michael, 'everything needs recording before we start covering over for winter or there'll be nothing worth digging next year.' He blushes, recognising he's put his foot in it again. 'I need all the hands I've got just to make a fist of our existing work!' Embarrassment turns to bluster.

'Then, give me Martin and ask the students if they want to get some experience working with me,' I suggest.

'Great,' he tones, sarcastically. 'I'll lose all of them that way. They're falling over themselves for the chance to work with a modern-day icon.'

'This isn't a battle to win or lose, Ernest,' Michael softens. 'At least,' wryly, 'not for you. And I've made provision in my will: there's funding for three more years of digging at least and it'll go to your department. After this, the dig is yours, to pursue whatever avenues you choose. But, please,' his voice shakes a little and it hurts to hear, 'I need this.'

I have to turn away. I make a show of going over to the table where the students were cleaning finds in washing-up bowls, but I can't focus on what's right in front of me and my throat is thick with pre-emptive grief. The urgency of my own excitement is now the urgency of a race against mortality. I feel the weight of the years and years he's been looking for answers. Of that solitary pursuit of some hidden truth. I'm not sure I even know what question he's asking; all I know is that I have to pursue it for him now.

I hear a few murmured words between the two men, then Montague leaves the tent.

'Eoghan.' I turn to face Michael at his call, masking my emotions. There's exhaustion in the deep lines on his face, and pain beneath. 'I need to get back,' he busies himself with pulling on his jacket and retrieving his walking stick. 'The nurse is due, then they bring lunch at one.' He's giving us both time to regroup.

'OK, let's head out.'

It's as we walk towards the bridge that I remember the standing stones. 'Michael, give me a second…' I stall him.

The stone is wonderfully cool beneath my fingers, in spite of the heat of the day. I run my hands down both sides of the first stone, then crouch by the one hidden in the hedge, trying to make out markings in the play of light and shade. Yes, they're there: carved divots at roughly the same height, the right shape and spacing for metal hinges. I can envision them in my mind: closing my eyes I see the landscape, two-feet deep in snow, the air cold and crisp, the threatening clouds with yet-to-be-shed snow, a heavy gate hewn from oak, dark with age and wear and bound with iron. And yes…still with my eyes shut, turning my face over my shoulder in the direction of the tents…a gate-house. It's a poor rough building, smaller, meaner than the rest but at least it's a home for Walter…

What the hell? Where did that come from? I open my eyes and stare at the tent, and I can almost see that tiny house, barely more than a hovel, imprinted on my eye, overlaid on the modern reality in front of me. My head swims and I put out a hand to steady myself, expecting to find the gate there and surprised to feel the hedgerow instead. I cover my eyes and struggle to focus. When I look again, it's gone.

Michael's standing patiently by the bridge.

'What?' he asks, seeing my face as I approach.

'Something…nothing,' I dismiss it.

He lets it go but as he turns to leave, he stumbles and only just manages to hold himself up on the railing; his strength has gone. I put my arm around his back and my shoulder underneath his arm, bending low to support him. It's a shock how fragile his frame is now. He was always a small man but there's almost nothing to him, so bird-like I'm afraid I'll crush his ribs. But there's inner strength and determination in him. And such dignity. He withstands my help without a word because he must, but as soon as he's seated in the car, he's his usual self and focused on the dig.

'Will you come back this afternoon to start?'

I fire up the car and turn down the track. 'No point until I can get the labour to start clearing. I'll come early tomorrow. I want to go back over your papers this afternoon,' I glance at him for permission. 'Now I've seen the site, it'll help me to put everything in context in my head. Maybe see some of the details differently.'

He nods. 'Good. You can do that while I have my afternoon nap.'

When I get back into the car from letting us through the gate, he's staring out of his side window.

'I want you to know, I'm not worried about dying.' I fix my gaze on the road ahead, understanding why he's turned his face away, though his voice is stable and quite normal. 'I'm very pragmatic about all that. Sam's well set, especially now she's got rid of that husband of hers. Never was right for her.'

I wait for him to go on, but he doesn't, so I take the opening he's offered. 'What happened there?'

'She hasn't told me much. She tried hard to make it a success, but I could see she was forcing it. Lasted longer than it needed to, in my opinion.'

'I thought your generation didn't believe in divorce.'

'I've come to terms with it more than most,' he accepts. 'I would never have wanted Marilyn to make herself miserable by staying with me.'

'Even if she made you miserable by leaving?'

'But she didn't,' he assesses. 'Of course, I missed her at the start, but it wasn't that hard to lose myself in work. I felt she was never really mine.' He says it so simply, my heart catches.

'Why not?'

'We were a mismatch from the start. I should have married an ex-student or someone I met through the faculty, not an usherette at The Regal. But she was lovely. So full of life. Carefree and easy-going, in spite of the deprivation she grew up in, or perhaps because of it. She struggled after Samantha arrived. It was like her life was being smothered inside her.'

'You didn't attempt to stop her leaving?'

'I didn't have any choice. I came home one night and she'd gone. Sailed to America with the US Army boy she'd met in The Eagle, according to her 'Dear John' letter. Not that I would have asked her to stay; better to let her go and think of her as being happy again.'

'When you love someone, set them free?'

'What is that, some awful pop lyric?'

I hesitate for a moment before asking, 'What about Sam? Is there anyone new in her life?' I try for nonchalance, but it sounds hollow to my ears.

He looks at me and I look at him. He doesn't reply.

* * * * * * *

Thoughts sit unspoken between us on the drive back. It's just as we're winding through York's city centre that he gives voice to them.

'We've started something, haven't we?'

'Meaning what?'

He scrutinises me. 'You're sensing things, aren't you? Like I did that first time.' I don't respond but that's an answer in itself. 'What do you think is happening?'

I frown back at him. 'Nothing in my experience can explain this.'

Heavy silence. 'Why you?'

I shrug because I really have no insight to give him; I'm as lost in the unknown as he is.

'I feel connected to them. Don't you?' he probes. 'I don't know how. I don't even know who 'they' are. But it's like they're reaching across time to me. To us. God!' he scoffs. 'I never thought I'd hear such New Age nonsense from my own mouth! But I feel it,' he insists. 'I feel them. There's something unfinished.'

Chapter Eighteen

York. 13th September 1976

'Hello?'

'Eoghan, it's Sam. I wasn't expecting to catch you at Dad's. I thought you'd be up at the site.'

It's surprisingly nice to hear her voice, soft and low on the telephone line.

'We were this morning.'

'We?'

'He insisted on coming, Sam. I couldn't have stopped him if I'd wanted to.'

'No, I don't suppose you could. I hope he's not too tired?'

'He's sleeping now. I dropped him off for his lunchtime check-up then came back after lunch to go through his papers.'

'Do you know if he ate much?'

'Some.'

'Which means hardly any, right?'

'Hmm.'

'Please, Eoghan, I need you to be honest with me. No sugar-coating.'

There's a tightness in her voice that I dearly want to soothe away.

'I think he was too tired. Maybe he'll be hungry by dinner.'

A pause as she takes that in. Of course, she doesn't need me to soothe her; she was always so strong in the face of the difficult moments in life. It gives her remarkable resilience in her personal life as well as her profession.

'What did you make of the site?'

'There's definitely something there. The only way to know what is to dig it. Who knows if it will tell us anything? Let's just hope it doesn't turn out to just be the village dumping ground,' I remark, drily, 'or my reputation will be in tatters.'

'How long?'

'Hopefully no more than a few days to know if we're onto anything. If it is, a couple of weeks should cover it if we work all the daylight hours.'

'I'll be back up at the weekend. See if you can have it wrapped up by then, would you?'

Teasing me. And I force a laugh because she too is trying to lighten the mood.

'He called it "unfinished business". What do you suppose that means?'

Considering for a moment.

'This has always been more than an anomaly of history for him. Something was drawing him to it. No doubt the shrinks would say he was trying to make up for letting Marilyn go by chasing down the tale of this woman.'

I go to the question that's hovering between us.

'Were you serious when you said you'd seen her?'

'Yes.' Defensively.

'What did you see?' I sense her reticence. 'Come on, Sam. I need honesty too.'

'Just don't ridicule me.'

'Scout's honour.'

'Thanks, that's not reassuring.' She takes a breath. 'It was the first time Dad took me to the site. We were going fieldwalking. I think he'd been there the year before with York Uni. It must have been a year or so before he moved north.'

'Stop stalling. I don't need context, I need data.'

'Still as blunt as ever.'

'You can take it.' She was always the only one who could.

'I saw a young girl. Aged maybe ten or eleven, though she was small of stature so could have been younger. Red hair bound in a single plait hanging all the way down her back, so long she could almost have sat on it. A thick woollen cloak dyed green – a mantle, I think they call it? – all the way to her ankles, with a matching hood over her shoulders. A dress underneath, the same length. Leather shoes, up to the ankle, almost like little boots. Green eyes. The biggest eyes you've ever seen, set in such a pale face. Proper Celtic colouring.'

'Where was this?'

'Over by the church. She appeared to be looking around.'

'Looking around?'

'I know, sounds stupid, right? But that's what it looked like to me.'

'How did she look? I mean, was it how you imagine seeing a ghost would be?'

'She wasn't solid, but I couldn't see through her either. I know that sounds contradictory, but I don't know how else to say it. She had a light around her. I've never seen auras but if I did, I think that's what it would look like. A moving, rippling light, translucent but coloured – the kind of brilliant blue they use to paint the Virgin Mary's cloak whenever you see paintings of the Madonna and child.'

A moment to absorb the information. The detail and specificity of it. The resonance with what I dreamt. Then the harder question that it naturally prompts.

'You knew The Obsession was real,' trying not to accuse but failing. 'Why didn't you say anything before?'

A sound of…what? Frustration? Self-blame?

'Because he was already consumed by it. I didn't want to feed that. I know. I'm not proud of myself. But I did what I thought was for the best.'

'And now? Why the change of heart?'

'Because it's the only thing keeping him going.' Her voice is harsher, the words caught in her throat. 'It's the only thing that's making him happy. I can't take that away from him.'

'He certainly seemed happy today, messing around with the finds, directing the students.'

'If that were enough, it would be easier. But it's because he hopes you'll find what he hasn't been able to. He believes in you, Eoghan.' The pause is heavy with history. 'So do I.'

There's nowhere to hide from that. False modesty would resound emptily. Promises of success would be equally hollow. I don't know what to say, so I change the subject.

'He was talking about your mother earlier.'

A heartbeat passes.

'Really? Why?'

'It just…came up.' Pause. 'Have you never tried to find her?'

The response comes fast; too fast. 'I've never felt the need.'

'You don't want to know the woman who gave birth to you?'

'Don't over-romanticise it, Eoghan.'

'Unfeeling pragmatist.'

'Hopeless romantic.' Wordless smiles. The old banter. 'My childhood may not have been typical, but I never felt the lack of anything.'

'You're so self-sufficient.'

'Always.'

'Maybe that's what attracted me in the first place.'

'I thought it was because your friends started flirting with me.'

'Not "friends". Just Dean.'

'You can't blame him. After all, he didn't start it.'

'You were flirting with him deliberately?'

'Of course.'

'But you didn't like him.'

'No. But you needed something to make you see what was under your nose.'

'Ow. You manipulated me!'

'It was for your own good.' I love her laugh. Always have. 'What do you really think of the site? I don't want facts. What's your instinct telling you?'

'We're on the right path, Sam. I know it.'

An audible sigh. 'Thank God. I so want him to find some peace.'

I hesitate, knowing I need to go against Michael's wishes but that I can't have this knowledge hanging between us.

'What is it?' She knows how to interpret my silence.

'He doesn't want me to tell you, but Michael's been funding the dig.'

I can almost hear her frown. 'I thought it was a department programme.'

'They're not interested in the site. Montague's there almost under protest. Michael's funded it from the beginning, all three years. And they're not exactly being careful with the budget.'

'That doesn't matter, the money's irrelevant. It's that he felt he had to keep me in the dark. I guess that's my fault for making it difficult for him.'

'Don't say anything to him, will you?'

'Don't you think too many things have been left unsaid already?'

Now that's a comment loaded with meaning. I can feel her waiting for me to respond. And I would, if only I knew what to say.

'Tell Dad I called, will you? And call me if there's anything I need to know.'

There's a click and the dead line buzzes in my ear.

Chapter Nineteen

Threfield Percy. November 1318

Her room is in darkness, the flames in the fireplace already beginning to die down, some logs glowing inwardly but others blackened and smoky at the edges, too damp to take properly. Chill air seeps through the walls and door, sucking away what little warmth there is.

The mattress filling digs into her legs in places, even through her shift, and the straw smells musty; perhaps it hasn't been refreshed since last it was used, whenever that might have been. The air smells stale too, and the room has a feel of neglect or disuse, home only to the bed, a stool by the fire and a few chests that must relate to Geoffrey's business.

She likes that he didn't send her away when he sat down to brief the steward after supper. The solar was welcoming with the fire lit, candles around the room and some long-forgotten cushions found to enhance their comfort. From the Hall came sounds of servants clearing the space, putting away the trestles to make room for the household's men to sleep on the floor; that gave way to the more subdued sounds of conversation around the fire and the occasional shout of triumph or dispute from the dice-throwing in one corner.

Geoffrey and Richard sat across from each other before the fire, Geoffrey leaning back in his chair to straighten his left leg and ease the swelling around his knee from so many days' riding.

A pile of clothes and sewing materials lay on the table, her work assignment from Amicia. Drawing candles near, she turned her stool that she might discretely listen to the men's talk while she sewed.

Geoffrey attempted to engage Ralf with their plans, but the boy showed no interest, and when his unruly behaviour became disruptive Geoffrey dismissed him; he went without a backwards glance.

It was Richard who noted her interest and drew her into their discussion. This was a new world to her. At home, they had known and welcomed many of the leading merchants from the nearby market towns, but her father's and brothers' natural sphere was managing the land or fighting, whether in training or in battle. This talk of trade routes, international fairs, competing merchants, contracts, prices and profits was new to her and her mind was eager to absorb it.

In Richard, she felt a kindred spirit. Geoffrey was not adept at running the manor and left the management of its rhythms and routines, its politics and disputes almost entirely to his friend. Richard had adapted ably from the mercantile world to his new life and seemed well versed in its challenges and complexities. Even so, she could see what changes her mother would have made, where it would benefit from a woman's guiding hand; if Amicia had no interest in the day-to-day activities perhaps she might help him, and maybe he might teach her about the business in return.

This is a strange place, her new home. Geoffrey is kind to her and protects her as her father might have done, but he has his failings as a husband, father and lord. He would have been happier left alone to pursue his business for he is not strong enough to be master of his own house, and the guilt of that knowledge presses down on him. No wonder he is content to be away so often.

When she considers Amicia, sympathy arises; she sees how much pain she bears in the way it muddies and reddens the light around her. There is darkness there too, though, as if the pain has infested her mind and turned her away from the empathy for others that might counter her selfishness. The way she twists and dominates those around her, winding them to her will, is contorting her own soul, did she but know it.

And it reaches out to affect the hearts of those around her. Fear and suspicion – beyond the accepted wariness of a stranger in their midst – surrounds many of those she has seen in the village and in the manor house this day. Though none more so than the reeve, who appeared after supper to acknowledge his lord's return, but did so with such poor grace that it verged on insolence; he is clearly Amicia's man, for the hue that surrounds him mimics the shades of his lady's own.

It seems strange that he has been allowed to hold his post for so many successive terms. Of course, each manor has its own practices, but re-electing the same reeve every year is inviting his own self-interest. One among several strange notions in this distant place.

And yet, for the first time in longer than she can remember, she's at ease here among hills and valleys that are not so different from home, for all that the manor seems poorly matched to what she knows. More than that, within her are the stirrings of a freedom she has not experienced before. Such she might have known had she been betrothed and joined her future husband's household, but her father had hesitated to start negotiations with neighbours and kin, and then the uprising put paid to any such thoughts. But suddenly here she is, relieved of the oppressive uncertainty of the last three years, removed from her own family's oversight and drawn into a world where, one day, she will stand as lady, with all the duties and care and privilege that have been instilled in her from birth.

Hesitation arises only when she reflects on the boy who will give her that status, and who she intuits he could become. His disrespect for his father does not stand well with her. Without respect for kin, the Church and the king, we are little more than savages; her father taught her that. Even in raising an army, he did so not against the king but against the injustices being meted out in his homeland. This boy has learnt from his mother only to consider what pleases him, not what is owed to others; the blustering and selfishness in him today could so easily become brutishness and cruelty. Can the Percys overcome the influence of his mother and the weakness of his father to train him into the kind of man she might be proud to call husband and lord?

She turns onto her shoulder and pulls the coverlet up against the increasingly chill night air.

And as she closes her eyes for sleep, she wonders about the man who has stood at her shoulder, watching it all unfold. She senses his presence but cannot see him clearly, always at the edge of her eyes, disappearing if she turns her head. He isn't among the dead; it isn't the same as when she sees Grandfather or Father's younger brother, who died when just a boy and played with her as a young girl.

It is a reassuring presence, and she is glad he has travelled with her from Wales. It was only today as she sensed him again that she realised he had also been there on the day her father died. She had paid him little heed then, one soul among so many she had sought to shut out from her confusion.

Though she cannot see him, yet she knows something of him: his Celtic blood, like hers; the way he experiences things beyond the physical world, like she.

One more thing she knows: he is there because of her.

* * * * * * *

I wake to darkness, disorientated by the unfamiliar room.

I lie still for long moments, hearing my own breath loud in the quietness and trying to calm my breathing; the adrenalin that has shot through my veins takes a while to abate.

It was her. Again. In my dreams, inside my mind. I know it with the same certainty I find on a dig; the kind of knowing that comes into my head as a fully-formed thought, rich and textural in detail, sure and clear. I can see her, lying in bed, thinking over her day, her journey from Cardiff, the new people she has met, the new place she now calls home.

But already the concreteness of the images is dissipating, like smoke filtering out into the night air. I visualise the room, the bed, the fire, the storage chests, but the harder I reach for the thoughts, the more they elude me.

I dare not move as I attempt to empty my mind, hoping the thoughts will return, sensing that my here-and-now will drown out this ethereal other place.

And I catch the slightest echo of a thought, a whisper of connection, a single fragile thread tethering me to her world and she to me.

And then, it's gone.

Tuesday

Chapter Twenty

York. 14th September 1976

It's two hours before the indigo inkiness of the sky starts to lighten. Prone on the bed, I watch the night slowly subside before the approaching dawn, relaxed but not finding sleep again. Drifting in and out of consciousness, in that strange place of half awareness, I catch glimpses, fragments of her world again. But they're gone as soon as I open my eyes and my hard-edged reality intrudes.

The monastic quality of my small room is reflected back to me as I shave: a single bed, one wooden chair, a heavy 1930s-style wardrobe, a basin with a tiny oval mirror above. It appeals to me; I want uncomplicated right now. A spartan room and a basic existence suit me when I'm focused on a dig.

I'm too self-sufficient, I know that. Women want to get close, and I enjoy being with them, but I have no interest in letting them in. And too many of them want to change me; they believe there's a deeply caring man inside, waiting to be released by the love of the right woman. Maybe there was once. Call it habit or a single-minded focus on work or distancing, it's easier to keep women at arm's length.

Except Sam. The thought comes unbidden but with enough force to make me stop shaving, mid-stroke. What was that? A ghost of what was there before? A trace of old memory, long-suppressed? Or something new? My body feels alive at that thought. The hope…the hint of something more sparks within me something that's been absent for a long while.

But this is not the time.

* * * * * * *

The pub doesn't start serving breakfast until seven; too impatient, I leave without eating. The clear air has that invigorating nip to it of the seasons crossing over.

The lights in Michael's flat are already on – I guess he isn't sleeping well – but I don't worry about dropping in to see him: he'll be expecting me to focus on the dig. With the lanes empty and my foot hard on the accelerator, it's less than a quarter of an hour before I'm parking the Volvo at the edge of the field. There are no other cars around yet; I take a deep breath of the crisp air as I grab my toolkit and rucksack. My heart is pumping harder as I almost run across the bridge, eager to make the most of these moments alone.

I touch the standing stone as I pass through the gateway, my talisman for this dig. And smile as I imagine the stone almost responds beneath my fingers.

A morning mist has rolled across from the river and is swathing the valley floor in an opaque blanket. It has that quality of being both beautiful and a little disturbing, distorting the senses, muffling sound and blurring sight in a white, damp cloud. The birdsong is more distant, the rising sun is veiled and weak, and the cold wetness touches my skin with an unnatural clamminess.

I can only see some twenty yards ahead, so the known features form their shape gradually: the tents and trestle tables, waiting for the workers; the division in the path, upper and lower; and, more distantly, the lumpen structure of the church.

Unzipping the tent is a reassuringly mundane sound in this eerie stillness; as I tie back the canvas, I push aside an irrational wariness that someone might suddenly appear behind me. There's a pile of tools in the near corner, shovels and forks and picks heaped on top of each other, and I grab a selection. I want to assess the mound before anyone else arrives, to set a plan of attack for rapid progress.

The mist deepens as I head along the lower path. The atmospheric conditions that shroud the world have a timeless quality; has she seen the same kind of haze in her era?

And suddenly I remember – no, it's like I'm seeing it again – the snow on the ground, all around. Blown into drifts up against the front of the parsonage and the three little cottages, scraped away from the door in the north wall where I entered the church yesterday, presumably by…what was his name? Walter atte Gate.

The closer I get, the more it builds into a powerful sensation of tension and exhilaration in one conflicting, swirling morass, a juddering dissonance between then and now.

I breathe hard, leaning on the handle of the pick-axe until, gradually, the dual-vision fades, and I'm left standing alone in the mist with the dense, dark mound ahead of me.

Before yesterday's strange reactions can repeat, I step straight up to the edge of the mound and toss the tools down on it, claiming with force and forged metal some sort of dominion over this pile of earth and nettles…and God knows what underneath.

Pushing my hands deep into my jeans' pockets, I pace out a wide circle, assessing. The mound is uneven in shape, with more soil banked up on the south side than the north, perhaps from however the building fell in or was destroyed. Nettles cover a good two-thirds of the area, scrambling up the shadier sides and dominating the summit, dense, tall clumps, one of the few plants flourishing in spite of the drought. There's nothing to indicate masonry close to the surface, so we should prepare to be digging down some way before we hit anything material. It's a big area, maybe a day-and-a-half's work for three or four of us; let's hope Montague delivers on his promise to find me some strong labour.

We can take the mound down a layer at a time; roughly stratifying the spoil heap is better than nothing and a couple of students can sift through what we remove to ensure we don't miss anything. The soil can go behind the mound between the edge of the wood and the damp area that's bordered by the rushes; there's enough room there to lay out three chipboard panels.

I'm itching to get working. This is me in dig mode now: head down, ploughing on, total focus.

Throwing my rucksack on the ground, I pull out a pair of workmen's gloves as a measure against the stingers and, optimistically, my tool roll; I know it's highly unlikely I'll need it before tomorrow but there's something about being ready to get into the details that sets my nerves tingling and my mind buzzing.

I grab a scythe and set to with a vengeance. After a minute of hacking clumsily, I find my rhythm, swinging smoothly from my hip.

Twenty minutes later, I'm sweating and breathing hard. Unnoticed, the sun has broken through and dispelled the mist, and a brilliant blue sky is rapidly emerging overhead. But the nettles are down, so I can start digging out the roots. I strip off my jacket then head back to the tent to grab three large chipboard panels, awkwardly dragging each back along the path and lining them up behind the mound. As I drive a fork into the top part of the soil, that familiar excitement escalates within me: now the dig really begins.

* * * * * * *

An hour later, a shout from the path breaks my concentration. Three large lads are approaching, one raising his hand in acknowledgement of his call-out. He introduces himself – the son of the farmer who owns this land – and two of their summer labourers, one a local boy, the other a student who's dropped out for a year.

I send them to the tent for more tools. Beyond, there's movement, a few people milling around; setting up for breakfast, I hope.

'See if you can find a couple of wheelbarrows as well,' I shout at their retreating backs.

I've cleared most of the nettles and turf. Now we're into the first layer of topsoil. Paired up, one digs, one barrows the spoil onto the first heap, turn and turn about to keep up the productivity: it's going to be a long day.

The soil is pleasurable to work: the sand ridges of this region make it easy to break up and centuries of detritus from the woodland have mixed in to create a rich, fertile loam. In the silence of focused effort, with muscles straining, blood pumping and hard breathing, a pleasurable stillness fills my mind, a place out of time.

When they ring the bell for the morning meeting, I ignore it. The buzz of voices becomes a pleasant background noise, like the sounds of wildlife in the trees and the grass and the reeds. I'm at one with the world. I catch the smell of smoke on the breeze; maybe they're burning stubble in the fields today.

The morning meeting breaks up and a gaggle of students head in our direction. For a moment, I'm irritated by the intrusion: I feel an affinity with the farm lads – that robust straightforwardness that comes with being connected to the land – and an irrational resentment of these cocksure kids, so confident of their place and position, their right to be here. But then, I straddle both those worlds and I do so with my own ease and self-assurance, so I soften towards them. Besides, one of the boys brings a plateful of bacon sandwiches.

Standing back from the mound, I cast an eye over the rapidly growing first spoil heap. Here and there, darker pieces show against the light soil, and I pick one up. It's a fragment of wood, blackened by burning. With a jolt that almost makes me drop it, I realise the smell of smoke is back. And that it's not coming from the fields, it's all around me. Thick in my nostrils and the back of my throat.

I glance from face to face in the group, but no one else has reacted. They're integrating already; laughing and chatting, breaking down – or maybe oblivious to – the social boundaries I'd perceived between them, united by age and interests more than they are divided by backgrounds.

I lift my head and look around me, wondering if I can see whatever it is I can smell.

Suddenly, I start coughing, hard, like I'm choking for air. And then I sneeze, three huge sneezes. One of the female students blesses me, smiling at me with that usual open interest. I thank her and pull out my handkerchief to blow my nose.

It's only as I fold the cotton square to put it away again that I see the black marks and, in the same instant, notice a taste in my mouth from the coughing and a strange tightness in my chest from straining to breathe.

My lungs are full of soot.

Chapter Twenty-one

Threfield Percy. 14th September 1976

This day is as hot as any we have known over this inferno of a summer and the sweat has been streaming down my back.

But suddenly I'm cold all over, goosebumps rising on my forearms and the back of my neck. I stand still, my muscles going rigid as my brain tries to make sense of it. My heart is thumping fast, that kind of palpitating fear of an undiagnosed medical condition. The fear of not knowing, not understanding.

I step away from the group as nonchalantly as I can, moving instinctively towards the shelter of the church.

My breathing is quick and shallow, and I force it to slow and deepen, doing it under cover of taking a breather. I know the group is still in front of me but almost don't see them, unable to focus properly. Except to notice that the farmer's son is watching me curiously. I can't even raise a fake smile to reassure him. Our eyes lock, and I sense he knows something.

I turn away, wiping the sweat off my face with my handkerchief. Hesitantly, I blow my nose again. But all sign of the smoke has gone; if it weren't for the stain still visible from before, I'd believe I've imagined the whole thing. Shoving it back in my pocket, I pull myself together.

Now I catch sight of Montague standing to one side, arms folded, watching the group at work. He's focusing on them to avoid looking at me; his simmering resentment at my presence seems to have grown overnight.

I've set two of the students to clearing that overly elaborate path between the mound and the church; we might as well see what it looks like and confirm where it goes, and it keeps them out of my way during the heavy lifting phase. The rest are sieving through the spoil heap as we create it. We're making faster progress than I expected; with luck, we might hit our first structures soon.

Montague turns away, giving me only a cursory acknowledgement as he does so, and trudges back up the hill.

Determined to push everything else out of my mind, I return to the mound and grab a shovel.

* * * * * * *

By the time I look up again, the sun is beyond the meridian and there's a knot of onlookers gathered in the lea of the trees, students taking a break from the dig up top to watch our progress or, in some cases, to watch me. I've stripped off to the waist. I'm lean from all the work I do, not overly muscular but pretty well-defined. Martin exchanges a wry smile with me as he arrives to call everyone for lunch; I shrug my shoulders as I button my shirt.

'It looks like you're getting on well,' he remarks, walking alongside me, glancing back over his shoulder at now two mounds of spoil from our digging.

'It's good to have strong labour,' I nod towards the three farm boys striding ahead. They, too, are attracting attention from some of the female students; the male academics, side-lined for now, have clustered together and are deflecting the lack of focus on them with noisy bluster and banter.

'Anything turned up so far?' Martin enquires.

'Some rubble, a few larger pieces of masonry, bits of charred wood, pieces of roof tile. What you'd expect from a building that's collapsed in on itself.'

We join the queue waiting to have soup and sandwiches doled out by the team allocated to catering for today. Everyone takes turns with the essential but less glamorous roles on the dig; pity the one who's responsible for the latrine.

'How's the undercroft looking?' I respond.

The grin on his face tells me everything. 'More promising by the inch,' he affirms. 'And we're chasing down the lower entrance, like you suggested. There's so much coming up. Like they just upped and left, leaving behind whatever was in the cellar – barrels and bottles, storage jars, even spoons and knives.'

'Maybe that will cheer Ernest up?' I speculate. 'Make him feel the dig is worthwhile after all.'

'I get that this may not be the most exciting thing he's worked on,' Martin accedes, 'but our local archaeology group loves this place. Always has. In fact, I called one of the guys last night to see if he can come over after work and he bit my hand off. He's a metal detectorist. Bought some amazing kit a couple of years ago. I thought maybe he could scan the site for you?' He suggests this a little hesitantly, as if fearful of treading on my toes. 'After all, we've not investigated any of that area so far. And I'd like to think we'd done everything we can for Professor Langley.'

His consideration stirs me. Would that Montague shared it. 'Martin, I'm very glad you're on this dig,' I respond warmly. 'And I'll take any resources I can to bring Michael some answers.'

* * * * * * *

It's gone five by the time Ed Burroughs arrives with his kit, but he's eager to get going when Martin introduces him. I've seen his kind before: pasty-faced from some office job he hates, eager to spend what spare time he has outdoors, nerdy to the point of obsession about his hobby. In other words, he's just what I need. He starts with a slow sweep of the spoil heap, then progresses to a methodical linear progression across the area between the mound and the wood.

There are about two hours of daylight left but work has slowed during the afternoon, and I know the farm lads are feeling the strain as much as I am; my muscles haven't worked this hard in months. I promise them a pint in the local pub if they manage another hour. By then, we'll have broken the back of it.

It's been pleasant to have the students working around us. Their constant chatter is a cheerful backdrop while the four of us have ended up less vocal the harder the work has become.

So, I'm relieved when one of the students pulls me over to take a look at the path they're digging out. Between three of them, they've been exposing a cross-section of the path to see the tiles and understand their situation and are chasing out one edge to confirm its trajectory.

Within the exploratory trench, most of the tiles are still in place and look surprisingly pristine; a few are cracked but many are whole, their green glazing brilliant in the sunshine. But it's the girl who's followed the line of the path who shouts out to me.

'Professor Bren! You might want to take a look at this.'

She stands as I approach, brushing down her debris-covered knees and straightening her chestnut hair. 'Professor…'

'Just Eoghan,' I correct her. She smiles.

'I think I've hit a wall,' she breathes excitedly.

I kneel down to inspect the area she's exposed. The work is shoddy: there's little finesse in how she's removed the turf and dug down to find the ochre-patterned edging tiles. But the line is clear and matches what I'd anticipated, curving from the church's west door to, now, within eighteen inches of the mound.

She crouches down beside me. Closer than she needs to be. 'I thought I'd lost the line,' she explains, pointing to the final tile, 'or that maybe there was a break with a missing tile, so I just kept going. And then I hit this.'

Three inches down, just above the level of the tiles, she's partially exposed two surfaces of a light-coloured stone, about a foot wide and eight inches deep.

It's a long way from justifiably being called a wall but there's no doubt it's masonry: I can see marks where they've faced the block. I draw my fingertip along one, imagining the mason chiselling the sandstone to expose the right line. I see him running his hands, rough and swollen from years of work, over these same lines, brushing the dust away, appreciating the quality of his own work. I consider him as a master mason brought from York, garnering both resentment and curiosity in the local workers whose talents have been passed over for this high-end construction, resentfully standing aside to watch the intruder at work, much as Montague stands over mine.

I'm strongly tempted to take over the excavation but force myself to step back. 'Good work,' I encourage. 'All of you,' taking in the other students as well. 'Get it recorded then get washed up. We'll head to the pub shortly.'

Half-an-hour later, the tools have been downed and a washing-up bowl with hot water from the kettle removes the worst of the dirt. Chatter and laughter are now the order of the day, everyone satisfied with their efforts and enjoying getting to know one another.

I hand the farmer's son a £5 note. 'Get the first round in. I'll say goodbye to Ed then meet you all down there.'

Martin's coming down the lane as I head back towards the site and falls in beside me. 'I said we'd meet the rest of them at the pub,' he informs me. 'Professor Montague left earlier for a faculty meeting so it's just us.'

The metal detectorist has moved across the site, towards the area covered in reeds.

'Ed,' I hail him. 'We're heading out.'

But he can't hear me, headphones over his ears and listening intently to the electronic blips of his equipment. As we approach, he squats down, pulling a trowel out of his back pocket to pick away at the ground.

A strange tingling starts in my hands, like pins and needles in my fingertips, and there's an overwhelming urge to quicken my pace, like I'm being dragged towards him. Bemused, Martin is startled into keeping up.

The soil here is wet, heavy loam; if it was a fishpond, it must be fed by underground springs or the river because it's still soft underfoot and water rises up around the sole of my boot.

Ed catches my eye and grins, knowing he's got something interesting. I hunker down beside him, watching closely as he sinks his trowel into the darker soil, using it to feel around for what he's detected. With a frustrated grunt, he drives the trowel deeper until his knuckles are sinking into the sludge too. I experience with him the jarring as the metal of his trowel hits metal beneath.

It's in moments like this that time slows down for me. I hear the stillness of our surroundings, now bereft of human noise, settling back into nature's quiet conversation. I sense a light breeze from the west, just tickling my hair. I feel the strain building in my knees where I'm crouched on my haunches and Martin's tension alongside mine, bent over next to me, braced with his forearms on his thighs.

I try to stay patient, to respect my fellow expert's careful process and equal intensity.

Painstakingly, he wiggles the trowel around until he finds the edge of the object, then follows the line to get a sense of it. To judge by his movements, it's about five inches long, but not wide. He works to excavate those dimensions in the soil above it but it's so wet here that the hole refills almost as fast as he digs it.

Slowly he scoops his way through the sludge, then he sinks his hands in to feel his way towards the object. His mouth firms shut in concentration but gives way to a smile as his fingers find metal. He inches his way along it, one way and then the other, scoping out any weaknesses, anything that might create risk in lifting it. Satisfied, he slips his left fingers underneath even as he works the trowel in from the right. And gradually, the ooze slips back and the mud yields up its prize.

I find I'm holding my breath and I think Martin must be too because the silence around me is intense.

Ed has both hands around it now, working the worst of the mud away from the metal with his thumbs. As he stands, so do we.

'Someone must have rued the day they lost this!' he laughs, exhilarated by his find. Holding it out on the flat of his hand, he shows us a large, heavy key, wrought in iron with a detailed roundel at the top, a thick shank and surprisingly complex teeth. Though it's somewhat corroded from the water, still it's a solid and sizeable piece. Too big for a chest. Maybe for a door?

'Here,' Ed gestures to me to take it from him. As I do, I immediately fumble and drop it; thankfully, Ed manages to catch it mid-air. 'Hey, watch out!' he laughs. 'We don't want to lose it again!'

But I have never felt less like laughing. The instant the key touched my skin, blackness swept through me, the blackness of terror and hatred and despair. In that instant, all light goes out of the day and I am surrounded by pitch night, so consuming that I lose all sense of self, falling into an endless darkness.

Martin's hand on my arm brings me back. Ed has stepped away to wash the mud off his hands. I don't know if I've lost seconds or minutes in blank unawareness. But I notice the key is now safely resting in a plastic box at his feet.

'Eoghan?' Martin is watching me closely, frowning in concern.

'I...er...I...' I search desperately around for something to excuse what's just happened. My head is pounding where it's bruised, and I stem the pressure with one hand. 'I felt a bit dizzy. Probably just the concussion.'

'Should you sit down?'

'Don't fuss, Martin!' I snap, pulling away. My impatience shocks me as well as him. I put a hand on his shoulder. 'Sorry. Let's get to the pub,' I encourage him, turning my back on the site and trying to shut down thoughts that are now racing in my head. 'I think I need a beer!'

Chapter Twenty-two

Marston. 14th September 1976

The public bar in The Fox is vibrant and welcoming, alive with the buzz of happy young people. A glazed door shows the snug beyond where three older farm workers hunch over their pints, pipes and cigarettes.

Josh, the farmer's son, breaks away from his compatriots to bring us a pint each and my change.

'Cheers,' I toast him and Martin. 'We've earned this today.' We drink long draughts and ease settles in. 'I can't stay long,' I warn. 'I must get back to report to Michael.'

'As long as you leave some money behind the bar!' is Josh's laughing rejoinder.

There are fifteen students crammed into this small space, boys by the bar, girls around the table in the bay window. The air smells of fermented hops, oiled wood, polished brass, ancient lath-and-plaster walls and centuries of smoke, both wood-burning and tobacco.

I feel the inner entrance door pushing against my back and step aside to let someone in.

'Dad!' Josh greets the newcomer. 'I thought you might be in. Pint?' He signals the landlord. 'This is Eoghan Bren, the guy the professor asked us to help.'

A small, whippet-like man – it seems impossible that he could have spawned the strapping, six-foot son beside me – looks at me with a narrow, assessing stare as we shake hands. He recognises Martin with a nod.

'Colin Felton,' he introduces himself. 'You're the one poking about by the church, then?'

'For Professor Langley, yes,' I respond, figuring Michael's name might help me more than being linked in his mind to Montague.

'Hmm,' he mutters. 'He's a good man, that one. I was sorry to hear he's ailing.'

'He's very glad you're letting us work on the site,' I acknowledge. 'And thanks for lending us your lads today too.'

'You needing them again tomorrow?'

I shake my head. 'No, they've done enough today.'

'Good. The missus ain't too keen on the boy being involved,' he reveals, receiving the glass from his son. 'She and the other women, they don't like that place. It's nowt but old women's talk, but still.'

'What's their issue?' I sound only mildly curious, but my own experiences have stoked rather more than that in me.

He looks uncomfortable. 'You know how women are,' he flicks it off. 'Taking fancies at the slightest thing.'

'At school they said a witch was buried up there,' Josh leaps in.

'What rubbish,' his father contends.

'Nanna didn't think so,' Josh defends. 'My grandmother,' explaining to me, 'she used to talk about it sometimes. Told us tales of seeing a woman in black, one who was buried outside the churchyard. But then she had "the sight", like her mother before her, but it seems she didn't pass it along to Mum.'

'That shows what little you know,' his father disagrees gruffly. 'She sees things alright. She just doesn't talk about them.'

'Anyway,' Josh changes tack, his feathers ruffled, 'it's all just women's stuff and nonsense.'

'Are you implying it's nonsense just because a woman said it?' The girl with the chestnut hair has appeared at my elbow and Josh makes room for her with a grin. 'Just because men close their eyes to things they can't explain, it doesn't mean those things aren't real.'

'So you say!' Josh taunts her, jovially.

'What do you think, Professor? Eoghan,' she corrects herself. 'Isn't there "more in heaven and earth than is dreamt of in our philosophy"?' I smile at her precocity; students can't resist showing off.

'I don't think we should ever dismiss something just because we don't understand it.' Martin surprises himself as much as the rest of us with his interjection. 'I mean,' flustered, 'haven't you ever experienced something you couldn't explain?' looking to me to shore up his faltering position.

'You looked like you did earlier,' Josh intervenes, watching me closely.

I fold my arms, swirling the dregs of my pint around in the glass. 'There's nothing I can definitively say was supernatural,' I evade.

'I've seen one of your presentations, Professor. Eoghan,' the girl – Petra – presses. 'And Professor Montague was talking about how you personalise the people whose things you're excavating.'

'Not in approving terms, I suspect.' I laugh it off, but I can see by her face she won't be dissuaded. 'That's a bit different,' I justify. 'It's like putting together what I find at the dig with what I know from the history. It makes the experience more real for the reader. Brings it to life, if you will.'

It's a line I've used so often that it just falls off the tongue. But I know the truth is more than that. That from the first dig at fifteen, I've sensed aspects of those other times, sometimes predominantly one era, sometimes several overlapping and merging. But my awareness of the people who farmed these fields and walked these streets, who loved and laughed and lost in those houses…that's real and it's personal.

'Is that all?' Petra persists, turning towards me so that we're face-to-face. 'I mean, you can sense when there's something there, can't you?' she suggests, meaningfully looking up into my eyes.

And then she puts her hand on my bare forearm.

I feel an electric charge go through me, but it's not attraction, it's repulsion, a charge pulse of energy that rejects her touch, almost violently throwing her off. And it's not from me. Petra steps backwards, off-balance, and bumps into one of the students behind her. For a long moment, she stares at me with startled eyes, then turns as the student's half-abusive, half-jocular response breaks through her shock, spurring anger in her. She curses him and pushes roughly past, fighting her way through to get back to the other girls at the table. She shoves her way onto the window seat, forcing the others to shuffle around to admit her, and is immediately engulfed in a sea of questions and concern.

I stare after her, trying to read in her face what she felt. But the stare she returns is hard and defensive. And whatever she's telling her friends is causing them to look askance at me as well.

* * * * * * *

I make my excuses shortly thereafter, glad of the twilight stroll back up the lane to the car and the drive back to York to clear my head. By the time I arrive at Michael's flat, my mind has refocused on the dig, not the odd happenings of the day.

I knock as I push the door open, just for form's sake. Michael's on the phone and looks up as I enter.

'Eoghan's just arrived,' he tells Sam on the other end. 'Why don't you talk to him first and I'll listen in.' He hears her response then holds out the receiver to me. I take the desk chair he's just evacuated and watch him sink, painfully slowly, into his armchair; he fills only a fraction of the space, shrunk back in one corner, and positions a cushion to prop himself up.

'Hi, Sam.'

'He's tired tonight.' It sounds like she is too.

'Mmm.' My noised response confirms I'm seeing what she's sensing.

'Too tired even to ask questions.'

'Mmm.'

I glance at Michael. His gaze is distant, unfocused. Or perhaps inwardly focused, distracted.

'OK, tell me what you've been up to today so he can hear. Paint a picture for him.'

'OK.' I collect my thoughts for a second. 'We've had ten of us working on the site. Montague was true to his word and got me three lads from the farm to help clear the undergrowth and remove the soil, so we've been able to work quite fast. I knew we'd only find stone and rubble in the first couple of feet, so we shifted the spoil and some of the team are going through it. It's when we get below that we'll get to what interests us.'

'What makes you think that?'

'Sorry?'

'I guess I assumed the mound was just where the grass had grown over the top of what remained of the building.'

That gives me pause. Good question. Why wouldn't the finds largely be above ground? Because I know they're not. I just know. And I haven't even stopped to question how I know.

'I'm working on the theory this building had a cellar.' Justifying. And a little defensive. 'They've uncovered an undercroft at the manor house, and I think this is the same. I'm assuming everything collapsed into the lower level. Maybe they robbed out what was left of the stonework and reused it, or that might have fallen in as well. The stonework we've found so far supports the latter.'

'OK. What else?'

'There's quite a lot of charred timber in the spoil, so a fire is looking plausible. We've got a good look at the path from the church now and we've just hit some stonework that looks like it might be in situ, so that could be the first signs of what's left of the walls. And a metal detectorist has been along; he found a substantial key near the pond area. It would be nice to think it's connected to the tower.'

'Anything else?'

'Give me a break, Sam! That's not bad for day one!'

'Sorry, I guess we're all a bit impatient.'

Well, one of you is: Michael's not even looked up. I hesitate before responding. I know what I need to tell them, but I'm reticent to do so, remembering the disbelief in Michael's eyes when I told him about Llywelyn Bren's execution.

'What is it?' How does she sense my hesitation down a phone line?

I sigh. 'I dreamt about her last night.' There's movement as Michael turns his head towards me.

'The Woman?' Sam asks.

'As a child,' I confirm.

'And?' she invites.

'She was at Threfield Percy. Came there from Cardiff, some weeks after her father was executed. Llywelyn Bren's children were dispersed afterwards, and someone decided Christiane,' there's a crack in my voice as I say her name, some emotion catching the back of my throat, 'should be taken in by the Goscelin family and betrothed to Ralf Goscelin.'

'She *did* come to the village.' Vindication in her voice.

'Yes, she came here. But I don't know what happened next.'

'If there was a marriage, Dad might find some record of it? I know the parish records were destroyed. But maybe somewhere.'

'I don't know when they got married or if they even did,' I continue my side of the conversation for Michael's sake but I'm seeing no evidence that this is engaging him. 'But there are other historical details we can verify. On her journey, they stopped at Kirkham Priory. The prior at the time was a Catalonian by the name of Robert de Veteri Burgo. And there was a prioress visiting from Molseby Priory, Lady Alice de Lacy, who must have been in her early forties. Oh, and Geoffrey Goscelin's steward, a man called Richard Prudhomme.'

'What does Dad think?'

'Michael?' I prompt.

'Write them down for me,' he concedes. 'I'll see what I can find in the morning.' The Michael I know would never have waited until tomorrow if he had an excuse to dive into the historical records today. There's a slight sheen on his skin, like he's sweating but cold at the same time. 'You'll have to excuse me, my boy. I think I must lie down for a bit.'

'Of course. Hang on, Sam.' I drop the receiver and rise to help him up, but he bats me away as soon as he's steady on his feet. I watch him cross to his bedroom door and close it behind him. Something's bothering me about his mood tonight but I can't put my finger on it.

'Enough about the dig,' I tell Sam, moving to cradle the phone against my shoulder and grab of piece of paper to write the names down for Michael. Absentmindedly, I start doodling beneath the words. 'How was your day?'

Now that Michael's gone, she drops the façade. 'Long. Early. Long. Same old same old.'

'That doesn't sound like you. You love your work.'

'Maybe I need a change.' That's definitely not like her. I'm not sure I can take this, both of them in an off-mood.

'Take it easy. You're dealing with a lot at the moment. Will they give you a break…when you need it?' She knows what I mean but can't say.

'Probably no more than is required. The hospital is short-staffed. But aren't we always?'

'Tell me if there's anything I can do.'

'You're already doing it.'

'Sam?'

'Hmm?'

I feel a compulsion to tell her, or maybe just to be able to tell anyone. I pause: Michael has closed his bedroom door, but he can probably still hear through the paper-thin walls. 'Some weird stuff happened today.'

'What kind of stuff?' She waits.

I keep scrawling as I think about the emotion and disorientation I felt this morning at the site. The strange happenings with the girl in the pub, that haunted look in her eyes. And the smoke from the fire that destroyed the building, as tangible to me in the present as it was when it happened.

That makes me reach for my handkerchief and stare again at the soot stains, just to prove to myself they're real. I want to talk to her about it but it's hard. I don't want them to think I've become fanciful. Partly because I don't want them to worry that I'm not up to this, partly because I know how he'd look at this with his logical, grounded historian's eyes, partly because it feels alien – and yet so natural – to be confiding in Sam again. She would understand and might even help me make sense of it.

'There's something about this site. It's getting under my skin. And incidents that feel a little…sinister.' The words sound like nonsense even to my own ears, and I make a noise of disgust at myself. 'Never mind. It's probably nothing. Just my imagination.'

She waits, in case I change my mind, then accepts my reticence.

'How's your head?'

I stop to consider because I've not really paid attention to it during the day. 'Nothing to report.' Then, nonchalantly: 'Does concussion have any ongoing effects I should watch out for?'

'Headaches and dizziness predominantly. Nausea, problems with balance or disorientation. Maybe blurred vision. Difficulty concentrating. Aggression or depression. Disturbed sleep patterns.'

No inexplicable manifestations then. I laugh hollowly inside my head.

'Any of those bothering you?'

'No, doctor.'

'Eoghan,' earnest now, 'if you're at all concerned, please see someone. I can't get back there until Friday night. Please, don't hesitate.'

She waits. I feel the intensity of her concern vibrating down the line; it's a long time since someone cared about me like that, and it feels good. I hold my breath and the moment between us is alive with unspoken tension.

'Sam…'

'I've got to go. Talk tomorrow?'

Disappointed. 'Sure.'

I stare at the phone after she rings off; the handset pings as I replace it on the cradle. Lost in my thoughts, I drum the pen on the desk in a staccato rhythm, staring absently at my scrawls on the page, then screw the paper up in frustration.

I look in vain for a waste-paper bin and head to the kitchen instead. As I open the bin, my mind registers how much waste food is already in there. Not just the leftovers from a man with diminished appetite; it's a day's worth of food, untouched.

I stare at the bin, considering, then wait for long moments, in case Michael decides to come back now the call with Sam is over. But all is quiet. And yet all is disquiet.

* * * * * * *

I force myself to eat supper at the pub, my body ravenous but my appetite gone. The food settles heavily in my stomach, appropriately matching the weight I feel oppressing my heart.

After that, all I need is a bath to shed the dirt of the day and ease my muscles. The landlady confirms there's enough hot water as long as I stick to the regulation six inches and asks me to take only half-an-hour in order to respect the needs of my fellow guests for the shared bathroom.

The aged enamel tub has the characteristic rusty brown water stain between tap and plug hole, and the tiling and lino have seen better days, but the cast iron radiator is pumping out excessive heat, so the room is pleasantly relaxing.

I run the taps longer than I should but, with my long legs forced to bend, my knees are still sticking out of the water as I sink down to allow it to flow over my chest.

My mind is thick with thoughts, as clouded and fog-bound as the site was this morning. The warmth seeps into my limbs and, as I lean my head back against the rim of the bath, I close my eyes.

Chapter Twenty-three

Threfield Percy, February 1322

In the three years since she last saw her betrothed, he has gained both height and breadth of stature, but his arrogance has also grown entirely unchecked.

'I'm telling you, if Percy will let me go, I will fight for the king!'

Frustration suffuses Ralf's face with blood and his body is rigid with tension, one hand aggressively pointing his intention towards his father, the other in a fist at his side.

'Then it's as well that Percy has more sense than to let you!' Lady Alice retorts, her voice cut with ice.

Geoffrey sits back heavily. 'Retake your seat, Ralf,' he requests with a gesture and a sigh.

The boy submits sulkily, folding his arms across his chest and slumping down on the stool. Beyond in the Great Hall and the kitchens, the household is a hive of activity, clearing away after the meal celebrating his long-overdue return. And yet he seems hardly to care that they have slaughtered the fattened calf for this prodigal son's return.

In truth, he almost looked handsome in his blue-and-gold Percy livery when he arrived yesterday. His shoulders and chest have been broadened by training, yet he still has a litheness about his frame. He looks tall for his age too, standing a head above herself. Resplendent enough to please his mother's eye, for sure, but what Christiane sees underwhelms her.

Three years ago, he had been a self-centred and sullen boy. Now, he is an arrogant and attention-seeking almost-man, more interested in carousing with the reeve and his closest crowd last night than in paying the respect due to his parents. He revels in everyone's attention after such a prolonged absence and behaves as if his deigning to visit were a blessing to them.

She thinks back to the day she stood at his side before the priest to make their betrothal vows. Her third day in Threfield Percy. He wore a rich red tunic, green surcoat and matching hose, and seemed to feel as much pride in his attire as he felt dislike for her. She had found an adequate blue gown from among those Amicia had discarded; though it was the closest fitting, still it swamped her small frame, even tied in at the waist. By contrast, Amicia wore a gown of scarlet edged with fur and cut close to emphasise her waist and hips.

They were brought before the priest in Amicia's upper room, Lady Alice by Christiane's side, Geoffrey and Amicia beside Ralf, with Richard Prudhomme and Simon Reeve to witness the event. The skies had cleared and the briefly bright sunshine outside even penetrated the heavy stained glass to dazzle the room with jewel-like colours.

The priest tried to bring some solemnity and weight to the short commitment ceremony, adjuring them and their kin to hold to their promises before God. He seemed ill at ease throughout and blushed strangely when Amicia insisted on taking from him the signed betrothal document the moment the ink had dried.

The prioress had responded warmly to the request for her to stand surety for Christiane's betrothal, returning at once with the boy who had relayed the message to her at Kirkham Priory. That night, at the prior's behest, she visited Amicia to assess her condition and see if her knowledge might shed light on what ailed her. Like others before, she diagnosed an underlying corruption of the black bile as giving rise to her melancholy, though she observed too the strange sensitivity in the skin and eyes to light, and swellings in the joints.

'More worrying, though,' she confided to Christiane as they sat together afterwards, 'is how little distraction she has. Time weighs heavily on her, with too little company to balance out the natural propensity of her mind towards pitying herself. You might do much,' she encouraged, 'to bring her out of herself, even if she is unwilling or unable to remove herself from that self-imprisonment she mistakes for security.'

Christiane knew it to be her godly duty, but her future mother by marriage was not making it easy to like her. Amicia had hardened her stance in opposition to a betrothal celebration and Geoffrey capitulated after a second painful discussion. Instead, the news was announced to the household at dinner at noon on the day before the ceremony, and Richard was tasked with informing the rest of the tenants. Though Geoffrey accorded Lady Alice great respect in the food he ordered to be served at each meal during her brief stay, she felt compelled to raise with him her concerns at the lack of due ceremony being addressed to the new couple, and particularly to Christiane. From nearby but out of earshot, Christiane watched him accept the chastisement with the resignation of one who knows the justice of the arguments but finds himself unable to deliver a different outcome.

Christiane was grateful that Lady Alice seemed inclined to extend her role as protector and guide. As she departed the morning after the betrothal, she assured Christiane she would visit as often as her position might allow; she had frequently kept her word in the years since.

Ralf left the same day, having said not a word to Christiane beyond the promises he was forced to make her before the priest. He seemed deliberately to avoid even looking at her, ensuring she was aware of the loathing and resentment he had for this betrothal and for her.

It could not have been more different on the day he returned. He arrived without warning just as dusk fell, riding into the courtyard at such a pace that he had to rein his horse in hard until its hind legs almost slipped from under it; only by launching himself from the saddle did he avoid being thrown.

As the horse regained its footing but danced skittishly out of Ralf's reach, he shouted for someone from the stable to attend him at once. Two stable lads appeared in the doorway, but it was Geoffrey's squire, David FitzAlan, who pushed past as they gawped uselessly at the stranger and, bowing swiftly, came forward to help.

Talking to the horse in that soft voice of his, David caught the reins and calmed the animal, stroking its forehead and leaning his cheek close to its muzzle. Ralf slapped the younger boy heartily on the back in a falsely jovial greeting.

Returning from an afternoon of reading to Amicia, the disturbance attracted Christiane's attention and she hesitated by the entrance to the kitchens. In the fading light, he caught sight of her.

The men were still working outside though it was now deep into winter, arranged blessedly close to the blacksmith's fire or in the shelter of the barns, and there were comforting noises from their exchange of banter and from the animals that had been stabled or penned against the worst of the weather. And yet she suddenly felt isolated and under threat, like predator and prey, deeply uncomfortable under his gaze; it seemed to demand much that she knew she would be unwilling – yet expected – to give, and to come from one who was used to taking what he wanted.

Her breath felt stuck in her chest, and she found herself at a loss how to greet this man-boy, at once a stranger and her betrothed.

'Christiane! Come inside at once, child.' Geoffrey had appeared at the door to the Hall, beckoning her into the warm light. 'You'll be chilled to the bone if you stand there a moment longer.'

He had not seen his son behind his mount. But she saw the shock register in Ralf's eyes as he realised who she was; he had mistaken her for one of the servant girls. The resentment of the child and the curiosity of the man warred within him, until the old childish petulance won out and he snatched the reins from David, dragging the horse towards the stable, not even stopping to give his father the proper greeting.

* * * * * * *

The festivities to mark Ralf's return show no sign of abating as they rise from the dais and withdraw to the relative calm of the solar.

A sumptuous supper with the promise of music, dancing and games – more precious for the fact the usual privations of Lent are just around the corner – have enticed the entire village to the Great Hall. With little warning to prepare for the event, there was no time to find minstrels and players to mark the occasion, but there is plenty of wine and ale for all, several different dishes of food – including the largest side of beef they had stored in the pantry – and music from William Child and Stephen Crow.

Good fortune brought Lady Alice to Threfield Percy this same day, intending to visit Christiane and to minister to Amicia, checking whether the poultices she had prescribed upon her last visit had eased the pain and inflammation in her joints. That meeting, though, has been postponed until the morrow, as Amicia will admit no one but her beloved returned son today.

The blessing in disguise is that it has allowed Alice and Christiane to pass the afternoon together, in conversation and in tending to several sick villagers. On each visit, Christiane gleans a little more healing knowledge from Alice, fast becoming competent in her own right.

In the solar, Geoffrey and Lady Alice settle themselves close to the fire; Geoffrey has, over time, enhanced the solar with tapestries on the walls, and the room feels homely as they draw near the flames for warmth. Approaching, Christiane discovers they are discussing her and hangs back in order not to intrude.

'It is good to see the child so well settled here now,' Lady Alice remarks, receiving a cup of wine from the servant. 'It took a while, but the people are more accepting of her at last.'

'They are,' Geoffrey recognises, 'though not aided by my wife. Thankfully, Christiane's winning ways seem to bear her into people's hearts. And I must say,' he admits gruffly, 'with her interest in the running of the manor and her support for Richard, things have been much easier for me since she came to Threfield Percy.'

'For your good wife too, I believe. When I last visited, I sensed that Christiane's daily presence was making her a little less fretful.

She has such a soothing way about her. It was much in evidence with the tenants we were helping this afternoon.'

'Calming, you mean?'

'That and more. I've heard tell of it but have never seen it for myself until now: people whose very presence seems to have a healing effect on those close to them. At least,' she caveats, 'on those who are open hearted.'

'In which you would not include Amicia?' he clarifies.

'Your lady wife, I'm afraid, seems too fixed in her obsessions with her illnesses to be aided as she might be,' she notes, somewhat severely, having little patience with those who do not help themselves. 'And yet even she seems to feel some benefit from having Christiane near.'

The doorway to the Hall darkens suddenly and Christiane looks up to see Ralf staring hard at her. It is a mistrusting look, challenging too, and she wonders what she has done to justify it. Instinctively, she takes a step away from him, towards the light of the solar.

'Ah, there you both are! Come on in,' Geoffrey beckons them to sit. 'Come, Ralf. Tell us how things are with our cousin Percy.'

'I was not intending to stay,' Ralf negates. 'The games are starting…' with a longing look back towards the Hall.

'But you spent all of last night with Simon Reeve and the rest,' Geoffrey protests. 'You cannot mean to do so this night as well?'

It is clear from the look on his face that he certainly does intend that, even though he will be starting his return journey northwards in the morning.

At that moment, Richard Prudhomme arrives, ushering in servants with sweetmeats.

'Richard, you must join us as well.' Geoffrey seems in an expansive mood, more light-hearted than Christiane has seen him in a while. 'Come, have a drink. There is much we should all discuss while we are together.'

'Such as?' Ralf, refusing to sit in childish protest at being detained, seems set on being argumentative.

'I'm sure you would care to know how things in the manor are proceeding?'

The grunt his son emits is non-committal at best.

'Come, sit. And you, Christiane. No, here by me; leave your mending to another night. Richard, tell my son how his future inheritance is faring.'

'Progress has been good, another year of steady improvement after the Great Famine.' Richard takes up a standing position facing the family semi-circle now gathered around the fire, still supervising servants coming and going with tasty titbits, more logs for the fire, a fur to cover the prioress's knees, more candles to brighten the room. 'The harvest was the best we've seen these many years, and it's satisfying to see the grain stores finally returned to more normal levels.'

'More than that, Master Prudhomme,' Christiane inserts. 'It's thanks to your careful stewardship that our seed stock is now back up to the levels of before the rains. At last, we will be able to sow the full demesne lands again this spring.'

'Indeed, Richard,' Geoffrey re-joins, 'Christiane speaks well, and I thank you for your continued efforts on our behalf.'

'I was intrigued to hear your plans for next year as well,' Lady Alice prompts Christiane.

'There are pieces of land on the edge of the woodland we feel could be usefully brought into cultivation,' directing this towards Ralf, though he does not acknowledge her. 'Now the livestock levels are increasing and we have sufficient feed for them, we could benefit from more grazing land and fields to sow.'

'So, you expect to make more money?' Ralf's ears prick up.

'Some, in good times,' she affirms. 'And some fat to help in leaner times. There is no family in the village that did not lose someone through the famine. Save yours.'

The shrug he gives speaks his lack of concern for that fact. 'How soon?'

'This is not a quick process,' she caveats. 'We must seek permission from Lord Percy to assart the land first. And we should give it over to grazing for the first two or three years in order that the soil's fertility might increase before we sow.'

'Mayhap there are other ways to raise more funds, then?' he pushes. 'Simon Reeve was suggesting the fines might now be increased as the tenants are better able to pay.'

Richard's face expresses his discomfort. 'Master Reeve speaks out of turn. Conditions have been improving for all, but we must not take too soon from the tenants.'

'Why not?' Ralf demands. 'I shall soon need a sword and Percy's master breeder has a horse set aside for me. I'll take whatever monies the manor can give me.'

'We would do well to be wary,' Christiane supports Richard. 'This winter has been harsh. Ploughing should have started three weeks ago at Candlemas, but snow has lain on the ground here since Christmas, never warming enough to thaw, and most days bring another layer to settle upon the existing.'

'You are too cautious,' Ralf disagrees harshly. 'Mother backs me up. She assured me I would have the funds I need!'

Christiane sits back, stung by his criticism and hurt that he does not acknowledge all they have achieved.

'And the well-being of your manor does not concern you as long as you have your money?' Lady Alice chides.

The look he gives her is disdainful. 'You expect me to care about the petty lives here when bigger issues are playing out at court?'

'You speak of the king's dispute with the Marcher lords?' she discerns.

'Dispute? What a milksop word!' he mocks. 'This is all but internal war!'

'Temper your words, my son,' Geoffrey warns uneasily. 'Show Lady Alice the respect that is hers by right.'

The prioress sits more upright in her chair, leaning forward to engage with Ralf. 'You consider yourself expert on the political situation, I suppose?' she provokes him.

'I care not for the politics,' he dismisses high-handedly. 'But I am interested if there will be an opportunity to fight.'

'And how will you decide whose side to take in the argument?'

He seems confused by her question. 'Why, I take the king's, of course! When he is ordained by God, any who stand against him are sinners.'

'Indeed?' Lady Alice warms to her subject. 'Even though he tramples on the freedoms and rights of the Marcher lords that were established centuries before he was born?'

'And why should he not? As their lord, he can do as he pleases!'

'You answer like a child!' Christiane's protest burst from her. 'Even a king owes responsibilities to his people, just as you will in time to the people of this manor as their lord.'

'What do you know, girl?' he spits.

'More than you, it seems,' Geoffrey taunts.

Ralf's face flushes a deep shade of red and he rises in fury from his chair. 'I'm telling you,' he shouts at his father, 'if Percy will let me go, I will fight for the king!'

'Then it's as well that Percy has more sense than to let you!' Lady Alice snaps.

For a long moment, anger and rebuke hang in the air, stinging the room into silence. It is only at Geoffrey's bidding that Ralf retakes his chair, with pronounced bad grace.

They settle into silence, only the crack of logs falling in the fire breaking the uneasy peace.

'To be fair,' the prioress concedes with a sigh and a frown, ashamed that she has become so heated herself, 'whilst I sympathise with their cause, I cannot but condemn the Marcher lords' wanton and destructive rampage through Glamorgan. It is difficult to justify the extremes to which they have gone.'

'The king calls them the Contrariants,' Ralf seeks to display his knowledge.

'That he may,' she retaliates, 'but that does not make them wrong. The trouble is the king has always been a lazy man except where his favourites are concerned; only in their interests will he stir himself. Though the Marcher lords have succeeded in forcing Hugh Despenser out of the country, the king will not rest until his favourite is restored. And the lords will not rest while their powers are threatened. I fear the implications of such heightened strife between the king and his great barons.'

'Even your cousin Lancaster seems reluctant to get involved,' Geoffrey observes.

'He was so for some time, but I fear he will not maintain that stance much longer,' she infers. 'Whether he willed it or not, he now harbours the Marcher lords in his lands. And the king has declared he will bring his army to raise Lancaster's siege at Tickhill Castle.'

'Which he never should have attacked in the first place,' Ralf accuses.

'I confess, I do not understand my cousin's reasons for that action,' the prioress muses. 'Though he has ever mistrusted the castle's constable as the king's spy in the north.'

'I fear a direct confrontation is coming,' Richard adds. 'And we must be careful ourselves: too often Yorkshire lands are caught in the midst of these fights.'

The prioress nods.

'You are fearful, I think, of what this means for your cousin Lancaster?' Christiane reads the tenseness in her face.

'You see shrewdly, little one,' she sighs in acknowledgement. 'Henry is the king's cousin and the queen's uncle, as well as being the richest man in the land; I cannot imagine the king will hold against him for too long. And yet...' she worries. 'Edward has never forgiven him for executing Piers Gaveston. Years may have passed since the death of his first favourite, but he harbours his discontents deeply, does our king.'

Geoffrey shifts uneasily. 'And where stand our closest allies in this, the Percys?' he queries.

'The letters from my cousin suggest my lord Percy is playing a careful game, for now,' Lady Alice responds. 'It is lunacy to set oneself up against the king, but equally he always has a need to collaborate with Lancaster and his fellow northern lords. Much rests on them in protecting the kingdom against the Bruce and his Scottish rebels; to stand together in that regard makes it difficult for him to oppose Lancaster in any other.'

'But the king is the king,' Ralf resorts mulishly to his fixed position.

'Is he? Or is the king, in effect, my Lord Despenser now?' Lady Alice frets. 'It seems the king has no appetite to reign without him.'

'And would you, Ralf, fight to support the man who spends his days conducting acts of piracy in the English Channel?' Geoffrey inserts. 'Who threatens our own business and the very monies you are hoping to glean from us for your armour and your horses and who knows what else?'

'Who do you mean?' Ralf feels misgiving.

'Hugh Despenser, of course. He has been running pirate ships in the Channel since he was exiled in August. You did not know?' Geoffrey queries. 'Hardly a ship makes it to or from England without being raided, even the large, well-defended Genoese vessels. We have had to delay all manner of shipments for fear of being attacked.'

'And this,' the prioress' voice is dry with dislike, 'is the man you would fight for?'

Ralf rises angrily, spurred into self-defence by his embarrassment. 'Does no one care that to fight for the king could be my chance for greatness? To be noticed. To be raised up. Why else would you send me to train with Percy?' he appeals to Geoffrey. 'How am I to progress in this world if not by fighting? I will be no merchant, nor a stay-a-bed lord neither. I have seen too much to live within the narrow bounds of your little world,' he scorns. 'I am made for greater things. Mark my words: I will find a way to fight!'

* * * * * * *

'I feel I should say something to ease him,' Christiane hesitates.

The gathering broke up shortly after Ralf stormed out of the room, and she and Lady Alice retired to her chamber to ready themselves for bed. But now she hears him return to the solar, calling angrily for wine.

The prioress huddles beneath the covers, feeling her body ache with the dampness in the air.

'If you must, be quick, child,' she instructs. 'I wish to sleep.'

Drawing her mantle over her chemise and motioning to the maid, Edith, to stay in her truckle bed, Christiane raises the latch to open the adjoining door. Ralf is slumped in his father's chair by the hearth, nursing a goblet and with the wine jug on the floor beside him. To judge by the number of logs he has added to the fire, he seems to be settling in for a while.

'My lord,' Christiane calls his awareness to her.

'What do you want now?' he grumbles. 'Haven't you all had your say already?'

'I see your disappointment, my lord, and wish only to understand your position better.'

He scowls at her, a little disbelievingly, a little drunkenly. 'I made myself clear,' he complains.

She pulls up a stool to sit across from him. 'Humour me, my lord. You seem so eager to rush into battle. Why so when there will be plenty of opportunity for that in your lifetime?'

'I knew you didn't understand,' he criticises. 'How could you? You cannot imagine how good it is to be in the thick of fighting, the exhilaration of overcoming your own fear and driving down your opponent.'

'Are you not concerned for your well-being? If not for yourself, then for those who are reliant upon you?'

'Farmers and merchants?' The wine slops onto the rushes as he gesticulates dismissively with his cup. 'What time have I for such as these? Or,' he asks, pointedly, 'do you mean you?'

'I hadn't even thought...'

'Do you know,' he interrupts, 'I couldn't wait to get away after our betrothal, back to Percy's household? That's where I belong. And even when we are wed and the land is mine, I shall still want to be away from here as often as I can arrange. In faith,' as the thought occurs to him, 'you must be prepared to stand in my stead here, seeing to my "responsibilities to my people",' throwing her earlier words back at her. 'So, it's much more important that you learn to manage this paltry backwater; I'm sure it will suit you well. And since Percy wasn't even inclined to give you a dowry to bring to the marriage,' he disparaged, 'you can earn your way instead.'

His comment stings. She tilts her head to one side, considering him. 'You would not wish me with you at court, then, my lord?' she nettles him in return.

He almost chokes on his wine. 'Never!' he spits. 'The stain of your family's betrayal will never be wiped out. Why would I want anyone in the king's court to associate me with that?'

Now his words stab deeper and a dark flush rises in her cheeks in anger, but she manages to control it. 'I have no wish to argue with you, my lord,' she assures him.

'And yet you did tonight!' he opposes, resenting her restrained response and resorting to anger to assuage his guilt at the pain in her face. 'A man's betrothed should not gainsay him before others,' raising an admonishing finger. 'Least of all before his own kin. And is it too much to expect my kin – and my future wife – to be proud of me for wanting to go to war?' he carps. 'To take a chance to raise my fortunes? To prove myself before the king and Percy and anyone else? Do not fret for my safety: I am stronger and faster and better trained than all the squires. I am ready for war!'

'You cannot expect them to be happy that you would fight for Hugh Despenser,' seeking some fellow-feeling in this selfish boy.

'And why not? 'Tis the king's fight, after all.'

'But it affects your father deeply. And the prioress. If you understood their positions, I'm sure you would find more sympathy in your own.'

'Nor never mind that he condemned your father to death,' he sneers, leaning down to refill his cup. 'Don't think me so naïve, girl, as not to know your own motivation in opposing me.'

She blanches. 'You mistake me, my lord!' Feeling her anger rise, she pushes to her feet to move away.

He seems pleased that his taunt has garnered a response. 'Don't deny it, girl,' he advises. 'You were so quick to defend your father's name before, I'm sure that hasn't changed.' He leans back in his chair, looking her up and down in a hard, assessing manner. 'For certain, you are comelier than you were then; pray fortune that will continue. But,' his face turns brutal, 'know that your pleasing looks are not sufficient to overcome the stain of your family in my eyes. I may be forced to marry you one day but do not expect me to place you at my side.' He sees how his words strike home, and he rises with a leering, malice-filled grin. 'Though,' stepping towards her, 'I shall be very happy to bed you!'

He moves so fast that she has no time to react. Grabbing her throat with one hand, he pushes her up against the wall, so hard that it drives the air out of her. Such is the disparity in stature and strength between them that his hold almost lifts her off her feet, and her breath is tight in her constricted throat, her hands scratching at his, trying to loosen his grip.

He laughs, exalting at the disparity between her feebleness and his strength, then crushes her mouth beneath his, pushing his body up against hers. Her whole being revolts, and she tries to push him off her, to pull her mouth away, but he has her trapped against the wall. Her head thumps painfully, desperate to be free.

And then, in an instant, all her revulsion vanishes, and she is standing outside her own body, an onlooker, a witness to his assault. The pounding in her ears stops and her panic drains away.

She watches Lady Alice appear and hears Ralf yelp with pain as Lady Alice holds tight to a handful of his hair and yanks him backwards. Edith stands close behind her, ready to intervene if needed.

'Get off me, old woman!' he orders, scrabbling at the prioress's hand just as Christiane has fought against him.

'You go too far!' she accuses, pushing him across the room and putting herself between him and the girl. 'Has no one taught you how to respect a lady?'

'Lady!' he baulks, touching his sore head. 'She's no such thing!'

'She is worth ten of you, ungrateful boy!'

'What is this?' Blinking in sleepy confusion at the scuffle, Geoffrey appears at the door. 'What's happening?'

'Your son seems to think it is acceptable to attack Christiane!' the prioress exclaims.

'It was just a harmless kiss,' he defends. 'She's my betrothed: I have the right.'

'But that doesn't put you in the right,' Geoffrey reacts, coming to stand by the girl to reassure himself she is well. She looks at him strangely, not quite meeting his gaze but unmoving and fixed within herself. 'She deserves your respect and consideration.'

'I might have known you would take her part over mine!' Ralf whines. 'Mother warned me you had become too caring about her.'

'Christiane is part of this family and has become a true help to all of us,' Geoffrey reasons. 'You should be grateful to her, not resentful. Certainly, she deserves to be treated better by you!'

'She has both of you wrapped around her finger!' he derides. 'Well, know this, girl,' pointing at Christiane's face, though she does not raise her eyes to his, 'when we are wed, I shall be the one holding the leash and these two shall not be permitted to protect you.'

'And when that day shall be still sits with me,' Geoffrey warns. 'So, take heed, my son, or I shall refuse to fix your wedding day until I see an improvement within you!'

The threat finds its mark, stunning the boy into silence; his face glowers his displeasure at being thwarted and he slinks from the room.

Geoffrey sighs heavily and nods at the Prioress. 'We shall see you in the morn,' encouraging her to remove the still, quiet girl.

Lady Alice puts her arm around Christiane's shoulder to guide her towards their chamber, chivvying Edith ahead of them both. Pulling back the coverlet, she hands Christiane's disrupted mantle to Edith and directs both girls into bed.

As the prioress comes round the opposite side to settle herself too, Christiane turns on her side, frowning slightly.

'I'm not sure Master Ralf really cares to have me as his wife,' she concludes. Lady Alice looks at her in surprise; how can the girl be so calm?

'If that were true,' the prioress assesses wryly, 'there would be nothing like a father standing in the way of it to make a boy like him want it more! Anyway,' she changes tack, 'never mind what that boy says. He will be brought into line when the time comes. Now, go to sleep, child.'

Christiane closes her eyes obediently and lies listening to the sound of the prioress's breathing as it softens into slumber.

But she cannot fall asleep while she waits for the thumping of her heartbeat to subside.

Because, inside, her blood is racing. Not at Ralf's actions or at the sting of the insults he had thrown at her, but because she can feel an almost engulfing anger in the man who has been by her side throughout. That same indistinct but specific presence she has felt before, evading her eye but so real to her, just as he had been three years ago.

She can still feel him there, in the shadows of this room. Watching protectively over her, needing to know she is safe, raging still.

She's elated that he has returned. And reassured by powerful feelings of being protected, cherished and loved.

He has taken all the negative emotions from her and borne them within himself, his rage dissipating her own fear and anger. She has never felt so clear in her mind, so calm in her body, and it leaves her with an incredible trust that all will be well.

Even so, she looks forward to Ralf leaving in the morning.

Chapter Twenty-four

York. 14th September 1976

The world rushes in on me in a confusing, blinding whirlwind. I put my hands out to steady myself, grabbing the sides of the bath, swallowing hard until, gradually, everything slows down.

It's then that I realise the bathwater is stone cold, as is the air in the room. And there's a strange buzzing and flickering from the bare lightbulb in the centre of the ceiling, like the crackle of a loose connection.

I've lost all sense of myself in this time.

I scramble up as fast as I can. My limbs are stiff and unresponsive, and I rub them hard with the towel to bring back some feeling. My skin prickles painfully as the blood starts to flow again. I pull on enough clothes to make it back to my room in semi-decency and pad barefooted down the hallway.

Flicking on the light, I stop again as a wave of dizziness hits me. I lean one hand against the wall, eyes closed, waiting for the weakness to subside. The roughness of the wood-chip wallpaper under my fingers offers a touchpoint back to reality.

Because a moment ago, I was standing beside her. And it was so real. The stifling heat by the fire, the damp cold near the external walls. The brilliant colours of the new tapestry hangings. The dull gleam of the pewter ewers they serve the wine in. I can still feel the foul smell of the tallow candles in the back of my throat, at odds with the sweetness of newly laid rushes on the floor, strewn with lavender and rosemary.

And I feel all those emotions surge through me again. I have never felt anger like it. An overwhelming cocktail of fury at him, intense protectiveness towards her and frustration that I could do nothing to intervene.

And what comes in response to that is a huge desire to inflict pain. I want to grab that arrogant, insolent boy and pound his grinning face until all the rage has gone.

Suddenly, I can't stand to be in this room. I'm penned in, the space too small, the hermetic sanctuary now a prison cell. I need air. I need to see the night sky. I need to walk, to run…to hit something. Anything to get these uncontrollable emotions out of my system.

I throw on the clothes that are to hand, grab a coat and run down the stairs, through the bar, ignoring my hosts and their regulars alike, and rush out into the street. The detached, rational part of me knows they must think I'm a madman.

Night has settled in, bringing with it cooler air. It's so good to draw that into my lungs, and I breathe as deeply as my ribs will allow, long, refreshing drags of crisp air.

My head clears a little, but my body is still humming. I pace out a long loop around the Museum Gardens' perimeter, down by the river, walking fast to burn it off, stepping into the road impatiently as I overtake anyone else on the path. By the time I return to Michael's street, my breath is coming fast from the exertion and my heart is pumping. I stop on the pavement opposite his front door to reassess. But the buzz is still there, like my body is overcharged with electricity. I half expect to see sparks coming out of my fingers. And my mind is playing those images over and over. When he grabbed her by the throat, I wanted to do the same to him. When he pushed her up against the wall, I wanted to ram his head into it. When he kissed her like that…if I'd been able to, I would have thrown him across the room. I've never thought of myself as a violent man, until now.

And the impotence of not being able to do anything – not to cry out, not to call for help, not to stop him – is tearing my body apart.

I start walking again, up and down the road; I have to keep moving. I focus on my surroundings to ground myself, anything to stop my mind playing that scene again and again. Staring at the red brick wall of the house opposite, counting the bricks in one layer and then the number of layers from top to bottom. Pressing my hands against the huge slabs of sandstone in the Museum Gardens wall, feeling them carved and cool to the touch, tracing the roughness of the mortared joints between. Even taking my shoes off and walking up and down the narrow strip of grass to feel the turf beneath my feet.

Now I really do feel on the brink of insanity.

I put my head in my hands and close my eyes, but that just makes the buzzing louder in my head.

In despair, I lean back against the wall and knock the back of my head against it, three times, trying to drive some sense into myself.

Michael is watching me, standing at the first-floor window of his flat. With the light behind him, he's in silhouette and his face is hidden.

Not now, Michael. Not now. Don't ask me to explain this to you. Please. I can't. I can't talk to you now.

He watches me a moment longer, then turns away. I know I have to go to him, though every cell of me is screaming against it. I shut my eyes and clench my fists, giving in to all the resistance within me. And then I let go.

* * * * * * *

Lamps are lit in every corner of the flat, spilling warmth throughout. It's jarring to me, and the tension rises again. By the frown on his face, he sees it too. Without a word, he leads me through to the kitchen. There's an uncomfortable, drawn-out wordlessness as he makes tea. The Englishman's panacea.

Still silent, he goes back to the sitting room; when he takes the desk chair, I feel he's inviting me to take his armchair, though it seems an unnatural inversion to do so.

Instinctively, I close my eyes and let my head rest. I'm exhausted. Without my noticing it, the buzzing in my head and limbs has stopped, and now I feel empty.

He's waiting for me to speak. I don't want to. I'm not ready to share this with him. The ticking mantle clock marks the moments as they pass.

'Do you know Marilyn and I are still married?' His voice comes to me as if from a distance. I open my eyes, but the expression on his face is inscrutable.

'What?'

'I never filed for divorce. Unless she's dead, Marilyn and I are still married,' he reveals. 'I've heard nothing from her since she left. I was thinking someone should tell her. When I've gone.' I can't find the words to reply, not even some platitude. 'I wonder sometimes how she dealt with that,' he ponders, contemplating his cup of tea for insight. 'If she and the airman stayed together, they would have known she was already married. Did that stop them or did they just pretend it had never happened? Or did she meet someone else? Perhaps she had another family.' He smiles. 'I do hope she's found happiness, of her kind.'

'Meaning?' I try to concentrate on what he's saying, to engage with his train of thought.

'I wasn't equipped to make her happy: she needed someone who could be devoted to her, who put her at the centre of his life. I could never do that for her. My work was already the most important thing to me; I'd never give that up.'

That strikes a chord. 'Is there no way to have both?'

'I never found it. But then, she was gone before we really tried.'

'You loved her though?'

'Very much. But I was endlessly surprised that she felt anything for me, which is why I never expected it to last.' His smile is regretful, almost apologetic. 'I always thought you and Samantha would fare better,' he reviews.

'Why?'

'It's different for your generation: you're more independent, less reliant on each other. That neediness can be stifling. I thought you would be more resilient than we were.'

I'd thought so too.

'How was it? When Marilyn left?' I'm stepping into territory I never expected to explore with him.

'I slipped back into the old habits and just let myself focus on the work. The hole she left behind didn't take long to diminish.'

'Diminish, but it didn't go away altogether? Does it ever?'

His gaze is direct. 'You tell me.'

I'm not ready to go there. 'Has Sam never shown any interest in knowing about her?' I deflect.

'None. I've spoken about her over the years but it's always one-way traffic. I tell Samantha what I remember because I feel I should but she has no questions for me. I think she sees Marilyn as nothing more than the woman who brought her into this world; otherwise, she's an irrelevance. She has no need of her.'

'Do you think that would ever change?'

'I doubt it. I don't think she needs that relationship. She's always been so strong within herself. Like you.' He leans his head to one side and looks at me with a wistful smile. 'Single-minded too. She decided she wanted you the moment she saw you. I don't know how she knows these things. I guess she has a strong intuition. It was just like that,' he recalls, 'when she decided she was going to be a doctor. Nothing could divert her. I remember the school calling me in to discuss her career options, wanting me to convince Samantha to pursue nursing instead of being a doctor. I sat in that cubby-hole of an office with its cold white walls and paint peeling off the steel-framed windows,' a reminiscing smile ghosts across his lips, 'and I listened to the man talk for ten minutes about why a woman can't be a doctor. Then I advised him not to get in Samantha's way.'

He rests his elbows on the chair's arms and steeples his hands, tapping his index fingers against his bottom lip.

'I didn't notice until the end of that first summer how she felt about you. I was too consumed by the project, as always,' he confesses. 'When I eventually did, it worried me: I could see you didn't see her that way. You liked having her around but mostly because you went from being the baby of the family to having quasi big brother status. For you, it was all about the dig, and it was just fine if she tagged along.'

'You gave me my first taste of archaeology. You started this addiction,' I smile.

There's a warmth between us as he smiles back. 'I thought her feelings would fade once we went away but she was just the same the following summer. I was so worried about it I even thought of saying something to you. I should have known better: Samantha always gets what she wants.'

'But she didn't, did she? Because we didn't last.'

The bitterness in my tone causes him to hesitate. 'You lasted longer than most,' he consoles. 'Had a more successful relationship than most people as well, from what I saw.'

'It always felt easy,' I begrudge. 'Just being myself with her. Of course, we argued and fought like anyone. But she never asked me to be other than what I am. Except once.'

His pause tells me there's a loaded question coming. 'Is that why it ended?'

'What do you mean?'

'Well, from the outside, it looked like you were heading in different directions, and it pulled you apart.'

'That's not how I would describe it.' Sadness and resentment are still there, not far below the surface. More than I knew.

'Enlighten me.'

'She drove me away.'

'How?'

'Pretty much insisted I should take the job in London if I still wanted to be with her.'

'Did she?' He stops to consider that for a long moment. 'So, the woman who never asked anything of you gave you an ultimatum?'

'That's about the sum of it.'

'Doesn't that strike you as...' choosing the word with care, 'inconsistent?'

'What's your point?' I challenge.

'I think she let you go.'

'I was the one who had to make the decision,' I argue. 'I was the one who walked away.'

He nods. 'And yet she created the circumstance to let you do so.'

I don't want to hear that. What's been suppressed for ten years is surfacing with surprising momentum. 'I thought she would fight for me. Apparently, I wanted us to mean more than we actually did. She knew me better than anyone. Knew what my work means to me. Of all people, how could she ask me to compromise on my career?'

'If she'd held on, you would have ended up pulling away anyway, and she would have known that.'

'And then she had to go and marry that idiot almost immediately afterwards!' I justify.

'Yes, not her finest moment. At one point I even wondered if she'd married him so she wouldn't come running back to you.' I raise an eyebrow at that one. 'If it's any consolation, I think she's been paying for it ever since.'

'How?'

'I could see it was a mistake almost immediately. He wasn't strong enough for her, not like you. You and she are so similar, you respected one another's drive and ambition. Paul was threatened by her success, and he made the mistake of trying to squash her into a box that suited him. She even went along with that for a while, working on his happiness at the expense of her own, just to keep the peace. I dare say I've not helped,' he allows. 'I left them to get on with it. Followed my own path here, chasing phantoms.'

'Phantoms? I thought this was what you wanted?'

'I did. Maybe part of me still does,' he admits heavily, 'but it's not like before. When the doctors gave me the diagnosis, my first reaction was desperation to finish the work. Ernest was already geared up for the dig and I encouraged him to expand it as much as possible, to accelerate the work. I promised him whatever funding he needed. But as summer's worn on, it's come to mean less to me. When I faced the fact that I would die not knowing what I want to know, it felt less bad than I expected. I discovered that what I really wanted was to spend time with Samantha. And you.'

'But you told Sam not to tell me.' That hurts.

His nod is unapologetic. 'I did. But I was on the verge of changing my mind when she arrived with you. She always could read my mind.'

'And now?' I return. 'How do you feel about the dig now?'

'I've reconciled myself to not knowing and I don't think I can go back to hoping like I did before. I'll play along for Samantha's sake because she hopes I'm hanging on for this. And your enthusiasm is pretty infectious,' he smiles, paternally.

'How can you not want to know?' I'm incredulous. 'I saw her again tonight. Don't you want to know?'

'You did?' In spite of himself, it pulls him in. But then he thinks better of it. 'No,' he retracts. 'I can't keep doing this.' And I glimpse what a drain this has been for him.

Now that he doesn't want to know, all I want to do is tell him everything. The details are overwhelming me, not least because I have no frame of reference for what I'm experiencing. Not that I'm expecting him to either, but holding it inside, leaving it unspoken, feels like putting the Big Bang in a bottle.

He sees my internal battle, understanding it better than anyone. 'That's why you were outside tonight?' he surmises.

I nod. 'I was in the bath…and then I lost all awareness of myself. Woke up ages later.'

He sighs. 'Then you had better tell me about it.'

Now he's given me an opening, I hardly know where to start, and I feel that pent-up force well up inside me again. It's choking my throat from the inside, pushing up through my oesophagus, stopping my words and yet crying to get out. I push to my feet because I have to: it's either move or explode. I feel his eyes on me as I stride across the room to the far window and stare down into the street, standing where he stood as he watched me below.

'I've never seen you so agitated, my boy,' he worries, calling me back to him, resting his chin on his interlaced fingers.

'Agitated doesn't even come close.' I can't tell if it's anger or scorn or bewilderment in my voice. 'I don't know what to do with these…' I gesture helplessly as I sink into the chair again. What are they? Dreams? Visions? Hallucinations? 'To watch that girl go through the execution of her father. Her life uprooted, her family left behind. Forced into being part of a family she doesn't know. And then attacked by that…worthless boy!'

'Attacked?'

I have to stop the anger before it consumes me again. 'Ralf Goscelin,' I push the thought away with one hand. 'It wasn't serious. But I don't like him.' What a pathetic phrase for what I actually feel!

He reads my resistance to giving him more. 'She's come to Threfield Percy?' he prompts.

'After the execution. God,' I empathise, 'how is she even finding her way after that? Though she does seem to be,' I reflect, closing my eyes and seeing her again so clearly. 'I mean, she's really integrated into the life of the village in the three-and-a-bit years she's been there. She knows what's happening in every household, who's sick, who's thriving, who's struggling financially, who's fallen out with their family. She's built a relationship with Amicia, somehow. That's no mean feat given how temperamental and self-centred and avaricious that woman is, how little concerned for others, least of all Christiane. She's still a girl, fourteen years old, and she's practically running the manor with the steward. Everything she gleaned from growing up in her father's household, watching him and her mother make decisions about their tenants and household, she's applying all of that here. The Great Famine casts a long shadow over her life, so she's looking for ways to protect the tenants if they face another crisis. Christ!' with sudden realisation. 'Little does she know what's ahead of her! Civil war in England, war with France, the plague. Assuming she even lives that long.' That gives me pause; I feel sick at the thought of Christiane dying. 'What do we know about any of the family?' I turn on Michael. 'Ralf – when and where does he die? What about Geoffrey and Amicia? There must be something in the records that gives us an indication of what happened to her.'

Michael shakes his head, mutely. He doesn't know even how to start answering my questions. I think he's struggling to follow my train of thought.

'Is there any mention of marriage?' he asks. I shake my head. 'At that age, it would be premature.'

'I thought they tended to be child brides?'

'A common misconception. You might see it among the greatest families, but the majority of ordinary people would marry in their late teens or early twenties.'

'I hope it's not too soon,' I mutter. 'They're not a good match.'

'Marriage is essentially an economic contract anyway,' Michael warns.

'Very romantic!'

'I know, but we have very different perspectives on romance from them. Women were technically property, passed in ownership terms from father to son.'

The factual detail seems to ground him, so I follow his train of thought.

'What does it mean that she brought no dowry?' I wonder.

'She didn't? No, I don't suppose she would if all her father's lands were confiscated. That's not good for her: her dowry would be what she would fall back on once her husband died, assuming she outlived him. It would have been her husband's to use during her lifetime. And Goscelin could probably do with it; Threfield Percy wasn't a wealthy manor. It produced only £10 or £12 a year in income for the family.'

'Give me context for that?'

'It's the lower end of the land-based strata. The earl of Lancaster made £1,000 a year, the barons anywhere between £300 and £700. The lowest of the landed gentlemen were little better off than the most qualified artisans. A master mason might make £10 to £17 a year, so could a lawyer or physician. Most landowners would have more than one manor; it could be seen as a slight that Percy gave his niece only that one, though he may have been assuming her husband's business would support them.'

'Did that do well?'

'I've not looked closely but a middling merchant might have £500 in capital, equating to income of £100 a year.' He stops, checks himself. 'You really are seeing this?' He sounds half bewildered, half jealous.

I run one hand through my hair, distracted. 'The question is how? And why do I only see what's gone before? And only from her perspective? I can't read anyone else's mind. But when I come to, I know everything she knows up to that point. For instance, I know about the letters Lady Alice receives from someone she corresponds with in Percy's household, a cousin of her dead husband. How she keeps abreast of court politics and hears tales of Ralf's behaviour, his misdemeanours with the serving girls, his frequent brawls with other boys. All of which she shares, unexpurgated,' feeling a little critical of the prioress, 'with Christiane.'

I shake my head in dismay as more of the details come back to me. 'I know how Amicia's joints feel when Christiane puts her hands on them and prays,' I reflect. 'How warmth flows through her fingers and into Amicia, how it soothes Amicia and makes Christiane's body tingle. How Amicia treats her as little more than a servant girl, there to do her bidding. To dress her. To read to her. She reads English and French as well as Latin, did you know? And writes. Endless letters dictated by Amicia that she sends to anyone she knows in the outside world who might be of benefit to her. Pleading, whingeing letters, expecting them to have sympathy for her condition and to send her treats and precious things to make her feel better. How she squanders whatever money her husband can make,' real distaste flickering through me now. 'And the way she controls the people of that village, the fear she instils in them. There's something so strange there. Christiane doesn't know why, but Amicia has a terror of someone bringing something to the village. She's certain it's going to bring her death.'

I lean forward in my chair, gesturing for emphasis. 'Christ, I even know how Christiane felt when she had her first period! If you ever want to know how medieval women deal with pregnancy and menopause, I could soon be your resident expert!' I laugh harshly at the absurdity of it.

'Do you know, though, there's something so different about how they think? The medieval mentality, I've never thought about it before. They're so much more connected to…God, they would say. To whatever you want to believe is out there,' I shrug, ill-equipped in such matters. 'whatever it is – if there even is anything – that's beyond the physical. They see themselves, every one of them, as a microcosm, a tiny individual replica of God's entire world. I've never felt a fraction of that absolute faith in my entire life!'

I sink back into the chair, shaking my head. Michael's watching me, still bemused. Like he doesn't know what question to ask first.

'What's she like?'

'In what way?'

'I don't know, Eoghan. Just tell me about her!' he demands.

I almost resist. But it's such a relief to be talking about her. 'They're more mature than we were at that age, more mature even than the graduates we teach, with her running the place and Ralf ready to go off to war.'

'They had to be,' Michael muses. 'When you're lucky to live to thirty, I guess you get on with life.'

'Michael,' I switch tack, giving him a direct look, 'I know exactly what's under the mound. I just don't know why or how it's collapsed.' He waits for me to go on. 'I'll tell you now, tomorrow or the next day we're going to start finding red clay rooftiles that were brought in from the Midlands. Charred timbers from the bigger pieces of furniture that won't have burnt through, from the table from upstairs, the bed, perhaps the floor joists. The stone steps leading down to the lower floor and the circular basement wall. Maybe even some of the artefacts, if the place hasn't been looted: silver-bound ivory caskets, wooden chests, jewellery and gemstones. Perfume vials from the Middle East,' remembering that unmistakable smell. 'And pieces of coloured glass – not stained glass, hand-painted. Heavy pieces, thick like the bottom of a bottle. The most iridescent red and blue and green. Fitted with such heavy pieces of leading that it looks clumsy and awkward compared with normal stained glass. But it's needed because Amicia believes it will keep out the sunlight that hurts her. She's so afraid of it, it's unnatural. She's not stepped out of that tower in over a decade. At least, not in daylight. She insists on mass being held before dawn and after dusk so she can attend. But even so she appears in these layers of black cloth, head to toe, to avoid light touching her. The children of the village are petrified of her. And the priest, he's more terrified of her than anyone. Do you know, he has a family, a wife and two children?'

The look on Michael's face cuts me dead and I realise what I'm saying is hurting him. These are the things he's always wanted to know but it's come to me instead of him. It's a betrayal. He's given years of his life to this, and at the eleventh hour, it's rejected him in favour of me.

'Michael,' I falter. 'I'm sorry...'

His raised hand forestalls me. 'It's too late,' he denies. 'Please, no more. I don't have the time and I can't start to hope again.'

His words bring me back to what I saw in the kitchen this evening. And I understand what he's saying.

'Michael,' I start, and stop. How do I say this to him?

He sees my dilemma and anticipates me. 'Just say it,' he permits.

'I saw the food in the bin earlier.' I don't know how to frame the question, but he anticipates it for me.

'They insist on bringing the food whether I eat it or not. And I know Samantha checks in with them to see how much I'm eating. So, I give them a clean plate and keep them all happy with the pretence.'

'You've stopped eating?' I just have to say it out loud.

He doesn't flinch. 'How long do you think a man can survive without food?' His voice is horribly calm and determined.

Mine is stuck in my throat. 'I don't know. A few weeks maybe?'

'Hopefully less in my condition.' He's holding my gaze with as much strength and determination as the man I first met twenty years ago.

'Michael, please, hold on a bit longer.'

'Don't ask me to do that.'

'But I'm finding those answers you've been searching for.'

'Those questions aren't important to me now.'

'But they are to me!' I defend.

He grimaces. 'Then answer them for yourself.'

'But I need your expertise.'

'No, you don't,' he rejects. 'You've seen more than I've grasped from a decade of pursuing this. My boy, I can't wait for this disease to waste away at me, cell by cell.' There's no anger in his voice, just acknowledgement. 'I'd sooner go this way. It seems kinder, to me.'

How can I argue with that? I could no more watch him fade away than he could stand to experience it. But it makes all of this so much more immediate. I want to ask when he stopped eating, as if I can gauge how much time we might have left, but neither of us wants to do that calculation. I'm adrift in the ocean, not knowing how far it is to shore or even which way to go, knowing only that I have to keep going. That the only thing I can focus on is The Woman.

He reads the acceptance in my face, and I think having a co-conspirator eases him.

'Will you just tell me something,' he requests tentatively, unable to help himself.

'Anything,' I affirm.

'Goscelin…was he kind to her?'

He catches me off guard and my retort becomes sarcastic, laden with the anger from before. 'The boy? He's arrogant, immature, selfish and brutal; what do you think?'

'Not the boy.' His voice seems rusty, like mine was some moments before. 'The father. Geoffrey.'

I frown, taken aback. 'He seems protective of her, like he's trying to stand in for her father.'

'What's your impression of him?' I can't see Michael's face properly, so I don't know what he's getting at.

I reach for a memory of Christiane's impressions. 'He doesn't fit easily into the role of lord of the manor. He's a merchant who somehow fell in with the Percys and got stuck with that life when he married Amicia. He'd sooner be away, trading, travelling. He maintains a semblance of peace by appeasing his wife. She's a difficult woman, wrapped up in her self-importance and whatever her illnesses are. He brings her gifts and panders to her foibles, basically to pacify her and give himself an easier life. But he's a decent man and there's a strong friendship between him and Richard Prudhomme, which speaks well of him. And he stands up for Christiane, protects her from his wife and son.'

His face, in profile and shadow, is inscrutable. 'That's all?' I nod. The nod he gives is almost imperceptible. 'Thank you, my boy,' he embraces the knowing. 'Now,' drawing himself up in his chair, 'let me say something. And I know you won't like it, but it's the right of the dying to be demanding. I don't want you to be caught up in this mess, just like I was.

'I was watching you outside. I know that look. I've felt it too. There's nothing like it. The first time, I felt completely out of control, didn't know what to do with myself, how to deal with it. But it made me feel more alive than anything I've known. And I felt I owed it to her. I think it's something to do with Geoffrey. I can't say why but I've always been drawn to him, felt an affinity with him. I dream of him sometimes. Just vague impressions, really: feelings of failure and weakness and guilt.

'In the last few days, it's like she's let me go…or I've let her go. And I can't tell you what a relief that is. Like I've lived in semi-darkness for years and suddenly there's brilliant sunshine all about. I don't want you to get lost too.

'What I want, in what time I have left, is to be with those I love. Samantha will be here when she can. And you're here. And it's brought me so much joy to be able to see you.'

He's looking at me steadily, hoping I'll intuit what he can't bring himself to say. He's asking me to give up the dig and focus on being with him.

I love this man like I love my own father. I owe him everything. He started me on this path, showed me the way to who I really am.

But however great that love is, I can't do what he wants. Because everything that I am is now inextricably entwined in this. With her.

Once more, he reads my face and I watch the sadness spread through his.

'I know,' he regrets heavily. 'I can see it in you: you're here but you're not. She's got her grip on you. No one could understand that better than I. I'm so sorry, my boy.' The sadness, regret and guilt I see in his eyes almost – almost – reaches my heart. 'I've brought this on you. And I just hope you're stronger than I was. Otherwise, it's going to destroy you, just like it's destroyed me. Thank God I won't be around to see it.'

Wednesday

Chapter Twenty-five

York. 15th September 1976

When I wake, I'm a mess.

My nose and throat are dry and rough, my eyes struggle to focus and my head is so heavy I let it fall back on the pillow and just lie there, waiting to come round more gradually.

What's wrong with me? I feel like I've been through a major drinking session, but I didn't touch a drop last night. Mercifully, the pub was just closing when I returned last night, otherwise, given the circumstances, I might have been tempted.

Lack of sleep, maybe? My brain was racing when I went to bed. I know I kept going over and over things in my mind. Each time I dropped off some thought would jolt me awake again.

Several minutes pass until I cautiously open my eyes. The sun streaming in the window – where I neglected to draw the curtain last night – is higher in the sky than it should be.

I'm late.

I'm never late. And that darkens my mood even further.

Forcing myself to throw off the blankets, I shiver in the morning air, goosebumps rising on my forearms. I pull on extra layers; even though I can see the sun and clear skies through my bedroom window, I think I'm going to need them. I hope I'm not coming down with something, I don't have time for that just now.

The landlady unlocks the public bar door to let me outside, teasingly scolding me for not taking breakfast yet again, but the smell of fried food is making me nauseous. I raise a smile for her, trying to be polite while escaping as quickly as possible.

The traffic makes it slow-going getting out of York and I'm getting more and more tense, drumming impatiently on the steering wheel. My mind is moving slower than I'm used to, only now registering that I'm even later than I thought. Maybe I should have asked for a wake-up call, but I've never needed it before. Oversleeping is not something I have to contend with.

The number of cars already parked in the field makes it awkward to find a space for the bulky Volvo and I have to manoeuvre several times. I run across the bridge, along the river path and towards the camp.

Shit. The morning meeting is already well underway. I should have been here an hour ago to go through the dance with Montague, making my case for appropriate resource for the day's work. He'll think I'm slapdash and careless, arrogant even, and I suspect I look as bad as I feel. I didn't stop to wash or shave.

Montague catches sight of me as I approach and there's a hint of triumph beneath his reprehensive glare. He hands over to Martin to allocate the tasks and storms off, unnecessarily theatrically. More than a few heads turn my way. And the girls are giving me very different looks from their open interest yesterday.

I ignore all of them and head to the tent, grab a random collection of tools and sullenly head off down the lower path. I trust to Martin to make sure I have some workers.

As I approach the site, I feel the slightest apprehension for the first time, wondering what it's got in store for me today. But everything is calm: the sun has chased away the shadows, it seems. There's even birdsong.

I pull off the tarpaulins protecting the soil as Martin leads a small group towards me: five in total, three men, two women. Only one appears to be a student.

'The group's already thinning out,' Martin confirms after he's introduced me to everyone. 'Students and faculty getting ready for term, I think. But it's great we've got reinforcements from our local group. I put in a few calls last night and we might expect one or two more tomorrow.'

'What about you?' I ask. 'I assumed you'd prefer to be working on the undercroft.'

He gives me a shifty look. 'The students are well underway with that,' he asserts. 'I think I can have more of an impact here.'

'Meaning Montague wasn't going to give me anyone, so you stepped in?' I deduce.

'I'll do what's best for Michael,' he states, plainly. That gives me a stab of conscience. 'How's he doing?'

With no idea how to even start answering that, I shake my head mutely, but he's distracted anyway.

'Look out,' nodding over my shoulder, back up the path, 'he's on the way.' Martin ducks away, wisely leaving me to it, and the rest of the group turn away too, trying to look busy.

'Montague,' I start to forestall him.

'You're late,' stating the glaringly obvious. 'I can't be wasting precious resources waiting for you to arrive whenever you deign to turn up. It's unprofessional. And you know better, which makes me think that you're doing it to disrespect me.' He's properly angry and invading my personal space in an attempt to intimidate me. 'And you think you can get away with it because of Michael. Well,' wagging a finger in such a ridiculously priggish way that it's all I can do to keep a straight face, 'count yourself lucky I've given you anyone to work with.'

He turns his back before I can answer, or perhaps because his courage deserts him. I shake my head and swallow the chastisement without complaint.

Thankfully, Martin steps up. 'OK, what's the plan?'

'Let's work in two groups of three,' surveying the site and the workers. 'Martin, you take one team, I'll take the other. Work fast: this is about getting as far as we can in the time available. That takes concentration, so rotate the diggers, say, every thirty minutes. One digging, one sifting, one overseeing. You'll miss things. It's not a criticism, it's just a fact, so one person keeping a watchful eye while they're resting will help. If you find anything meaningful, shout out.'

* * * * * * *

God, what a frustrating day! I sling my rucksack in the footwell behind the driver's seat and slam the door. The car rocks on its axles. I'm dirty, sore and grouchy.

It's been one aggravation after another. Tools that break. People getting called away. We couldn't get a rhythm going. It was just a back-breaking slog. And, periodically, Montague hanging around like the spectre at the feast. Perhaps he'd sooner we failed.

Just before lunch and again before the close, Martin pulled in a couple of students and got them working with a camera and graph paper to record where we were at, but he might as well not have bothered. Eight hours' labour and nothing meaningful to show for it. A pile of soil, some stone from the walls and bits of roof tile.

If I didn't know better, I'd start to question what I expect to find. But this knowing allows no room for doubt. Somehow, that just makes my mood worse.

The air in the car is warm from a day in the sun but I still feel cold. I haven't eaten, too embarrassed to show my face at lunch and wanting to make up for lost time. Much good it did me.

I collapse into the driver's seat and turn the ignition. The engine coughs twice, then nothing. Oh, come on!

I smack my hands against the steering wheel and relish the jolt of pain up my arms at the aggression. But when it's gone, I slump back in the seat, closing my eyes.

I'm glad I got away without seeing Montague again. How he revelled in being able to tear a strip off me for being late. Like I'm some recalcitrant schoolboy! He may be head of department at York, but he's achieved a fraction of what I have in half the time. My work is changing the face of archaeology. What's he contributed? Really?

And the worst of it? I didn't get a feeling of her being there today. Not one. The site felt as flat as a pancake. I tried to focus myself, hoping I could find whatever it was that tapped into her before. But that just drained me until I became tetchy and short with everyone on the team.

What if I've lost it, that connection? I don't know how to control it. I don't know what's causing it to come in.

Five days ago, life was normal: presenting at conferences, having a beer down the pub.

Then I get knocked on the head. God knows if that has anything to do with all this. Can I trust anything at the moment?

And the only woman I've ever loved comes back into my life after ten years, bringing back all kinds of memories and thoughts that I've not gone near in all that time.

Then she tells me Michael is dying, the man who, other than Dad, has been the greatest male influence in my life. Who didn't even want me to know. Who's decided he's given up, so I have no time to adjust to losing him.

And all of this…this…what is it? It's like that intuition I've always had, but to the nth degree. Souped up like high-voltage electricity. Making no sense whatsoever but completely undeniable.

A rap at the passenger window jerks me upright. Martin gestures at me to let him in. I fight an instinctive but unjustified resentment at the intrusion and stretch across to pop the lock.

He glances at me as he settles into the seat. 'Flat battery?'

'Who knows? Mechanics isn't my forte. I'll give it a minute and then try again.'

He nods. 'I'll wait. If it doesn't work, I'll give you a lift to the garage.'

'Thanks. It's been that kind of day,' I laugh it off but it rings hollowly.

'I could see that. Tell me to keep my nose out of it…' he opens.

'In all honesty,' I admit, 'I'd be glad to talk.'

'Don't take Ernest's lecturing to heart,' he advises. 'His nose has been out of joint since you arrived. It's no surprise he took the opportunity to put you in your place. But he's not so bad, really. He's helped Michael a lot with this, particularly over the last three years.'

'I guess so.'

'Believe me, he could have made sure the dig never got off the ground. He has the influence to do that around here.'

'You're right, I know.'

'Academic egos at war,' he re-joins. 'It's not the first time I've seen it.'

I start to object but Martin's wry smile stops me. He's right: my ego is easily as big as Montague's.

'And this should be about Michael, not me?' I infer.

'I have a lot of time for him. And he talks about you a lot, so I know you're close.'

'I've known him more than twenty years.'

'He said you met in Ireland. Whereabouts?'

'Glendalough. County Wicklow. We're farmers and Mum taught in the village primary school, but money was always stretched so we took in summer boarders most years. Michael and Sam first came in the summer of '54. A Trinity College project at Glendalough Priory; Michael took me along one day.

'He got you hooked on archaeology?'

'From that first time, I was enthralled. Slowly and painstakingly clearing away the years of dirt to reveal some artefact from centuries past, compiling a picture of people's lives, piece by piece, to be able to re-construct lives long after they were dead and gone…it just seemed miraculous to me. And I felt I could sense their lives, their passions, their motivations. The difficulties they faced, the triumphs they enjoyed. Like I could receive that knowing from the materials I held in my hands.

'Michael saw it and fostered it in me from the beginning. After my Leaving Certificate exam, I went to stay with him and Sam. He was still at Cambridge then and gave me access to the library and his colleagues in the department. I spent hours talking to the faculty staff, sucking up their knowledge. I started volunteering for every dig I could fit in, from local historical groups to university ones. And it felt natural to choose Michael's college for my degree.'

'Your parents were OK with you leaving?'

'They didn't need me: my three older sisters all married local men and they now work the farm with Dad. I think they were relieved I could find a stable career; it was a tough time in Ireland, economic depression, huge levels of emigration.'

'I can see why this dig means a lot to you,' he surmises.

'I'll admit,' a little hesitantly, 'it's coming to mean more than I expected. This has been Michael's thing for a long time but I never engaged with it before. There's something…' I stop.

'Something…like what happened in the pub last night?' he intuits.

'What do you mean?' warily.

'That incident with Petra.' He's watching me acutely. 'From where I was standing, it looked like she was pushed.'

'I didn't push her,' I protest.

'I didn't say you did. And I'm not saying what, but something shoved her away.' He frowns. 'It's spooked them too: the female students. They refused to work with you today, said they'd work on the top site or they'd leave. En masse.'

'I didn't intend to disrupt everything.'

'It's not you,' he contends. 'Or, at least, it's not just you. There's something about the site, always has been. The locals have felt it for years; that's why there are so many superstitions about this place. But,' correcting himself, 'there's something about you and the site. Michael too, I think, though to a lesser degree. Like you're at the epicentre of whatever it is.' He shakes his head, uneasy with the idea. 'Look, I'm on your side and I'll do whatever I can to help but we're almost out of time.'

'More than you know,' I admit, heavily.

'You mean Michael?'

'I think he's given up.'

'Think…or know?' He reads the answer in my face. 'That's a shame. Though I can't blame him: you can see the pain he's in.' He pauses, a moment of shared sadness. 'Oh, I almost forgot, I have something for you,' reaching into his jeans pocket and unwrapping it from a handkerchief. 'Philippa spotted it in the spoil as she was about to leave.' He drops something small, hard and sharply angular in my palm.

It's a shard from those ghastly painted windows, blood-red.

Suddenly, my whole body is vibrating, tingles running up and down my spine, my thighs, my arms. I can feel an energy flowing between her time and mine, a bridge between then and now, reaching across the ages, resonating in both, present in each simultaneously. My hand closes around the piece and I feel it digging into my palm and fingers, becoming ever more specific to me in its original form. In my mind, I know its placing within the window frame, its proximity to other pieces, the lead that held it in place. And the white hot, searing heat that released it from that casing.

I gasp and drop the shard, feeling it scorch my skin. Martin retrieves it from the floor, which gives me enough time to cover my shock.

'At last, something more interesting than limestone blocks!' I joke.

Martin's look of curiosity says I'm not fooling him, but he lets it go.

'Hope for a better day tomorrow,' he advises. 'Give the car a try now.'

Of course, the engine starts immediately. I can feel how the mood has lightened, within me and around me.

Martin nods with satisfaction and gets out of the car. Which gives me a moment to check with my eyes what I know I feel in my skin: raw and blistered burn marks are already forming on my hand.

And all I can think is…thank God she's back.

* * * * * * *

I bump the car over the sun-baked tyre ridges carved into the field, a watchful Martin visible in my rear-view mirror. The country lanes are joyfully clear, but even as I hit rush-hour traffic in York, I feel more relaxed, less fraught.

I wait at the turn into Marygate to let an ambulance exit the narrow lane, then pull up on the curb to park the car.

And my heart thumps as I realise Sam is standing by her little sports car, nervously flipping her car keys around her index finger as she waits for me.

Just as fast my heart leaps into my throat as I realise the ambulance was for Michael.

Chapter Twenty-six

York. 15th September 1976

'I'm heading straight to the hospital,' she cuts in. 'I want to be there when he comes round.'

'He's unconscious?'

'He was on the floor when I walked in. The nurse says he was fine at lunchtime. Even so, he could have been lying there for hours.' Her voice is strained.

And resentful. Wanting to blame me for not being there. Wanting to lash out at someone. Instinct makes me want to defend myself, but I also want to let her have a target for the emotions she can't deal with.

'How come you're here?'

An awkward lift of her shoulders. 'An instinct.' She's anxious to leave.

'Want me to go with you?'

'No point,' she blocks, 'they'll only let family in.' It's not intended but that exclusion stings.

'When will you be back?' thinking I'll wait in the flat and maybe organise some supper for her.

'He's not coming back, Eoghan.'

She deliberately misconstrues my meaning, but it's her tone that throws me off-balance: normally so composed, she's as close as I've ever seen her to falling apart.

Emotions buttoned down, she gets in the car and drives off.

* * * * * * *

Heavy-hearted, heavy-limbed, I walk upstairs to a space that is flat and empty without him. I've never noticed before how much an individual imbues a place with themselves. This no longer looks like Michael's home; it's just an inadequate flat, typical of so many university residences, too small for a man who has written his life so large in mine. Dusty where the cleaner has been neglectful. Cluttered with papers that lose their relevance without him to give them meaning.

But I can reinject that meaning, keep alive what has meant so much to him. Detain his essence here a bit longer, hold onto normality. For now.

I pull out his desk chair and apply my natural sense of order to this chaos of documents. A pile related to the site, another for everything else. Suppressing the traitorous voice that says those too will have to be sifted through soon enough.

But when I lift a half-drunk tea-cup to retrieve the papers beneath, the act is like a bridge too far, like I'm trying to claim an inheritance before the appropriate time. I shake it off; I need something to think about so that I don't imagine him lying unconscious in that ambulance or Sam staring out of the window in an aseptic hospital waiting room as she waits for news. I can't think about him. And I can't think about her. Which means I have only one thing to focus on: The Woman.

* * * * * * *

When I stand to stretch my aching back, the daylight has almost gone.

I've been back over everything, revisiting what Michael took me through on Sunday with the overlay of my new insights. Now I understand what he means about Christiane's absence from the records. It's like a physical hole.

Here is Geoffrey's and Amicia's wedding, recorded in Percy documents. Ralf's entry into the world too: it looks like Amicia chose to give birth at her cousin's home. Wanting Ralf to be born amid her kin and kind, explains the voice in my head. There are accounts of Threfield Percy's annual profits and consequent obligations to its overlord, right through the period up to the Black

Death, with similar annotations in the ecclesiastical records from York. And details of Geoffrey's dealings with the Percy family and household: purchases of fleeces and cash advances against the right to future fleeces; sales of trade items, principally cloth but also Mediterranean and Middle Eastern oils and spices, wines from France, silver plate, oak storage chests. Even Geoffrey's son, Hughes, appears in the 1330s, by when he has taken over the family business, though there's nothing to show Geoffrey's death or will; Amicia's death is penned, blackly and briefly, in the Percy family details in 1349. Ralf's marriage isn't there, either, which would interest me more. Nor is the betrothal document.

But Ralf and who looks to be his son appear in Percy's annals, ranked in campaign lists from the wars against Scotland and France, with gifts from Percy in thanks and recognition.

New detail comes in a letter from Wales, dated yesterday, following up on a telephone conversation, enclosing Xerox copies of the documents they had discussed, promising to revert following further review.

My heart leaps to see her name marked in Glamorgan scrolls. The seventh and last child of Llewelyn Bren to be disposed of after his execution.

Scrawled marginal notes in Michael's spidery – and weaker – handwriting conclude his colleagues in York's history department have confirmed that Robert de Veteri Burgo was prior at Kirkham until his death in October 1321 and that Lady Alice de Lacy held her position at Molseby until 1337. A first corroboration.

Reaching across to turn on the desk lamp, I'm attracted to a faded colour photograph, sticking out from underneath other papers.

I'd forgotten he had this, a copy of the one in my rooms in Cambridge. I sit back heavily in the chair, the rest of the papers forgotten in reliving the moment caught on camera.

Early summer in Cambridge, nearly the end of my first year.

Formally dressed for dinner with the Master, Sam and I as Michael's guests; I was uneasy in my ill-fitting suit, conscious of how it compared unfavourably with those of more affluent backgrounds around me, and the overlay of the fur-trimmed gown on a warm summer evening was making it worse.

The photographer grouped the three of us together on the lawn; other guests chatting over drinks are blurred in the background against the backdrop of the college's aged yellow stone and rose garden in full bloom. I'm standing between the two of them, a little gangly still at nineteen.

Two rapidly downed glasses of wine in, I've draped my arms with feigned nonchalance around these two people I love. Michael's not altogether comfortable with the familiarity of my gesture, particularly with colleagues nearby, but he tolerates it; I was aware of his pride in me that evening when those same colleagues fondly recalled my earnest questioning in prior years.

Sam is tucked in under my shoulder and her arm is around my waist; she's every inch my girlfriend and I couldn't be prouder of that fact.

She fitted in so easily with my new university friends. Living in Cambridge, with her father being part of the same college and with her own wide circle of female friends locally, we became a wide and well-integrated social group, bridging the town-and-gown divide. At first, it felt to me like a natural extension of the friendship we'd always enjoyed when I stayed with them during my school holidays. Until the day I acknowledged it was something more.

It was an evening out in the Lent term which she spent flirting with one of my friends. At the time, she was revising for her A levels, and I started to imagine her going off to uni in London, surrounded by men all wanting to be with her. How typical of my self-centredness not to have known sooner. And how typical of her that she had known a lot longer.

It took me even longer to realise she understood me more than anyone else. More than my family. More than my friends. More, even, than Michael, who saw the historian – and tolerated the archaeologist – in me but was frequently blind to the other dimensions of my life. That was the start of something special.

Is it excusable that I didn't know how special until it was gone? When it comes so early in life, how can you know?

We were happy. Not just that first-flush-of-love kind of happy. Something deeper, more sustained. Something based on how easily we got along together, how much we enjoyed spending time together. Though also how comfortable we were to be apart, to be ourselves as individuals as well as a couple.

Was Michael right: did she engineer the split for my sake? She knew that position in London would have tied me down and stopped me working in the field so much. She certainly made it look like she was asking me to compromise to be with her. She'd had enough of me being away so often and for such long periods, she said. She'd given the long-distance thing a chance: years of me being away, working on my doctorate, and then increasingly called on for different digs.

Of course, she knew how I'd react. Which means Michael was right: she let me go so I could be happy.

Have I been? In work, that's an unequivocal yes. I lose myself in it for hours, days, weeks at a time. I'm sure it makes me quite difficult to be around. I know I'm not always easy to work with: I'm never the greatest expert on the era of a dig but no one knows as much as I do about rescue archaeology techniques. And colleagues' snail-like progress and rigid adherence to old-fashioned processes can be intensely frustrating.

But the process makes me deeply happy. As does the feeling of piecing together someone's life. The Roman who built his villa amid the recently conquered Britons: what was his relationship with his family, with other immigrants and with that subjugated community? The woman who ran the brothel in London: what brought her to this state, what ambition drove her to run a business, to raise herself up from penury, what responsibility did she feel for the lives of the other women? As I dig, they talk to me about their experiences, how it felt to live there, what their preoccupations were, their worries, hopes and dreams.

I get that many in my profession think my insights are a stretch. But is there anything more human than to want to tell stories for others? To tell again the lives they lived? Isn't the whole purpose to find truths from their existence to enlighten our own?

If she let me go so that I could be happy, then I must acknowledge she did the right thing. Because I have been.

But am I now? For that matter, at thirty-six, am I any better equipped to be happy than I was then?

I'll admit, I still don't quite understand the impulse behind taking the role at Cambridge. Accepting some curtailment of my fieldwork…why? No one asked me to. I had no reason to. And yet it felt like the right decision. Ironic that I could do so easily – and for no apparent reason – the one thing I wouldn't do for Sam.

Sam. The only one I've ever let in. Others have expected too much from me. Recently, I've felt on safer ground with the married ones, no strings attached.

Whatever drew me to her before, it's still there. That stillness at the heart of her. No, it's more than that. There's a deep knowing at her core. That strong sense of direction and focus. That sureness in herself.

I love her inquiring mind. How she'd sit and read book after book on so many different subjects while Michael and I worked or talked about a dig. How she'd pick up everything we were saying even when it seemed she wasn't paying attention and ask the most insightful questions. Michael always included her; he'd stroll out of the finds tent to show her something and then contentedly disappear inside again.

The front door creaks as she pushes it open. I haven't even heard her footsteps on the stairs, lost in my thoughts, memories. And dare I say it, hopes?

I don't turn round but the floorboards yield as she comes to stand behind me where I sit at his desk. She rests one hand on my shoulder as she leans across to take the photograph from my hand, then props her side against me. As she silently stares at it, I move one arm around her waist and feel her ribs expand with a long-drawn breath, then both her arms come round my shoulders, and she rests against me.

****

She's lit the fire while I've been making tea in the kitchen; it's not a particularly cold night but she's in need of the warmth. She's put on Michael's old arran cardigan, misshapen from age and oversize on her small frame, and she's sitting on the rug, leaning back against his armchair, like she's a young child again settled at his feet as they read to one another.

'Sure you don't want to eat?' offering the doorstep sandwiches I've just made.

She shakes her head again as she receives her mug, drawing her knees up and wrapping her arms around them. She nods towards the photograph, laid on the floor in front of her.

'Life was so simple then.'

I sit next to her, legs stretched out in front. Shoulder to shoulder. Friendly. Supportive. But with an underlying tension.

'Does it have to be complicated?'

'I don't think it has to be. It just is. The older we get, the more complications we accumulate.'

'Tell me how it went at the hospital,' I encourage.

She almost smiles. 'They wanted to restrict me to visiting hours, so I played the 'I'm a doctor too' card as long as they would allow. But in the end, they insisted I leave. They think he's not that close, yet.'

'How is he?' Needing to know but almost not wanting to ask.

'Disorientated. Only partially aware. He's dehydrated, so he's on a drip. He has moments of lucidity, then his mind drifts and it's like he's talking to people who aren't there. He smiled at one point;

I've never seen him smile like that before. He looked so young.' She pauses, thinking. 'I wondered if he felt like that with Mum.'

I don't think she's ever used that word in her life in relation to Marilyn.

'He says they're still married,' I tell her. 'Did you know?' A shake of negation. 'I think he wants us,' a heartbeat of connection in using that word, 'to make sure she knows.'

She goes very still, the way she does when she's internalising, dissecting and deciding on something. It's a strange stillness: not rigid or tense in muscular terms, but her body holds its current position while her mind is occupied elsewhere.

'I can't think about having her in my life in normal times, let alone consider finding one parent because of losing the other.' Subject closed. 'I remember that dinner,' a smile tugging at the corners of her mouth as she touches the photograph with her toe. 'It was our one-month anniversary.'

'It was?' I tease.

'Clearly it meant more to a schoolgirl than a sophisticated undergrad!'

'The eighth of May 1959,' I prove her wrong. 'The day you first kissed me.'

'You actually remember.' That surprises her.

'The anniversary of VE Day.'

'There had to be an historical reference point! Typical you.' She laughs, and it feels good.

'It should have been sooner,' I admit.

She nods. 'Even when you eventually worked out what you felt, you took your time doing anything about it.'

'I was wary of crossing a line.' This is old ground but we both seem to want to re-tread it.

'Because of our friendship or because of Dad?'

'Both.'

'Just as well I did it for you, then.'

'Walking back from dinner,' I recall.

'All the way to my door, like the gentleman your mother taught you to be,' she can't resist.

'Too much of a gentleman to kiss you goodnight.'

'It's a good thing I wasn't too much of a lady to ask!'

Caught off-guard by her suggestion, I had been slow to respond and, amused but impatient, she had grabbed my collar to pull me close and kissed me. I smile in remembrance. So does she.

'I kept all your letters,' she shares.

'I burnt all yours in fury,' I quip.

'No, you didn't.' She sees through me.

'They're in a shoe box under the bed in the flat,' I admit.

'You're a romantic at heart,' she assesses. 'Though you don't like to think so.'

'You were never that romantic,' I compare.

'More than you might think,' she defends.

'So, you'd get married again?' Where did that come from? The words are out before I think them, and instantly the air between us is charged with something.

'Who knows,' she resists. Then concedes: 'Maybe.'

Well, if we've already crossed the line… 'Michael said something earlier.'

'Hmm?'

'That your…ultimatum,' I want to avoid recrimination but it's the only word that comes, 'was actually your way of letting me go.'

A moment of that stillness again. Thinking. Weighing up the risks of being honest? 'It was the dig in South America that did it.'

OK, then. Time for the truth, it seems. 'Because I was away for so long?'

'No. Because I'd never seen you happier. When you came home, all you wanted was to go back for more.' Her face shows the resignation she recalls. 'I didn't want to get in the way of that. Not only for you,' she admits, 'but for me too. We'd both been putting part of ourselves on hold by trying to make the long-distance thing work.'

'You never really wanted me to join the department in London?' Just to be clear.

Shakes her head. 'Teaching instead of research? A desk instead of a dig? That's not you.'

A piece of long-held anger resurges for a moment, then breaks loose. I stare into the fire as I mentally picture it drifting away, diminishing, until it disappears. But another backwards glance reveals a resentment that remains. 'Why did you get married so soon afterwards?' I try not to accuse but that wound is sore.

'You sound angry.' I don't answer but I know she can read me. 'I'm not sure you have any right to be,' she suggests, softly. She never did let me get away with self-indulgence.

'You always told me you didn't want to get married.' Now it is an accusation.

She shuts down. Wraps her arms around her knees, rests her chin, purses her lips. She does that: she won't lie to me but if the truth can hurt, she won't say it. What she means is: I didn't want to get married to you.

Impasse. Old resentment meets old self-justification. It will take time to adjust to what I now know. To forgive.

She hurt me. Deeply. But it seems she also freed me. I wanted the life I've lived. The freedom to take up any and all requests to be on a dig, to fly off anywhere in the world at no notice and with no-one else to consider.

It puts a different slant on everything. She'd made it a clean break. Made it clear we wouldn't see each other again. I'd assumed it was a reaction to my rejection. What did Michael say? Her way of not letting her resolve weaken.

I file the thought away; it's the sort of thing I'll resolve when I'm digging. A long time ago I learned that I don't need to obsess about things; my mind just processes them subconsciously and then the thought or the answer pops into my head when I'm focused on my work.

And it means I don't stay angry for long. I certainly never could with her. Nor could she with me. Neither of us ever conceded a point but we did love each other too much to make the other feel bad for long.

'How has life been for you, since?' Offering an olive branch. She accepts it.

'Since the split from Paul? It's a relief not to be pretending any more. Not keeping up the façade for friends and colleagues.'

'Why do people do that to themselves?'

'Because everyone else does?'

'Not the best reason I've heard.'

'But nonetheless true.' She helps herself to a sandwich. 'What made you take the job in Cambridge?'

'I was just wondering the same thing,' I admit.

'You still love the digs.' That's never in question.

'I've been on sites for twenty years, and I'll probably be on one on the day I die,' I consider. 'It still calls to me like nothing else. But,' reflecting even as the thought forms in my mind, 'I feel the call of Cambridge too. This ancient city, full of knowledge, full of inquiry. Young minds too, full of questions. There's something there for me, I just don't know what it is yet.'

'Has it restricted your being out in the field?'

'A bit. Not enough to frustrate me. Maybe it will in time.'

Silence. Is she wondering if I'll be around enough to make things work…if we decided to give us another chance? I know I am.

'What's this?' I'm unconsciously testing the burn on my palm as I think and it distracts her. She turns my hand up to inspect the injury. The blister has subsided, leaving an ugly red mark in the centre and two thin perpendicular lines, joining nearly at a right angle on one corner: the lead welding that held the painted glass, branded into my skin.

How do I explain that to her? 'You won't believe me if I tell you.' I laugh it off but that just makes her more curious. 'It's from a piece of glass from the dig.'

'How can a six-hundred-year-old piece of glass burn you?'
'Because of the fire. The one that destroyed the tower.'
'What?'

'Don't ask me how but, when I held it, I could feel the heat of the fire in the glass, in the lead that doesn't even exist around it now. It's like…' I cast around for something to explain it that doesn't sound completely absurd, '…like it's still carrying the memory of what happened before it disappeared beneath the earth.'

I expect her look to askance at that, but she just looks thoughtful.

'Why do you call it "the tower"?'

'Probably not the best description,' I concede, 'but it reminded me of a picture of Rapunzel's tower in one of my sisters' book of fairy tales. It's like an ugly, squat version of that. With an ugly, soul-twisted occupant to match.'

'And a strange red-haired child as her saviour?'

'Or in need of saving?' I ponder.

'Here we go again,' she sighs dramatically. 'Eoghan the hero.'

'Sam?'

'Hmm?'

'Am I going mad?'

'Clearly,' she teases, then sobers suddenly. 'But please don't. I can't cope with you and him at the same time.'

'I'll do my best,' I promise.

I reach my arm around and she turns in towards me, resting her cheek on my shoulder.

'Eoghan?'

'Hmm?'

'Have you said everything to him you want to say?' Oh, shit. She thinks we don't have much time.

'Have you?' turning her question back on her.

She nods. 'Not that there's much to say…at the end. Anything I've not said before has become rather meaningless.'

'He and I never really talked about religion,' I confess. 'Does he believe in God?'

'I think his parents took him to chapel growing up. He never told me much about them or his upbringing.'

'I suppose he hardly paid attention to the present, let alone think about spiritual versus physical concerns.'

She smiles at that. 'Always with one foot in the past.'

'Do you want me to stay tonight?' I don't know where I'd sleep but I feel I should at least offer.

I feel her shake her head. 'I'll sleep in his room, head to the hospital first thing. You should come to see him tomorrow. For evening visiting hours, after you finish on the dig.'

I'm silent. Knowing that she wants me to promise I will go. Knowing that I should. And knowing that I can't.

Even as I think of Michael, lying on a bed in a darkened hospital ward, his physical form fading fast, already a shadow of the man I love, holding on by the last few threads of this life…even as I think of him, my thoughts are overridden by images of the site and I feel again that inexplicable but undeniable draw to…her.

'Oh, Eoghan.' Despairing, because she sees the battle within me and sees me lose. And hurt because she's losing too. She pushes me away.

Thursday

Chapter Twenty-seven

Threfield Percy. 16th September 1976

Is it very wrong that I feel so good right now? Standing halfway down the scree slope with the midday sun warm on my back, a soft breeze in my face and a bright blue, cotton-flecked sky above me. Hearing distant chatter and laughter and activity from the upper dig site I've just left. Excitedly anticipating the return to my own dig with several more hours to build on this morning's successes. Mentally energised from an engaging debate with Ernest and Martin about what they are finding at the manor site. Chemically stimulated by two cups of strong coffee, drunk while watching the students work as we pontificated about their output.

With everything that's happening with Michael and knowing how distressed Sam must be, how can it be that I feel more content, more centred, more like myself than I ever have before?

Like I'm connected to the whole world. More: like I'm connected to everything, to everything that was and to everything that now is. As if time and place have ceased to be borders to my perception. I feel...full of myself. With such vigour in my body and such clarity in my mind that anything seems possible.

From this place, all of it takes on a different sense of proportion. Michael's disease no longer looks like a tragedy hanging over us so much as a gradual releasing of attachment, with little to keep him here. Sam's sadness is a natural adjusting to the anticipated loss.

And this...thing with Christiane? What is that? Consciousness connecting? Kindred spirits? People talk about that happening within a lifetime, can it also exist across time? Or could it be the same consciousness – projected into two different moments in time – able to break beyond the narrow confines of what we normally expect to see and hear and smell and taste and touch?

But why?

The question rises strongly within me, a visceral sensation that starts in my legs and increases as it travels through my gut and heart.

Is it like Michael talked about feeling for Geoffrey, a sense of responsibility or obligation? A need to act, to help?

Suddenly, instinctively and without knowing why, my body hums with alertness.

And then, she's here.

I know it before I even turn my head to look, sensing her presence in how my skin prickles, in the pulse beating in my forehead, in the tension of my muscles.

I don't know how but she's right here, not ten feet to my right, where the track would have run in front of the tenants' cottages.

She's just walked out of the front door of the nearest cottage and turned to walk away from me down the lane.

She's alive with a vibrancy I've never experienced before, that I have no paradigm to define. A vivid energy, almost luminescent, shifting and adapting as she moves.

It gives her a compelling presence: there's a brilliance, an inner beauty about her that's so much more than can be bestowed by flesh and bone. Though, my God, she's physically attractive as well. She looks to be…what…nineteen or twenty? Even the poor quality of her shift and mantle can't disguise the curves at breast and waist and hip. Wearing her head uncovered and a long single plait of the thickest red hair hanging all the way down her back: still not married then.

A breath I didn't even know I was holding forces its way out of my mouth in a loud sigh, then I draw in a deep lungful of air.

And catch my breath as she stops on the path. As if she's heard something.

She doesn't look behind but her head lifts, listening, alert, aware. And turns just an inch to the left, as if she's trying to listen.

She can't. There's no way she could have heard me. I stand stock still, like I'm trying not to startle her. Feeling like I'm intruding. Or spying on her.

And the more I watch and wait, the more the world around her is revealed to me. The vibrant green leaves of the hazel that hedges in each household's livestock. The mud of the lane rutted by cartwheels and churned up by cattle and horses' hooves. A sky as brittly brilliant in its blueness as the one above me, but with heavier rain-filled clouds scudding rapidly from the north.

The air is so still I can actually hear sheep cropping the grazing land beyond the hedge and bickering among the children tasked with shepherding them. The shout of one man to another from up the slope behind me.

Turn. *Turn!* I urge her in my head.

She almost does. Moving her head so I can see her face in profile, a frown on her forehead like she senses me but can't see me.

It's seconds that feel like minutes.

And I'm jolted back to the present by a hearty slap on my back.

'Coming?' Martin enthuses as his momentum carries him beyond me down the hill, filled with the same eager anticipation I knew moments ago. He stops some steps ahead, noticing my hesitation. 'What is it?'

'Martin,' I start, caught between my world and hers. 'Did you see…?' I stop.

He waits, then prompts: 'See what?'

I push my palm against my eyes, rubbing the confusion away.

'Never mind,' I dismiss it. 'Let's go.'

* * * * * * *

He's here. How is he here? Why now, after so many years? It's been so long, she has doubted her own memories; he seemed like a shadow of her youth, something she might have conjured in her mind or maybe dreamt about.

But he is here, she knows it, though she doesn't dare turn her head, fearing he will disappear if she tries to look at him. Always on the edge of her vision. Almost there, but not quite. She stands as still as a deer that scents a predator. Waiting. Wondering. As if she can hold the moment, hold him here, with her.

She feels so safe whenever he is here. Watched over, protected. At times she has wondered if that was why he disappeared: had she no longer any need of him? Her guardian angel. Her spirit companion. Her watcher.

Does she need him now?

She feels his presence, standing behind her on the main lane, becomes aware of him from the prickling of her skin and scalp. She's cold one instant, flushed with heat the next, and her heart beats so hard it fills her chest.

He's here for me. Always for me. She knows it with every sinew in her body. And she is glad he is seeing her now, a full-grown woman, no longer a child.

Though she can't see him, she knows him just the same. And knows him to be the same as he was before, in his age, his stature. So, too, his mind and heart.

Only, with a different intensity this time. An intensity that means she knows what he is feeling: the same excitement and elation running through her.

And the same strange sense of connection.

She is being drawn to him, wanting to turn around to face him. The compulsion starts in her gut and seems so strong that it almost overtakes her.

Stay! Be patient, her mind implores. *I don't want to lose you again.*

And then, whatever holds them together breaks loose, hard and fast as the snapping of a bow string. And he is gone.

No! She spins to look behind her, only to witness the empty space she knows she will find.

And is utterly bereft.

Chapter Twenty-eight

Threfield Percy. 16th September 1976

I feel so disorientated, so disconnected from reality that I assume it's going to be difficult to concentrate during the afternoon. But it isn't. Almost the opposite: I'm driven to progress as fast as possible while this feeling of connection to her still grips me.

There's real excitement around the site now with finds coming thick and fast. It took a couple of hours to clear a large amount of rubble first thing: stones from the walls, some whole, some smashed, some still mortared, many with evidence of heavy implements having been used: the demolition used to cover what lies underneath.

A cairn over a grave.

Beneath, there's clear evidence of the fire. The roof tiles are smoke-blackened, with cracks and flaking consistent with extreme temperatures. Large timbers from the roof trusses are burnt to a fraction of their original size and crumble at a touch. With luck, some of it will give us good material for dendrochronology. At least, that's what the trained archaeologist in me thinks; the rest of me knows it's an unnecessary detail.

We're getting down to ground level now, which should mean we're getting into the remains of the upper floor.

Since lunch – when the chatter was all about what we're finding – our ranks have swelled with more students, though still only the male ones; the women continue to avoid me. Our small dig area is getting cluttered but there's plenty to keep everyone engaged. The first hour is filled with that delicious quiet intensity, heads down, eagerly scraping, fully expecting to find something soon. Discoveries emerge one after another until almost every digger is painstakingly easing the soil away from an object and the very air seems charged with anticipation.

Even Montague is finding it hard to hide his delight at what comes up: shards from both Mediterranean pottery and local earthenware; the blade of an eating knife; metal hinges and clasps from caskets and chests; a small hoard of silver coins, though the pouch that held them has rotted away; fragments of intricate jewellery in tarnished silver or burnished gold; more glass and some lead joints from the windows.

And a tiny glass vial, broken at the neck and with a deep crack from the base up through the body. But, to me, so instantly recognisable that I can almost smell the oud again.

* * * * * * *

We break mid-afternoon when tea and biscuits are being handed round back at the tents. The noise levels rise rapidly as the two dig teams converge and compete for glory with their latest discovery: it's the chatter of youth and passion.

Martin and I stand on the periphery, shoulder to shoulder, watching the group. He reluctantly admits he has to return next week to his office job with the district council; it turns out that, with no wife or family commitments, he's used his full annual leave quota to be on the dig this summer. The more I see of him, the more I like this quiet, considered, considerate man.

With my back to the tents, I'm facing the standing stones and get distracted by a short, round, slightly stooping woman hesitating at the entrance to the site. She's dressed exactly as I would imagine a farmer's wife of the older generation would look: a tired cotton summer dress that may have been her Sunday best once but now does for everyday wear; tan-coloured tights thick enough not to ladder easily; and practical but clunky low-heeled, lace-up shoes. Beneath a silk scarf that's tied under her chin, her silvered hair is in curls, cut short to keep them in check; I imagine them set in curlers at night with a pink hairnet over the top. She's only lacking the kitchen apron to make the picture complete; but she would, of course, have removed that for going out in public, even if she's only walking down the lane to the people working on her husband's land. She reminds me of my grandmother.

But her face, when she picks me out of the crowd, betrays tension and unease. She's reluctant to step within the village's boundary.

As I start to move towards her, I see her beckon over a local woman who volunteers on the dig with her husband. Everything about the exchange reinforces her resistance: the way she holds out a piece of paper at arm's length, as if trying to keep even this long-known neighbour at a distance; how her eyes look anywhere but at her friend's face as she delivers her explanation; the vigorous head shake as the younger woman turns to point towards me; and the hurried departure, turning her back as soon as she can and scurrying back up the path towards the footbridge.

The woman's shrug tells her equal bemusement, and she has a rueful look on her face as she approaches me.

'That generation,' she smiles with incomprehension as she hands over the paper. 'How can you be so afraid of a piece of land?'

'You don't worry about the old superstitions, then?' I ask.

'I'm a woman of science. I live by what I can test and measure,' she asserts. 'She says Professor Langley's daughter needed to get a message to you,' gesturing to the folded sheet in my hand. 'It sounded urgent, otherwise she wouldn't have dared come so close.' With a wry smile, she steps away.

'Any news?' Martin asks as I focus on the words.

Even as I digest the message, my detached brain wonders if the brevity of the note comes from Sam's instructions or the old woman's reticence. Either way, all it gives is the number and floor of the ward they've put Michael in, the hospital's address and two words: "Please come".

I hand it to Martin instead of explaining because there's an internal conflict within me. He seems to understand.

'You should go,' he presses, weighing in with the angels.

'There's too much happening here. I can't leave while we're making such fast progress,' giving voice to the counter-argument playing in my head.

And while Christiane feels so nearby, a third voice adds silently.

'I'll take care of that. The site will still be here tomorrow. Michael might not be,' he warns, trying to soften his words with sympathy.

'I can go this evening. A couple of hours won't make much difference.'

Who knows what I might miss out on here? What if she appears again? What if we find something significant?

'How much will you regret it if you don't get to say goodbye?'

'We've already said everything we need to say.'

And I don't trust anyone else to feel what I feel when things turn up. What if something comes up that only I can truly understand? The voice is working harder to deflect that one; Martin's getting close to the bone.

'Then be there for Michael,' he insists, his tone hardening somewhat. 'And for Sam.'

'You don't understand,' I dismiss him. 'It's more important to find answers for Michael. We're so close. Can't you feel it? There's something here and I want, I need to find it for him.' I sound manic and Martin's face shows his disquiet. I shake my head, my stubborn streak kicking in. 'I'm not going,' I insist. 'There's work to do.'

'Do you think we can't manage without you for half a day?' exasperated now.

I dump my mug down, spilling my half-drunk tea. 'Enough, Martin,' I demand, a little too loudly. Heads turn and Martin shuffles with embarrassment. 'That's enough slacking,' I command the group. 'Back to work,' and I stalk off towards the site, not waiting for them to respond.

There's wariness in the eyes of my dig team as they dribble back to the site, loosely corralled by Martin. He looks my way but doesn't speak, and his tight lips and tense shoulders convey a barely suppressed unease.

It sours the afternoon, dampening the earlier excitement into a sullenness. That just frustrates me further as the pace of work noticeably slows and they start making stupid mistakes: breaking pieces that should have come up whole, getting ridiculously excited about finds that turn out to be mediocre at best.

And all the while my head is chastising me for deciding to stay, cursing me for being a pig-headed idiot. And underneath that, a nasty niggle, knowing I'm letting Sam down; there'll be hell to pay for that. I shut down the insidious murmurings about me failing Michael too.

Which makes me more and more aggressively focused. Pushing the team to work harder. Vocally critical of the amateurishness and awkwardness of their techniques. Dismissive of their naïve and ignorant conclusions. Thrusting them aside so I can take over when their clumsy slowness irritates me.

Together, we join in a downward spiral from tetchiness and frustration to blame and resentment. Then, for me, guilt.

The finds are just as good as they were this morning, but I've lost all joy in them.

And Christiane's absence settles into a silent, simmering anger within me.

By the time Montague rolls around towards five, my short fuse takes only the tiniest spark to ignite.

Oblivious to the mood, he strolls up with a hearty conviviality, presuming he'll get a warm welcome after this morning's collegiate interactions. He takes one look at me and one at Martin but seems unable to read the situation and blunders straight into the path of my wrath.

'OK,' he claps his hands, 'time for everyone to call it a night.'

'Not yet,' I negate with a growl. 'There's more to finish tonight.'

'Come on, Bren,' he cajoles. 'It's been a good day. Time to celebrate. I'm buying the first round,' he proffers a bribe, jovially.

'I said not yet.'

'Come on, lad,' placing a fatherly hand on my shoulder. 'All work and no play…'

'I said no!' I shout. 'And I'm in charge of this dig!' Christ, I sound like a petulant child, even to my own ears.

'No. You aren't,' he contradicts, stung by my rebuke. 'And I'm saying these guys have done enough for one day.' Pompous, bombastic bastard.

'They're my team,' I persist, straightening to my full height. 'I'll decide when we're done.'

'If you want to stay, that's your choice,' he asserts. 'I'm taking the team to the pub. Martin,' he instructs over my head, 'get things wrapped up. Now!' He gives me one a hard glare, then strides away before I can come back at him.

Martin chivvies the team, and I don't miss their relief at being released, nor the speed at which they make their way back up to the camp.

Only Martin waits.

'Just go, Martin,' I direct, turning my back.

I hear him hesitate for several long moments. 'Maybe I'll check back in a bit?' he offers. I ignore him and he gives a resigned sigh before he, too, heads up the path.

My body is full of tense anger; I want to shout or to hit something, just to find relief. This is not like me: I'm usually the calmest, most contained person I know. I internalise everything. I don't get into arguments. And I never shout. Ever.

I'm becoming a different person on this dig. What's happening to me?

Don't be absurd. There's just a lot happening right now. With Michael. With Sam. It's disrupting my usual equilibrium. And I know how to find that again. There's always been one thing I can rely on: my work. Work through it. Keep going. This is all about the dig now. It's all about knowing what happened to Christiane.

I turn my back on the rest and sink onto my haunches. The soil beneath my fingertips grounds me; I feel the warmth of today's sun in it and it connects me back to every previous day it's been here, through sun and snow, wind and wet, season after season. As the sound of the others falls away, I reconnect to this place. It reclaims me for the past, without anyone to hold me in the present.

I slide my fingers over the piece of glazed pot I'm carefully exposing, the edge sharp where it broke. The world around me falls away, narrowing down to the point of my perception, to this sliver of time and space. The expanse of the rest of the world dissipates behind me, even my peripheral vision disappearing as I focus only on what's in front of me. And the bridge it creates between me and her.

Chapter Twenty-nine

Threfield Percy. August 1326

Just a moment before she saw him, she had been so happy, joyful that old Martha had finally – however hesitantly – allowed her to help ease the unceasing pain in her lower back. It means so much to her to have built this trust, to have overcome her long-held resistance, to bring relief. Waiting until Martha was alone had been the right approach, beyond the sight of her daughter's ever-mistrustful eyes.

It will be some hours yet before Agnes and the other women return from the Malton fair. Time enough to have Richard send old Martha some meat from the pantry; Agnes ensures her aged mother is well-supplied with vegetables, milk and cheese from their land and animals, but some meat is sure to strengthen her too.

She shakes off the slight melancholy that settles on her, that strange feeling of emptiness in the place he has, so briefly, filled. There are always reasons to be content, and always more in the village who are in need of her attention; she has no time to stand here, letting her heart grow cold, while she pities herself.

Geoffrey's kindnesses alone give her a life with such comfort that she should count her blessings. She is as loved as if she were truly his daughter; more than that, she likes how he has drawn her into his business as he might have done his own son, had Ralf shown any inclination.

Perhaps Hughes might one day have reason to visit them again; she has rarely seen Geoffrey as happy as he was when reunited here with his first-born son, full of gratitude to his sister and her husband for raising his son alongside their own. Geoffrey rarely seems proud of the manor he owns, but he flushed with pleasure in welcoming those guests. Their trip north and introductions to the Percy family went well too, enough to promise expectation of a long alliance, fruitful on both sides.

That was two summers past, and with the turmoil at court – the heightening tension between the king and his queen, fostered by her brother, the French king – making travel difficult, they were unlikely to see Hughes again any time soon.

As she turns towards the row of houses at the foot of the hill, a woman is waiting for her by the first cottage's gate.

'The blessings of the day to you, Mary,' she calls.

'God give you peace, my lady,' the other woman salutes her respectfully.

'How goes the day?' opening the conversation so Mary might choose her subject.

'It's baking day, my lady,' she starts, wiping her hands absent-mindedly on a rough cloth. 'My turn with the bakehouse, though I'm fair behind where I should be.'

'All is well?' she encourages, letting the conversation take its necessary path.

'I wondered if I might use the bakehouse today on promise of payment, my lady? We haven't yet caught up since Will replaced the sheep after the floods. But the reeve has promised him several days' labour on your harvest, so he's sure to have sufficient soon,' she affirms.

'That's an easy one, Mary,' nodding her assent. 'I will tell Master Prudhomme to expect the payment later. And thank Will for me for helping with the harvest. We're fortunate it looks to be a good one after such a torrid time in the spring.'

'Perhaps we may look forward to a good harvest feast?' Mary ventures with a smile.

'For sure, Elias would be ashamed to send out anything but the best from his kitchens!' she laughs. 'I must away. I fear I am already late for sitting with my lady this afternoon. I shall see you at tonight's dinner.'

As she turns to leave, horses' hooves thud down the hill and her heart lifts with joy.

'Walter!' she calls towards the gatekeeper's cottage as she hurries towards the gate barring the path. 'The Lady Alice arrives!'

She raises her hand and her friend waves in acknowledgement as they slow before the gate, waiting while Walter gives them access.

'My dear child!' Lady Alice nudges her mount forwards to come alongside Christiane, holding out her hand in greeting. 'It has been too long.'

Christiane kisses the prioress's hand and looks up at her warmly, brushing the mare's neck to soothe her. 'I am so pleased to see you, my lady. You are good to give us your time on such brief notice. I know how much the priory demands of you. How was your journey?'

'Uneventful, thanks to Master FitzAlan here.'

'I would trust no-one else with your safe delivery,' Christiane smiles at the young squire, which raises a pleased flush in his cheek.

Alice cups the girl's face with one hand, scrutinising her thoughtfully. 'You are much grown since last I saw you. I should call you 'child' no longer, Christiane. And you have become the beauty that you showed promise of being.'

Christiane smiles gracefully at the compliment. 'I have so much I would discuss with you,' taking the prioress's hand in both hers. 'But we will take care of your needs first. Master Prudhomme awaits your arrival at the Hall and Edith stands by to help. Please take any refreshment you desire.'

'You are bound for the lady Amicia's?'

'I am. At least for a few hours.'

'I'll come down shortly to see how she fares.'

'That's kind. I'm sure she will be grateful for your attention.'

'I doubt that,' Lady Alice smiles, knowingly, 'but bless you for thinking it.'

With her nudge of its flank, the horse kicks away up the slope, David following. Only a year or so younger than Christiane, he ought to be returning to his father's household soon, but his father seems in no rush to reclaim him. And David's continued service here is welcome since Ralf is equally disinclined to return home.

Though, is that also about to change? It is the reason for Lady Alice's visit now, to coincide with Ralf's arrival. Long looked for but equally long delayed, the news of his intended return was unexpected when it finally came a few days ago.

In the instant it became known around the manor, the mood altered; the very air seems heavy, like a thunderstorm is brewing. The more so as Ralf has ordered a feast for tonight and commanded that all the villagers attend. Geoffrey extended the news unhappily, wary for not knowing Ralf's intent.

She is uneasy in herself, as if the balance of her world has tipped. She cannot help but wonder if fulfilling their marriage commitment is now on his mind and perhaps the reason for his arrival. In truth, she is surprised – though not unhappy – that the betrothal has been left unfulfilled for so long. Geoffrey would not welcome her broaching the subject, she senses, but she has trusted that he will address it at the right moment and finds joy instead in the relative freedom and ease her current position gives her.

As she raises her hand to knock at Amicia's door, she is suddenly forced to step back, making way for the pale priest and the sweating reeve, the latter mopping his brow and cursing that place's oppressive air.

'Christiane!' Father Peter greets her as he always does, with warmth and pleasure in his voice, though his tone and expression change in the next moment. 'Child, you're later than she anticipated,' a whispered warning. 'You must expect a chastisement, I fear.'

She smiles her appreciation. 'You are good to worry about me, Father.'

'You should put more effort into pleasing your lady, girl,' the reeve admonishes her, high-handed and opinionated as always. 'There can be few better ways to express the gratitude that is appropriate for one in your position.'

'Your guidance is ever appreciated, Master Reeve,' she replies courteously, refusing to rise to his provocation. Many of the villagers have little time for the reeve, tolerating him for his position not his person, yet she has some sympathy for him. Yes, he chooses to accept the preferential treatment constantly meted out to him by Amicia, but he has sacrificed the trust and comradeship of his community for it, and she has wondered more than once if he feels lonely with neither kin nor true friends.

His chest puffs up at her reaction and he steps ahead down the lane with more spring in his feet than usual.

'Father,' she stays the priest's departure with a hand on his forearm, 'I've been meaning to ask after your…after Joan and her family.'

'My *wife* and my *children*,' he fills in for her, softly. 'I hope that we can recognise them for who they are, even if only between the two of us,' raising a wary smile.

'Are they well? Do they have everything they need?'

'They are well, thank you. You are kind to ask. There are few in the village who would dare to, for fear of speaking of what my lady has dictated should simply cease to exist.'

'You must miss them,' she sympathises.

'Every day. Though I find some contentment in this new way of life that the Church and my lady have forced me to adhere to.'

'I'm glad. And your continuing care for your kin reflects well on you, Father. I hear of others who cast their spouses off without any concern for how they would fare apart from them.'

'I owe much to you for helping me with that. The archbishop's command was clear enough, but the lady Amicia was stricter even than he.'

'You will let me know if they need anything that I can help with?' she asks.

He nods. 'I bless the day the Lord sent you to us, Christiane,' he remarks, though his eyes are sad too. He touches her head briefly and is gone.

Taking a breath, she readies herself for Amicia and steps inside. The perpetual heat embraces her as soon as she opens the door and almost smothers her as she pushes it to, turning the heavy key in the lock.

'You're late!'

The snapped criticism reaches her before she has put her first foot on the upwards steps. She ascends quickly.

'Forgive me, my lady,' she opens, crossing to where Amicia is sat before the fire, kissing the outstretched hand in formal greeting. 'I was speaking with Elias about the dishes he is preparing for your son's return.'

It is a calculated distraction. 'Good. How many dishes has he planned?'

'Fourteen in total, my lady.'

'What roast meats?'

'Goose, partridge and venison, as well as the usual woodcock and rabbit.'

She nods in approval. 'I shall look forward to my portion tonight. Make sure you tell Elias not overly to spice the partridge: it is my favourite, but you know how my stomach cannot withstand a heavily spiced sauce.'

Christiane smiles her assent, knowing the cook to be well-versed in, and always considerate of, Amicia's specific preferences.

'Who were you conversing with at the gate?' Amicia's mood changes as quickly as her subject, and her query is sharp and challenging. 'The reeve thought it might be Lady Alice.'

'Yes, my lady. Master David fetched her from the priory.'

'She will present herself here shortly, I trust?' Respect for her status and position remains paramount in Amicia's eyes, regardless of – or perhaps the more so because of – her withdrawal from the world. She demands that the manor's life should continue to revolve around her, wherever she chooses to be.

'I believe she intends only to refresh herself first. Such a warm day will have made for a dry and dusty journey.'

'Even so, the people need to see that she puts my needs first. If she does not arrive soon, you shall fetch her to me.'

Christiane casts around for some entertainment to distract her. 'Shall we continue our game?' nodding towards the draughts board.

'I am too tired,' retorting dismissively. 'Read to me instead,' waving a hand in the direction of her books.

'What would please you most today?' turning the books over. 'A romance?'

'Too frivolous today. Read to me from the Book of Hours. I feel the need of God's healing grace. Perhaps it will help to ease the ache in my joints. I barely slept last night for the pain. And hand me some wine,' indicating the jug on the table. 'The reeve brought me some special wine he procured from somewhere. I'm glad to have someone who understands what relief these small pleasures bring to my dark days.'

Having done as she is bid, Christiane settles on the low stool Amicia makes her use and starts to read the day's lesson and prayers. As her soft, melodic voice rises and falls, Amicia rests back in her chair, closing her heavy eyelids. The day is warm and, as often happens with Christiane nearby, her aching body starts to ease.

As she comes to the end of the prayers, Christiane turns the page and studies a beautifully detailed image the transcriber has inserted into the book: a picture with the Virgin and Child seated in the centre, flanked by depictions of Amicia to her right and Geoffrey to her left.

'You have stopped. Why have you stopped?' the complaint breaks through her thoughts as Amicia opens her drowsy eyes.

'This picture,' she muses. 'I had not noted it before.'

'Show me!' comes the demand. 'Ah, yes. I commissioned this shortly after we were married. Before Ralf was born. Before God chose me to carry this terrible burden of a life beset by illness.'

'It would be usual for Geoffrey to be the one seated at the Holy Mother's right hand,' she appraises.

'Clever girl!' Though it isn't Christiane's cleverness that pleases her so much as her own. 'I wanted a permanent record of my higher status. They might make me wed a man below my standing, but people should remember that I am a Percy by birth. As,' her face shows fierce determination, 'in my eyes, is Ralf.' Her stare dares Christiane to disagree.

'As he must also be in my Lord Percy's eyes,' she concurs. 'Perhaps that is why he has needed to stay away so long.'

Amicia gives her a sharp look, uncertain whether Christiane intends a compliment or criticism. 'Ralf is the most adept of all Percy's squires, as we know from the letters from my kin. Percy must find it hard to release him, I'm sure. The reeve said you stopped to speak to someone else,' changing the subject swiftly to regain her dominant footing. 'It was Mary again? What did she want this time?'

'Only to ask for more time to pay her bakehouse dues.'

'Again? That is the third occasion.'

'Master Prudhomme has promised Will some labour for the harvest, so they are sure to be able to pay from that,' she reassures.

'That is not acceptable,' Amicia disregards. 'If you allow for one, all shall ask and then where shall we be?'

'It has not been easy for them,' she advocates. 'They lost nearly all their flock to the murrain after the spring floods, and lambs were so scarce they had to pay almost three times the price at market.'

'That is not my concern. Go, immediately. Tell her she may not use the bakehouse unless she has the coin to pay for it.'

'That will affect more than her family alone, my lady,' unable to stop her protest at the injustice. 'She shares the work with four other households, and they are all dependent on the bread she will produce today. Not to mention Father Peter's daily loaf.'

'You are too soft-hearted, girl. No, I tell you it will not do. If they cannot pay then Will must give his first day's labour for free.'

'My lady, that is hardly an equal exchange!'

'Fairness is irrelevant,' raising her voice, harshly. 'This is about sending a message that there is no shirking what is due to this manor. To me. And you will not gainsay me, girl,' growing in anger. 'This manor is *my* birth-right and I will have that right respected! I am already too lenient with them, allowing you to talk me into so many attending the Malton fair today.'

'The summer fair brings them important income, my lady. Many would struggle the rest of the year without it.' These were old and well-trodden discussions.

'Income, yes. But what else will they bring back with them? Sickness or poisons or evil potions? How am I to control them outside the manor?' There is an edge approaching fear in the pitch of Amicia's voice.

'Walter and Margery have been tasked with inspecting what they return with, just as you ordered,' Christiane defends.

'And where is my share of what they make today? I must have my share!'

Christiane holds her tongue, forever frustrated by Amicia's selfishness but knowing from bitter experience that continuing to disagree will get her nowhere.

A sudden hammering at the door makes them both start and exchange a look of surprise. No one would dare intrude in such a demanding way. Except…

'Ralf!' Amicia's face seems lit from within with sudden joy and Christiane's heart pities her for such a rare elation; would that she could find some happiness more often, they would all benefit from it. 'Go! Go!' she exhorts Christiane. 'Quickly, girl. Let him in!'

The hammering continues as she runs down the stairs, surprised to find her heart beating faster. Her hands shake as she fumbles in releasing the heavy lock, feeling the door reverberate as it takes another hammering.

'Patience!' she calls. 'I am here.'

'Open the door, girl! Do not make me wait any longer!' comes the rough rebuke.

The moment she pushes the door ajar, it is wrenched from her hands and thrust open. 'In God's name, what took so long?' he demands, then stops dead.

Chapter Thirty

Threfield Percy. August 1326

She hasn't seen him in four years; how he has changed. The stockiness has gone, displaced by height that balances out the breadth of his shoulder and chest. He must tower over his own father now. Maybe even over the blacksmith, the largest, strongest man on the manor. His hair is long and well cut, his beard too is well shaped and shows off strong lines in his jaw and cheek. Blue eyes hold her gaze with ease and sureness; to her they carry a knowing, as of one certain of his place in the world.

She becomes aware he is scrutinising her as much as she is him and a blush heats her cheeks. She steps back into the shadows, as if to hide herself, but that makes it worse: it allows him to step forward into the small space between the two sets of stairs, barely sufficient for one person let alone two. His tall frame rises over hers, and she feels an unease at his dominance.

'Ralf! What's keeping you?'

He seems not to hear his mother's supplication and his brow takes on a deep frown, as if his mind is preoccupied with some perplexity. 'You are not…' he mutters, giving a slight shake of the head. 'You cannot be…' He leans back, as if to give himself more room to assess her. 'Christiane?'

She drops her head, embarrassed now by the intensity of his look. 'My lord,' refusing to meet his eye.

'Ralf!' The command from above is short and biting. Both of them know that tone, and he snaps out of his revery.

'I am coming, my lady Mother,' he calls upwards. About to push past Christiane to head up the stairs, he checks himself and steps back, inviting her to go first.

Amicia has raised herself to her feet, something she scarcely attempts without aid these days. And Christiane catches a glimpse of the loving being that still exists beneath the mask of this disease-damaged woman.

'My boy!' she cries, holding out her hands. 'At last!'

And whether by instinct or calculation, he finds the right response in the moment, taking one of her hands in his and kneeling before her, bowing his head so that she might place her hand in blessing upon him.

As he rises, she falters, her enfeebled body unable to sustain such elation. He catches her fast and supports her into her chair, taking the cup of wine Christiane offers and holding it to her lips. As she starts to revive, she continues to allow him to serve the wine to her, her eyes never leaving his face, and small murmured endearments escaping her lips as she touches his hand, his face, his hair, proving to herself that he is substantial.

Standing to one side, it seems to Christiane that a silent communion is happening between mother and child, a wordless reunion of two souls bound by something more than blood; they understand one another.

In time, his mother's attention becomes too much for him and he pulls away, which only causes her to hold more tightly to him, to hang onto his hand with surprising resolve. He breaks away for a moment but only to pull up a stool so that he might sit alongside her. But then he turns his attention to this startlingly beautiful woman, standing quiet and patient in the shadows.

'I have interrupted your reading, I perceive,' he notes the open book on the table. 'You read to my mother often?'

'She is an adequate reader,' Amicia answers for her. 'And you know how much I need something to occupy my mind.'

'You have sufficient distraction, I trust?' his eyes straying back to Christiane.

'Never enough. I live as withdrawn a life as any anchorite!' his mother claims. 'But,' tempering her tone, 'you know how well I accept this half-life I must live, the patience with which I bear the burden that God has placed upon me.'

He nods his head in distant recognition, but his eyes remain fixed on the younger woman. 'And Christiane helps you?'

'She is here most days,' she allows. 'But how could she better employ her time? She contributes so little to the running of the manor.'

'It is good you have someone to read to you. Someone better qualified than that priest of yours.'

'She has proven useful to me,' she begrudges. 'Writing letters that I might keep up with news of you. In principle, it seems such a waste to me, teaching a girl to write. Reading, I grant, has some merit, not least to ensure we are not being cheated. But writing? My father never thought it necessary for me, so I don't see why it should be so for another.' Receiving no response and realising Ralf remains distracted by the girl, she rambles on. 'Though I concede, there is some benefit in having Christiane scribe my letters for me. Father Peter is so slow and awkward to the task. Christiane's being that much quicker has enabled me to send more letters than ever before. Though we so rarely receive any back, I can't help but wonder whether she writes as clearly as I would wish.' Frowning at his continued inattention, she raps him on the knuckles. 'But never mind her. I would know about you. I hear some of your success in Percy's household, but I would know more. Are you still the best swordsman he has in training?'

Christiane turns away and busies herself, tidying the trinkets and jewels Amicia has spent the morning putting on and gloating over. Picking up Amicia's two favourite gowns she has tried and then discarded that morning, she quietly moves down the stairs to return them to their storage.

She hears the rise and fall of mother's and son's voices – hers more than his – for several moments more and then the creak of timbers from his foot upon the stair.

'Will you not speak to me, Christiane?' he asks, stopping at the foot of the lower stair. 'Have you no word to say to your betrothed after all this time?'

'Your lady mother is pleased to have you here,' she responds, folding a gown over her arm. The defensiveness of the gesture is not lost on him.

'My mother is always pleased to see me,' watching her closely. 'I am more interested in whether you are.'

'You are always welcome back, my lord,' she evades and turns away, finding his scrutiny too intense.

'That is not what I asked.' She starts in surprise: suddenly he is close behind her, though she hasn't even heard him cross the room. She forces herself not to turn, but he puts his hands upon her shoulders, and his exhale is hot on the back of her neck. Even without looking at him, she is all too aware of the size and strength of him compared with herself. 'You have become a beautiful woman since I saw you last,' he breathes.

She holds herself still, hesitant to move. 'What brings you home, my lord?' The question breaks from her, unbidden.

His hands still. 'You will find out soon enough, Christiane. Though,' considering, 'now I am here I wonder whether I might not kill two birds with one stone, so to speak.'

What does that mean? And how should she react? The uncertainty hangs in the air between them, notching up the tense feeling in her stomach.

A knock at the door breaks through and they turn as one to look in that direction.

'Oh!' Christiane's hands fly to her face, her eyes wide. 'I forgot to lock the door! Please,' her eyes implore him, 'please, my lord, do not tell your lady mother.'

His smile suggests he enjoys having the upper hand. 'What's my silence worth to you, Christiane?'

She narrows her eyes. 'Don't play games with me, my lord. I ask not to protect myself but to reassure my lady. She wouldn't sleep at night for fear she is not as safe as she should wish.'

He pauses, stalled by her answer. But as another knock comes, she steps around him and heads for the door, making a show of turning the key within the lock in case Amicia might be listening for the sound.

Lady Alice steps in from the afternoon's brilliant sunlight. 'There, now I might greet you properly, my child,' she tells her, warmly.

'Did you find everything you needed, my lady?'

'And more besides,' she reassures. 'I thought it judicious to come down as soon as I might.'

Releasing Christiane, she addresses Ralf, standing at the foot of the bed.

'Master Ralf, God's greetings to you,' holding out her hand.

He bends his head in homage, though the manner of his bow is discourteous. 'My lady prioress. I had not thought to see you here,' he speaks warily.

'News of your imminent arrival travelled fast,' she returns.

'And it would appear you travelled even faster,' he retorts.

'I take my duties to Christiane very seriously,' she admonishes. 'As I'm sure you would expect me to.'

'I am glad to hear you are taking good care of *my* betrothed.' His emphasis is heavy with meaning and Lady Alice bridles visibly.

'I have come to attend your mother and see to her health,' she informs him coldly. 'But no doubt she would sooner have time with you. Be good enough to say I will return when she is alone. Come, Christiane,' she commands. 'Walk with me,' and disappears back through the door.

Watching for Ralf's reaction, Christiane cannot read his guarded expression.

'You should go with her,' he permits, looking beyond her towards the door. Christiane dips her head and turns away. 'I shall see you later,' calling out an afterthought as she leaves.

Lady Alice is waiting by the covered walkway. 'This is new. And looks expensive,' she remarks, pointing to the tiles with her toe.

'My lady wanted something to brighten up her walk to mass. It's the only time she steps outside her home,' defending against the prioress's raised eyebrows. 'I can see why she should want the experience to be beautiful.'

'And there was no better use for the money?' pursing her lips in disapproval, then leading the way up the lane. 'Still too tender-hearted, my child,' with an indulgent smile. 'So, did he say why he is here?'

Christiane shakes her head. 'You do not trust him,' she surmises.

'I may be unjust,' relenting a little. 'Perhaps he has changed in temperament as much he has matured in stature.' So, she isn't the only one to notice. 'But what I hear from my sources in the Percy camp leads me to believe otherwise.'

She nods to the tenants as they make their way through the village. At the path behind the houses, they encounter Richard Prudhomme heading towards the fields.

'Back so soon, my lady?' he greets the prioress.

'Master Ralf has arrived,' she conveys archly. 'We deemed it best to leave him with his mother.'

'Ah.' Knowing and sympathy are bound up in his gentle response, and the prioress can't hide a wry smile.

'How goes the harvest, Master Prudhomme?' she enquires.

'We are faring well enough. The hay barns are full, so all that spring rain came to some good after all. The grain yield looks promising too. If the weather holds for another couple of weeks, we should get it done.'

'Perhaps tonight's feast will spur everyone on,' Christiane hopes.

Lady Alice catches the fatherly tenderness in Richard's glance towards Christiane as she turns to head up the hill.

The Hall is a hive of activity with servants scurrying hither and thither in preparation for the night's celebrations. Christiane passes on Amicia's instructions for dinner to Elias Cook and requests sustenance for her guest.

With the sun dropping towards the west, the solar is already darkening. Christiane welcomes Lady Alice into the best chair and waits to supervise the servants arriving with candles, wine and sticky sweet dates. Their scent intermingles with the woody and earthy aromas of the sun-softened room.

'A special treat from my lord's most recent ship from the Levant,' Christiane explains as she offers the dates.

Lady Alice settles back in her chair, savouring the cloying richness of the fruit, and takes a goblet of wine.

'You have made this such a pleasant place, Christiane,' she praises, taking in the intricate tapestry on the wall and soft cushions on the chairs and stools. 'It does not compare with Alicia's palace, but it conveys a genuine sense of welcome and care.'

'I am glad to make use of what Alicia discards. Had we the money for glass and lead, I would choose to enlarge the windows here but that can wait.'

'The manor's income will not suffice?'

'It is just too small to flourish. At home, even Papa's smaller manor was twice the size of what we have here.'

'Thankfully, you have Geoffrey's business to sustain you. Particularly with Amicia's spending.'

'I cannot begrudge her when she has so little joy in her confined life, though I worry that Geoffrey is so unfailingly generous that he sometimes does not leave enough to invest in the business as he should. I see the guilt he bears for that, wondering what he will pass on to Hughes and Ralf in due course.'

'Ralf hardly seems to care what he inherits.'

Christiane hesitates, unwilling to criticise but unable to defend. 'He's shown no sign of wanting to be involved, nor even to understand what obligations will fall to him in time. I fear he will adopt his mother's attitude, seeing the manor only as a means to fund the way he wants to live. I shall do what I can to protect our people against that.'

'They are fortunate they have you. You show such a strong inclination to help people, I still believe you would have been a wonderful gift to the Church,' Lady Alice muses, then laughs at Christiane's expression. 'You never look so rebellious as when I suggest that!'

'I could not bear to cloister myself away in such a narrow world!' Resistance burns in her throat like vitriol before her cheeks brighten with shame. 'Forgive me, my lady, I mean no disrespect. But your calling is not mine and never can be!'

'I understand your fervour, my child. Indeed, I shared it, once. But circumstances change and so did my attitude. Do you think,' pondering suddenly, 'it is because you see people's light that you are so inclined to help them?'

'When I see so clearly that they are out of sorts, I can't help but want to aid them.'

'It's always with you?' Lady Alice grows curious.

'It never goes altogether, though at times it grows or diminishes. I'm never sure why,' she assesses. 'Sometimes I might wish I couldn't see. It's hard when someone is in deep in pain and I am unable to reach them.'

'Do you take that on yourself? What they're feeling?'

'I try not to but it's not easy, particularly with those close to me. When I was growing up, my brothers' moods influenced me, especially with William and Roger, the ones closest to me in age. Roger's temperament could be so dark, and I tried hard to make him happy, but I often lost my way because of it.' Lady Alice reaches across and holds Christiane's hand, knowing her pain as memories of her family revisit her. They sit in silence for a long moment, both lost in Christiane's thoughts. 'And you, my lady,' raising her eyes to Lady Alice's face. 'I see the change in your light too. You have never been the same since the king executed your cousin Lancaster.'

The skin of Lady Alice's face tightens around her eyes and mouth. 'You see that in me?'

She nods. 'It's there now. Just at the thought, your light dims and loses its brilliance. Like a cloud passing over the sun.'

'It is an open wound in my heart that deepens whenever I think on it,' she admits. 'The shock not only of losing my kinsman but also of knowing our king believes he has the right of life and death over every man in the kingdom.' Her body stiffens in resentment. 'What he did that day fractured the bonds of trust and loyalty that must exist between a king and his barons.'

'It is strange to hear you speak of loyalty when my lord Lancaster was accused of rising against the king.' As was her own father; the unspoken thought hangs heavily on her heart.

'But that is the greatest loyalty, to the Crown and to the people,' Lady Alice disputes, 'to be prepared to stand against the king when he has been led astray. A king must always put the interests of his people first, but Edward puts his favourites above his people, even above himself.'

'You cautioned me once for speaking out against the king's favourites,' Christiane reminds her.

'I did,' Lady Alice recalls, 'and I should take my own advice. But,' her passion is roused, 'now we stand in fear of invasion from France, with the queen threatening war and Frenchmen being arrested across the country.' She shakes her head in disbelief. 'Enough of that talk for now. There's sure to be time for that after dinner tonight. It is good of Master Geoffrey to arrange such a celebration for Ralf's return,' she deliberately digresses.

'It wasn't my lord's idea.'

Lady Alice is taken aback. 'It wasn't?'

'I thought better than to mention it in my letter. The request – in truth, it was more a command – came from Ralf.'

'From Ralf? To what end?'

'That is unclear.'

Lady Alice frowns in bemusement. 'It cannot be to announce your marriage, then. He could hardly do that without having first engaged with me. Though it is high time the matter was resolved.'

'My lord seems in no more of a rush than Ralf in that.'

'He should be. If he cares for you as I think he does, Master Geoffrey should want to secure your future.'

'I know you are concerned about the lack of a record.'

'Concerned? Thanks to Amicia, there is nothing to prove your betrothal ever happened, child! Only the word of a handful of people, any of whom might be induced to lie should Ralf change his mind. How does that *not* concern you?' she posits.

'If Ralf wanted to do that, surely it would have happened by now?'

'On the contrary, the longer this goes unresolved, the more time there is for him to be drawn astray.'

Christiane pauses at that. 'What makes you say that, my lady? Have you heard something?'

'Nothing of that sort. But,' she muses to herself, 'perhaps I should raise this with Master Geoffrey while all the parties are now here? Yes, indeed,' resolving her mind. 'The time is come. I must seize the moment tonight!'

Chapter Thirty-one

Threfield Percy. August 1326

But that is not to be.

By the time the last light disappears from the sky, Lady Alice's determination has waned. Seated next to Christiane, on Geoffrey's left hand, she becomes ever more silent and watchful as the feast progresses.

Disapproval emanates so strongly from Lady Alice's face and rigid frame that Christiane hardly needs to see the dark red shade surrounding her to know what she is feeling. For herself, she finds an unfamiliar tension rising within her, a tightness within her chest that gives her a strange sense of foreboding.

It starts even before they have cleared the first trenchers. Almost the entire village is here: the tenants, their wives and children, many straight from the fields and a long day's harvesting; other women back from a fruitful day at the market, rejoicing in their financial gains; the household servants who are not otherwise occupied in serving the meal; the blacksmith and his apprentices; the old miller; even Margery, though Walter has remained behind to keep watch over the gate. All overseen by Richard Prudhomme, with Simon Reeve taking pride of place alongside him to emphasise his own status.

It doesn't take long for the muttering to start. No one is averse to enjoying a feast at their lord's expense and many are eager to make the most of the night, particularly the extra ale that has been bought from the ale wives who took advantage of the short notice to exact a high price.

But soon some start to ask why they have been thus summoned. An oppressive cloud of suspicion settles over the room.

Oblivious to this, Ralf is intent on creating an atmosphere of celebration. Unable to sit still, he is moves feverishly around the Hall, engaging with the high and low tables alike. Asking their opinion of each new dish as it appears. Calling for more drink as soon as a cup is drained. And he wants everyone to know the credit for this feast lies with him.

Between the courses, he calls forth tumblers he has brought with him from Percy's household. As they leap and throw each other about, he claps and cheers louder than any. And as Percy's fool apes his behaviour and casts out awkward jokes that land close to the knuckle, he laughs the hardest and entices others to do the same.

Slowly, his behaviour infects the Hall.

At first, many awkward glances are sent Geoffrey's way, taking their lead from his reaction, unused to such freedom. But Geoffrey is unwilling to intervene, though Christiane can feel how ill at ease he is himself.

Unleashed by Ralf's unrebuked example and fortified by quantities of ale, they make up for years of being suppressed. The noise grows and grows. And Ralf feeds off their response, raising his voice to be heard across the Hall, slinging his arm around the shoulder of one man after another, smacking kisses on the cheeks of their wives and daughters, clasping the waists of girls who serve the food or clear the emptied dishes. The more lascivious his attentions become, the more detached and distant Christiane feels.

By the time the minstrels take up their instruments and the servants clear a space for dancing, the room is ready for mayhem.

And Ralf leaps forward to encourage them, calling for more ale, more wine, more dancers. Clapping the beat with the musicians, urging them to a faster and faster pace. Throwing himself into the thickening throng, grabbing the girls and whirling them round. Pulling half-reluctant men into the crowd, laughing with them as they throw off their restraint. Pairing and mis-pairing men and girls, married or unwed, like the Lord of Misrule at Christmastide.

Then he stands back to survey his work. With his arms folded across his broad chest, he watches the revelry unfold and stares intently towards the silent and awkward figures on the dais.

His father, his face a picture of discomfort and mistrust, anxious hands tightly clasping the carved arms of his chair.

Lady Alice intensely disapproving of this debauched display.

Christiane doesn't need to look at him to sense Richard's deep unease and to know he is also hesitant to act, unable to intervene without his lord's lead.

And the conflict warring within the reeve, who has shrunk away to distance himself, arms folded, face hidden in shadows, caught between the disapproval he knows his lady would voice and gainsaying her beloved son.

And for herself? She tries to meet his gaze steadily, to ensure her face gives nothing away beyond perhaps a slight curiosity. But, beneath, her wariness is increasing.

He scowls at her, wanting to disrupt that calm, complacent exterior. He wants to intimidate her, as he intimidates all those who meet him in the lists, with sword or staff.

He sees himself as strong and fearless. Everyone in Percy's household proclaims him a success, and he expects their respect here too.

Calling for wine, he empties the cup at a swallow and demands another. That's one thing he could be assured of here: good Gascon wine. He is pleased to benefit in that way from his father's trade.

The minstrels strike up another tune, a lively dance, and it propels him across the room before his mind connects. Her breath sticks in her throat as he stops before her at the dais and holds out his hand.

'A dance, my lady!' As much a command as a request. Even before she can respond, Lady Alice's hand comes down on her wrist to stay her movement. Ralf glowers at her intervention. 'May I not dance with my betrothed, my lady?' he challenges.

'Perhaps if you were more sober,' Lady Alice rebukes him.

'I can hold my wine with the best of them,' he disagrees angrily. 'Believe me, I am capable of more than a mere dance tonight!'

'Enough, Ralf,' Geoffrey advises, leaning forward, belatedly moving to temper the situation.

'When all others are enjoying themselves,' Ralf counters, sweeping his arm towards the throng, 'should she not also join the celebration?'

'And what,' Lady Alice cuts in, icily, 'are we celebrating, my lord?'

The noise of the crowd hushes as they watch the dispute and, distracted, the minstrels lose their beat. Fury flushes through Ralf's face, feeling his dominance falter. The dance stops and he turns to face the waiting crowd.

'Are you not entertained?' he demands, sweeping his arms wide. 'Have I not given you the best celebration tonight?'

Murmurs start, each looking to another for reassurance. They are out of their depth, bemused and confused by this unexpected display.

And it is making them suspicious. Christiane feels the nervousness building within them, and her own anxiety notches up, moving from her stomach to her chest and neck.

Feeling the weight of others' need for direction, the blacksmith hesitantly steps forward. 'And what would you have from us, my lord?' he raises, his tone respectful but wary. 'Will you not tell us the purpose of tonight's gathering?'

Men edge nearer the blacksmith, seeking safety in numbers, while the women fall back behind them, drawing the children with them. Christiane's head pounds a painful beat.

A recklessness overtakes Ralf. He draws himself up, his blood pumping as he seeks to regain his hold, standing before these people. His people. Seeing himself as a leader of men at last. Empowered by a sense of responsibility that gives him a swagger and swells his status. Experiencing the thrill of fulfilling everything he has trained for since the age of seven.

Tension now grips every person in the Hall and their response reaches out to Christiane like a thick wave, invading her mind.

Unable to defend herself, her throat closes, stopping her breath. She rises without thought, wanting to speak, wanting to put an end to this, but she can only put her hands to her neck, trying to stop the panic.

Oblivious to her pain, Ralf surveys the men, looking from one to the next, as if to draw each of them to him with the force of his command.

'I need fifteen of our strongest and best-trained men,' he raises his voice high, shouting into the stunned silence of the room. 'My Lord Percy commands it, and I shall lead you,' breathless with excitement. 'We are going to war!'

'No!'

The cry that flies from Christiane's lips springs from the instant response of almost every person there.

Fear crashes down on them and it swirls in her head, darkening her sight and closing her ears until all she can sense is her own blood pounding in her head. All the life floods out of her limbs until she can no longer hold herself up.

And blackness consumes her.

Chapter Thirty-two

Threfield Percy. August 1326

'How dare you!'

Christiane has never heard Geoffrey so enflamed. His face is white with anger as he squares up to Ralf, standing his ground even though he is a head-and-shoulders shorter than his son now.

Somehow, Richard caught her before she fell and, supported between Geoffrey and Richard, she has been guided to a seat in the solar. Lady Alice applies a cold cloth to her brow.

The crowd in the Hall seems reluctant to disperse and sounds of dispute filter through to them in the solar.

'How ungrateful they are!' Ralf complains, pacing the room with unrestrained indignation. 'I thought feeding them would assure their goodwill. Instead, I am met only with whingeing and complaining. Such ingratitude!'

'How dare you!' Geoffrey explodes with righteous anger. 'How dare you announce such a thing without first speaking with me!'

'I have my orders.' Ralf is defensive in the face of his father's sudden and unusual displeasure.

'And you didn't think to convey them to me?' throwing his hands up in despair. 'How will that appear to the people here? I am still lord of this manor, Ralf!' He turns his back and sits down heavily in his chair, trying to regain control of himself.

Ralf folds his arms across his broad chest, planting himself squarely in the middle of the room.

'You cannot expect them to welcome such news,' Richard hints.

'Whyever not?' Ralf retorts.

'We are in the midst of the harvest,' Richard explains, his voice tight with barely contained frustration at his lord's son. 'They fear to leave their homes when so much work is yet to be done.'

'We always knew this day might come,' Ralf justifies. 'It is our duty to supply fighting men when required by our liege lord.'

Christiane leans forward, pushing Lady Alice's administering hand aside. 'And we will fulfil our obligations, my lord,' she asserts. 'But you must understand, you would take a fifth of our men, and the strongest among them, maybe never to return. The consequences for the manor and each household could cut deep and long.'

'I'm so glad my betrothed has concern for my safety!' he snaps, petulantly. She bites her tongue. 'My Lord Percy gave me a fortnight to muster. 'Tis a long day's march to York, perhaps two if they are as feeble in walking as they are fearful of fighting! That gives you nine days to make ready,' he demands, self-importantly.

Christiane looks from Geoffrey to Lady Alice and sees reluctant acceptance on both their faces. 'Then we have much to do,' she assesses, looking towards Richard. 'We must find additional help for the harvest. Perhaps some men from the kitchens might be freed up to work in the fields?'

Richard nods, his face grim. 'And we may be able to provide the midday meal for a few days, to free up more of the women.'

'I care not how it is done,' Ralf dismisses haughtily, feeling his command wane, 'only that we are ready to leave at dawn on the tenth day.'

'We shall need to equip the men too,' Christiane ignores him. Richard nods, folding his arms in resignation.

That catches Ralf's interest. 'Have they been training as Percy ordered?' he demands.

Richard raises his head. 'Every Sunday after mass. They are adequately adept with the longbow. Some of them,' he caveats, uncomfortably.

'You will pick out the best of them for me,' Ralf insists.

Richard glances at Christiane, holding back his words.

'We cannot spare all our best men,' she speaks for him. 'Some must stay to help with the land.'

'And would you have me risk more deaths by taking men I can't trust to fight as well as they should?'

'No...'

'No,' he quarrels. 'Would you have me risk my own death from having less than capable men around me?'

At that, Geoffrey's simmering anger boils over. 'You care for no one but yourself!' he accuses, looking like he wants to throttle his own son.

Ralf draws himself up to his full height. 'You are unfair!' he complains. 'And I shall prove it to you, Father.' His father raises an eyebrow in sceptical response. 'There is one other matter we should conclude while we are all together,' he pushes, his voice strangely firm. 'Before I go, Christiane and I should be wed.'

'Absolutely not!'

The denial is out of Geoffrey's mouth before he even is aware of the thought, so powerful and immediate is his reaction. From where she sits, she sees his face suffused with outrage as he glances in her direction.

'No?' Ralf challenges, disbelieving. 'She is my betrothed, and it's high time we should be wed. I can give her my protection by marrying her, in case I should not return. And my mother has already given me her blessing,' he finalises.

Geoffrey turns slowly to stare his son in the face. 'But the decision is not hers to take,' he contradicts, his voice shaking, unused to such conflict. 'It is mine. You are not yet of age and will obey me yet.'

Lady Alice opens her mouth as if to intervene, ready to lend her weight to Ralf's suggestion, but Geoffrey raises a hand to forestall her, and she sinks back on her stool.

'On what basis would you deny me, Father?' barely containing his haughtiness.

'Based on your arrogance and impetuosity. You are clearly far from ready,' Geoffrey spits scorn.

'In what way am I not ready?' he raises his voice. 'I am about to lead our men to war,' gesturing towards the Hall. 'I have made myself the most feared of Percy's squires, able to best even his strongest and most experienced knights. How is it my own father cannot see how ready I am?' thumping his hand against his chest with pride.

'Ready to fight, maybe. Ready to die, for certain,' Geoffrey mocks. 'Ready to be a husband to a wife? In that you are still but a boy!'

In the instant, he knows he has gone too far. Red in the face, Ralf bites back his response, staring hard at his father. But his father stares him down.

Lady Alice cannot hold back. 'My lord,' she counsels, 'your son speaks some sense. I, for one, would sleep better knowing Christiane's position is secured. The betrothal has already gone on longer than is normal. Could it not be formalised now?'

Geoffrey swings a displeased eye on her, but his respect for her causes him to pause. His mouth tightens as he weighs her opinion.

And in that instant, Christiane feels ripples of energy flow up and down her arms until her fingers tingle, almost painfully. In her mind, she catches a flicker of remembrance, as if this moment has happened before. As if she has stepped out of place, crossing time, and is watching her beloved Papa consider in just such a way. Sitting as Geoffrey now sits. Looking at her thoughtfully as he turns over some words from her mother in his mind. And it is as if both become one. Both present. Both focused upon her. One overlaid on the other in her vision.

'Christiane?' the father-men turn towards her, their faces softening with concern. Her father's face. Her father's loving concern. But Geoffrey's words, Geoffrey's attention. 'My child?' seeing her frowning and unfocused. 'What say you on this?'

'Papa.' Her lips frame the word, though no sound comes out. The longing, the yearning hold her heart in a merciless grip.

Geoffrey leans across and covers her hand with his, conveying his reassurance through its pressure. 'Tell me,' he encourages.

She feels lost, unable to guide herself or even to know her own heart. Only in his gentle gaze does she find ease. 'I obey you in this, as in all things, my lord,' she replies.

A sound of disgust from Ralf, frustrated and furious, breaks the moment of thrall. When she turns her gaze back to Geoffrey, the image of her father is gone.

Geoffrey looks towards Ralf, ascendancy in his expression.

'You have my answer,' he shuts down the argument. 'You shall not marry Christiane until I say so.'

Ralf stares back, dislike twisting his face. 'Let's see what my lady mother has to say about that!' he re-joins, then turns away and slams out of the room.

Chapter Thirty-three

Threfield Percy. 16th September 1976

I come back to my broader awareness with a jolt. I have no sense of what time it is, but it must be late because the sun is setting behind huge, dark clouds. The day's light holds on longer, but it too will be gone soon. The air is cold and a firm wind has whipped up, chasing the clouds across the sky.

Every muscle screams with pain from being tensed too long. I step back to survey the site, but I must have stood up too quickly because my head spins and the world swims in my vision, moving around me, even as my detached mind recognises it must be me that's moving. I stagger forward and fall to my hands and knees, trying to still the physical world, but it keeps swinging around. Closing my eyes just makes it worse, feeling the gyrating movement within me now. Nausea rises within me so rapidly that I can't stop it and I vomit in the grass.

Sweat breaks out all over my skin, setting off a compulsive shivering. I know I'm going to black out, and I sink onto my side, clutching my arms around my chest for warmth. The last thing I feel is the first large drops of rain that start to fall.

My voice whimpers in my head.

Christiane!

Chapter Thirty-four

Threfield Percy. August 1326

She wakes with a start, unsure what has stirred her but with an immediate unease gripping her. She lies still, feeling for an unauthorised presence in the room: there is none. Only Lady Alice, flat on her back and snuffling in her sleep, and Edith on the truckle bed below, still as the dead.

She can't shake the feeling of something amiss. It brings her fully awake, alert and watchful. It must be the early hours of the new day; lines of lighter night show around the window shutters. Dawn is not far distant, though enough that the birds are yet to start their dawn chorus. She rests in the silence of the night, trying to take comfort from the rare peace; it's so unusual for there to be no sounds from the manor, from the village, from the animals.

Even as she thinks the thought, the screech of an owl scrapes through the night air, and her gut tightens with apprehension.

Softly, so as not to disturb her guest, she swings her feet to the floor. The wood is warmly welcoming beneath her bare feet and the air touches her softly, no sign yet of the morning chill of late summer. She has no need of her mantle.

The door creaks on opening, as is its wont, and the floor echoes a reply as it gives beneath her slight weight. The room beyond lies in darkness, the bones of its furniture visible as heavier dark. The door to Geoffrey's room is sunk in deeper shadows, firmly closed.

She looks into the Hall where the room is lighter for having no shutters on the high windows. The tables are pushed back and sleeping forms line the floor close by the walls; just the reassuring sounds of sleeping bodies, hefty with food and drink, no signs yet of any stirring to the upcoming day. One of the kitchen cats slowly pads its way across, pausing to look at her; its eyes catch and reflect the sinking moon, making them flash supernaturally.

Muffled sounds from Geoffrey's room catch her attention. Frowning, she stands at the door, leaning her ear towards the wood, holding her breath to hear.

There are noises on the other side, but she can't make them out. Scuffling, maybe. A grunt from a man. She hesitates. She so rarely goes through that door – and never at night – that to do so would be an intrusion. But the apprehension is overwhelming her, a tight knot in her chest. Breathing hard against it, she grasps the handle and pushes open the door.

It's even darker in here than in the solar, no candle or rush to cast a light. She picks out the usual forms in an instant: chest after chest ranged against the walls, the large oak bedframe projecting its dominance into the room. It takes a moment more to realise what else is there: Ralf, standing over the prone form of his father, casting aside a pillow with one hand.

As her eyes adjust, she takes in more details. How his face is beaded with sweat that glistens in the greyness. The shock on his face, his eyes deep-set in darkness as he takes in that she's there.

And a colour around him she has only ever seen once before, when Hugh Despenser condemned her beloved father to death.

She starts forward, compelled by dread.

'Is my lord unwell?' Her voice is thready with fear.

He doesn't answer, just stares at her. Different emotions chase across his face: surprise gives way to calculation and then – it horrifies her to see it and is so quickly covered over that she immediately doubts she has – to triumph.

'Something made me come to check,' he starts to explain.

Her body is so leaden she has to force herself to move towards the bed, called towards Geoffrey but hesitant to come too close to Ralf.

'Christiane,' his voice seems to catch on some deep emotion, 'I think he's dead.'

No! The anxious knot in her chest drops to her stomach, the dread filling her like a lead weight. She knows it's true even as her mind shelters in denial.

And in a flash of understanding, she also knows Ralf has killed him. That the pillow had been covering Geoffrey's face a moment before she entered.

She sees it as clearly as if she had witnessed the act for herself. She tries to take a step forward, as if to approach Geoffrey herself, but Ralf moves fast to block her way.

'Don't, Christiane,' he advises, his large body obliterating any view.

'What happened?' The question demands its way out of her, and she knows there's accusation in her tone. Knows too he has heard it, from the narrowing of his eyes before he controls his features once more.

'I was sleeping,' there's a tremble of distress feigned in his voice as he nods towards the door to the adjoining room. 'I woke unexpectedly and, somehow, I sensed something was wrong. I came in to check on my father…'

'Why were you leaning over him when I came in?' Half of her cannot help but push, even as the other half registers that there is danger in doing so.

'I was feeling if there was any breath...'

'And the pillow?' she interrupts, direct and accusing.

His body stiffens with resentment, as if she were unjustified in her distrust of him. 'I was just moving it out of the way. Christiane,' he grasps her hand, 'I know you feel his loss too.'

As he tries to draw her to him as if to comfort her, she twists away and manages to slip past him. Quick as a flash, she lays her hands on Geoffrey's chest, hoping, praying to feel something…anything. A heartbeat. A breath. A tremor of life.

But even in the darkness she needs no further proof. Geoffrey's spirit no longer inhabits this body; she knows it with every sense she has. His skin is still flushed, as he often was after a heavy meal and a quantity of wine, but no spark now animates that face.

She touches his cheek, softly, tentatively. Still warm. But already cooler than normal.

'An apoplexy, perhaps,' he suggests, with almost a shrug of dismissal in his tone. 'He was no longer young.'

She barely hears him as a tide of emotions floods over her, sinking into a bottomless well of loss for the man who has been a father to her for more years than her own beloved father, who has sheltered and protected her, nurtured and encouraged her, loved and cared for her.

Even as grief consumes her, the implications of her loss creep in, invidious and invasive. She is as isolated and alone as the day she arrived in this place. As vulnerable and uncertain as that kinless, homeless child. What is to become of her now?

Because now, this man standing in heavy silence so near to her holds her life in his hands. Just as surely as he held Geoffrey's only moments before.

Wariness creeps a warning across her skin.

He's standing too close to her.

The stench of wine is heavy on him, a rancid, sour smell that turns her stomach. She tries to move away, but he anticipates her, roughly grasping her arm and turning her towards him. His limbs carry the clumsiness of sustained drinking, and his eyes are blurred and unfocused as from a long night of disturbing dreams.

He catches her scent as he turns her, the sweetness of rose water and lavender, and breathes it in.

She senses the change in Ralf's body and how the atmosphere becomes charged with threat.

He pulls her towards him slowly, almost gently, as with the tenderness of a lover. She resists, pulling away.

His eyes fix on her mouth, a teasing smile on his lips as he allows her to resist for a moment, knowing he is the stronger, then exerts his dominance and inexorably but tauntingly slowly draws her towards him.

'Don't fight me,' he warns.

His voice is gritty and deep, half warning, half inviting. She shakes her head in disbelief.

He growls at her denial. 'You obey *me* now, Christiane!' and snatches her to him, his arm hard around her waist, holding her close, pinioning both arms with one hand. With the other, he grabs her hair and tilts her head upwards, then clamps his mouth to hers. It is a rough, merciless, selfish claiming; elation sweeps through him as he realises no obstacle now stands in the way of him having everything he wants.

Furious, she pulls her arms free and braces her hands against his chest, levering herself far enough back in his arms to see his face.

'Enough, my lord!' she demands. 'Have you no respect for your father?' She can't bring herself to look at the still body beside them on the bed.

'Damn my father,' he growls, and kisses her again. 'I want you, Christiane,' he breathes.

'No,' she tries to push him away once more. 'This is not right!'

'I have wanted you from the moment I saw you at my mother's yesterday,' ignoring her. 'God's teeth,' kissing down her face while bracing her head in his hands, 'you're a winsome woman now.' His breathing is laboured, his breath hot against her cheek and ear.

'Don't, my lord,' she pleads.

'Don't resist me, Christiane,' he cajoles. 'Give me comfort this dark night.'

'No!'

But he's oblivious to her opposition. And she's feeble to his control. He backs her towards the door to the other room. The harder she struggles, the harder he holds her until he bodily lifts her off her feet, his arms like bands of iron around her chest and waist. She kicks out blindly, but her feet connect with hard bone, and it hurts her more than him. The door bangs as he kicks it open, and it crashes against a chest behind.

Please God, let someone hear.

This room is darker than the other, with no window to admit any relief. Full too, of Geoffrey's prized acquisitions, ready to trade. No more.

Grief grips her heart as loss bites again.

The truckle bed has been moved in here, an intrusive shape in the middle of the room, the chests shoved roughly aside, forced to yield space.

He's kissing her face and neck as he moves towards the bed, his hand roughly grabbing her breast.

She tries to claw at his face, to inflict pain to bring him out of this stupor, to raise him to awareness of what he's doing. Having to believe that he cannot know himself what he does.

He drops her so suddenly that she loses her footing and staggers against him, then he grabs both her wrists, transferring them to one hand. 'Do not scratch me, little cat,' grabbing her chin, his voice low and threatening.

And she understands he knows exactly what he's doing. God knows, maybe he's even done it before.

Urgency grips her as he pulls her against him. She tries to fight harder, wriggling her body to try to slip out of his grasp.

'Yes,' he breathes with a laugh, 'keep moving like that, little cat. You are making me hard.'

She leans back, and spits in his face.

His lips curl with distaste. He holds her from him, his hand still around her wrists, and slaps her face with the other. It is only his hold on her that stops her from falling. Tears sting her eyes, shock ripples through her body.

He throws her down on the bed and she curls up protectively, her arms over her head and stomach, trying to protect herself. Her head buzzes with dizzying darkness, hardly aware of him standing over her.

Suddenly, everything slows.

She can see and hear and feel everything that's happening to her but she's experiencing it from outside herself.

The cold night air against the skin of her legs and lower body as he grabs the hem of her chemise. The tearing of the material as he yanks it up halfway. The softness of the lawn as her hands scrabble to push it back down. The callouses on his hands as he grasps her wrists in both hands and shoves them out of the way. The unyielding bone and muscle of his arm as he thrusts under her waist, lifting her bodily as he moves across her. The coarseness of the hair on his thighs as he uses a knee to push her legs apart. One hand holding her wrists, the other moving to position himself between her legs.

She closes her eyes. Forces her mind to focus elsewhere. Cuts herself off from what's happening to her body.

Feels her own breath held. The straining in her chest as she refuses to let it out. The pounding of blood in her head and behind her eyes.

She hears his breathing come faster, grunting, sweating. Feels the weight of him pressing her down into the mattress, straw ends sticking into her flesh like needles.

And senses...*him*...nearby. No, not near. Everywhere. Huge, intense anger, filling the room. All around her.

Help me, her mind demands, despairing. *Can you not stop this?*

And then anger to match his. Feeding off him, turning against him.

Like a white heat in her heart and guts.

Fury at the man pinioning her to the bed, pressing her down as he lies over her, focused not on her but on his own body, his own demands. Impotent outrage that her weaker body can do nothing to stop this. Trapped, suffocating, helpless, sinking down again into dark despair.

Rising back up with anger, red as blood.

How can you watch this and yet do nothing? her mind cries out in rage. *What's the point of you, if not to save me? Why will you not help me?*

Chapter Thirty-five

Threfield Percy. 16th September 1976

Someone is shaking me. Hard. There's blackness all around, so dark I can't see anything. But I can feel hands gripping my shoulders and shaking me so violently that my whole upper body is reverberating with it.

And the full force of the rage I felt a moment before for Ralf is turned on this unseen person.

'Stop fucking shaking me!' I shout – at least, I think it's a shout, though my body feels so disconnected and resistant to command that I'm not sure it comes out that way.

But, somehow, the action breaks me loose of whatever held me bound and my vision clears. Then I realise Martin's crouched beside me, leaning over me anxiously.

'Shaking you?' he defends, bewildered and shocked. He rocks back on his heels as if to put a safer distance between the two of us. 'I was trying to hold you still!' defensive and indignant. He reads the scepticism in my face. 'Eoghan, you were having convulsions. I was trying to stop you hurting yourself!'

'Don't be absurd!' I dismiss. But a cold weight of fear drops into my stomach.

I push against it, struggling to sit up. The sudden move makes my head rebel and I cover my mouth with one hand as nausea burns the back of my throat. I feel wetness on my skin and simultaneously notice the rain drumming on my head and neck, that my soaked shirt is plastered to my chest and that rivulets run down Martin's half-resentful, half-fearful face. The darkness all around is the depths of night, compounded by a heavy storm.

I've been here for hours. Unaware. Out of control. Lost.

The panic spreads through my chest and guts, into my arms and legs. Pervasive. Gripping. Paralysing.

And then I remember her fear, and it consumes me in an instant. Her total helplessness and vulnerability. Her powerlessness against Ralf. Her despair at the loss of Geoffrey. Her anger at me.

And my anger floods through me again, so intense that I hesitate to close my eyes, expecting to be overwhelmed by it. It swirls through and around my body, coalescing into a tight ball at the base of my throat, threatening to block my lungs with an all-encompassing need to act, to take revenge.

Then the black, leaden, impotent guilt intensifies my anger into a red, molten rage. And my head explodes with a sharp, stabbing pain behind my eyes.

'Eoghan.' When Martin's voice reaches me, I realise that's the third time he's said my name, each notching up with anxiety until it's the tightness of his tone that cuts through my oblivion. When I meet his gaze, he raises his hand towards my face, but hesitates in his uncertainty to touch me.

I take my hand away from my mouth. 'What?' I demand. Hearing my own voice shake with emotion only elevates my fear.

He motions helplessly at my hand, momentarily unable to speak.

I stare where he directs. And watch the raindrops hit the blackness on my fingers until it streams down my palm and wrist.

I'm bleeding.

I put my hand to my face again and feel the difference in the blood and water on my skin. Feel it run over my top lip and into my mouth, salty and tannic, dilute with rain.

'It's nothing,' I dismiss, sounding calmer than I feel, pushing the base of my palm against my nostrils to staunch the flow. 'I used to have nosebleeds all the time as a kid,' I lie. 'It'll stop soon.'

It's partly true. I remember having a couple of them and my mother sitting me in a chair, pinching my nose to make it stop. But there's more blood here than I remember.

'Didn't you just have a concussion?' Martin rationalises, handing me a handkerchief. 'I really think I should get you to hospital. Let's get you to the car and we'll work it out from there.'

Hospital. Shit! Michael. I need to tell him. He needs to know what happened to Geoffrey. He has to understand he didn't fail her. The memories fill my mind again. Everything she was experiencing through her senses being translated through mine.

'Yes,' I concede. 'The hospital. I need to see Michael.'

'I meant for you,' Martin disputes.

'I know. But this is more important.' Confusion, frustration, bewilderment mingle on his face, and I know he's remembering how I refused to go earlier. 'Martin, please,' praying he'll forgive. I need his help now. 'Please just get me there. It's all about him now.'

* * * * * * *

I know I'm making no sense to him, but it doesn't matter. He's seen me at my worst and yet he's still here. Thank God for Martin. Because by the time we get to the hospital, I'm in an even worse state, my temperature shifting violently from too hot to too cold.

He insists on coming into the hospital with me. I know the ward I'm heading for, so I walk straight through reception without checking in, knowing Martin will cover for me. He stops when the nurse in charge calls out to us, and I sense his momentary hesitation between wanting to follow me and needing to comply with her strident demands. She wins; I leave him to it.

There's a directions board by the lifts. It seems to take me an age, but I find the ward. And then remember that Sam's message earlier had told me which floor it was anyway. Idiot. Wasted time.

Seconds drag as I wait for the lift to arrive, impatiently counting down from only the second floor. Feeling a wave of vertigo flood through me, I prop myself up against the wall, closing my eyes and breathing as I wait for it to pass.

The lift pings and I hear the doors slide open. *Move*, my brain urges my body. But the dizziness is overwhelming and when I open my eyes, I see blackness encroaching from my side vision.

I close my eyes again, but the moment of sight has given me enough to work with. I can judge my distance to the lift opening and feel my way into the gap. Sweat breaks out all over my skin as I grab the side rail in the lift and sink to the ground, dropping my head between my knees.

Someone gets in. I ignore them, waiting for the weakness to pass. He sighs and reaches alongside me to press a button. The shushing of the doors sliding shut is amplified in my ears, as if we're in a long tunnel.

The lift shudders from its standstill state and begins a long, slow climb, its machinery vibrating through my feet and hip bones. The weakness starts to dissipate; cautiously raising my head, I open my eyes to see Martin standing on the opposite side of the lift, half-seated against the handrail, arms folded, gnawing on his lip.

As the lift jolts its way into alignment with the seventh floor, he leans forwards, grim-faced. 'Can you stand?' He proffers a hand to help me up.

Deep breath. Grasp the hand. A hard pull and he has me on my feet.

The light from the lift spills into darkness, the corridor lights turned down, the wards beyond in deeper shade. Small pools of electric light puddle at three points, one to the left, two to the right: desk lamps at the nurses' station for each ward.

I turn left, guessing that Ward A is the first of the three. My shoes, wet through, squeak on the linoleum. Martin keeps pace with me; I think he expects me to pass out at any moment. And the way my feverish body feels, he may be right.

The duty nurse behind the desk stands as we approach, startled that anyone is arriving this late at night.

'Visiting hours are ten until twelve and four 'til seven,' she conveys in a chastising whisper. 'Come back tomorrow.'

I scan the ward: six beds, three on each side, two with those curtains on a wheeled frame surrounding them.

I shake my head. Bad idea. 'I need to see Michael,' I insist. 'Michael...' I stop. I can't remember his surname. That freaks me out. What's his damn name? I put my hand to my forehead as if that will stop the world spinning around me.

'I just told you,' standing to reinforce her authority, 'you can't visit anyone until tomorrow. You'll have to leave.'

'I'm not leaving until I've seen him,' I return, struggling against the pounding that starts in my head, a persistent thump, thump, thump. My eyesight blurs. Martin's hand is on my shoulder; I don't have the strength to shake him off.

'Are you drunk?' the nurse accuses, mistaking my slurring.

I lean forward to place my hands against the desk, bracing myself against the unconsciousness that's pushing at my peripheral vision.

She mistakes my intent and reaches for the phone receiver, dials two numbers. 'Security, Ward A, seventh floor. Immediately,' she orders with a sharp tone.

'Nurse, please,' I hear Martin advocate for me. 'There's no need for that. He just wants to see Michael Langley. Professor Langley.'

I don't see her face, but I do – just – catch a sharp intake of breath. And then the sound of footsteps.

'Sam,' I start, holding out a hand as if to grasp hers, as if to convince her, but she evades me. 'I found the truth about Geoffrey. It wasn't his fault. Ralf murdered him. He couldn't be there to protect Christiane.' A frown fills her eyes and face. 'He needs to know,' I assert. 'Michael. He needs to know. It wasn't his fault. You see?' I beg her to understand, to make sense of this even though I can't. 'It wasn't his fault,' I repeat, weakly.

I expect to her be angry with me. And she is. Or was. But there's no passion behind it.

'Where were you?' she asks, simply. 'I asked you to come but you didn't.'

They're the words of someone who has played the thought over and over in their mind, fuelled by disappointment and blame, until they've become so weary that they've lost touch with the emotions that first sparked them. Someone who is feeling so much more that there's no room for those lesser emotions.

So, I know the truth before she says it in how she's shut herself away from me. Because there's nothing coming from her now, no worry, no disappointment, no compassion. Grief has closed her off and turned her in on herself.

Her words sound the death knell as she turns away from me.

'You're too late, Eoghan. He's gone.'

* * * * * * *

She won't let me see him, even though his body is lying behind one of those privacy frames, not ten feet away.

Martin takes charge because now I can't think at all. My mind is numb. My body too.

He drives me back to the pub and straightens things with the landlady who resents having to unlock the door for me so late. With hushed undertones, he delivers the news of Michael's death as an excuse for the state I'm in, walks me up the stairs, helps me out of my wet clothes and puts me to bed.

And, still, I feel nothing.

I just close my eyes. And let the darkness consume me.

Chapter Thirty-six

Threfield Percy. August 1326

Ralf's inert body is heavy and hot against hers.

He makes no effort to relieve his weight on her, seemingly oblivious to how his shoulder presses against her cheek or how his thrust-out arm covers her nose and mouth. The sweat and staleness on his skin catches in the back of her mouth; the smell makes her gag. She only knows he is still awake by the roughness of each intake of breath, pushing her harder into the mattress, oppressive and stifling. Where he has shoved her shift up around her waist, she is exposed and unprotected, invaded where his legs still hold her thighs apart. She lies still, eyes closed, and wills him to move.

Unnaturally long moments pass, and she tries to turn her mind away from her body, and from Ralf's. Tries to reach for *him*, that other presence. But the room is empty, hollow and still. They are the only two there.

She senses his decision to move before it happens, in the tensing of his shoulders, in a slight lessening of the pressure on her chest as his back muscles tighten.

Don't look, her mind warns. He levers himself off her and the mattress dips as he awkwardly edges himself off the bed. When the wooden floor creaks as it takes his weight, she rolls onto her side, her back towards him, and draws her knees up, pushing the cloth back down to cover her lower body.

She hears him pull on his braies, tie the leather at the waist. He clears his throat, as if he would speak to her and, like a child, she covers her exposed ear with one hand, turning her face into the bed. *Go away*, she silently urges. *Leave me be*. And fights back the prickle of tears that threaten from behind her closed lids.

A sigh. A heavy tread on the boards. A pause. And the quiet unlatching and relatching of the door and his footsteps crossing that benighted mausoleum beyond. Then, silence.

She waits for the emotions to come, for the tears to start.

Waits for the emptiness of her mind to fill, for some reaction to surface. But nothing comes.

What she catches instead is an echo. An echo of his anger, the rage that filled this room, engulfing her. It washes over her like a wave through time. Less than the first but in essence the same. Ebbing like the tide.

And she reaches for the thought of him, for the memory of that anger, as if it can reconnect her with him to let her draw strength from him. She can't let her reaction out: it's so big it might consume her. But his anger gives her a line to hold onto.

And as she clings to him, she feels herself detach from her own body again until she sees her own foetal form on the bed.

And there, from the darkest depths of his anger, his love reaches out to claim her.

It encompasses her, as enfolding as an embrace, as fierce as fire, as emboldening as truth. Her soul sparks with something she has never known before and expands like an eagle reaching out its wings to take flight. To soar. To fight. To hunt.

In her mind, she feels herself lifted, swept up by the wind, rising in the air. She rises with the joy of it, higher and higher. Strong. Powerful. Free.

But his anger holds him earthbound, unable to unshackle. And when she notices, she plummets with the leaden weight of it, a chain around her frame crashing her back down to earth.

Into her body on the bed.

For an instant, a bottomless despair engulfs her. Then the fire of blame ignites in her belly, and she curses him again, crying out for justice, for help, for relief.

With an answering flash of guilt, he breaks away. And is gone.

Chapter Thirty-seven

Threfield Percy. August 1326

Slowly, her senses reassert themselves. The throbbing across her left cheekbone comes first; when she tentatively touches it, she finds the skin has split. There is an awkwardness to her breathing where the power of his grip has crushed her ribs. Bruised soreness between her legs. Fluid on her inner thigh.

She turns her mind away, reaching instead for sounds of the household stirring.

How much time has she lost? Night's grip is loosening; a rosy lightness from the door to Geoffrey's room suggests dawn isn't far away.

Geoffrey's room. Yet his no longer. Drawing her legs close, she curls inwards in defence against the grief thickening inside her, holding herself to hold back her emotions.

This is not the time for tears, her mind urges into the emptiness. *They can't find you in here.*

She has to move before someone comes in.

Somehow, she forces herself to sit up and to confront the dilemma Ralf's actions have created for her.

Her heart demands justice, for Geoffrey and for herself. To expose Ralf as fully as he has, physically, exposed her. To make others know he has committed these most sinful acts: depriving this gentle man of his life; brutalising and violating her for his own satisfaction. Her heart cries out for their sympathy to ease this outrage that burns within her.

But, with creeping doubt, her head undermines her heart. Why would they believe her when she didn't actually witness the murder? And what if they accused her of willingly accepting his desires?

Suddenly, all she wants to do is clear away any trace of what he has done to her. To pretend that it has never happened. To wash away his sin. To feel clean and whole again.

The thought drives her to her feet and through the door to the bedchamber, her thoughts intent on the ewer and bowl set out for Geoffrey on the chest by the door.

Moving swiftly, with eyes averted, she almost can't see the body on the bed as she passes. But as she reaches the door and leans against the chest with her back to the room, she is breathing hard against the sickness threatening within her.

Grabbing a water-soaked cloth, she raises the hem of her chemise and blindly scrubs at the stickiness on her thighs until the water, rose-stained, runs down her legs and over her bare feet.

And then her heart leaps into her throat as the latch rattles and the door is pushed open, letting light spill in from beyond.

Richard Prudhomme stops dead.

In the pale pre-morning light, his eyes scan quickly across her slight frame and take in the rest of the room.

'What in Heaven's name…?' he starts, appal and disbelief etching into the deep lines of his face.

'No!' Christiane denies, realising what has flashed through his mind. 'It's Geoffrey,' still unable to do more than half-turn in the direction of the bed. 'He's dead.'

Even in the weak dawn light, she sees the colour drain from his face. 'No,' a whispered, tortured echo of her denial. 'Please, God, no.'

She stays where she is as he crosses the room to the bed. He checks for breath, then leans over the body, hands braced on the mattress, head bowed in prayer for the departed.

Slowly, she turns towards him, her heart thumping with nerves, her soul straining for relief. Hoping, praying that she can put her faith in this kind man.

'I think Ralf killed him.'

For a long moment, Richard doesn't move; only a tightening in his face reveals his response to her words.

'What makes you say that?' His voice is filled with despair, as if he already knows the truth of what she has uttered.

'I woke, and something made me come to check on my lord. When I opened the door, Ralf was standing over him, with a pillow in his hand.'

She looks at the bed and her blood runs cold: after all that has happened, he's had the presence of mind to put the pillow back where it belongs.

'Where is Ralf now?' he asks, his voice taut as he stands upright and turns towards her.

'I know not,' she whispers. Then realises Richard is now looking at her closely, his eyes narrowing as his mind put the pieces together.

He hesitates before asking the question but knows he must. 'What else, my lady?'

She drops her eyes, takes an involuntary step backwards to distance herself from the truth. She knows he is looking closer at her dishevelled state, recalling what she was doing when he entered; it makes her want to cover herself. Slowly, he walks back, coming to stand before her, close but still at a reassuring distance.

'My lady,' he urges softly, trying to look into her downturned face. 'What else has happened here this night?'

The tears fill her eyes and stopper her throat, tight knots making it impossible to speak, even should she wish to. Mutely, she shakes her head, closing her eyes against what she cannot acknowledge. When the tears run down her cheeks, he growls at the tumult of thoughts tumbling through his mind, clenching his fists against the dark emotions building in his chest.

'I will kill him for this,' he swears, his voice strangled with pain and revenge.

'Don't do that,' she pleads, raising her face to him so he can see all her anguish. 'There are enough angry men around me. I don't need your anger. I need you to think for me.' Her voice catches with distress, and she drops her eyes to regain control of herself. 'We don't have much time. The household will be stirring soon, if they aren't already. And I can't think straight. I need you to help me think.

Please, Richard. Help me.' Knowing what she is doing, she reaches out tentatively and places her hand on his arm. Knowing it is the first time she has ever touched him, the first time she has used his Christian name.

He looks into her upturned face and knows he would do anything for this woman.

'What would you have me do?' he asks, gently.

'Help me to know what I must do. Should I make known what he has done here?'

'To Geoffrey…or to you?'

'Either. Both.'

He steps away from her, turning back towards the bed, trying to marshal the conflict of thoughts within him.

As he thinks, a strange stillness settles on the room, and she becomes alert to sounds emanating from the Hall: the low hum of men's voices as the first wakers greet one another; a dog barking outside; the wooden bar on the stable door being heaved off its iron rests. Time is against them.

Still yet he stands, thinking. And the longer he does, the sicker she feels. Hatred clenches his jaw and anger deepens the lines around his eyes. Both release at a dawning realisation that compresses his lips into a thin line, distaste curling his upper lip, until it too surrenders to a strange hopelessness that draws his eyebrows together before settling into helpless resignation.

And then a peculiar resolve takes over, replacing his tenderness and hardening his expression.

He draws a breath to steady himself as he turns back towards her.

'You are going to have to be strong,' he cautions, slowly approaching her, his hands low and calming. As he does when he gentles a horse, she registers absurdly. 'There is only one path you can take now: you are going to have to wed Ralf, and soon.'

'No!' Her refusal is pure instinct. 'How is that the answer?'

'I know it seems…' he starts.

'How can I wed the man who killed…him?' she interrupts, pointing at the lifeless form on the bed. 'Who did what he…did?' helplessly gesturing towards her lower body and feeling panic threatening just below the surface.

'Stop now, my lady,' he orders, not unkindly but more firmly than he has ever spoken to her. 'Your tears will help neither of us in this. Come.' Opening the door, her escorts her from the room and, with only a brief further glance, closes the door on the corpse. 'Sit,' he suggests, before crossing to close the doors to the Hall and her bedchamber. Edith stirs as he does so, so he beckons her over. 'Your lady has had a shock,' he conveys in hushed words. 'Fetch her some wine from the buttery but try not to be seen and speak to no one. Do you understand?' The sleep-drowsed maid nods, glancing with concern at her mistress as she slips into the Hall.

'We haven't much time,' Richard warns.

Christiane nods. Her maid's anxious departing glance has brought her back out of herself, reconnecting her with reality and with her responsibilities. Taking a deep breath, she feels the mist in her mind dissipate. 'Tell me your thinking.'

Her calmness relieves him enough to speak plainly. 'With all my heart, I want revenge on Ralf. If what you say is true, and every bone in my body tells me to believe it, then he has taken my greatest friend from me. The man who stood by me when the world would have abandoned me. I owe my life to Geoffrey, and not avenging him is like betrayal. But he would not want me to lose everything because of him. Nor you.'

'You're saying we shouldn't tell anyone what Ralf did.'

'What happens if we speak out? If they don't believe us, we lose everything. Both of us. And if they do, what happens to the manor?'

'Percy will reassign the lordship,' catching the thread of his thought. 'And who knows who will come or how they will treat the people.'

'You could be thrown out with nowhere to go.'

'You paint a stark picture, Master Prudhomme,' she reflects bleakly.

'That makes it no less true.'

'But must I marry him? A man who has no respect for me, for his father, for his people?'

He hesitates, discomfited. 'But what if there's a child?'

Fear cuts through her. 'There couldn't…' she whispers, the implications rushing in.

'What's worse,' he presses, his concern for her surfacing, 'is that he could discard you. He is his own man now; what if he decides not to fulfil his father's commitment? He can't be allowed to dishonour his father. And you,' he argues. 'But he tied his own hands with his announcement yesterday, when he said he wanted your future to be assured before he left. We must play him at his own game.'

'Though Geoffrey is barely cold? People will expect a proper time of mourning.'

'There is no time, my lady!' Frustration is making him impatient.

'I see your sense, Master Prudhomme,' she accepts reluctantly.

'I'm glad,' nodding his reassurance. 'Because we have need of you, my lady.'

'Of me?' Surprise lifts her voice.

'We have not only lost our lord, but we are also about to lose our most able men.'

'These will be difficult times for those households,' she weighs his warning.

'They will need your leadership. And compassion,' he affirms.

'Mine?'

'If not yours, then whose? We cannot expect it from the lady Amicia.'

'What about you?'

'They respect me, but they do not love me. I am and always will be an outsider.'

'As am I,' she protests.

'Not if you're married to Ralf. More than that,' he hastens to reassure. 'They've seen you grow up here. Many have benefited from your attention and kindness. You've earned their trust. If there are doubters, you will win them over. And someone must protect them from Amicia.'

'Surely Ralf can do that?'

'Perhaps. But he will not often be here. And he will not come into his inheritance until he turns twenty-one next summer. She can do untold harm before then.'

She sits back, her brow furrowed. 'Those are the terms of Geoffrey's will?'

He nods. 'The manor goes to Ralf because it came through Amicia. The merchant business is split equally between Ralf and Hughes, though I'm sure Hughes is the one who will have the running of it.'

She resists. 'How can I do this?'

'How can you not?' he pushes, increasingly blunt. 'No other man would take you now. You are friendless and dowerless. Geoffrey was your shield and he protected you the best he could. But he is gone,' with harshness in his voice to cover his own distress. 'You have no kin to help you. You have not the money to induce a convent to take you. Where would you go? To some town? To do what? What skill or service can you offer? And what if you are with child because of this? What would you do then?' The darkness of the choices he presents is a cold hand clutching at her heart, and he reads it in her face. 'Forgive me for speaking harshly, my lady,' he tempers his tone. 'Think about it this way,' he urges. 'You need not be friendless and alone. You will be lady of the manor.'

'And you, Master Prudhomme,' straightening her spine and lifting her chin to look him directly in the face. 'Will you stand by my side?'

'As long as I have breath in my body, my lady.' It is an oath easily given.

'Perhaps I am not entirely friendless, then,' she hopes. She looks towards the windows. 'The day dawns.'

And into the hushed stillness, a bell starts to toll. A mournful dong, dong, dong. Christiane rises.

'That tells us where Ralf went,' she concludes. 'To tell his mother her husband is dead.'

'And the Lady Amicia wants everyone to know she is a widow,' Richard adds.

Already they can hear the gentle awakenings in the Hall turning into confusion, rising to commotion. As Edith returns through one door, Lady Alice emerges through the other, disturbed from her bed.

'What is it? What has happened?' she demands.

Christiane's eyes meet Richard's once more, and a silent pact is made.

'My lord has died in the night,' Christiane announces. 'An apoplexy, I fear. My lord Ralf has been to inform his lady mother and now we must tell the rest. Edith,' she instructs, 'please help Lady Alice to dress. Our people will be gathered soon, and we must be ready for them.'

Chapter Thirty-eight

Threfield Percy. August 1326

By the time Christiane and Lady Alice are properly attired, a large crowd has gathered in the Hall. Men, women and their offspring, all huddled together in a cacophony of confused chatter. Richard stands at their head, stone-faced against Simon Reeve's relentless probing for information. The sun is not yet high enough to penetrate the darkness in the body of the Hall and the rushes and candles around the room add a solemnity.

Hidden in shadows by the solar door, Christiane hears Ralf's arrival before she sees him, with a hushing whisper across the gathering.

The people part as he makes his way from the door to the dais, striding with purpose and poise, his faced fixed, his gaze unwavering.

It seems to her he has grown in stature in the darkness.

As one, the corpus of the manor turns to follow his path, eyes drawn by this new spectre of command. And not a murmur is heard as he steps up onto the platform and centres himself before them.

'It is my saddest duty,' speaking with such control that the room holds its collective breath, 'to convey that my beloved father, our revered lord, has died this night. Compelled by some impulse, I sought to check on him before dawn and found him struggling to breathe. Try as I might to aid him, I was too late, but I was blessed to be with him when his soul departed. He died in my arms as I prayed for his redemption.' He pauses dramatically and a sigh ripples around the room in sympathy. 'I have this moment returned from informing my lady mother, who is as stalwart in her bereavement as you would all expect.

'I have spoken to the priest,' he continues. 'We shall bury my father tomorrow. Work may cease for the morning. But,' an edge entering his voice, anticipating the reaction his next words will raise, 'we have precious little time to spare. Nothing else has changed: our men must be ready to leave for war as planned. It is essential we hasten to complete the harvest work, so there will be no remembrance feast until that is done. Only when we are ready can we take time to mourn his passing.'

His eyes move slowly across the heads before him, holding the gaze of any who might challenge him. Not a murmur comes.

He nods, slowly. He owns these people now and they will obey. With a curt lift of his chin, he sends them away; after only the briefest hesitation, they turn as one and file out of the Hall.

And now you mean to deal with me, Christiane recognises, seeing him glance towards her, with just a tiny flicker of uncertainty crossing his eyes. Or I must deal with you.

'Lady Alice,' she steps back into the solar and addresses the silent older woman, 'give me leave to speak with my lord alone. There is much we must discuss.'

'Should I not stay to advise you?' Lady Alice queries out of habit, though there is a new determination in Christiane that says her advice is no longer required. The balance of their friendship has shifted.

Christiane shakes her head. 'There is no need. I shall convey to you what we decide,' she reassures her.

Ralf arrives as Lady Alice departs. He closes the door behind her, leaning back against the wood with his arms folded across his chest. It looks forced: he is trying, and failing, to hold onto the feeling of control that uplifted him on entering the Hall.

'Christiane, I fear you were gravely mistaken in what you thought you saw earlier,' he opens, his eyes wary. The light around him, already grey and murky, deepens a shade; you are lying, she sees.

'I had already concluded that for myself, my lord,' looking him directly in the face. His expression betrays his surprise, but her tone seems to reinforce her acquiescence to him. She uses his momentary confusion to take control. 'My lord, we must be wed before you leave.'

He is not quick enough to conceal his dismay at her words. 'You cannot mean that,' he contests, levering himself off the door. 'To do it so soon after my father's death, people will think it unseemly.'

'You said you wished to see my future secured before you leave for war,' she reminds him.

'But the situation is different now, Christiane,' as if he were educating a fool. 'The Church would never allow it.'

'Then you will inform your lady mother and she will manage the priest as she always does,' she rebuffs. 'I am sure you would want me to be protected. Me...' meaningfully resting her hand on her belly, 'and your child.'

'You cannot know if you are with child,' he protests, coming closer to her.

'And you cannot know that I am not,' she challenges, lifting her chin to stare him down. She sees his anger spark at the realisation he has been trapped by his own actions, just when he believed he had taken his freedom. *At the price of your own soul*, she thinks.

He puts his face close to hers, menacing and fierce. 'Have it your way, Christiane,' he allows. 'But I promise you this: if you aren't already carrying my child, I shall make sure you are by the time I leave.'

'When we are wed, I shall of course be an obedient wife to you,' she affirms.

'Oh no, sweet cat,' he taunts, dragging one finger over her cheek. 'I mean to have you every night until I leave. Wedded or no.'

Her own anger flares in response. 'That would not be seemly, my lord. And Lady Alice will stand in your way.'

'Then I shall send the interfering woman home tomorrow after the old man is in the ground,' he promises, grimly. '*I* am your lord now, Christiane, whether you like it or not, and you seem to desire to be my wife. If I choose to take you to my bed now, I will let no one here stop me. Do you hear?' He grabs her arm in a pinching grip and pulls her towards him. 'I want you, Christiane,' he breathes into her face. 'And I will have you.'

Sickness rises within her, but she forces it down. 'By force, if necessary, it seems,' she retorts.

'You cannot blame me for that, little cat,' with a brutal smile. 'That's as much your fault as mine. Teasing me all night until I wanted you so badly.'

Her stomach turns in distaste, but she holds grimly to her goal. 'Then you will go to your mother?' she pursues. 'And tell her we will be wed?'

He releases her arm, and she takes a step back, trying to keep her breathing steady, hoping he can't sense the rapid thumping of her heart.

'You mean it?' he doubts, some unexpected vulnerability breaking through. 'You wish us to wed before I leave?'

You have left me little choice! her mind protests in outrage. And tears press at the back of her eyes. But in the next moment, she sees the blustering boy beneath the façade of command and an awareness of her own strength surges within her.

'I do, my lord,' she nods her agreement. 'It is time we were wed.'

He shakes his head in disbelief and raises his eyebrows. 'Then we shall go together to my mother,' he decides, smiling a little grimly. 'God help us both.'

* * * * * * *

'Have you told them?' Amicia's voice, strangely lively, reaches down to them even before they close the door. As they ascend, Christiane takes in how the older woman's cheeks are bright with colour and her eyes sparkle; she has never seen her so energised. But a moment later, Amicia's face clouds with displeasure. 'What is she doing here?' she demands, frowning at the sight of Christiane.

Ralf steps forward to speak but Christiane moves to address Amicia herself and he retreats to a nervy distance.

'I am come to condole with you on the loss of your husband, my lady.'

The flash of elation is not masked quickly enough. 'He was a poor husband,' Amicia cannot help but counter, her chin raised stubbornly. 'It was a marriage I should never have been forced into. And yet,' belatedly tempering her opinions, 'I find myself sad at his passing.'

'He showed you great generosity,' Christiane re-joins. 'And tolerance.'

That earns her a sharp look from Amicia, but Christiane's gaze is steady, and Amicia is the first to look away. 'Perhaps he did, from time to time,' she concedes, ungraciously.

'I am here, my lady, because we need to discuss his burial. And,' looking towards Ralf, 'our marriage.'

'Marriage?' Amicia scorns. 'How can you contemplate that with my husband not yet in his grave?'

'My lord,' a pointed nod towards Ralf, 'intimated last night that you had given him permission to wed before he departs to join Lord Percy's army.'

Amicia shrugs dismissively. 'That was last night. Before this happened.'

'But the passing of your husband is not all that occurred last night. And Ralf's actions carry consequences.'

'Ralf's actions?' Amicia questions disbelievingly.

'Must I be blunt? He chose to take what he does not, yet,' heavy with insinuation, 'have a right to.' She can feel Ralf's discomfort from across the room, and he crosses his arms across his chest, self-defensively.

'And so?' Amicia chooses to be difficult.

'And so, we need to marry now. In case there should be a child.'

'Or I could have you cast out with nothing, ungrateful girl!' Amicia spits, her face flushed.

'And risk my making known the truth?' Christiane fights down her cold fear.

'Who would believe that you did not consent?' Amicia scorns. 'The more so if you *are* with child. 'Tis well known a girl can only conceive if she has enjoyed the act!'

'You no more believe that old wives' tale than I do, my lady,' Christiane challenges. 'And I believe you know what your son is capable of when something suits his purpose.'

She means only to hint at what she knows of Geoffrey's death. But as the words leave her mouth, an unquiet notion worms its way into her mind. Had Ralf come here this morning to break the news to his mother…or to confirm that the act was done? The traitorous thought slides into her mind with the smoothness and subtlety of a serpent.

Had Amicia known what Ralf intended? Condoned it? Encouraged him to it? She looks from mother to son and the notion becomes a knowing.

Slowly, Ralf raises his guilt-ridden eyes to hers, and it is as if he is seeking her understanding. For his weakness in being controlled by his mother. For his selfishness in disposing of his own father. For his brutality towards her.

And because he sees that she sees him truly, he rebels against his mother. 'I shall marry Christiane,' he addresses his mother while still holding Christiane's gaze. 'And, my lady Mother, you shall instruct Father Peter to make it happen.'

'No!' Amicia opposes, grabbing her son's arm with surprising intensity, forcing him to look at her. 'You could marry anyone now. She is not worthy of my son!'

'You told me to free us of my father!' he blames her, shaking her hand off, aggressively.

'I did not tell you to take this whore!'

Both are stung into silence.

And Christiane feels the silence bind the three of them together with invisible, indissoluble bonds.

Secrets to be kept.

Friday

Chapter Thirty-nine

Threfield Percy. 17th September 1976

I don't want to be awake. So, I keep my eyes closed and ignore the noises from the pub below – customers are being served so it must be late morning already – while smelling the mustiness of the warm air and feeling the glare of the sun on my face, turning the inside of my eyelids dark red.

I don't want to be awake because then I'll have to face what a failure of a human being I've become.

There's an empty world waiting for me this morning.

So, I keep my eyes closed and think about Christiane instead.

Part of me wonders how she can stand the thought of having that man as her husband after what he did to her and what she knows he did to his father. Another part of me knows exactly why because I've seen it through her eyes, felt it through her emotions. She feels vulnerable: her life is tenuous, dependent on the weather and the whims of other people for her home, her food, her well-being.

They don't even see it as rape, and there's certainly no thought of seeking justice in any kind of legal way.

But I can't help seeing it with my own, modern perspective and feeling such anger at his brutality. Taking what he wanted. Using her in some twisted way to suppress or release what he'd just done to his own father.

How dominant men are in that world. Of course, I know they still are in mine, but it's even worse then.

And, yet, in some ways she has power, practically if not nominally. When he's not there, she's in charge of that whole manor. Though, technically, Amicia is and will be until Ralf turns twenty-one next year. But that weak and selfish woman will only ever suit herself, not do what's needed for the sake of so many others.

Am I being judgemental? She's certainly very sick. I wonder what Sam would say her illness is?

Sam.

Michael.

And there it is. The yawning, black, desolate hole, waiting for me to fall in. Michael. So much more than a father is. That's not a reflection on Dad. I love both my parents very much, and I'm forever grateful for the loving, happy childhood they gave me. But I have a real affinity with Michael. He inspires me and he mentors me, and he's welcomed me as a colleague. And he loves me. He never says it: he's a naturally reserved man, as so many in academia can be. But I've never doubted that he loves me, and I like to think he sees me as a quasi-son. He's forgiven my every failing. Me leaving Sam. Me not being there for him these last few years. And now he's gone. That quiet, solid, reassuring love is gone.

And in its place…emptiness. A deep, dark void.

Step back. I can't go there. Not yet.

Reach for another thought.

Sam inherited that forgiving nature.

I have never let her down as badly as I did yesterday.

It's unforgiveable. I tell myself I love this woman – still – and yet I'm not there for her at one of the worst moments of her life.

Have I lost her too? If there was ever any chance of us being something to one another again, I've probably killed that.

Is this what Michael felt like? Is this The Obsession?

He never said he was experiencing anything like this. But then, would he have told me if he had? He must have thought he was losing his mind.

Am I losing mine?

I have never felt rage like it. Mine and hers. At him and at me.

And I have never felt so helpless. So impotent. Wanting to intervene, to stop him, and utterly unable to do so.

I'm a prisoner in witnessing it. And I wouldn't be without it.

That moment I realised she was aware of me. Woah. I can feel it again: the shock that injected through my system. I have goosebumps on my arms even now. It's like a feedback loop: aware of her being aware of me.

How is any of this possible? It's absurd.

And I know my rationality has gone. That's my only excuse. I'm not thinking straight. I'm running on pure instinct.

Like that impulse to see Michael as soon as I knew about Geoffrey. Would it have meant anything to him? What was Geoffrey to him, really? But it was such a strong need to tell him that Geoffrey had been murdered, that it wasn't his fault he wasn't able to help Christiane.

Too late. I failed him.

And I failed Sam. She won't be angry with me. She should be, but she won't. If she's disappointed in me, it's because she knows I can be better than this.

And I want to be. Even if my actions don't show that.

Why am I so consumed by Christiane's story? What do I feel for this woman? How can I feel anything for someone who's been dead for six hundred years?

But how can I not feel something? Who could experience what she's going through and not feel something for her?

I can't put a name to it. It doesn't fit any normal paradigm.

But it's pulling me away from my own reality. Disconnecting me, severing me thread by tenuous thread from this time and this place. Drawing me into her world. And I'm losing myself there.

Losing those I love too. Michael. Sam.

All I have left is Christiane.

* * * * * * *

When the taxi drops me off at the site, they're finishing lunch. But there's hardly anyone here.

What's happening? Where are they all?

Martin spots me and approaches with evident wariness.

'Eoghan,' he halts at a slight distance, 'I wasn't expecting to see you today.'

'What's happening?' Brusque. Rude. Because it's another rug being pulled from underneath me.

He draws me to one side with a hand on my arm. 'I'm so sorry about Michael…' he starts, but I shrug him off.

'What about the site, Martin?' I demand. I watch as two of the students take tools from the tent and start removing the canvas.

He sighs. 'Montague gave the order for the site to be closed as soon as he heard about Michael.'

'Why? There's still work to do.'

'But without Michael, there's no money,' Martin excuses.

'Damn the money,' I dispute. 'I'll pay it myself, if needed.'

'You may have to. No one's been paid for this week's work as it is.'

'Then tell them I'll pay and get them back to it.'

'Eoghan, there's no point,' he defends. 'We were finishing this weekend anyway. It's only brought things forward by a couple of days.'

Everyone is deserting me.

'Please, Martin,' that choking helplessness again. 'Stay. Help me.'

'That's just it. You think it's all about you, don't you? Not Professor Langley. You.'

His face shows me his frustration. And I can't blame him. I've abused and rebuffed him in return for his kindness and consideration. He pushes his hands into his jacket pockets, shakes his head. 'I'm sorry, Eoghan,' he refuses. 'I can't. I have to help Mother this weekend. You have to understand,' he justifies as I turn my back, 'I've been neglecting my responsibilities for weeks now.'

'That's fine,' I disregard him, walking away. 'Do what you must.'

I walk down the path, steadfastly facing towards the dig site.

I'm on my own.

* * * * * * *

It takes them a couple of hours to finish clearing away. No one dares come near me. I hear their muted cheeriness as they say goodbye to one another. As they go, Martin walks halfway down the path, halting before he gets to the church. I raise one hand, a dismissal, a farewell.

His boots crunch on the gravel.

They're gone.

It's a beautiful afternoon. Blue skies. Warm sun. Birds twittering in the hedgerow.

The silence soothes me, as does the work. I'm not even frustrated by how slow it is now I'm on my own.

The team has gone down about eighteen inches below ground level, then there are string markers squaring off three different focus areas where they've gone deeper, one by the doorway where stone steps are being revealed, one opposite to chase down the limestone wall that circles the site and the largest in the centre of the plot, painstakingly pursuing the tale of the building's destruction. That's the one for me.

It's a wide area, almost six feet by six feet, and I methodically remove another layer across the whole square. Each time an artefact comes up, it's another thread of connection to her. I start to imagine she's here with me, watching over my shoulder, eager to see what I'm carefully releasing from the soil.

I work mindlessly until the warmth of the day wanes and the chill on my skin brings me back to my surroundings.

I stand to flex my muscles, bending my back to ease out the kinks.

The shadows have lengthened into evening, the shade of the trees stretching towards me. Something catches from the corner of my eye, a movement in amongst the greyness. No, a movement *of* the greyness. Like the shadow of someone moving in the twilight.

My skin prickles, and I become acutely aware that I'm alone. I wish Martin were here.

Maybe it's time to concede for the day. Thoughts of the cosy bar at the Red Lion entice me and my stomach growls.

The car is where I left it yesterday; mercifully, it starts at the first turn of the key. Michael's car. As I push the gearstick into reverse, I notice Michael's flat keys, tucked under the dashboard. Perhaps I can go there instead?

I still want to feel that connection to Christiane. The only thing that can fill the voids of my life.

Chapter Forty

Threfield Percy. August 1326

The rain starts just as they gather outside the Great Hall to see the men off, a soft drizzle that begins as dampness in the air but soon hardens until it soaks into their hoods and cloaks.

A sombre atmosphere hangs over the crowd in the cloudy dawn, the eagerness of those ready to depart conflicting with the anxiety in those who remain.

The men have had time enough to reconcile themselves to their duty and most seem more excited than nervous. Though all knew their being called to a muster was a possibility, it was so many years since it had last happened that only old Edward, the last of that generation, could tell the tale from first-hand knowledge. More than one had sought him out for a quiet discussion in recent days; for many, this will be the furthest they have ever travelled from the manor in which they were born.

Some contemplate only the long walk ahead to the muster site; some think beyond that to the prospect of battle. Who knows what faces them? The king has been expecting an invasion for weeks, gathering men on the east and south coasts and putting the watch towers on alert for signs of ships. Will they even have to fight? Perhaps his forces will be sufficient to rout the queen's army then and there? Though it is said that mercenaries from all over Europe have been enticed to join the queen by funds from France and Hainault.

None even knows on which side he will be fighting. Percy has yet to declare his allegiance, though Lady Alice and Ralf both assume he and the other northern lords will follow the Earl of Leicester's lead, and he is sure to take the queen's turn against the man who executed his brother, Lancaster. Perhaps Percy will wait to see who else will flock to her banner against the king and the hated Hugh Despenser before aligning his cause to hers? All they know is that the tension pervades all of England, even their remote part, with little else talked of in the marketplace in Malton.

Christiane is glad of Richard's reassuring presence at her shoulder, standing in the shelter of the Hall door. Together, they watch the families cluster in small groups to share their farewells, some wives openly weeping their fear, some trying to smother it for the sake of giving strength to their men and reassurance to their children.

The men are well equipped, at least: Robert the blacksmith has fired his forge day and night, pushing his apprentices for long hours to hammer out as many weapons as they have materials to make. Ralf's sword has been sharpened and each man carries at least a new knife at his belt.

And now, Robert Smith too stands with the men ready to depart. Christiane pleaded with Ralf to leave him behind, but there was little chance of her winning that argument. Instead, she prays for their fast return; the apprentices who remain are adequate to simple tasks like shoeing the horses, but she questions their competence should they need to mend a broken plough, and that season lies not many weeks hence.

At least they have largely completed the harvest and what little work remains is manageable if the rest of them pull together.

And they did them proud with last night's feast. Who could blame them that it became even more rowdy than usual? There are some sore heads this morning, especially among those departing.

The sombreness morphs into a strange solemnity as Ralf mounts his horse and settles himself in the saddle, a signal that mutes the chatter of the gathering.

The priest steps forward as the men form paired lines behind Ralf's horse and the families fall away to the edges. David FitzAlan takes the rear of the line, walking like the rest of the men and leading his horse by the reins since it pulls the pack ponies behind. It has been his own choice go; he was not called to do so by his father.

Father Peter raises his voice as he makes the sign of the cross over Ralf and the men, but the wind whips away the sound of his blessing and some shuffle their feet, impatient now to get moving. They will join up with troops from other nearby manors on the York road, all setting out at dawn, and expect to encounter long-standing friends and kin.

Ralf turns in his saddle to take one last look at Christiane. It is as much of a farewell as can pass between them, both finding themselves stilted and awkward with one another this morning.

He has been true to his word: Lady Alice departed, with much resistance and displeasure on her part, as soon as Father Peter finished the mass for Geoffrey's soul. And he came to Christiane's chamber the same night to claim her.

She knew he would come; she didn't doubt his intent for one moment. But his hesitation surprised her. He stood awkwardly by the door, taking in the scene with Christiane plaiting her hair and Edith putting linens away in the chest, as if he needed her permission to go through with what he promised. Or perhaps to redeem himself in her eyes? She saw the uncertainty in him, and herself ordered her maid to leave them together, reinforcing the command with a reassuring nod in response to her questioning frown.

'I know how to please a woman,' he told her as he drew her towards him, seeming to want to make up for his earlier brutality.

She had blocked out the thought that she was breaking God's law in allowing this to happen before their wedding, reminding herself that this man would be her husband, the father of the children she knew it was her duty to have.

He didn't sleep in her bed that night, nor any night thereafter. Edith would wait nearby and creep back into the chamber shortly after he departed, a fierce protectiveness surrounding her as she met her mistress's gaze.

That he didn't sleep in Geoffrey's chamber either spoke eloquently to Christiane, even more than seeing how the knowledge of his sin was weighing down his mind, seemingly worsening day by day. Only the prospect of soon departing seemed to alleviate the darkness that he carried with him, distracting him to some degree.

If he had hoped to bury his guilt with the body of his father, he had not succeeded. And it wasn't for want of appropriate show and ceremony, though that was driven principally by Amicia's desire for due respect to be shown to her as the grieving widow.

What a figure of fear Amicia had made at the funeral mass, clad in heavy black to protect her skin and eyes from the sunlight. And the sun had shone brilliantly that day: God's own tribute to a flawed but well-meaning man. Everyone sweated in the close air of the church, and yet Amicia still refused to uncover; it was telling that, in her fear, she evoked a similar response in others, rather than pity or even ridicule. This was sure to add grist to the mill of the supernatural tales the villagers told one another about her.

And everyone was there to see. Simon Reeve had ensured a full attendance, employing cajoling and threats in equal measure. The church was so crammed with every man from the village, whether they wanted to be there or no, that many of the women and the children were pushed out to congregate in the churchyard, almost out of earshot of the priest's low-voiced venerations.

The contrast could not have been greater with their wedding ceremony, as if Amicia wished as few people to witness that as possible. At least her beloved friend was there, though only at the priest's insistence; for once, Father Peter had stood up against Amicia's opposition. He resented being forced to permit this untimely union, but he would ensure no one could later challenge him on its legitimacy. And who but Lady Alice could have witnessed for Christiane?

Up to now, she had given little thought to what her wedding day would be, but even so it was far from what she might have imagined. Without family and with so little attention or ceremony, it could almost have passed for an ordinary day in the manor.

Bless them, at least Edith and some of the household women had made her a bridal bouquet, with roses and rosemary from the garden and greenery from the hedgerows. And Edith dressed flowers in her hair, chattering away brightly as if this were the happiest day of Christiane's life, hiding in pretence the truth they both refused to speak.

News of the sudden wedding was received with a predictably mixed response across the manor. The more practically minded understood why they should wed before Ralf departed for war, and some hoped it might be a love match that made the couple too eager for each other to wait. Of course, most expressed surprise that it should come so soon after Geoffrey's death, and with that came the inevitable speculation that this haste was born out of necessity. Christiane kept her counsel and met their curious looks with outward calmness.

But as she walked – alone – from the Great Hall towards the church, she felt their eyes upon her, stopping in their work to watch her pass. She fixed her gaze ahead, uncomfortable in their scrutiny.

Hold your head up high, my child. She heard her father's voice as clearly as if he walked by her side.

She held the flowers tightly, a talisman of caring, as she approached the small group at the church door: Amicia and Ralf, Lady Alice and Father Peter. Even Richard was not there, ordered by Amicia to stay away; she had seen him earlier heading for the fields, grim-faced.

Lady Alice had given her a small smile of encouragement, but she felt the older woman's wariness alongside her own. Lady Alice had wanted a chance to speak her mind before the wedding, but Ralf had been careful to prevent that, and part of Christiane was grateful: for all that Lady Alice had advocated for the wedding before, she was concerned by the rush, but Christiane's own mind was set and talking would not change that.

That strange detachment had settled in again as she took her place beside Ralf, facing the priest at the church door. She heard him pose the formal question to Ralf, heard Ralf repeat the words that claimed her as his lawful wife. Saw Father Peter turn his eyes to hers and recognised the earnest caring in his expression as he softly asked if she wished to have Ralf as her lawful husband. At her affirmation, he joined her hand with Ralf's and held them together in both his as they spoke the words of acceptance to one another and pledged their faith.

All from a distance. All from outside herself, looking in on the scene without emotion, without a feeling of connection. Then they passed through the church door to hear the wedding mass.

The air inside the nave smelled of sun-heated stone and lead, of warm wood and incense. As she listened distantly to the gentle rhythms of the priest's Latin, she thought about the maternal tenderness of the women who had given her the flowers in her hair and hand, and the paternal protectiveness she received first from Geoffrey and now from Richard. She thought about Geoffrey, his body close by beneath the stone floor and, catching an echo of his love, knew the joy he would have known as she became a part of his family.

She thought about his tenderness for his wife, the pity and care he had always shown to this troubled woman, even though she never wanted him as a husband.

And the responsibility and regret he carried, but never expressed, about his son. This man who now stood at her side as her husband. A flawed and marred man, the sum of his parents' weaknesses, yet desperately trying to break the shackles of how they had shaped him.

She realised how she had been caught up in that too, felt the weight of hate she had been suppressing for days, a leaden anger holding her down.

Closing her eyes, she let the priest's words wash over her and prayed to find forgiveness for him. Prayed with a fervour she had rarely known before.

Until, suddenly, a breath filled her chest and a wave of relief rose up within her. It was like she had been holding her breath ever since Geoffrey died.

And in the next moment, she had to bow her head to hide her smile. Because, in that gentle quietness, that rush of relief, she felt *him* return.

For days, she had been trying to ignore the absence of him. Hollow days and restless nights that had dragged by as she kept herself busy with the harvest and the preparations, focusing on the men who would leave and the families they leave behind. Anything not to face the emptiness at the centre of her world, the void at the very heart of her that grew with each day that passed without him. Anything not to face the fear that she might have driven him away with her anger, that she might have broken whatever this thing was that bound them together.

But now, here he was.

And a sense of all-encompassing love enfolded her, as present and yet intangible as a soft scent floating on a summer breeze. A love that settled deep within her, filling her from the inside with reassurance and knowing and strength.

And now, looking across the crowd at her husband, she knows how much she is in need of that strength. To cope with the way Ralf looks at her with longing but no caring and returned to fondling the kitchen girls barely a day after their wedding. To tolerate Amicia's vengeful harshness towards her, resentful that her son has taken Christiane's side against her, resorting to giving her painful nips and pinches at the slightest misdemeanour. To remain hopeful when the priest informs her that Amicia is refusing to admit their marriage to the family and church records, warning that Amicia will take any opportunity to drive Christiane out if she sees Ralf might make a better marriage.

And to stay steady of heart when Ralf forces her to move into Geoffrey's room on their wedding night. It is an act of brutal ownership, taking command of the space and of her, trying to stamp out the last memories of his father. She closes her eyes and mind against that and determines to find a way to make the space her own after he has gone.

She gives a nod of farewell to Ralf, and he turns away, shouting a command that starts the lines of men moving away from the Hall, Richard and the villagers following on behind.

She watches them go and withdraws her mind towards *him*, seeking that inward reassurance.

Change is happening all about them. The departure of their men is shifting the life of the village. Looking at the groups trailing tearfully after them, what she sees is those who are left: the women and children, the weaker men, the old and infirm. A protectiveness towards them all settles within her, seeing their uncertainty as their men disappear down the path, not knowing when they will return or even if they will come back at all.

She walks back into the Hall, briefly emptied of people, and her mind dwells on their future.

Change is coming for her too. Because Ralf has also made good on another promise, though she has not told him; that is her small, petty act of defiance. Everyone would say it is too soon to be sure, she justifies. But she knows it as surely as anything she has ever known. She is carrying his child.

Chapter Forty-one

York. 17th September 1976

The sun has set by the time I park the car opposite the flat.

It's surreal picking up the post from his pigeon-hole by the door. The letters have become an unfinished conversation: someone's written to him who will now never receive a response.

There are noises from the flat above, some heavy-footed person walking across creaking floorboards. In the darkness, it's reassuring to know I'm not alone.

Now I'm here, I climb the poorly lit stairs with some reluctance, anticipating the cold and empty flat, devoid of his warming presence. At the same time, something is drawing me there.

Inside, I turn on every light to chase the shadows into the corners. Clattering around the kitchen helps too: setting the kettle to boil; opening and closing cupboards to find tea, crockery, cutlery. I drop the fish and chips I picked up on the way back onto a plate, still wrapped in grease-stained newspaper, heavily salted and with the acid smell of vinegar making me salivate.

I carry my makeshift dinner – supper and a cuppa, as Mum would say – over to his desk. It's abnormally tidy after my previous organising of his material and I regret having invaded his space; I wish it could go back to being the unholy mess that would let me pretend he's still alive.

I think about him sitting here, eating his meals, alone, like this. Thinking about Christiane. Going over and over the papers, looking for some sign of her, hoping for some inspiration about where to turn next. To an historian like him, there must have been nothing worse than the absence of her in the records.

Leafing through Michael's post as I eat, I pull out the one with a Cardiff postmark. A covering letter from Professor Alwyn Ross at University College says he's enclosed records of prisoners held at Cardiff Castle and from Hugh Despenser's papers, marking what happened to each member of the Bren family after Llewelyn's execution.

I hardly notice the food I'm eating as I open the photocopied documents he's sent. It takes a while to tune my eyes into the elaborate, cramped writing. Most of it is in Latin, still the clerical language of the court at this point, but as I get used to the script, letters resolve into names.

There she is. Christiane Bren. Named at the end of a long list of other Brens: Gruffydd, Ieuan, Henry, Meurig, William, Roger. Her brothers.

It's a shock to see her name in ink. My name.

I go back to Alwyn's letter. He says he recalls a reference that he's still trying to locate that Lleucu Bren lived out her life in the earl of Hereford's castle in Brecon, dying in 1349.

1349. A year that resonates down history. The height of the Black Death in England: the greatest plague mankind has ever seen.

Does Christiane survive to see that?

What must that be like, living in fear of a disease that's sweeping its way across the country, with no understanding of what's causing it, how to treat it or how to avoid it?

It's an event I have scant knowledge about, but now there's a strong urge to know more. There's bound to be a book about it on Michael's shelves.

I mindlessly finish off the chips as I methodically work along the bookcases, though method is pointless here: if there's logic to the order, it eludes me, being neither chronological nor thematic. It raises a wry smile that I'm still not able to fathom Michael's untidy mind.

Eventually finding two books, I take up Michael's favourite position in his armchair by the fireplace. I wonder if it will make me feel closer to him, sitting here in his room, in his chair, reading his books.

But I can't settle. I get up to take my dirty plate back to the kitchen. Then again to turn off all the lights except the standard lamp he used as a reading light, hoping to create a cosier atmosphere. And a third time to ignite the gas fire, because suddenly I feel a chill in the room.

I stare absently at the blue-yellow flames as they lick at the firebricks until they glow a heated orange, drinking my tea, the books unopened on my knee.

Slowly, the tension in my muscles eases and the weight of food in my stomach works its soporific magic, slowing down my thoughts, releasing my concentration.

I'm tired. Emotionally drained.

I must have dozed – maybe for no more than a few moments – but I jolt awake as the books fall to the floor.

And instantly know the atmosphere in the room has changed.

Though the fire is on full-blast, it's icy cold. And there's a strange buzzing in my ears…no, in the room. Maybe the fire's faulty? Frowning, I lean forward to twist the knob off until the gas stops.

But the buzzing continues.

And then I nearly jump out of my skin when the telephone rings.

Chapter Forty-two

York. 17th September 1976

'I thought you might be there.'

Sam. 'Where are you?'

'London.'

'Why?'

'I couldn't stay. The undertaker came to the hospital this morning. After that, I spoke to the funeral director, told the Master and Dad's department head. And then I got in the car and just drove.'

I can hear the pain in her voice, though she's holding it together. Like she always does.

'Sam, I'm so…'

'Don't,' she interrupts. 'There's no point being sorry. You made your choice. That was yours to make. And you chose not to be there.' Her tone isn't blaming or criticising, but it is harsh.

I don't know what to say.

'I was calling to let you know the funeral is on Thursday at eleven at Holy Trinity church.'

'I'll be there.' There's a weighty silence between us at the hollowness of that promise. 'Is there anything I can do?' Internally, I wince at the trite words, but I feel at a loss to know what to say to her. We've never struggled to communicate before but there are barriers between us that didn't exist before. Hurt. Regret. Disappointment.

Her delayed response seems to suggest she's actually considering my offer. 'I need to start clearing the flat. The university will want it back soon.' She doesn't say it, but I guess she's wondering whether she wants to do it herself or would sooner I did it for her.

Even now, my instinctive response is that I don't want it to interfere with the dig. God, I'm a shit. 'I'm sure they'll give you time.'

'Perhaps.' For which read: that tells me you don't want to do it.

Guilt overcomes my reluctance. 'But if you want me to start on it, just say.' Too little, too late.

'Don't worry. I'll take care of it.' Dismissive.

'Can I take the papers relating to the dig?' Can I sink any lower in my selfishness?

'Take whatever you want.' She sounds defeated.

Silence stretches out; both of us are struggling to find something to say. And yet – the slight glimmer of hope makes my heart beat a little harder – neither of us wants to end the conversation. Is it just because we're the last link to Michael for one another…or something more?

'How's it going at the site?' She reaches for the one subject she knows I will talk about.

'Montague sent everyone home the second he heard the news.' I don't even attempt to keep the blame out of my voice.

'So, the dig's over? I'm relieved.'

My hackles go up. 'Why?'

'Because you're as obsessed as Dad was.'

'I'm not giving up, Sam.' Stubborn determination in my voice. She knows that side of me so well.

'I wish you would. What are you carrying on for? It's too late to give Dad any answers.' And it's because I know her so well that I pick up on that break in her voice.

'It's not about him now. It's about me.'

'So, you're still digging?'

'Yes.'

'Just you?'

'Yes.' Almost pugnacious now.

'Want to tell me about it?'

Does she want to know? Or does she want to prolong the conversation? Maybe she just needs to be talking to someone right now. Maybe she's too drained to talk but doesn't want to let go. At least she's talking to me. Not to a friend. Or her ex-husband. I so hate the thought she married someone else.

'Eoghan?'

'I'm here.'

'Lost in your head as usual.'

'Hmm.'

'Want to tell me about the dig?'

Where do I even start? So much has happened.

'She got married. To Ralf. The son of the lord of the manor.'

'Who? The Woman?'

'Christiane.' I feel irrationally irritated that she doesn't use her name. 'Married him even though he raped her and murdered his father. And now she's pregnant with his child. And he's taken all their strongest men off to fight for the queen's army against Edward II and Hugh Despenser, who, of course, had her father executed. But she's amazing, a natural leader we'd say these days. Even though she's so young by our standards, only nineteen. Though that's not so young for their day. I mean, boys became men at twelve and by thirty you were middle aged. The Black Prince led his first battle at sixteen. Of course, she learnt by example from her parents and brothers. But I think it's also innate in her. Coupled with how much she cares about the people on the manor. How much she finds ways to make each of their lives better. And she's more excited than daunted by the prospect of running the manor while Ralf's away. Even if she has to manage her way around her mother-in-law. I wonder what you'd make of Amicia's illness. She reminds me of your great-aunt. What did she have?'

'Aunt Lily?' She pauses, struggling for the answer. 'A form of lupus, I think.'

'That's it. But maybe other issues as well. The sensitivity to light. The lack of vitamin D from not going out in the sun.' My mind snaps back to Christiane. 'And I think – I don't know how – but I think she senses when I'm there. When I'm watching what's happening in her life. There was a moment at the village when it was like my time and hers crossed over. And this incredible energetic connection…'

I stop. I'd never expected all of that to spill out of me.

Prolonged silence.

'And you can tell all of that from some shards of pottery?'

It's hard to read her tone. Trying to be light-hearted, but there's something else underlying it.

'Meaning?'

'I thought you were going to tell me how far down you've dug or what's come out of the soil. But it's all about her.' Is that resentment? 'Is this just you extrapolating? Like you usually do?'

How can I possibly explain to her what's been happening when I don't understand it myself?

'It's like that dream I had in Cambridge. It comes in dreams. Or when my mind drifts as I'm working at the site.' I'm downplaying it. And, somehow, she can tell.

'How's your head?' Always the doctor.

'Right as rain.' Too quick to throw that off.

'No headaches? Memory loss? Black-outs?'

'I'm fine.' Keep her away. Don't let her see. I regret saying so much. This is between me and Christiane.

Keep her out of it.

Where did that come from? I receive the words as clear as day. I don't hear them: they're in mind, but they're not coming from me. My skin prickles uncomfortably.

'Sam, I've got to go. I'll call you tomorrow.'

'Eoghan, wait…'

I cut the call abruptly without waiting to hear her response and stare around the room.

But whatever was here, it's gone.

Saturday

Chapter Forty-three

Threfield Percy. May 1327

The unexpected arrival of a messenger brings blessed relief from the endless court session.

How can one small manor have so many squabbles to settle? It gets worse with every month that passes, dragging the hearings out longer and longer each time. Richard and Simon Reeve do their best to mediate the disagreements and mete out the prescribed punishments, but it is wearing them all down.

Of course, Amicia isn't helping. Three times she has increased the fines for transgressions over the last nine months, and it is causing a deep-seated discontent. Everyone knows she is taking advantage before Ralf comes into his inheritance; she took one third as her dower after Geoffrey's death anyway yet is still determined to extract every last farthing she might.

But she is a symptom, not the cause: the truth is, Ralf's decision to take the men to war is having unexpected effects on their lives.

They weren't away that long. Most were home by Advent, full of tales of traipsing across the English countryside with Percy's army, though they never engaged directly in battle.

They met up with the queen's army at Gloucester and were at Bristol for the week-long siege that brought down Hugh Despenser the Elder, the father of the king's favourite.

As they chased the fleeing king and Hugh the younger towards Wales, they were welcomed like heroes into towns and cities wherever the queen and her son led them. They laid waste to Despenser manors and, to hear them talk, took strange delight in the act, seemingly careless that they were devastating the lives of people to whom Despenser was as remote a lord as Percy was to them.

But it was the death of this hated lord that most preoccupied them. Some had seen men executed before, but nothing like this. Christiane's skin crawled to hear them talk with such relish about what they had witnessed; emotions warred within her, glad to know retribution had come but tainted by remembering how it felt to be on the other side of that act.

They came back different. Thrilled with their experience beyond this narrow world, elated to have survived. And less compliant.

Violence and disagreements erupted in the village, little things at first, just drunken arguments, but soon escalating.

It worsened when Ralf returned at Christmas, bringing monies that had been shared out from Despenser's treasury for those who met the call to arms. That sudden unlooked-for good fortune divided with resentment and jealousy those who had gone from those who had stayed, turning neighbour against neighbour.

Thank Heaven they didn't know Amicia had taken half the money for herself before they even knew about it.

Yet still she wanted more.

The Great Hall is full, and the smell of bodies is heavy on this late spring evening. The sun set soon after the session started and though the night air is now cool outside, the heat of the many candles causes every man's face to glisten and redden.

Simon Reeve presides. He loves these moments of undisguised power, sitting at the centre of the dais with Father Peter at his side to record the proceedings. He is Amicia's voice in the room, giving licence to Amicia's greed and his own craving for status. Richard stands by, trying to rein in the heavier penalties, but Simon is happy to take his mistress' lead, further motivated by some of that money coming his way. That brief period of financial abundance is quickly turning into real hardship for the tenants and Christiane is powerless to prevent it.

Simon announces the latest increase in fines at the start of the meeting and resentment ripples across the crowd of men and women standing in the body of the Hall. Some shuffle uncertainly, reconsidering whether to bring their cases forward tonight.

But it doesn't stop them. James Crow accusing Clement Hering of moving the stone markers to grab land from their strip in the third field. Anne Wragge alleging Hilary Ketel allowed their pig to stray into their toft and trample the spring cabbages underfoot. Reginald Ketel charging Anne Wragge with having slandered his wife, though everyone knows her to be the most vicious gossip among them. Henry Child demanding repayment of a loan that Gilbert Wragge has failed to make good. Robert de Windt drawing a knife to threaten Letitia Fraunceys in her ale house, alleging she has watered down his beer.

It grieves her to see such bitterness among them.

She tries to adjust her weight in the chair. It is awkward to breathe tonight with the babe sitting up high and pressing towards her chest. Her back aches incessantly, her skin is sensitive to the touch and her hips feel so loose and out of place that she hardly knows her own body anymore. She longs for a good night's sleep, but no number of cushions and bolsters bring her comfort and turning over in bed is such a feat that she lays overly long on one side until her joints ache even worse.

She doesn't have to be here – Richard and Simon are more than capable of handling the court – but Amicia's abuses weigh heavily on her conscience and Ralf's prolonged absences make her want to be present for her people all the more.

That is about to worsen: a curt missive from Ralf yesterday informed her another muster has been called to defend the border lands. Percy's negotiations with the Scots are going badly, with Robert Bruce continuing to demand the independence Queen Isabella promised him in return for staying neutral in her war against the old king.

This time, more of their men are eager to enrol, enticed by the hope of further rewards. It makes her wary, knowing some of them are ill-prepared, particularly against the experienced Scots. And they are hearing talk from York of the army's Hainaulter mercenaries being attacked by the local men; only when the new young king rode through the streets could they quell the violence. It seems all of England is a tinder box, waiting to spark into fights.

She feels it in her own manor whenever a stranger steps into their midst. The walls and gates are supposed to make Amicia feel safer, but they foster only suspicion and superstition and fear among their people, creating a divide between them and the world on the other side of those barriers. Only now they are also starting to turn against each other; the notion constricts like a knot in her stomach.

I am weary of all this battling, she meditates, resting her hand on her round belly. What kind of world are you coming into, my child?

Suddenly, the heavy outside door slams open, banging hard against the wall behind and making everyone turn towards the interruption. A wave of antipathy makes the messenger halt, looking uncertainly around until he spies her and threads his way through the crowd towards the dais.

'My lady,' bowing before her. 'You are the lady Christiane, I hope? Daughter of Llywelyn Bren?'

A Welsh voice! Her heart leaps into her throat. How long since she last heard that soft lilting accent, the gentle tones of her childhood? The warm love of home floods through her.

'I am, sir,' she affirms, hardly able to speak.

'My lord Gruffydd sends greetings, my lady,' drawing a letter from the leather pouch strapped across his chest, 'and bade me deliver this into your hands alone.'

'Gruffydd! My brother? After all this time, how?' Stunned, she receives the parchment from him in disbelief. But as she does, she becomes aware of the stillness of everyone in the Hall, their eyes turned towards her, and feels the hostility that is being directed towards herself now as well as towards the messenger. Because the messenger has addressed her in Welsh and she, unthinking, has responded the same.

In that moment she becomes an outsider to them again. She looks around and sees the distance in their eyes. Never mind how many years she has lived among them, how much she has helped each and every one of them at times, she has marked her separateness from them, and their suspicion of her difference reasserts itself.

Looking slowly around the Hall, she meets theirs gazes, wanting to reassure and reconnect. Nothing.

'Follow me,' she instructs the messenger in English, turning towards the solar. At her nod, Richard steps forward to nudge the reeve to restart proceedings.

She closes the door behind them with relief.

'Where did my brother send you from, herald?'

'Senghennydd, my lady.'

Home. The yearning for her childhood hearth rises powerfully within her.

'How is my lord brother?'

'He fares well, my lady. And sends his blessings to you.'

'Are any of my other brothers with him?'

'I know not…' His voice trails away and she grasps that the boy is struggling to form his words, his body almost dropping with weariness.

'You have travelled far this day?' she surmises.

'Since first light, my lady.' And he looks like it, the dust of the road covering his leggings and shoes.

Frustration makes her frown. She wants so much to talk with one who has, not so many days ago, been in Gruffydd's presence, but her well-drilled courtesy overrides her selfish desires. 'Edith,' beckoning her maid over. 'Will you take Master…'

'William, my lady.'

'Master William to the kitchen and make sure they feed him well? And have Master Prudhomme ensure he has a bed for the night. A fresh mattress and good blankets.'

'Thank you, my lady.'

She smiles, a warmth in her heart she has not felt in so long. 'I thank you, Master William. You have brought much unexpected joy to me today.' She presses a coin into his hand. 'God bless you for that.' She glances at the parchment in her hand, eager to know the news. 'Now, go. But see me before you depart in the morning. I may have questions for you.'

She settles in Geoffrey's chair by the hearth and unfurls the paper.

Chapter Forty-four

Threfield Percy. May 1327

The Lord's blessings and joy be with you, much beloved sister.
I am overjoyed to have found you at last. We have long sought to know what became of you after they sent you away from Cardiff, none more so than our revered mother, yet we had naught but hearsay to go on until these last weeks when we uncovered records from Glamorgan's chamberlain about your departure.

There is so much to say that I am sure you would wish to know, more than I can convey in this one letter. Rest assured; we are all well. Our dearest mother conveys her deepest love and well wishes to you. She lives in hope of seeing you again someday and I pray the Lord will make this happen. She resides in my household for now and is a great support to my beloved wife, Aelwen, and dotes on our son, Llewellyn, and two daughters. Indeed, you will rejoice to know you have eleven nephews and nieces, between myself and our brothers, and they would be most glad to meet their aunt.

For myself, the greatest news I can convey is that, thanks to our just and merciful Queen Mother Isabella, I was restored to our father's lands this Christmas past. I can call myself Lord of Senghennydd and Meisgyn at last. You alone will know what deep and abiding joy that brings me, for even as a child you understood my love for this land and people better even than our brothers.

Knowing not what you experienced at the death of our brave father, yet I am sure you will be glad that the demise of the devil responsible for this injustice was in no small part due to the efforts of two of your own brothers. This November last, my lord the earl of Chester, in whose service Ieuan and I have been for many years, sent us to aid the earl of Lancaster in his search for the king and the traitor Despenser as they fled through our homelands. The king thought his popularity in Wales would draw allies to him, but our hatred for his treacherous friend was stronger than that love, not only for the murder of our father but also for his many abuses across Glamorgan since then. Perhaps even the Almighty Lord deserted him in the end, for we found him and the king stumbling around our darkened hills in the middle of a terrific storm, with barely a dozen men in their company.

Should I tell you about Despenser's execution, my beloved and most gentle sister? I hesitate to do so, knowing your soul is too pure for such words. And, yet, I am compelled to write, even if you will not read it.

I watched him closely in every moment of his execution. I witnessed his suffering and knew it to be at least the equal in pain and distress of what he inflicted. They tied him to a hurdle and four horses dragged him through the streets to Hereford Castle while the people blew trumpets and banged drums until we were all quite deafened by the noise and threw at him anything they might lay their hands on. New gallows were erected, some fifty feet high, so that all who came might see, and the crowds were mighty that day. When they stripped him naked, I could see the words and Bible verses that had been cut into his skin. They threw a noose around his neck and hauled him up to those gallows, and his eyes bulged and his face turned dark red as he struggled for breath. I could see the relief in him as they loosened the rope and he gasped for air, life fighting within him even as he knew worse was to come. They lowered him onto a ladder and strapped him on so that he might not struggle or fall to a quick death. The executioner climbed that ladder, and at each step, each time he weighed down another rung, the fear increased in the coward's face until he was crying openly and begging to God and the Queen Mother for mercy. But there can be no mercy for such a devil, and there was justice in his punishment, for it was the same he meted out to our father. I watched the executioner's knife hack away at his body just as he had ordered us to watch our father's suffering, you and I and our brothers and mother. He screamed in agony when his male parts were cut off and his belly was sliced open, and his intestines were ripped out. The executioner was very skilled in his work for I swear it was only when he cut that black heart out that the light went out of his staring eyes.

God forgive me, but my heart swelled with vengeance at the sight, little sister, and still does at the memory. I have carried such hatred for so long that it is hard to let go. But I pray now that I may find some peace, and you, too.

Mayhap I have said too much. If so, I ask your indulgence and forgiveness, beloved one, and turn my mind to thoughts of better days.

I hear tell you are wed to Ralf Goscelin, who serves in my lord Percy's retinue. Lord Percy is a good man who is much loved of both our new king and my lord Lancaster, and he sits on our king's council so is certain to continue to benefit from the Queen Mother's gratitude. I liked him well enough when we encountered one another in the queen's army, so I have good hopes that you will thrive in his care.

Would that I had such good things to report of your husband. He has some repute as a fighter but also as a hot head, which makes him more of a blunt sword than Percy would wish. I sought him out in Gloucester last month after hearing of your marriage, but he seemed little interested in acknowledging our kinship. If you have any sway with him, keep in Percy's good graces. He is a just lord but, like many, has a strong sense of his own standing and can become heated when he is disrespected. It seems Goscelin's decision to marry without first seeking Percy's permission rankles with him.

I understand your husband comes into his majority shortly. It is for this reason that I hesitated a few weeks before writing, for I was awaiting news that I know will be important to you.

Although our beloved father had not finalised a dowry for you, I know he would have wanted to be assured of your lifelong comfort and ease, and I take that responsibility on myself now. With the aid of our dear mother, we have secured a small property adjoining our own land, which now I give to you as your dower lands. It is not a large income but should bring you some £6 or £7 a year, I trust, and if you will it, I shall run the manor on your behalf alongside my own and send the monies to you each Michaelmas. I convey this knowledge only to you, my beloved sister, and trust you will know how you wish to proceed.

I can hardly number the years since last we saw you. For a long time, the world was not a kind place for those who bore the name of Bren, but our Lord God is smiling on us now, little one. In my mind's eye, I see you as the beautiful and capable woman I knew you could become even as you ran rings around us as a child, adored by all, always there whenever we turned around, eager for Father's every word and attention. I remember you surrounded by our dogs, who were never as joyful as when they could sit with you, that little red-haired scrap of a thing, fierce and determined and passionate, and yet also thoughtful and considered and kind.

May the Lord's abundant blessings be with you always, my beloved sister, and I trust that I may hear from you soon.

In God's just name, I am your loving brother, Gruffydd.

Chapter Forty-five

Threfield Percy. May 1327

For long moments after she finishes reading, she sits unmoving.

It is overwhelming to know her family are safe. All of them. Her dear mother, such a reassuring presence in her youth; she remembers the feeling of incredible stillness at the heart of Lleucu, underpinned by her unshakeable faith and trust in God. Her adored brothers: how she had been in such awe of Gruffydd and Ieuan, the mingled tenderness and irritation she felt for the teasing younger ones. She even finds herself missing the dogs, her constant companions when the brothers were too busy training to fight to pay any heed to her. She smiles, wishfully: might Gruffydd send her a pup from the next litter?

The thought of seeing them again is an immediate aching temptation. Might that even be possible? For sure, she can't leave the manor while Ralf is absent, but might he stay while she travels to see them? It seems unlikely: he has not shown her much consideration in the months of their marriage thus far. Indeed, she has hardly seen him for more than a few weeks altogether in that time.

The contrast between the deep love and security she remembers in Wales and the life she is living here is acute. She feels more kinship with the family she has not seen in almost ten years than anything there is for her here.

Will that change with the birth of this child? she wonders, resting her hand on the roundness of her belly. Will it ground her in a new way? After all, this will be their birthplace and she will belong to them. Can it fill this longing she now has for her own kin?

Blood is truly thicker than water, she appreciates. And on the eve of this momentous change in her life, Gruffydd is offering her freedom such as she has never known. *'I convey this knowledge only to you, my beloved sister, and trust you will know how you wish to proceed.'* She knows what that means: he will not inform Ralf about the dowry. It is his duty – and hers – to do so, for it is Ralf's by right to control and will only revert to her on his death.

But that means ceding control to Amicia as well as to him. Might she not do more good with this money by keeping it to help the villagers, rather than see it squandered on ever more luxurious indulgences for Amicia's comfort and pleasure?

She rises, energised by the thought, crosses to open the window and looks out onto blossom-laden trees in the moonlit orchard.

Can she enlist Lady Alice's complicity? Then the money might be channelled via her or held for whenever she has need of it, perhaps to help the villagers in leaner years when the harvests are poor or the animals fail to thrive.

And what of those improvements she has contemplated that could enrich them all? Enhancing the mill and developing a fishpond where the low-lying land floods each winter. She could take up Hughes' suggestion to bring Flemish weavers across to train the women in preparing cloth instead of exporting their raw fleeces to the lowlands. New, heavier ploughs could be produced if the blacksmith might be incentivised to take on sufficient help. And there is that stray thought she had one day about breeding horses, had they only the capital to get started.

Dreams. Untouchable dreams…until now.

Her conscience stirs. Is she being unjust to Ralf? He isn't to blame for his mother's selfishness. And yet he saw her brother weeks ago but has told her nothing. What would it have taken to get that news to her? Even as a single line in the letter instructing her to muster the men. Clearly, he cares nothing for her concerns.

She is a convenience to him, nothing else. He hardly has to think about the manor while he is away, free to pursue the dreams that drive him, of battle and status, increasingly engaged in the life and politics of the court now that Percy too is so entwined in the Queen Mother's and new king's affairs. He has not changed his mind in never wanting her with him. She tells herself she cares little that he leaves her here, that life means more to her left alone to run the manor. But Gruffydd's letter has reawakened memories of the closeness and tenderness she witnessed between her parents and her heart aches a little. Is such caring and tenderness not to be her joy too?

A hard kick, high in her stomach, jolts her out of her thoughts, winding her for a moment. *I am your joy.* The words flutter in her head with a warmth that is like teasing laughter. She bows her head, smoothing her hands over the bump. *You are my joy, my love and my life,* she thinks as the overwhelming emotions coalesce into a boundaryless love for this child, a love that fills her entire being.

And she becomes aware of the love emanating from another presence, close by her. He feels so present she could almost touch him, though she knows none of her human senses can perceive him. The emptiness that held her heart a moment before has vanished, driven away by a pervasive sense of wholeness, of belonging, of giving and receiving in the same moment, a circle of love, eternal and entire. A slow smile takes hold of her, inside and out, as her heart expands.

Then something snaps and the world pivots on its axis as pain rips through her and she staggers forward. A shout shoots from within her, at once an expression of sharp agony and a panicked appeal for help.

In that moment, there is no world beyond her pain. Only the all-consuming sensations that engulf her body and overtake her mind for endless, timeless moments.

As they ebb, she gradually becomes aware of the room around her again, but even that seems more distant. It is as if a veil hangs between her and what she knew before. Dimly, she perceives people gathering around her: Edith supporting her into the bedchamber, Richard briefly appearing at the solar door as they pass, taking in the situation and then moving as fast as his awkward limbs allow in the direction of the kitchens.

She sits on the edge of the bed as Edith strips her down to her shift, breathing hard.

Before long, Joan and Agnes appear, laden with sheets and cloths. The manor's most experienced midwives, they take charge of preparing the room, closing the shutters and lighting a fire in the hearth, then assume their practised positions, one on either side of Christiane. Edith cedes her place to them respectfully but a little reluctantly, remaining close by. Soon, a kitchen girl appears with the first of innumerable jugs of hot water.

And they settle in to wait.

When the priest arrives to take her confession, she looks over the precipice at the realisation that she might die this day; it grips her coldly, until another contraction seizes her, then the women push him out of the way even as he gives his benediction. The world shrinks down to this one room and everything beyond is disconnected and unreal. Each time the door opens, noise from the continuing court session filters through, hushed at first in respect for what is happening a room away, but soon disorderly again and increasingly raucous. When the door closes, she is enclosed again with this small huddle of women who mutter quietly among themselves as if speaking louder would disturb her.

She smells the herbs they use, rosemary and wild thyme, feels the slickness of the oils they rub into her skin, the hands that prod at her, feeling around her belly, testing the child's position. And, later, probe, personal and invading.

Cold cloths wipe coolness onto her face, while her hair and chemise stick to her clammy body. Hands on her shoulders and arms hold her as the contractions almost double her up in pain.

She moves between the waves of pain – and she can feel them coming, engulfing her then all-too-slowly ebbing, just like great storm waves that crash themselves against the rocks and slide off again into deep, dark waters – and periods of relief, of returning to herself. Though even those ever-shortening moments are characterised by the constant ache of her overstretched and distorted body, her limbs shaking uncontrollably at times.

The long patience of the women soothes her somewhat, moving quietly around the room, holding her as a contraction galvanises her body, resting in between until the next arises.

The noises outside the room disappear as everyone else settles down for the night, then grow again as the new day starts. She can't believe how this was dragging on and on. And the longer it takes, the more fear creeps in at the edges of her mind. Is this normal? Is something wrong? What is the look exchanged between the two midwives? What are they not saying? Is there something wrong with the baby? Or with her? What if they have to cut him out? Will she have to give her life to let him have his? So many babies die. Women too. Why not her? Please God, not him.

And somewhere in that isolated, enclosed and timeless room, the barriers of status and position that normally stand between these women disappear. Barely clothed and physically exposed, she is stripped of everything that makes her stand apart as lady of the manor. She has never been so aware of her own physicality, so focused on what her body is doing. It opens her in a most primal way, uniting them through what she and these women have in common, displacing what separates them.

Until the contractions are coming so frequently that the pain becomes her only reality. It surrounds her, consuming and containing her, until even the women cloistered with her and supporting her crouched position become distant and disconnected.

Everything beyond herself disappears as all her attention is forced into one limitless place, one timeless moment. And in that place, only two things remain real for her: the child within her…and *him*. Both separate and yet linked, an overlapping and intertwining of connection. Both present to her and, somehow, within her.

It is to them that she clings as her exhausted body cries out that it can do no more. It is they who call her forward as she begs to let go. They who hold her in a mindless stillness of connection until, at last, it is done.

As she collapses back on the bed, Agnes holds the babe while Joan clears his airways and wipes him clean, then lays him on fresh cloths and tightly swaddles them around him.

'Almost there, my lady,' she encourages. 'Just the afterbirth and then you're done. We're not finished…!' she protests angrily as the door is flung open, then stops short as Amicia pushes into the room.

'Over there!' Amicia orders the man who is carrying a chair for her, impatiently waiting for him to get out of her way. 'Bring me the child!' she demands as soon as she sits down.

Joan looks to Christiane for guidance, but she is too distracted as further contractions – easier now but still demanding – overtake her body.

As the midwives clear away the afterbirth and bloodied clothes, and clean and dress her, Christiane's eyes warily watch her mother-in-law cradling her son. It is a shock seeing Amicia here in her own bedchamber; it makes her look at the older woman with fresh eyes and what she sees scares her.

Perhaps she has become too used to Amicia's strange ways, has come to make too many exceptions for her.

What she sees now is an aged and twisted woman, old beyond her middle years, her skin as thin as parchment and yellow-tinged like tallow, so wasted that the bones of her hands stand out like crow's talons, an impression enhanced by the heavy black mantle wrapped around her fragile frame.

Such illness would elicit pity were it not also accompanied by such an unsettling expression on her face: there is something not far from madness in her eyes. And the way she is looking at the child terrifies Christiane. It should have been adoring; instead, it is greedily possessive.

Was she like this with Ralf?

Amicia feels herself watched and raises her gaze. 'I name him Henry, for Lord Percy and his father, my dear cousin.'

'My lady, his name must be agreed with my husband!'

'His name is Henry,' she persists, unperturbed. 'And we shall write immediately to Percy for him to become godfather to the child.'

'My lady Mother,' she dissents diplomatically, 'that is a great responsibility, and my Lord Percy may not be in a position to take it on. And the child,' her voice trembles with her own maternal possessiveness, 'needs to be baptised within a day.'

'The boy is a Percy!' Amicia insists. 'Percy knows it and will come!'

'It may take many days to reach Lord Percy,' panic rising, 'and many more for him to ride here. They are preparing to fight the Scots.'

'A Percy knows his obligations!'

'Please, my lady,' Christiane implores with fear equal to Amicia's blind stubbornness. 'You would not put your grandson's immortal soul at such risk!'

At that, Amicia's thin arms tighten around the child, clutching him to her breast. She is so small that the new-born looks strangely large next to her. And the sulkiness on her face is that of a petulant child.

'Edith,' Christiane instructs, retaking control, 'have Father Peter come so we may make arrangements for the baptism tomorrow. Then send messengers to Lady Alice at Molseby and the prior at Kirkham Priory to attend as godparents and tell Master Prudhomme he shall also stand as godfather.'

Amicia's jaw tightens at that: she hates the thought of a servant as godfather, but the choice of prior and prioress appeases her. Christiane prays they will come.

The last of her might is spent and exhaustion floods through her. All she wants is to be alone with her son.

The midwives sense it, and Joan comes forward to retake the child from Amicia. 'Our lady needs to rest,' she hints.

For a moment, Amicia's jaw juts in opposition but she allows the child to be taken from her without a word.

Christiane sinks back on the pillows and hardly perceives the other women departing as Joan eases the child into her arms. He snuffles quietly, his eyes contentedly closed. She touches a fingertip to the skin of his cheek and feels the oneness of them both.

The door closes and stillness settles in.

Alone, she can feel it again: that wholeness, that completeness of self, that connection.

Swept up in it, she knows it has been there all this while; it is only that she lost awareness of it when her attention was elsewhere. Now, undistracted, she turns back…and finds it still there.

He is still there.

Eoghan.

She hears his name in her head, a knowing that appears in her mind.

That knowing connects them beyond this time, beyond this place. It exists beyond this physical realm and cannot be bound by the natural constraints of this world.

Infinite and eternal.

Two souls; one stream. Focused into two minds and hearts, stretched across different times, yet forever one.

She knows all this with an unquestioning clarity as she cradles the child in her arms.

And as she raises her head, drawing the babe close, his presence increases in the room. More than the feeling of him. More than the emotion of him.

He is no longer a vague presence, he is present.

More than that: he is becoming visible.

She holds her breath.

He is standing at the foot of the bed, looking down on them. Tall, lean, strong. Fair-haired. Strangely clothed.

There is such tenderness in him that she can feel it in the room, deeper and stronger, more intense than anything she has known.

A smile touches his lips.

Then he raises his eyes to her face.

And she looks straight at him.

Chapter Forty-six

Threfield Percy. 17th September 1976

She looks straight at me.

Shock shoots through me.

I stagger back in disbelief and in the next instant I'm falling, toppling backwards. I land heavily on hard soil, bang my hip and smack my left wrist on a stone.

What the…? Where the hell am I?

This is the upper dig site. The solar.

But the last thing I remember is sitting in Michael's chair.

I struggle to my feet, cradling my bruised wrist, and try to piece my memories back together.

I slept in the chair in Michael's flat. Fitfully. Disturbed by bad dreams.

As soon as it was light enough, I came to the site.

But I was digging down at the tower. How did I get up here?

I'm standing in the solar, in what would have been Christiane's bedchamber, about where the foot of her bed was.

That connection ripples over me again.

She looked right at me.

She saw me.

She knew me.

I can see it all in my mind: the limewashed walls of the room and the tapestries she's hung for warmth; the shutters on the windows for her lying-in; the fire in the hearth and candles in sconces on the walls. I can smell the fattiness of the cheap tallow – only Amicia and the church get the good quality candles – and the oils they rubbed into her skin to help the process along. And underneath that, an earthy bloodiness; I never realised childbirth had a smell.

Edith combed and re-plaited her mistress's hair when she cleaned and dressed her afterwards; I don't think Christiane even noticed, between her exhaustion and only having eyes for the child.

Henry.

With a fluff of red hair and deep blue eyes.

He's in the records.

And Amicia. Now it's not goosebumps: my skin crawls with wariness. Christiane thought she was just on this side of madness but I'm not so sure; there's something very disturbed – and very disturbing – about that woman. Something very wrong, as if reality had fractured for her long ago. I could see it in her eyes when she looked at the boy. I'm not sure she even knows the boy isn't her son but her grandson.

Though who am I to talk about reality?

I don't even remember this latest episode starting.

And then, something moves.

Off to my right.

My heart leaps into my mouth.

There's nothing there. And yet there is.

It's happening again.

Her world is merging with mine, like a translucent image overlaid on my time.

The walls of the bedchamber. But I can see through them to the orchard beyond. And where my day is grey and overcast, hers is blue-skied and bright. Where the ground in my world is stripped back to bare earth, hers is lush green grass. The air is warmer. Blossom falls from the trees like confetti, dislodged by a gentle breeze that carries its sweet scent.

And she's here.

Her beautiful hair is covered by a wimple, as would be expected, but it's escaping around her face as she plays with two children.

They run around her, hiding from one another behind her skirts, and she tickles and teases them until they scream with giggles.

With their thick red hair, there's no doubting they're both hers. Henry. And Dafydd. Amicia anglicises it as David, but he's Dafydd to her.

And as she turns, laughing, she sees me and stops. The boys keep playing, chasing each other in between the trees, oblivious to her stillness, Dafydd toddling along behind his more agile older brother.

I love her.

You're here. I can hear her words in my head, though she doesn't say anything. *You look just the same.*

I smile at that because it's been moments for me but years for her.

Stay, she asks. *It's been so long.*

And she looks at me as if she would carve every detail of me into her memory. And I her.

She's heavily pregnant again. Ralf must be damn fertile because he's managed to get her pregnant on each of the rare occasions when he's been home.

I'm jealous. I hope she can't read my mind.

And realise with a shock that she doesn't. I know it because I know her every thought.

Can she hear me?

'Christiane.' I feel foolish saying her name out loud.

She smiles, seeing me speak, but shakes her head, with a vaguely helpless gesture of her hands.

She glances over her shoulder to check she's not seen.

And walks slowly towards me.

I hold my breath.

She stops a foot away and looks up at me.

Her skin is flushed, and the pupils of her eyes are so large I can almost not see the dark-ringed clear green that makes them so arresting. Her breath comes shallowly and fast. Like mine.

She lifts a hand, as if she would touch my face.

And then she's gone.

Something's wrong.

I feel sick in the pit of my stomach as the knowing drops in.

The blossom is still on the trees, but the day has darkened. Nightfall. Rain in the air. Clouds moving fast across the rising moon. Cool winds.

I turn back towards her bedchamber and see Christiane sitting on the end of the bed, crouched, waiting for the next contraction. The midwives are back. Agnes again, but the other is Mary; Joan died of the dropsy this last winter.

The child has stopped moving. She knows it. She's at full term, but she hasn't felt movement for days. Not since she saw me in the garden.

She looks up as I move to stand in front of her.

Is that why you're here? Her eyes show me her fear and confusion. *Why do bad things happen when you're here?*

That rips my heart open.

That she could think things go wrong because I'm here.

She's wrong: she calls me to her when she needs me.

The baby hasn't turned.

It's her third birth. Quicker than the first or second. But the breech birth makes it so hard, and her screams sicken me.

As Agnes coaxes one leg out, she rapidly recites the words of baptism so that the dead babe is shriven and can be buried in sacred ground.

Feeling around for the other foot, Agnes grasps both ankles in one hand and tugs as Christiane – despairing, silent tears flowing down her face – pushes the tiny, still form from her body.

They treat the babe as tenderly as any born alive. Clean and wrap her, even as they clean and reclothe her mother. Moving quietly, respectfully around the room.

She cradles the child to her. And lifts her eyes to mine.

Christiane's pain is so raw it almost brings me to my knees.

I mirror her despair. A black torment that is at once her pain and mine at not being able to help her.

She closes her eyes and shuts me out.

As I lose connection with her, the room disappears. So does the upper dig site, as if I'd never actually been there.

And I find myself back at the tower site.

Alone.

Darkness all around me.

And rivers of rain running down my face like her tears.

Chapter Forty-seven

Threfield Percy. 17th September 1976

'Sam, can you talk?'

'Hello, Eoghan. Nice to hear from you. I'm fine, thank you for asking. And how are you?' Sarcasm. Understandable.

'Sorry. How are you?'

'Shit, thanks.'

'Want to talk about it?'

'What is there to say?'

'I don't know. But don't people say it helps to talk about it?'

'People, yes. You, no. Besides, you're the one who needs to do the talking, right?'

I am. And I do. I tell her everything. About losing time, losing control. About thinking I'd come round at the upper dig site then actually coming round at the tower site. About the birth and the stillborn child.

'So, what do you think?'

'Honestly, there are so many thoughts going round my head right now that I hardly know where to start.' I hear the resistance in her voice.

'Am I going mad, Doctor?' A feeble attempt at levity, but I'm only half-joking.

'Yes.'

'Tell me what you really think!'

'Do you want my medical diagnosis or my view as a…friend?'

That split-second hesitation is laden with meaning.

'Either. Both.'

'As a doctor, I'd send you straight to hospital. Hallucinations and dreams and lapses in consciousness? All of that could be associated with your head injury. And didn't this all start after that?'

'Maybe.' Her describing them as hallucinations puts my back up.

'But you don't want to hear that, do you?'

Christ, she knows me well. Too well.

'They're not hallucinations.'

'Then what are they?'

'If I knew, I'd tell you!'

'At least tell me why you think they're not hallucinations?'

I have to think about that one.

'Because it's not coming from inside me.'

'How do you know?'

'What do you mean?'

'Well, it's all perception, isn't it? It's all being interpreted inside your brain, so how do you know if it's coming from outside of you or from inside your mind?'

'Are you trying to confuse me even more?'

'I'm just trying to understand.'

'All I know is that this is as real to me as anything in "real life". That, somehow, I'm tapping into her life. That I'm watching her live it. Feeling her emotions. Thinking her thoughts.'

'Like watching an old movie being re-played.'

'Yes. But more than that. Because I'm becoming part of the movie. Like she opens a door that lets me into her world. And however that connection happens, it's changing…increasing. Because now she can see me, even if she can't hear me.'

'All of which is impossible.'

'I know.' I pause. Try another tack. 'So, what do you think…as a friend?'

This is where it gets messy. And my pulse speeds a little.

'I'd say that you've just lost one of the most important people in your life and that you're trying to keep him alive by pursuing the one thing that kept him alive. Or trying to finish the one thing he couldn't.'

'Now you sound like a shrink.'

'That'll be Paul's influence.'

'Your husband?'

'*Ex*-husband.'

'I didn't realise he was a psychiatrist.'

'Psychotherapist.'

'Potato, potato.'

'Don't let him hear you say that.'

'I can't imagine I'm going to meet him any time soon, am I?'

'Hopefully never.'

'But,' coming back to the topic, 'either way, you think I'm imagining this?' I know I should let it go, that I should ask how she's doing instead. But I can't.

She pauses. Sighs. 'It is all just perspective, isn't it?'

'As in?'

'That it really doesn't matter where this is coming from. What matters is that it's real to you. But I wish you'd stop.'

'You know I can't.'

'You can, Eoghan. Just walk away. Go back to Cambridge. Or come to London. Come and see me.'

Does she know how tempting that thought is? But if I walked away from Christiane it would feel like betraying her. And how could I live the rest of my life not knowing? Not knowing what happens to her.

'Please, Eoghan. You're scaring me. It's like watching Dad all over again. But worse.'

'How is it worse?'

She doesn't answer. Because of how she feels about me. *Say it*, my mind urges her. *Say it*!

'I need to go.'

'Sam…'

'I'll call you tomorrow.'

And she's gone.

* * * * * * *

I drop the receiver back on the cradle.

Catching a glimpse of myself in the mirror over the fireplace, I stare myself down. *What are you doing, man?*

I'm completely lost. And completely hooked.

There's nothing I can use to explain this. It makes no sense on any level. I know that. I'm not stupid: I know how this must sound to Sam.

But I'm not doubting myself. Not really. This is real. I know it is. As real as Sam or me. It's as genuine an experience as anything I've known.

I know she's scared for me. Scared that maybe there's something really wrong with me.

And scared, I think, that I feel so much for Christiane. Not that she's any kind of rival.

God, what an awful thing to say. I know I'm in love with Sam. More now than I ever was before. It's like everything that was wonderful about her before has been amplified tenfold. And I know that without even needing to spend much time with her, like we recognise each other on another level.

And I love Christiane.

But it's a different love. I feel whole when I think about her, as if we're parts of the same. It's like loving myself. Not that I do particularly right now. Or, at least, I don't much like aspects of myself. But I can't not love her. And giving up on Christiane would be like giving up on myself.

I can't believe how badly I'm behaving. I look at myself from a distance and see what I should be doing or saying. But I can also see why I'm not. It's not a question of condemning or condoning. It just is.

I'm on a path. That's how this feels. That I'm on a path and I'm here for a reason, though Heaven knows what that might be.

What if... What if I'm here to change something?

Now that's a brain fuck, right there.

If I change the past, what effect does that have on the future? Or have I already done this in the past and it's just that it's happening in my present, so the future is the same?

What I do know is that I'm here because of her. Unequivocally, I'm here because she's calling me in. I'm not in control of when I step into her world. Truth is, I'm not in control, full stop.

I just hope Sam's still there when all this is over.

How much more selfish can I get?

Chapter Forty-eight

Threfield Percy. April 1333

The day is turning into the warmest of the year so far. As Amicia drowses, lulled by the book she has been reading to her, Christiane has an impulse to open the window, only to see Ralf striding down the path.

It is with mixed emotions that she watches her husband's arrival. He has given no warning to expect him, and her mind immediately goes to the practical implications: what food and wine are available, whether fresh bed linen is to hand. Then there is the disruption that inevitably accompanies his visits, which always have a purpose whether he wants money or men; he never comes back just to see his children or his mother or her.

But she can admit to herself, there is also excitement in the pit of her stomach. In part for the rare novelty of someone from the outside world being in their midst. In part because he is an attractive man, strong and well-built, and her body responds to him. Whether he is here for a few hours or some days, she knows he will want to lie with her.

'Your son arrives, my lady,' gently waking Amicia, then taking the stairs to unlock the door for him.

The appreciation in his eyes as he approaches makes her heart jump.

'You look well, my lady,' he greets her on the threshold. 'If I didn't know better, I'd think you were breeding again.'

'Since you haven't seen fit to return home since last year's harvest, that's hardly likely, is it, husband?' she retorted, tartly, and the meaningful glance he gives her flat stomach earns him a withering one in return; he laughs.

'Have you missed me, wife?' surprised to find himself in a teasing mood with her. He runs the back of his fingers over her cheek as he brings his face close to hers.

'Your mother misses you more!' comes the demanding cry from above, and he rolls his eyes, then follows Christiane upstairs.

'God's blessings to you, my lady Mother,' as he bends over her outstretched – and, he notes, heavily bejewelled – hand. 'My lord Percy sends his greetings and well wishes.'

The heated flush in Amicia's cheek and her nervous agitation bespeak her flattered self-importance at being remembered by her kin, as well as her joy at seeing her son again.

'How fares my dear cousin?' she preens. 'I hear the king continues to show him much favour.'

'For all the good it does me,' Ralf grumbles, his face clouding with resentment as he slumps into the chair opposite Amicia. His moods can be as changeable as hers. 'He still refuses to knight me. It's years since I came of age, and he even favours younger men over me!'

'How can he excuse such a slight to you and to me, his own blood family?' indignant on her son's behalf. 'You've proven yourself to him so many times. He knows you're the best swordsman in his retinue.'

They fall quickly into the old patterns of conversation, picking up right where they left off the last time he was here.

'I'm a strong leader too,' he justifies. 'Ask any of the men here who've fought with me.' He looks to Christiane for approbation. 'I can stir the weakest of them to unfaltering courage, and I organise them efficiently to ensure the strong help the weaker ones.' She smiles reassuringly as she hands him a goblet of wine and places Amicia's tray of treats before them both.

'I shall write to my cousin,' Amicia decides. 'I shall demand to know why he so abuses my kinship and ignores your abilities.'

'Nay!' Ralf immediately disputes. 'Do not put yourself out,' quickly backtracking. 'I'm sure I can find a way myself.'

''Tis no trouble for my only son!' She so rarely has a reason to stir herself that she is energised by the thought. 'You are a Percy, and I shall remind him of his obligations to his family.'

'Please, my lady Mother,' he pushes harder. 'Let it be.'

Christiane intervenes, sensing his discomfort. 'How long will you be with us on this visit, my lord?' she distracts them both.

'I am but passing through: I must leave for Newcastle in two days.'

'So soon?' Amicia pouts, child-like in her sulkiness.

'There's a war to be fought, my lady,' his eyes gleam at the thought, negligent of her disappointment.

'Not Scotland again?' she complains.

'Indeed. The king should have pressed his advantage when we routed them last summer. With his puppet Balliol crowned King of the Scots, Scotland was the king's to reclaim as his own, to bury once and for all that insulting treaty the Queen Mother made him sign at Northampton. Now Douglas and Dunbar have driven Balliol away, and the king is having to fight again. I shall join Percy at Newcastle. I'm here to enlist the men, so I can know how many to prepare for, then David FitzAlan can bring them to me in a fortnight. From there, we march to Berwick at the end of the month.'

'Are the Scots threatening to raid southwards again?' Amicia's voice rises anxiously. Christiane, seated on the stool nearby, places her hand on the older woman's, knowing the concern within her.

'It's unlikely at this time,' Ralf opines, less aware of her concern.

'But it could happen?' she presses. 'They've come so close before.'

'Though not in a long time,' Christiane soothes her.

'Do you forget how terrified Lady Alice was when they raided her priory?' Amicia turns on her, vehemently. 'If those barbarians will attack a house of God filled with defenceless women, what respect would they show for a sick and enfeebled noblewoman?'

'That was many years ago,' Christiane rebuts. 'And none of the women was harmed.'

'Maybe not physically,' Amicia bickers, 'but Lady Alice has never been the same since. And they all but destroyed her home and emptied their coffers and cellars.'

'You overstate it,' she tries to reason. 'And Lady Alice recovered entirely.'

'I feel so vulnerable. We can't even trust our own tenants. How many times have I told you we shouldn't let them go to so many of the markets?' throwing the criticism at Christiane resentfully. 'You have no idea how they talk about me when they're away. They gossip about all manner of things with people who have no loyalty to me! About my jewels and treasures. No doubt speculating about how easy it would be to rob me. I live in terror for days after they've been allowed out. Who knows what thoughts of invasion they encourage with their careless chatter. Or what threats or diseases they might bring back with them? No one understands!' she asserts to Ralf. 'No one cares how much I live in terror!'

'Hush, my lady,' Christiane softens. 'You are safe here. The walls and gate would deter all but the most determined, and I would confidently challenge any to get through that oak door.' Looking to Ralf to back her up, she finds him frowning in bewilderment. 'Husband,' she prompted, 'don't you agree?'

'For certain, it would take a bombardment worthy of the king's own army to break that door down!' he jokes, feebly.

'You think so?' Amicia breathes, her hand pressed against her chest to still the heart flutterings within.

'Mother,' he leans across to take her other hand. 'You are perfectly safe.'

'You should check the defences while you're here,' gripping his hand surprisingly hard. 'The walls always need repairing. Take the steward with you; you can instruct him on what needs to be done. Mayhap the fences should be higher? And that idiot Walter, he's fool enough to let just about anyone through the gate.'

'Walter may not be physically strong, my lady, but his mind is sharper than most,' Christiane is moved to dispute, feeling the injustice of her prejudice. 'And he takes his responsibilities very seriously. None more so.'

'I need to feel safe,' she appeals to Ralf. 'I don't expect *her* to understand, she cares nothing for me.'

'My lady, I'm sure that's not true!' Ralf disagrees.

Amicia backs down gracelessly, sinking in her chair. 'I'm tired,' she deflects, and the weariness is heavy in her voice. 'Let me rest awhile.'

Christiane and Ralf glance at one another, then rise to depart.

Amicia snatches at his hand again as he moves past her to leave. 'Come to see me again later. Just you. I trust you,' she asserts, desperately. 'Only you have my best interests at heart, my son. None but you.' She clings to his hand with both hers. 'Promise you shall come back soon. Promise me!'

'I shall, Mother,' he pledges. 'Let me do what I must around the manor while you rest, and then I shall return anon.'

'That is good,' distantly as she leans back. 'All is good when you are here.' She closes her eyes in dismissal.

Ralf raises his eyebrows in silent communion with Christiane, then follows her outside. She locks the heavy door behind them and hands him the key. 'For when you return later.' He stows it in a leather pouch at his waist.

'Is she often like that?' he broaches, walking with her along the lower path.

'That's the worst I've seen her in a while,' she compares. 'It must be the excitement of seeing you unexpectedly. She was agitated for many days after you departed last time.'

'I had no idea she was becoming so irrational.'

'I'm not sure she can help it,' she shrugs. 'She sees so little of other people that it distorts her view of the world. Maybe I don't help; I'm as complicit as others in letting her have her own way for the sake of a quiet life. And I pity her existence.'

'She shouldn't speak to you that way. In respect for my wife, if nothing else.'

Christiane can't help but smile to herself: how can he not see he is as bad as she in demanding due respect for status?

'What is it that makes her so afraid?' she questions. 'Sometimes she mutters about a curse, but I can't make sense of what she says.'

'I don't know all the details. Only that some woman threatened her with a vision of her death. It was when I was very young.'

Christiane lets it go.

'I should show you the changes we've made since you were here last,' she suggests.

'If you must,' he concedes grudgingly.

'It is your responsibility to know,' she chides gently.

'You know how little I care,' he returns. 'But if it would please you to show me, it would please me to please you.'

She smiles uncertainly at him. 'Have you been practising your gallantry, my lord?' she teases.

'Apparently I must, if I am to earn my knighthood, so Percy says.' He frowns his displeasure.

As they pass the newly dug fishpond, she talks him through the work underway.

'The upgrade to the mill is slower than I would wish, but my lady will not allow me to bring workmen in to progress faster. We have only Thomas de Welles to show us what needs to be done and we must rely on the labour of our own people otherwise.'

'What experience does he bring?'

'He built the mill on my brother's manor,' she admits, a little warily.

He absorbs the information without comment. 'I fear I shall make it worse for you by taking our strongest men away with me,' he almost apologises.

'We shall manage,' she assures him. 'As we always do.'

As they walk up the hill, they pause each time they encounter a tenant and Christiane brokers an update, navigating between the tenant's respectful diffidence and Ralf's sparse knowledge of who they are or what matters to them.

Near the summit, a woman is coming the opposite way, holding the hand of her little daughter to stop her stumbling on the rough stones. As they pass, she glances at Ralf as he stares at the young girl, and he, embarrassed, looks away, only to catch Christiane watching him. She nods to the woman, who bobs her head in response, understanding passing between them.

Christiane breaks the awkward silence. 'The child is well cared for. I do what I can to ensure they have enough for a good life.'

He meets her gaze with surprise.

'You know…?' he starts.

'Joan was born a bare seven months after Anne married Hugh. It doesn't take much to put two and two together.'

'And you knew it was mine?' She looks at him in that clear, direct way she has, and he feels guilty, not for betraying her but for underestimating her. 'You didn't have to do that,' he defends.

'I wouldn't have her disadvantaged for the nature of her conception. It was good of Hugh to take Anne on, suspecting she was already carrying another man's child. Goodness deserves its own reward. I have proposed that he takes on the running of the new mill when it's finished, to give the family more income.'

'Do people know?'

'If they suspect, they know better than to speak of it to me,' she smiles wryly.

'Where are our sons?' he asks, feeling a sudden impulse to see them.

'In all likelihood, they'll be with Richard, tending to the horses.'

'Richard?' He quirks an eyebrow at her familiarity.

'Master Prudhomme,' she corrects herself. 'I'll take you to them.'

Laughter and joyful shouting come from the stables as they approach, and it pleases her to see a smile overtake Ralf's face.

Leading him towards the open doors, she stops short as a small form comes hurtling towards them, fleeing from the chase.

'Henry!' she cries in warning, and he looks up just in time to see them, checks his path then, in an instant of recognition, throws himself bodily into his father's arms. 'Papa! Papa!' he cries with pleasure, then screams with delight as Ralf sweeps him off his feet into a bear-like hug.

'How you've grown!' Ralf exclaims, holding him tight to his chest. 'You're becoming quite the man,' he teases.

Henry wriggles to be put down. 'Look, Papa!' he demands. 'See how tall I am. I must be big enough to go with you soon. Then you'll have to take me with you, won't you?' he demands, every inch his father's son.

Ralf runs his hand over the boy's head with a mixture of pride and indulgent amusement. 'Soon, Henry,' he promises. 'Very soon.'

'Welcome home, my lord,' Richard comes forward, with Dafydd hesitantly hanging onto the tail of his surcoat.

'Master Prudhomme,' Ralf acknowledges his bow. 'Do you not know me, David?' amused by his younger son's wariness.

'Dafydd,' Christiane crouches to persuade him, using her soft Welsh version of his name. 'Come, greet your Papa.'

The four-year-old lurches into her arms and she scoops him up, bringing him close to Ralf.

'Say "hello, Papa",' she instructs.

'Hello, Papa,' he mimics.

'He takes after you as much as the other does after me,' Ralf remarks, strangely disconcerted by how the boy's clear green eyes hold his steadily; he is the first to look away. 'I hear you are making good progress with your horse breeding venture?' he addresses Richard Prudhomme.

'We are, my lord.' Christiane hears Richard's quiet pride. 'Our first three-year-olds will be ready this summer.'

'Where will you sell them?'

'Hughes is handling that for us,' Christiane responds, putting the boy down, though he clings to her hand. 'If we can't get a good price in York or London, we'll go to the European markets.'

'Before you do, send me warning that they're ready. We are always in need of strong horses for the army and Lord Percy may want to take them.'

'Only if he will pay a fair price, my lord. I would not have him take advantage of your kinship to our detriment.'

Ralf laughs. 'You strike a hard bargain, my lady,' and his eyes challenge her. 'Besides, if selling them at home will save you the cost and danger of shipping them, might there not be a fair middle ground? Then I get to keep Lord Percy on my side into the bargain.'

'You make a fair negotiator yourself, my lord,' she parries. And his gaze holds hers for a long moment.

'How many horses have we?' he turns to Richard.

'Twenty-two. Six could be ready for sale this year, two destriers, four coursers. The destriers were born later so if we keep them for at least another season, we can ask perhaps as much as £10. The coursers could command £3 or £4 each; we'll keep two mares for breeding and sell the others.'

'And thereafter?'

'There are seven from the next season, and all the adult mares are currently in foal.'

'Show me the destriers,' Ralf commands.

As Richard leads the way through the stables, the two boys run ahead to the flattened and fenced area beyond the yard where young lads are exercising the large, heavy warhorses. Richard calls them over and Ralf carefully inspects each animal.

'They're fine beasts. Percy would give his eye teeth to get his hands on them,' he appraises. 'You stable them at night, I presume?'

Richard nods. 'They're too valuable to leave in the fields.'

'Why destriers? That must have been a hefty initial investment.'

'That was my lady's choice.' Richard does not disguise his admiration.

'It didn't take much to see that the need for warhorses was increasing,' Christiane explains.

Ralf looks at her with surprise. 'You knew that when you started this three years ago?'

'How many times have our men been summoned to fight since we were wed, my lord?'

'Three or four, maybe?' he guesses.

'Five times. Twice in the last nine months. You've said it yourself, my lord,' she reminds him. 'Our king takes after his grandfather, the Hammer of the Scots. And if he ever finishes there, where will he turn his attention next?'

'France.'

'France,' she concurs. 'Which will only increase demand further.'

'Can we support the additional grazing requirement?'

'The assarted land gave us more pasture. It wasn't fertile enough for the crops we hoped to grow but it's adequate for grazing and keeping the horses there will change the fertility in time.' She has confounded him and the way he is looking at her – as if through new eyes – is surprisingly satisfying. And the attraction sparks between them. 'Thank you, Master Prudhomme,' she dismisses Richard. 'I'll take my lord to the solar. Have Edith keep an eye on the boys when you're done.'

Ralf follows her through the Great Hall; crossing that takes more time than he wishes, with tenants and servants stopping to greet him all the way. Christiane carefully manages their way through until they finally reach the solar.

As soon as she closes the door behind them, Ralf reaches for her. 'Have I played lord of the manor enough to satisfy you for now?' he breathes, one arm around her waist, the other hand pushing the covering from her hair and lifting her chin so he can bring her mouth close to his. Deliberately, he leans his body into hers until she backs up against the wall, and he pushes harder against her, pleased to feel her respond to him. 'Because I haven't seen my wife in months and I very much desire to take her to bed.'

Chapter Forty-nine

Threfield Percy. March 1333

'Leave that,' he orders. 'Come back to bed.'

She finishes folding the tunic she has retrieved from the floor and places it in the chest.

'Undo your hair,' he instructs as she sits on the edge of the bed, and he watches her unwind the long, heavy plaits and shake the flame-coloured thicknesses loose. 'You have become a beautiful woman,' he remarks, running his hand through the lengths of her hair, then shaping the curve of her breast and waist through the cloth of her shift. 'You were a little too bony for my liking before, but the children have changed you for the better.' He lingers for a moment, looking thoughtfully at her. 'I want to say...'

'What?'

'What you do for my mother. She won't appreciate it, but I want you to know that it doesn't go unnoticed.' She looks at him in surprise. 'I'm not the senseless block you take me for sometimes,' he throws out gruffly.

'It's hard to know each other,' she allows. 'You're away so much.'

'Would you want me here?' he arches an eyebrow. She stays silent. 'It wouldn't matter if you did,' he admits. 'I can't bring myself to be here. This world is far too narrow for me. Even knowing I had to come here now filled me with resentment.' He entwines his fingers with hers, as if to reassure that he isn't talking about her. 'They're little people with little lives, interested only in the weather and the crops and what their neighbour is up to. Obsessed with petty disagreements and imagined slights. I can't stand it.'

'This is how life is for many,' she muses. 'The simple rhythms. The seasons and stages of the year. The heights of the feast days. The joys and heartache of family, of births and deaths.'

'It's not for me,' he reiterates, a little aggressively.

'You are happy in your life?' she probes.

'As long as there's fighting to be done, yes. Thank God there's more promise of that now. Before, there was rather too much of the old king's taste for spectacle and events. Sometimes, barely a month went by without yet another masquerade.'

'You disapprove?' she surmises.

'I love the tournaments, but the king wants all the other frippery that goes with them. There is too much glamour and display at court.'

'I can see why it must seem very dull here by comparison,' she comments wryly.

'That side of things is not for me. I'd sooner be doing garrison duty at one of the border castles than languishing in that tedium. I'm glad it's changing, now the king's determined to control Scotland once more.'

'You're readying for another battle?'

'If he gets his way. We march on Berwick to besiege the castle, hoping it will draw the Scots army into fighting.'

'And that thought excites you?'

'There's nothing like it for me. Not even the pleasure of being with a woman. Though that's a good way to pass the time,' sliding his hand under her shift and pulling her down to kiss her hard. 'You know, you surprised me earlier,' he reveals as he releases her. 'Your insight in breeding the horses...I did not expect that. You're very astute.'

'And yet you wouldn't want me with you at court.' That rankles more than she wants to admit.

'I can't,' he resists. 'Even now it would damage me to be associated with your father's rebellion.' She doubts the truth of that: his actions have long been forgiven and his heirs reinstated. The illegality of the execution was even cited in the accusations against Hugh Despenser, according to Gruffydd. Why should Ralf hold out? His discomfort says he knows it too. 'Percy's sway is ever increasing,' he continues to justify. 'I should be in a good place to benefit, if I give them no cause to counter that.'

'Not being knighted rankles with you,' she presses.

'Less deserving men have already been knighted.'

'Why not you?'

'Because I disdain to indulge in the chivalric charades the king loves so much,' he resents. 'What does he want us to be: warriors or love-sick swains? But,' leaning up on one elbow, 'there may be another way. The king needs more knights in his army, and he's sent out a command: any man with income of £40 a year must become a knight. Can I get close to that number?'

Christiane tallies the numbers in her head. 'Not yet. Soon, maybe. There was £14 from the manor last year, including what we made by processing cloth instead of selling the raw fleeces. Hughes sent two weavers to train the women, but only a handful have taken him up on it so far. I'm hoping more may start when they see the money coming in.'

'How much did I get from my share of Hughes's business?'

'£20, there or thereabouts.'

'That much? It's as well the king looks favourably on merchants,' he judges wryly, 'since it seems I am more merchant than gentleman. My half-brother is doing better than I expected,' he concedes grudgingly.

'He works hard. And we're still benefitting from Geoffrey's foresightedness.' She feels his body tense at mention of his father. 'Especially those agreements he made to buy Percy's fleeces.'

He flops back against the pillows with a frustrated sigh. 'Still not enough,' he sulks. 'Unless,' hopeful of a sudden, 'we sell one of the destriers early.'

'That's poor economy,' she rebuts. 'To sell one today for £5 when we could get double that in a year's time.'

His face clouds at being thwarted, and he stares moodily around the room. 'Of course, it would be better if Percy knighted me himself, then he'd be obliged to give me more lands so I had enough income. But he won't do that.'

'Why so?'

'My lady mother's endless begging letters,' he growls. 'They cause much irritation.'

Christiane reviews. 'Even if we had sufficient income, I'm not sure we could sustain the cost of a knighthood. Your lady mother spends money as fast as any of us can make it.'

'I saw the new windows in the church,' he conveys. 'And the jewels. And the wall paintings in her bedchamber.'

'It's hard to begrudge her,' she sympathises, 'when she has so few joys in her life. Except her greed is hurting the people.'

'How?'

'She taxes them in every way she can. I've tried many times to bring the heriot payments and fines back down to what they were before, but Simon Reeve asserts her authority over mine and everyone is too afraid of her to resist. It's driving some of the younger ones away, to work in the towns or to marry into other manors. We're losing our labour and have to pay to replace it. And those who do remain are resentful; we're seeing no let-up in their belligerence towards one another.'

'What would you have me do?'

'Speak to Amicia. She has to yield to your wishes and the reeve takes his instruction from her.'

'I'll try, but I make no promises. Though I'll take pleasure in warning Simon Reeve: I will not have him disobeying my wife.' He pulls her into his arms, and she curls up against him. 'He might as well be disobeying me.'

They lie in silence for long moments, unexpectedly at ease with one another.

'I like how you've changed this room,' he appraises, taking in the furnishings in the bedchamber.

It is an unintentional drift in his thoughts but, in an instant, it brings both their minds to how it used to be, cluttered with

Geoffrey's trade goods. Ralf shifts and draws her closer, closing his eyes as he turns his face into her neck, seeking comfort.

'Guilt hangs over me,' he confesses, his voice suddenly stark. Christiane waits, sensing his need to talk. 'For long periods of time, I don't think about him. But when I do, it's like looking into the depths of my soul and finding only darkness.' She touches the arm holding her close, wanting to reassure him but not finding the words. 'When we're going into battle, everyone goes to confession the night before. It's better to fight with a clear conscience, with a pure focus on our just cause. But I can't...' his voice becomes rough. 'I can't confess my blackest deed. Only you know. And it gives me a strange ease to know that you do. Why don't you hate me for it? For what I did?'

She sighs and gives him the honesty they both need. 'I did,' she allows. 'But I can't carry that kind of hate, it exhausts me. So, you have my forgiveness, and I hope it helps you. But it's God's forgiveness you really need to submit to, for your soul's sake.'

'The older I get,' he contemplates, 'the more I appreciate how he tried to make our life work here, to make it palatable, especially for my lady mother. He wasn't my kind of man. Too weak to stand up to her, conceding to her on everything. He was no fighter, but that's who I am. It's been within me for as long as I can remember. It's where I feel most at ease with myself, facing down another man on the battlefield. I feel so alive, so confident in my strength and skill. There's a strange fire at the heart of me. Normally, it's damped down, but it flares up and burns red hot when I fight. It takes me beyond myself, and I become capable of feats beyond imagining. The only thing that comes close for me is lying with a woman. And that's too transitory; I lose interest in her as soon as my body's needs are sated.

'It's why I can't be here, surrounded by women and milksop men. Talk of crops and cattle bores me. Money holds no interest for me except for the quality of the armour and the strength of the horse I can buy. And I have to get away from my mother. I don't know how you can stand it; there's no room for anyone else's needs with her. She smothers me.'

He eases away from her until she rolls onto her back and looks into his face.

'I never expected to say any of this to you,' he registers. 'What is it about you?' he wonders, tenderly tracing her face with his fingers. 'You listen without judgement. And you don't need me to pretty it up for you, do you?' She shakes her head. 'I wonder if I could have been happy…here with you.'

'You're right, it's not who you are,' she submits. 'We must all follow our purpose in life. Those who fight, those who pray and those who work.'

'And you? Are you happy here?'

'There is much to keep me busy. It's better when I have little time to think too much on anything.'

'And…Richard?' he teases, half-seriously. 'Should I be jealous?'

'I am loyal, my lord!' she defends archly.

'I don't doubt it,' he reassures, not noticing the blush that warms her cheek. Pulling her into his arms again, he sinks back on the bed, holding her close and finding ease in his mind, even in his father's bed.

* * * * * * *

How odd it is to be intimate with a man who is almost a stranger. At once very personal and yet disconnected.

His body has relaxed into sleep, his breathing deep and steady, but she lies awake, listening to the sounds of people going about their business, the distant shout of children – perhaps their own – enjoying their young and unencumbered lives.

We have shared experiences that bind us, she understands. None more so than what happened in this very room. And a background and upbringing that unites us more than it divides us, however much he might think otherwise. We've both been trained to fulfil our roles, defined by the expectations of those above and below us in the hierarchy. And while we might sometimes strain to stretch those boundaries, there's little chance of breaking beyond them.

Yet being with him like this, it's like stripping off all the public trappings that define us, the clothes, the status symbols, the responsibilities. We're just two people, two bodies, two souls together, tethered to one another, finding meaning in being more fully ourselves for a fleeting moment.

And it's pleasant to be held by him like this, almost with tenderness, with caring and respect, if not with love.

But that's where the extent of it ends. Because it doesn't come close to what it is to be connected with...*him*.

The thought slides into her mind.

She has shut him out for so long. The tremor of worry is still there, that something bad always happens when he is near. But the yearning is strong. Wanting to feel that connection again. Wanting to feel the love that fills her whenever she thinks of him. To feel his love reaching out and enfolding her.

How misleading are the romances Amicia loves to read. Painting portraits of women who are virginal and pure, unattainable icons to be adored, worshipped for who they appear to be on the surface. Not real women, stirred in flesh and blood, desireful and yearning. Not women wanting to find a connection that makes them greater than themselves, wanting to share who they are beneath the surface. Not women filled with a love that gives and gives and gives.

Love isn't passive and saintly, demanding to be worshipped from afar. It's complex and earthy and enriching. It makes me more than I am.

Does that make me disloyal? I would not betray him in my body. I am everything the world asks me to be as a wife: I bear his children, I share his bed whenever he demands, I run his home and his manor, I care for his people. Outwardly, I obey every whim the world wants of me.

But inwardly, those are the bars of my cage and I want to feel free. Hemmed all around by expectations – those I have been taught to have of myself as well as those others have of me – is this my only way to feel that freedom: to choose where I give my love?

I can't hold him away any longer. I'm not fighting him, I'm fighting myself. Nothing is as true or as real as loving him. That connection…it makes me feel like I'm part of something greater than myself.

She can almost feel the resistance dissolving in her mind. And instantly, she is aware of him again. As if he has always been there, waiting for her.

'Eoghan.' She whispers his name to herself. 'Eoghan.'

Chapter Fifty

Threfield Percy. 18th September 1976

'Eoghan.'

I jump, jolted out of a trance.

I heard her. Did I hear it? Or is it in my head? Where is she?

My whole body is buzzing and my teeth judder uncontrollably. Like I'm a lightning rod and something in the atmosphere is channelling straight through me.

After a few seconds, my physical senses start to reassert themselves. The smell of wet soil, the clamminess seeping through the knees of my jeans. Dampness on the skin of my face, plastering my hair to my scalp. A tannic taste in my mouth, like iron. The sound of rooks cawing in the trees, a harsh, ugly interruption.

Then the wider world comes into focus: a mottled grey and cloudy sky, the woods curving away to my right, the marshy area that was once the fishpond ahead of me, the skeleton of the decrepit church to my left.

I'm at the dig site. The tower.

And she called me back in.

I feel elated. Not that I've felt shut out: I've worked all morning without being aware of her absence. To me, it's like she's all around. But I feel the joy within her at letting me in.

I stand up to stretch my stiff legs. How long have I been kneeling there? My tools are nearby. I must have been scraping away the soil when I reconnected with her world, saw her with Ralf. There are a few pieces in the finds tray; I shrug off the fact I can't remember digging them out.

It's so strange to know how she's thinking. Not only because she's from a different time but also because we're such different people.

She's very self-sufficient, like me, but I'm more solitary and she's much more interested in people's lives. She can't help it:

reading their emotions seems to compel her to want to make things better for them. I'd never seen an aura before seeing it through her eyes; she's never seen a person without one. She sees colours, but I think that's just energy she's interpreting as a particular hue. And from that she intuits what's happening to that person. No: what's happening *within* that person, in their thoughts, presumably.

She could see it in Ralf. How his aura changed from heavy grey to muddy brown when he talked about feeling guilt about Geoffrey. She's more merciful than I am; how she could forgive him for rape and murder is beyond me. Although maybe that's still quite raw because, to me, it's recent; to her, it happened years ago.

And there's so much satisfaction in her life that compensates for it. Being lady of the manor, in a position to help improve people's lives. Being a mother: she adores those two boys. The loss of her daughter is a constant presence. Not a heartache in the way I might have thought, except when she thinks about her directly. It's like each soul we interact with touches our lives and leaves their fingerprint on us. Alice – named for the woman who means so much to Christiane – left a permanent impression on her mother.

I wonder how it would change me, being a father.

Did it change Ralf?

If it did, I can't see it. He's almost as self-obsessed as Amicia. Nature or nurture? He has little or no interest in being around his boys. But their attitudes to raising children are so different from ours. Henry will leave home next year to enter Percy's household and start his training as a squire.

I stop abruptly. How do I know that? Is that my assumption or Christiane's expectation? Has there been a conversation at some point in her past that agreed this?

Everything I've known until now has come from accessing what Christiane has experienced up to the point when I'm connecting with her.

But this is knowing – it's not just assuming but really *knowing* – something that's going to happen in the future…in *her* future. How is that possible?

I'm losing sight of where her thoughts end and mine begin.

But there's no point worrying now: I'm in too deep. I have to keep going. I have to find answers. I have to know.

I grab my trowel and hunker down again, turning up my coat collar against the cold.

I fix my mind determinedly on the earth, shutting everything else out. The inane and contradictory chatter of my mind disappears, and I slip into that spaceless, timeless, limitless…beingness.

I'm aware it's happening because I catch myself, twice, when thoughts suddenly surface and catapult me back to my normal level of awareness.

But that stillness of mind is seductive and it draws me back in.

And, from there, something greater surfaces. Something that's there all the time but is hidden beneath the noise of this sensory existence.

Christiane?

Are you here?

Even as the question forms in my mind, I feel her presence. No, not presence. It's more like her…essence, distinguishable to me as her. But it's without the specifics of her human characteristics. In the same way as this mindless…place – for want of a better word – isn't defined by time or space, so too she isn't defined by her finite human traits or features.

On an impulse, I look up and notice a lighter patch of soil a couple of feet away, closer to where the students were digging down along the outer wall. The soil is quite dark all around this area, with remnants of burnt wood and other organic matter – decomposed cloth? – laid over the sandy, limestone substrate.

I shift over, all thoughts of my previous focus fleeing from my mind, and I start scraping away. It's muddy at the surface but quickly becomes drier as I slice off the layers. Something's driving me to get deeper as fast as I can, and my painstaking learning, practice and discipline all disappear as I force the blade almost vertically into the dirt.

I know where I'm working. It's where the bed stands. Stood.

I can see it in my mind. The heavy oak frame. The sumptuous drapery. A mural of a forest hunting scene on the wall behind.

Adrenalin shoots through my body: my heart speeds up, my breath comes high and shallow in my chest and my mind becomes alert and aware on another level, heightening every sense.

The day darkens as the dampness in the air turns from a determined drizzle into proper rain and the ambient temperature drops.

I'm conscious of it but it's irrelevant. The only thing that matters is whatever is under this soil.

The hole is becoming wider, maybe four inches across and at least as deep. I drive the trowel down hard again…and something makes me halt. Not like I've hit something. Like something pulled me back.

Suddenly, all my trained caution resurfaces. Whatever it is, I'm at the right depth. Now it's about carefully working my way around until I can reveal it.

I widen the hole enough to be able to get my hand and the trowel in at a shallower angle, enabling me to meticulously slice away slithers of earth, an eighth of an inch at a time.

I carve out another slice. And another. And another.

And there it is.

I stop.

Almost immediately, rain washes soil into the lowest part of the hole and it disappears again.

I lean across the pit, using my body to shelter it from the rain.

I hesitate to touch it, and nausea rises in my throat even as I use the tip of one finger to wipe the mud away.

I can see it again. Rusty brown from centuries in the soil yet still stark against the dark surrounds.

I know that colour. I've seen it before.
It's bone.

Chapter Fifty-one

Threfield Percy. 18th September 1976

Stupid.

How could I not have thought about that possibility?

Shit.

Now what do I do?

Is it her? That thought rocks me. But every instinct immediately tells me it's not. And yet I know my hand was being guided to uncover this. Why? Who is it?

Suddenly, my impulse is to put some distance between me and the site, and I'm almost propelled to my feet and away. But not far. Only to the shelter of the church, in the lee of the wall against the prevailing direction of the rain.

Think! My mind is moving painfully slowly. I lean both hands against the wall and bow my head, closing my eyes.

I have to inform the coroner.

Shit. Shit. Shit.

I don't want anyone here.

And I don't want to leave. I don't want to have to walk down to the farm or the pub and go through all the rigamarole of finding and then calling the local officials. Or, worse, having to go through Montague. Can you imagine the delight he'd have in rushing back to take control of the site? With a plethora of people in tow.

I don't want anyone here.

Is that my thought? Or coming from somewhere else?

Why can't I tell anymore?

Can I justify going a bit further? Of course. I've hardly uncovered anything. Even if I know – absolutely *know* within me – what I've found, they're not going to come out until I've uncovered more. Until I can show them for certain that I'm dealing with a body.

Better to keep going.

I stare at the sky, hoping the rain is going to abate. Is it my imagination or do I immediately feel it lessen? I'll give it a few minutes to see. Because, by rights, the site should be covered while I'm working around the bones to minimise environmental damage. And I don't have what I need to do that.

Could I create a makeshift shelter using the tarpaulin cover? Perhaps I could find some broken branches among the woodland and drape the tarp over the top?

You're overthinking this. Calm down. Breathe.

What is it about working on a skeleton that gives me a different kind of rush? Maybe it's the complexity because it takes so long to work around each element and it's only by uncovering multiple pieces that you can feel the unity of the whole. Maybe it's an affinity with this being another human, feeling more connected to the past in a specific, individual way.

Or maybe it's because the residual energy is so much more intense. That thought seems to drop into my mind.

Is that what I've been tapping into all this time? Echoes of the past, trapped in the fabric of what I'm uncovering, like an insect trapped in amber?

It makes sense that a person would feel different to me from an object. An object might be imbued with the spirit of the person who made it and even the people who used it. But bones…would they be a more intense coagulation, layer upon layer, of one person over a lifetime with everything they thought and desired and felt?

Who is this, Christiane?

My hands tingle as the question forms in my mind. If she's here with me, she's not answering.

I glance at the sky and see cloud breaks appearing. Time to work.

* * * * * * *

When I stop again several hours later, it's because the light levels have dropped so dramatically that I can barely see.

I squat back on my heels to assess my progress. It's been incredibly satisfying, painstaking work. Working outwards from my original hole, I've been able to establish a clear outline.

Fortuitously, the first bone I hit was a femur. Once I'd worked that out, it told me in which directions to excavate, aided by the fact the body was laid out straight and on its back, not on its side or curled up. I've got from the top of the skull to the phalanges.

But it's not in a grave: there are no signs of anything like a coffin and its certainly not orientated east-west. This body was buried by the collapse of the tower. And it was lying down at the time.

But I know nothing more than that. I don't know if I've shut myself off somehow, but I haven't had a single insight while I've been digging.

Not one. Not a feeling. Not a thought.

And now I've stopped working, I feel completely drained. I can barely force myself to stand.

I just want to go home.

No!

A hot bath. A hot meal. And bed.

Stay.

What a ridiculous thought. There's nowhere *to* stay. They took all the tents with them when they dismantled the site.

Stay.

Maybe I could. Dusk came and went an hour ago. It's not so long until it's light enough to work again. All I need is a couple of hours in the morning to finish the work. And then I'll know…

I could just sleep in the car. For a few hours. There's no harm. No one waiting for me.

Clean the tools, wipe the mud off. Pack them away. Haul the tarp over the site. Drive in the pegs to hold it down.

The moon is waning but there's just enough light.

Darker by the river, shadowed by the hedge. Night distorts everything. Have I gone wrong? No, there's the bridge. And the car.

Sink into the driver's seat.

This is absurd. It's a quarter of an hour to get back. I should eat.

Stay.

I could stop off at the pub. Get a change of clothes and have dinner at the same time. Sit in front of the fire in the snug.

Stay.

Too tired to argue. Can't fight you. Why do you want me here?

Close my eyes for a minute. Head nods forward, jolt awake.

Sam. She said she'd ring. What would I say to her? She won't understand.

I'm on my own.

Sleep.

I'm on my own. But I'm not alone.

Sunday

Chapter Fifty-two

Threfield Percy. 19th September 1976

I doze fitfully and wake cold and stiff, my neck aching with a painful crick. How long have I been asleep? It's still deep night outside. The thin moon barely picks out the outlines of forms, no detail, just layers of blackness.

Awkwardly, I clamber over into the back seat, thinking to stretch out. Of course, I'm too tall but even folded up it's an improvement. Except that I smack my shin as I go and swear loudly.

Now I'm annoyed with myself: why didn't I go home? For that matter, why aren't I just driving away now?

Because I want to be near her. Because I feel so close to her right now. It's not rational but it's compulsive.

I grab my bag to use as a pillow, then remember a picnic rug I saw in the boot. It doesn't cover me but it's better than nothing.

I close my eyes.

Sleep is no distance away.

* * * * * * *

I dream about her, riding in a panic to Kirkham Priory. It's snowing like the day she arrived, so many years ago. Worse, in fact: the snow has been blown in such drifts that it's impossible to open the priory's main gate more than a few inches; it's enough for Christiane to squeeze through, but David has to go to the postern gate with their horses. Her breath freezes in the bitter night air as the hosteller leads her across the courtyard.

Brother Anselm meets her at his infirmary, a warm, firelit haven in the darkness of the winter night.

Lady Alice is here: lying in a narrow cot in a tiny guest room. She looks strangely diminished, the planes of her face more angular – and fragile – without her wimple, her head bound in a blood-stained bandage. She's been unconscious since they brought her in; Anselm says she was thrown when her horse stumbled in deep snow.

Fear and guilt collide in Christiane. She hasn't seen Alice in months and now blames herself for not acting on her many impulses to visit the prioress herself. But the truth is she rarely leaves the manor: Amicia's mistrust has infected her.

She talks to her dear, unresponsive friend, updating her on all the news of the manor, just to have something to say: the second wolfhound pup her brother has sent: an Ajax to go with her Achilles, he said; Ralf's continuing hopes for war with France and his frustration that the king can't enlist sufficient men; David FitzAlan's unspoken reluctance at the prospect of having to leave again, and how she sees him struggle to live up to the martial role expected of him; the parallels with her own sons, Henry the fighter, Dafydd the scholar.

And about her realisation that Ralf has fathered another child in the village; it means the lack of further pregnancies is down to her, not him.

When she runs out of things to say, the long night settles into a waiting vigil. The gradual progression of the monks' services marks the hours. Lauds at two o'clock, Prime just before dawn. She listens to the opening and closing of cell doors, the soft shuffle of feet around the cloister, brief murmurs and then a deep voice leading the chanting.

She stands to stretch her body and leans against the doorframe, hugging her arms against the cold air as the music drifts past her and her mind wanders.

She feels the peace of the priory. It's different from the manor. Maybe it's the monks' spiritual focus, maybe it's the stillness of the valley, being a less exposed site than Threfield Percy. She recalls how the wind whips off the escarpment at times, driving the rain hard into her face. Here by the river, it's so sheltered, so protected and safe.

Yet I have come to love the manor as my home, she appreciates. Who would have thought that when I journeyed through here all those years ago? And who would have imagined so many aspects of the life I'm living? Least of all you, she wonders as she senses my presence. The veil between this world and the next is thin tonight.

As dawn nears, the night seems to enter a new level of stillness; the world holds its breath on the brink of the new day.

'Who is that man?' We both start at hearing Alice's voice. Her eyelids flutter open, but her eyes are unfocused. 'I dreamed about him. All around him was fire. He stood in the midst of it, but it never touched him.

'He's here for you, my child,' blindly reaching her hand towards Christiane. 'Something bad is coming. It's Amicia: she's calling it in.' Her eyes become distant once more as they slowly close. 'Only he can help you now.'

Those are the last words she speaks.

* * * * * * *

The dream shifts. I watch her walk into chaos.

There are men everywhere, shouting and shoving their way through the village, pushing their way into the houses in threes and fours, grabbing whatever they want.

There's panic among her people, they who have lived in fear for so long. They huddle together, resentful but helpless against the onslaught.

Christiane angrily confronts the commander on horseback, who thrusts a folded parchment at her in justification. They're purveyors, here to take whatever they need for king's army. Walter has tried to stop them at the gate but is brutally flung aside.

'Would you have our soldiers starve while they battle the King of France?' the rider ridicules.

'I would not have my own people harmed in the taking!' Christiane retorts.

Aggressive shouts announce the arrival of their men from the fields seconds before they are visible, charging down the slope, hardly slowing as they launch themselves at the purveyors, fists first, questions second.

Instantly, the men retaliate with an inflamed sense of righteousness on their side.

'Stop them!' Christiane demands of the commander. 'Now!'

Embarrassment and anger spur him to action; he drives his horse into the mêlée, forcing the men apart.

As the crowd clears, there is a man left lying in the dirt. Blood trickles from his ear. Richard.

'No!' Denial grips Christiane as she rushes forward. She crouches over him, feeling his chest rise and fall as he heaves for breath. But his eyes stare blankly ahead.

Not him too.

She cradles his head. The fight goes out of her, and I watch her watching helplessly as the purveyors' men continue to invade every part of the manor. Despairingly, she sees the hard-earned produce of their labour fill the king's carts: sacks and sacks of grain and vegetables and fruit, barrels of ale, chickens, geese, pigs, sheep, cows, horses, even their cloth and clothing.

Richard knows her no more.

* * * * * * *

I almost rise out of sleep, half-aware of my uncomfortable surroundings. It's still dark, too dark to see the time on my watch.

Her emotions swirl around me, thick in my head. Anger at what she sees as the king's betrayal. Guilt at letting her people down. Devastation at losing her stalwart friends.

Somehow, maybe because I'm still half-connected to the dream, I know what happened next. He had another stroke after being struck in the fight and it immobilised him. Not yet an old man but unable to take in water or food, it took him days to die. And she tended him to the end, dribbling wine from a cloth into his parched mouth as she watched him slip away.

Loneliness overwhelms her, burdened with the responsibility of caring for all these people alone.

How am I supposed to help her?

* * * * * * *

She's in the fields with the villagers as they harvest the meadows. It's a hot day and the air is thick with dust and the smell of freshly scythed grass. Her skirts are hitched up as she works alongside the women, gathering bundles to dry into hay.

She shades her eyes against the midday sun, one hand on her hip as she eases the backache from long hours of labour.

A boy is running up the path.

It's so long since she's seen him, she almost doesn't recognise that long, loping stride. Taller than ever. He must be almost his father's height now, though he hasn't even finished his training as a squire yet.

'Henry!' she cries.

This child-man is torn between throwing himself into her open arms and standing on his dignity in front of the tenants. Maybe for the last time, the child wins and he holds her tightly for a long moment.

'What are you doing, Mother?' he contends, taking in her dirty attire.

She laughs, the joy of his return bubbling up within her. 'Harvesting,' she smiles teasingly, though she rearranges her skirts for appearance's sake.

'But you shouldn't be doing base labour!' with such a frown of disapproval. He can stand on his status just as pointedly as his father and grandmother.

'Who else will,' she challenges, 'when your father has taken so many of our men away? The harvest won't wait.'

'Have you heard the news?' so filled with excitement he barely waits to receive her shake of the head. 'It was all the talk of the town as I passed through Malton.' He seems torn between wanting to share it and relishing the power of being better informed than she.

'Tell me!' she laughs, caught up in his mood.

'We've won a great victory! At sea!' he proclaims, apparently shocked by the news. 'We've destroyed the French fleet!'

'How wonderful!' she exclaims, amused by his passion.

'It is!' he expounds dramatically. 'The king was crossing to Flanders with the army, and they thought to block our approach, two hundred ships, all chained together, ready for battle. They're saying they were planning to capture the king! We even had the queen and her retinue in one of the ships. Can you imagine, women and children so close to a battle?'

'So how did we win?' she invites with a smile.

'It was the archers!' with such pride in his countrymen. 'They crushed the Genoese crossbowmen before the infantry even clashed. Men were jumping into the water just to escape but the Flemish slaughtered them as they came ashore. Three-quarters of their ships were destroyed or captured.'

He chatters away as he turns to head back towards the solar, assuming she will follow in his wake.

She's torn between pride and maternal worry for him. He's thirteen: not old enough to fight for another three years yet, but old enough to have that childish eagerness to be part of the fray. How is she going to feel then? Part of her wants him to fulfil the promise of his younger years, to feel the exhilaration of having trained for this. A bigger part dreads that inevitable moment, knowing that, however well he's been taught, however confident he is of his own abilities, all it takes is one arrow or one well-aimed blow and he could be gone.

'Mama, I nearly forgot the reason I'm here!' There's genuine remorse in his face as he halts suddenly at the brow of the hill.

'What is it?'

'David is dead.'

Her heart jolts in shock. 'Dafydd?' she whispers.

'No!' he swiftly corrects, understanding his mistake. 'Not Dafydd. David. David FitzAlan.'

She's instantly relieved. And just as instantly heartsick.

'What happened?'

He looks away, the inability of youth to engage too much with grief. 'They were camped outside Glasgow. The Scots raided at night, two hundred men against our thousands. But they caught us unawares and hacked their way through the camp so fast the men barely had time to respond. They slaughtered, and then they disappeared into the night. Father saw it happen; he sent me with a letter for David's father and wanted me to bring you one too,' drawing a parchment from the pouch at his waist. 'He knows how much you cared for David,' he condoles, and she sees him struggling against the distress of seeing one of his parents upset. 'But,' shrugging off his empathy, 'at least this victory means we shall be able to export our wool again now without fear of it being stolen by the French.'

Such youthful innocence still, able to absorb a loss and move on. When do we lose that resilience?

She stops at the top of the hill, looking down the valley to where the river is glinting in the sunlight. He doesn't wait for her; perhaps he's relieved that she's chosen to face her grief alone.

She's standing at the epicentre of her physical world, the three fields behind her, the village before her. The distant sound of children reaches out to her, and the smell of smoke comes from several of the cottages, the kitchens and the bakehouse.

Most of her people are scattered across the acres, working the land just as their parents and grandparents had before them, for generations back even before the Conqueror arrived. Lives woven in the warp and weft of the seasons, their individual tapestries formed by the shades of each experience, the threads of survival punctuated with moments of joy and sorrow.

In the stillness and sensing my presence, she sees her world in the light of new loss.

Suddenly, this place feels too narrow to her.

My world has shifted, she thinks, *and I haven't even noticed it happening. My dearest friends have gone: Lady Alice and Richard and David. This gentle man, who has been a quiet constant for me since I was a child. He was more present than my husband has ever been. He gave me reassurance and support without asking anything from me. Now he's lost to me too.*

She hugs her arms around her chest, wanting comfort. Foreboding settles over her.

What am I left with? An embittered, poisonous woman decaying her way through life. Weak men like Simon Reeve and Father Peter, sometimes well-meaning but both dominated by Amicia.

And a ghost.

A chill of vulnerability runs down her spine.

No one but you.

She feels so alone.

* * * * * * *

So alone.

This time I jolt into such wakefulness that I know my night is over, even though there's not yet any hint of dawn in the sky, like I've been ejected from the world of sleep.

So alone. Both of us, so alone.

The emptiness she feels mirrors my life too. I have colleagues but no strong friendships to speak of. Women who come and go, never more than temporary connections. My family would always be there for me, I know, but they're over the Irish Sea. I can't even remember when I last spoke to them.

Michael's gone.

Sam? Is Sam gone?

No one but you.

Her thought reaches into my mind.

I pull the blanket around me, feeling it's paucity, barely reaching above my waist.

And I sense what lies ahead for her.

Ralf's never here, an absent husband who sucks more strength out of the manor every time he recruits men for his wars, men who are all too eager to be away, to make more money from a few months' fighting than they do from working the land all year. Her sons are out in the world, building their own lives.

Without Richard, the horse-breeding business is failing. With insufficient labour, they're struggling to farm the land they have. Hughes's business progresses, but even he will struggle with the disruption to international trade that flows from war between England and France; the high export duties, restrictions on the trade in fleeces, French ships raiding merchant vessels.

And without David, managing the manor will become harder. At least he was here whenever the army wasn't deployed, whereas Ralf always returns to Percy's household instead.

It's strange to think that David's probably already been dead for several days, given how slow communication is in those times.

Does a man die in the moment his heart stops beating or when someone who knows him is told about it?

And what is she to me?

Rationally, I know she's dead, but she's also vibrantly alive. Is she dead because I know she already is, or will she only die to me when I witness her death?

What will it feel like to lose her? It could be years hence for her, but it could happen in a matter of hours or days for me.

My body is gripped with rejection of that thought. When I know, will she be lost to me? Will all these dreams and visions – whatever they are – stop?

She's drawn me close to her in those moments of death so that she's not alone.

But will I be?

Chapter Fifty-three

Threfield Percy. 19th September 1976

I need you.

I jolt awake. In that in-between space that bridges waking and sleeping, her voice resounds so clearly that I think I've heard it, not dreamt it.

But as consciousness asserts its dominance and the sound diminishes to a distant echo, my certainty fades.

So, I did sleep again, even though I was sure I wouldn't after those dreams. Images from them flow back into my mind but almost immediately recede; the more I clutch at them, the more they move frustratingly further out of reach.

Sitting up, I rub my tongue over my teeth, trying to remove the roughness of my mouth, and massage my stiff neck.

Outside, a thick white fog envelopes the car. It makes me wonder what this bit of land was in her time. The answer drops into my head in the instant the question takes form: it was rough pasture on the outskirts of land owned by Wharram, a manor centred several miles away.

And it strikes me just how remote Threfield Percy is. There's no through-road to encourage itinerant monks or merchants or entertainers to pass through and pitch their wares. No market to attract outside visitors. And, thanks to Amicia, a strong deterrent to day labourers seeking work. A dead end, in so many ways.

According to Michael's papers, even the nearby farmhouse didn't exist until the eighteenth century, built as a central domain when large parcels of land were consolidated by the Felton family.

It's eerily isolated. Cut off. Deserted.

A chill shivers down my spine and an unaccustomed wariness settles over me.

I need you.

The hairs stand up on the back of my arms. But at the same time, my heart thumps harder, not with fear but excitement. Because I heard her, as clear as day.

Grabbing my coat and pulling on my boots, I'm suddenly eager to get back to the dig site. That skeleton is waiting for me, an outline ready to be uncovered in all its detail today. What will it tell me?

It's only as I scramble out of the car that I notice something has been left on the bonnet. A thermos flask and a large packet wrapped in wax paper.

Resentment flares. I don't want anyone near me. I don't want anyone near the dig. This is mine and mine alone.

But then my stomach growls, loudly and painfully. When did I last eat? Who knows? There are thick doorstep sandwiches in the packet, filled with slabs of cheese and boiled ham, and hot, sweet tea to wash it down.

It must have been the farmer's wife who left this for me. Who thought of me even though she hates to come near the site. Who was also aware that I hadn't gone home.

And in that moment, I feel less alone.

* * * * * * *

Oddly, the fog is not as thick on the other side of the stream: the village is encircled in the blanketing greyness, cocooned from the outside world. Thankfully it means the air isn't quite as damp or as cold; just walking from the car, droplets had settled on my eyelashes and started to seep into my clothes.

An instinct makes me pause as I reach the boundary stone at the manor's outer edge. Standing on the verge of the village, my senses heighten and my head buzzes, like the noise around an electricity pylon.

Lightly resting my hand on the stone, I'm aware not only of the iciness of it beneath my fingertips and the roughness of the lichen growing on it, but also of the density compacted into the limestone, layer upon layer of compressed particles. The light ahead of me is different from what's behind, as if I'm looking towards deep winter, not late summer. I can smell wood being burned on a fire. Bread baking. And think I catch distant shouts, male voices.

I'm hesitant to move forward, but as I take a step the site draws me in and shuts a door on the world behind.

As I slowly progress down the path, in my mind's eye I can see the village so clearly. The heavy gate barring the entrance, its oak weathered almost as black as the iron that binds it. Walter and Margery's hovel, close by, windows shuttered against the cold, smoke seeping out through the thatch.

There's Mary Hering's house, better than Walter's but still relatively low grade; the thatch will need replacing this year. Then her father-in-law's where her husband, Will, grew up. After that, James and Maud Crow's, whose son Stephen died in Scotland, serving under Ralf. Beyond that, the parsonage, a longer building, three bays, not one or two; unlike many in his flock, Father Peter doesn't share his living space with his animals.

In a flash, their world accelerates around me: it's like watching a movie in fast motion, people shifting in and out of houses, up and down the road, animals herded hither and thither. Clouds shoot across the panorama at break-neck speed, flashing from rain to sun and back again, and the sky switches from day to night, night to day in less than the blink of an eye. It's dizzyingly fast and I instinctively put out my arms to steady myself, but the energies still whirl around me and I'm losing my balance.

Suddenly the earth shakes so violently that I fall to my hands and knees. A huge rumble tremors through the earth and into the ethers, juddering through my body so hard my teeth clatter. A sharp crack splits the air as a fissure appears at the base of the church's tower and jaggedly fractures its way up the wall to the window frame, shearing through weak points in the masonry. For a long moment, I think the wall is going to collapse and the façade of the building throws out a cloud of dust as it shudders, but then it holds.

January 1343. It's in Michael's ecclesiastical records, the day the belltower cracked in an earthquake.

1343.

Another leap forward in her life.

I stare at the ruined church ahead of me, seeing the crack in her time overlay the one in mine.

Last night's dreams. When were they from?

Lady Alice: she died in 1337, according to Michael's scrawled notes.

The king's purveyors, when would they have been active? He started preparing for war with France as early as 1338. It could be any time between then and this time.

And David's death? In her mind she thought of Henry as being three years away from being allowed to fight. Which would make him what, thirteen, maybe? If the battle he'd heard about was Sluys, that would be about right, making the year 1340.

And now it's 1343.

The years are disappearing. Her life is disappearing before my eyes.

I want to tell it to stop. Or at least slow down.

I pinpoint details to capture the moment. She's thirty-five years old when the tower cracks. Edward III has been king for sixteen years and will reign for another thirty-four. Ahead of him are the victories at Crecy, Calais, Poitiers and Neville's Cross, the loss of the Black Prince and Queen Philippa, and his ignominious final years with Alice Perrers.

And the Black Death.

It's five years until the first cases in England. Six until it reaches northern England.

A shadow falls across me. Though there's no sign of the sun.

* * * * * * *

One corner of the tarpaulin snaps in the wind as I approach but otherwise the site is intact and relatively dry. The wind picks up, rattling the reeds in the old fishpond; at least it'll clear any fog away.

I drop down by the steps, removing the tarp as I go, careful to avoid the deeper section where the body lies. Wedging the folded cover under pieces of masonry, I scan yesterday's output as I unwrap my tools.

It's not yet recognisable as a skeleton but it's enough to indicate the shape of a human: the top of what I believe to be the skull, bones that could mark the shoulders or upper arms, the edges of what may be the pelvis or hip joints, the femur I originally found and a smattering of what I take to be small bones from the feet. I've left the central portion – covering the vertebrae and ribcage – untouched.

There's no way I should have been able to scope it out like this. But all the time I was digging, I could almost sense the outline of the body in the soil. Nothing about them specifically but enough to give me a picture of its shape and position, arms folded across the chest.

My hands are tingling in anticipation as I crouch down and consider where to start.

* * * * * * *

'You have no right!'

The man's voice, aggressive and plaintively stubborn, breaks into my concentration.

He has the red Bren hair. Henry. Full-grown. Tall, lean, muscular. And angry.

With four people in it – five, if I include me – Amicia's small upper chamber is cramped and crowded. And with two combative men inside, it's oppressive with negativity.

Henry stands are the head of the stair, ready to storm out. His blood is up and for the first time in his life he's in outright conflict with his father.

Ralf has taken a position of dominance before the fire, though how he can stand the heat in this airless room is beyond me. Legs braced, chest out, arms folded, his very stance asserts control.

Amicia is in her usual chair, which puts her – in her mind – at her son's right hand. And yet, she seems to be enjoying this dispute: it gives her a twisted pride to see her son and grandson arguing about their roles in the king's upcoming battles.

'I have every right!' Ralf slams back. 'We cannot spare a single man from our army. It's my will and Percy's that we shall fight in Scotland. Leave France to the others.'

'I've had enough of fighting these damnable Scots,' Henry retaliates. 'One petty skirmish after another with an enemy who refuses to face us honourably on the battlefield, who stabs us in the dead of night before he slinks back into the mirky darkness from which he came! Where's the glory in that?'

'The king himself has made it clear how important our role is.' Ralf's stature seems to swell with the seriousness of his undertaking. 'If he's to fight the French, he can't leave the north unprotected. The Scots will rise, don't doubt it. And Percy and Neville must hold the border for the king.'

'You and Percy are welcome to Scotland. You're the old guard, it's right that you should fight the old battles. But I'm for the king, and I'm for France.'

'*Your* duty is to fight where Percy fights. You're pledged to Percy, and you will honour that pledge.' Ralf's face darkens the longer Henry holds out.

'Even Percy's own son has chosen not to be there,' Henry quarrels. 'He's pledged himself to Philip de Weston and will fight in the king's own army. I can just as well pledge myself to the son as to the father, so why shouldn't I?'

'We cannot spare a single capable man against the Scots,' Ralf growls. 'We are as critical to the king's success as if we were fighting in France's fields ourselves, and we do so with a fraction of the men. Think of the glory in that!' he urges.

'There may be glory but there's no money!' Henry's gestures are becoming as wild as his voice is loud. 'Every man with Lancaster is making himself rich beyond imagining as they scythe their way through Aquitaine. Even Dafydd benefits from the spoils even though he's never drawn a sword!' There's scorn in Henry's voice, overlying his jealousy of his brother.

'David's role is just as valuable to Lancaster as any in his army,' Ralf defends. 'More so, in fact. Most men can fight, but it takes intelligence and skill to be as trusted by Henry of Lancaster as David is. Diplomacy may be alien to you and me, boy, but you can still respect those who undertake it.'

Where is Christiane in this?

She sits at the table, her eyes focused on her work as the argument flows over and around her; she has such inner calm, the stillness at the eye of the storm.

Nearby, candles light the sewing she was working on – she's never not doing something productive – and strongly illuminate her face.

God, but she's beautiful.

The years are showing now – lines around her eyes and mouth – and she carries her maturity with both authority and compassion.

She's aware of me, I know. She doesn't look my way so as not to betray that awareness to the others, but her chin lifts fractionally as she registers the moment I arrive.

It's Christmas.

She's been going over the preparations for food, wine and entertainment. Tonight sees the start of festivities, when the Lord of Misrule will be appointed from among the villagers. She worries about what to expect: there's a restlessness among their people, so she anticipates more mischief than usual.

War is coming. Everyone in England knows. It's been long expected: it's two years since Parliament gave its support to war in France and authorised taxes for that purpose. Now, the king has set a muster date on St David's Day and the men are readying themselves mentally and physically for the moment they must depart. The women, too, knowing how much might fall to them while their men are gone.

She can tell this is more serious than what has gone before. This time, they will be away for a long time, many months at least.

She reads it as clearly as she reads a book, this different atmosphere in the air.

Something's changed.

The one thing she never has to worry about is whether they will have important guests to accommodate. Since Alice died, there's no one who visits. Threfield Percy has, to all intents and purposes, closed its gates to the outside world.

It's rare even for Ralf and Henry to be home, singularly let alone together. Is that what's in their minds? A last visit, should they not return? Her blood chills at the thought.

'Mama, what think you?' Henry appeals for support but before she can answer Amicia overrides her.

'The boy should go,' directing her instructions at Ralf. 'How much money have you ever brought back from Scotland? Let him go to France and try his hand there.'

'This is about more than the spoils of war!' Ralf cries. 'It's about defending England against two enemies who conspire to crush us. And for each man, it's about honour and duty, obligation and responsibility, to do what we must so that we might defend our own way of life, yours and mine.'

Christiane smiles to herself; it seems Ralf has finally accepted his responsibilities after all.

'We need every penny he can bring in,' Amicia whines, resenting her son's retaliation. Christiane sees Henry's uneasy shuffle and interprets the truth: her son intends to keep whatever he earns for himself.

Ralf takes a deliberate look around the tower, no doubt taking in the new, elaborate paintings of the heavens, planets and astrological houses on the wall and ceiling, and wondering how much the artist has commanded in payment. 'To fund your decorations, Mother?' he observes drily. 'Have you taken up an interest in astrology?'

'Do not mock what you do not understand,' she snaps, ready to argue with him on any subject now. 'I hear the French king never embarks on a battle without first having consulted on the alignment of the planets.'

'Let the French king do what he likes,' Ralf insists. 'Thankfully, our king is more interested in the terrain, the conditions and the strategic positioning of his forces!'

'Your scorn only betrays your ignorance, my son,' she rebukes him. 'You do not know what is coming.'

'And you do, Mother?' he disputes, needled. 'Pray, enlighten us.'

Christiane turns her eyes to her work again. I can feel her discomfort with the subject; she's heard Amicia's doom-laden prognostications before and doesn't share her relish for creating an atmosphere of fear all around her.

Amicia almost preens with pride to be the centre of attention and able to reassert her authority. 'They tell of a portentous alignment of the planets that presages many disasters, from floods and famine to a tremendous quaking of the earth.'

'So much we can already lay claim to right here,' Ralf mocks. 'Or have you not seen the state of the church? You will have to do better than that, Mother.'

'This is as nothing to what is already being seen in the East,' she expands. 'Floods that consume cities. Massive tremors that bring buildings crashing down around people's heads. Mountains exploding with fire that falls in flakes like snow but burns all the land and any who dwells upon it.' Now she has their attention, she forges ahead.

'Land so wet it is scarce possible to plough. Devastating murrains among the animals until meat becomes inedible. Starving people forced to eat dogs and, some say, even their children, driven mad by hunger.

'They tell of thunderstorms so violent and sustained that the sky appears almost the whole night as if it were on fire. Of a huge black dog that runs with fire darting from its jaws and sparks from its red eyes, that passes through doors that are shut against it and sets fire to whole houses and the families within. Of springs turning red and running with blood. Of the dead rising after a week in the grave, animated by demons and with their sulphurous breath carrying contagion from Hell.'

She stops, her face flushed and her eyes staring maniacally. Her animation has its desired effect: her male audience is rapt, and her dire warnings have settled a pall across them. The mood is sombre, verging on sinister.

Slowly and deliberately, Amicia meets the eyes of her son and grandson, nodding to herself as she confirms she's got them gripped.

'Mark my words,' she warns, her smile almost malicious, 'it is the end of the world: the Four Horsemen will ride across the land, and we shall know the faces of them all: War and Famine and Pestilence and Death. We must all be ready. God's judgement is coming.'

Chapter Fifty-four

Threfield Percy. 19th September 1976

The sudden screech of birds cuts into my consciousness and I'm instantly called back the present, seeing a mass of rooks rising into grey skies above the skeletal fingers of the wintry trees.

Only, they're not there.

Splicing between her world and mine disorientates me, and the landscape sways so much that I put my hands down to steady myself, even though I'm already on my knees.

As my vision clears, I get a jolt of shock: almost half a skeleton lies exposed in the soil before me.

Radius, ulna, humerus, clavicle, sternum, pelvis, femur, tibia, fibula, tarsals…

The names rise from deep memories: I'm back in my seventeen-year-old self, lounging on sun-warmed grass, propped up on an elbow with her textbook open in my hand, and Sam, slender and tanned in shorts and T-shirt, cross-legged before me, is explaining the human skeletal structure to me.

The second summer we were together.

I can feel again my impatient excitement in the days before they arrived, Michael and Sam.

The thrill of knowing he was allowing me to join the dig, my enthusiasm for talking to him about what I've read in the books he sent me.

And my eagerness to be close to Sam again.

Funny, I didn't see it at the time, but it's so clear to me now. Sam.

The memory evaporates as I stare at the bones.

I've yet to dig around the skull. I think I'm almost afraid to, as if it will make this person more real.

There's no avoiding it now. I need to finish the job, and then I'll have to think about alerting the coroner.

But not yet.
Not yet.

* * * * * * *

As I work, I watch her go about her daily life.

Most days she attends mass with Amicia in that inadequate little church, often with only the priest for company unless it's Sunday or a Holy Day.

There are interminable hours spent keeping her lonely and twisted mother-in-law company, however little it's appreciated. Reading to her, writing her endless stream of letters or just listening while she complains and criticises and lords it over everyone. She's witness to her malice towards those she sees as subservient, to the inordinate deference she expects from every tenant and vassal, to how she manipulates and corrupts Simon Reeve and to how she commands Father Peter as if she were his master, not the archbishop. The poor priest tolerates much more than he should, though whether through fear for his position – which is, by any standards, comfortable and easy – or through some misplaced sense of responsibility, I cannot tell.

I watch her work harder than any would imagine, and in ways none in her position would be expected to.

At harvest-time, she's out in the fields with them, gleaning the crops, even taking up a scythe to cut the hay or oats or wheat.

She makes herself an accessible presence around the village and in the Great Hall, knowing how often she's called to intervene in the most minor of day-to-day matters.

The village is struggling. Not visibly, maybe, but it is pervasive. Average crop yields have been lower ever since Ralf started depleting the labour force for war. The money the men earn keeps them going because they buy what's needed, but she frets about what will happen the next time there's a bad harvest and a surfeit isn't available to be bought.

I watch her with her people, see the care she brings to each of them. She attends the sick and supplies the poorest of them with food and clothing or labour and materials to repair their homes. Yet for all that they accept her charity, there's nervousness in doing so, wary that word of it will get back to Amicia; gossip and tale-telling are rife, providing plenty of fodder for the reeve to maintain his standing with his manipulative mistress.

The back-and-forth of claim and counter-claim at the manor court continues, and it feeds a deepening mistrust between households, even where kinship exists. The irony is that Amicia benefits from fostering it: each case results in fines – on one side or the other, or sometimes even on both – which wend their way into her coffers.

In spite of this, the villagers are still quick to prosecute one another. They retaliate against each perceived slight, protect their every right and become incensed about any disparity between their position and their neighbours'.

Nothing has stemmed the loss of young people to other manors or to York or Beverley or Lincoln; this backwater holds a future too narrow for the ambition and passion of youth. And the tenants' obligations to the demesne farm fall hard on those who remain, rigorously enforced as they are by the reeve.

When the long days are done, she sits with Philip of Ghent, her new steward, striving to stretch the manor's meagre income as far as they can, to meet their obligations to Hughes's business and to the Percy contracts, and to service Ralf's and Henry's all-too-frequent demands for money. What she earns from her dower lands disappears into that bottomless pit, to a husband who never stops to consider how their spending is sustained.

And yet, in spite of it all, she holds true to herself. That calm, centred spirit. That generous, forgiving soul. That deep, compassionate love.

* * * * * * *

I hear horses.

Startled, I look in the direction of the road, seriously expecting to see someone approach. Of course, the lane is empty.

But it makes me realise how late the day is.

And that my work is almost done. Standing to stretch out my cramped joints, there's no escaping the truth: it's time to report this in the right way.

No!

You don't understand. I must.

Don't.

I have no choice.

Not yet.

I feel the relief of that thought. Not yet.

It's too late in the day, I can justify. What harm is there in waiting until tomorrow if the site is adequately protected? Nothing will change between now and then.

Slowly, I clean the mud off my tools.

It's strange to look at the bones and imagine it as a body. The arm bones and several of the ribs are crushed where a great weight of material has crashed down. The skull has fractured into three pieces, but there are no obvious signs of injury. Given all the pieces of heavy timber we removed at the start and the stone blocks from the wall pushed in on top of them, it's little wonder there's such damage.

It feels momentous, finding this body. And I acknowledge how much has already been achieved here.

Though incomplete. That core question remains because I can't say how the village ended.

Are the answers even here?

I was so certain at the beginning, but now…

Am I as bad as Michael? As blind, blinkered, tunnel-visioned. Can I really hope to decipher the whole story from this one site?

But, in truth, that's not it any more, is it? This is personal. This is about Christiane. I don't know how she dies.

I stare at the bones, absent-mindedly wiping my trowel with a cloth.

And something slips into my mind from that summer afternoon with Sam. She'd been reading about how pathologists identified age and sex from the bones.

A book her father had given her.

I crouch down by the bones, studying them as I dredge up memories of what she told me.

There was the cranium, the ridges on the brow bones and the shape of the jawbone. To a discerning eye that could betray the heavier visage of a man.

But it would need an eye more experienced than mine to judge that.

The same is true of the pelvic bone. I know the angles are different in women, allowing for childbirth. I'd say that makes this a man, but I can't be sure.

The teeth? I'm still hesitant to touch the skull – some strange superstition has settled over me that I prefer not to scrutinise – but kneeling down I can get close enough to see.

Being that near the body is uncomfortable, like I'm invading its personal space. Ridiculous thought.

I count one side, then the other, and there they are: three erupted wisdom teeth.

And one more thing.

I'm about to reach for the tape measure when a different impulse grabs me.

The bone is almost entirely exposed anyway. It's a moment's work to slide the flat blade underneath and prise it upwards, slowly, gingerly, all along its length until its free and sitting loosely on the surface, crumbled earth all around.

Not wanting to touch it – what is this absurd reticence? – I use my cleaning cloth to pick it up and quickly wrap the material all around so that I don't have to look at it. Stepping back, it's strange to look at the skeleton without its right femur.

I drag the tarpaulin back over the site and pin it down, then shove the trowel into my tool kit, rough and awkward in my impatience.

The light levels are dropping rapidly. I stumble on the shale at the bottom of the hill where the two paths meet.

As I regain my footing and look up, I stop dead.

A rider is going past me. And behind him, a dozen men walking in a rough line, singing rowdily, arms around each other's shoulders. The rider turns in his saddle to cheer with them, elation filling his face. The celebratory heroes returning, brimming with tales of battle.

Crecy.

A shiver goes through me. Not cold. Not fear. Resonance.

I can feel them.

The pride in being part of that huge war machine, twelve of them among thousands of other archers, ordinary men like them who practised in the long summer evenings, hours of strengthening their arms and honing their accuracy.

The tension of long-held anticipation, waiting and waiting and waiting for the battle to start, balanced on a knife-edge between anxiety and excitement for long hours before the dawn.

The comradeship of seeing their leaders dismount and send their horses to the back behind the army, standing shoulder to shoulder, flanking the ranks of archers.

The thrill of seeing the king ride along their lines, exhorting every man to be the highest version of himself, invoking the honour of St George in bringing them victory that day.

The ripples of astonishment at seeing even the king dismount and stand alongside with them.

The exquisite torture of the moments before the battle starts, hardly daring to breathe. Seeing their counterparts fire their crossbows, hearing that sharp, high whistle of thousands of arrows carving through the air.

Then the exhilaration of watching those arrows fade and fall too soon, far short of their lines.

And the blast of jeering that burst from them, knowing their enemy was within range of their crossbows but they themselves were out of reach.

Loosing those first volleys, reloading and loosing, reloading and loosing, fast, fast, fast. Just as they had always practised. Six, seven shots per minute per man, thousands upon thousands of arrows rising high in the air, slicing with terrifying power and speed.

And from hundreds of yards away, feeling the wave of shock and terror that swept through the French army's frontline as they watched the arrows rise high, high, and then turn in their ominous arc and rain down upon them.

The blood of the Englishmen burned like fire in their veins that day beneath the banner of St George.

And when they were done, four thousand Frenchmen lay dead on the field of battle, in return for only three hundred of their own.

* * * * * * *

It's not a long walk down the lane to the red telephone box outside the pub but I'm glad of it.

My head's pounding, the second worst headache I've ever had. Thumping hard, pulsing until I can feel my blood pushing from my heart and smashing against the left side my skull where that bastard hit me.

Lights spill from every window of The Fox, warm and welcoming.

I know I won't be going back to the flat tonight, but am I presentable enough to go into the pub? I'm dirty but I don't think I smell too bad. Maybe I can wash up in the gents'. A pie and a pint are exactly what I need right now.

Every step away from the site is a lessening of whatever has a grip on me. My mind clears a bit more the further away I get.

But I'm far from free of it.
The bone still weighs heavy in my hand.
And I need answers.

Chapter Fifty-five

Marston. 19th September 1976

'Hello?' The phone starts bleeping at me and I pile coins into the slot. It takes a second for the line to click in. 'Hello?'

'Sam, it's me.'

'Eoghan. Are you in a phone box?'

'Yes. Outside the pub on the Marston road.'

'Where have you been? I've been trying to reach you all day. And most of yesterday.' Relief mingles with anger born of worry.

'I've been at the site.'

'What, all night?' I respond to her sarcasm with silence. 'Shit. You were. You stayed there last night?'

'I slept in the car.' I don't want to lie to her.

'Shit. Shit. Shit!' I can hear the worry now. I imagine her pressing her hand to her forehead the way she does when she's wrestling with something. 'This is out of control.' She says it almost to herself.

'Sam, I didn't call to argue.'

There's a moment of silence, a heavy sigh and the scrape of furniture. Pulling out a chair to sit down.

'OK. What do you need?' Is it years of dealing with Michael that makes her so tolerant? Or is that innate? Perhaps it's what makes her such a good doctor.

'Do you remember telling me about how to identify a skeleton?'

'No.'

The answer comes so fast I'm not sure I believe her. And I want her to remember. I want those memories to mean to her what they now do to me. 'That second summer at Glendalough. You were reading up on anatomy and archaeology, and you explained to me how pathologists identify characteristics just from the bones.'

'Dad bought me that book,' reminiscing. 'I always wondered why. Why he was trying to get me interested in your discipline as well as mine. Was he trying to push us together?'

'I don't think he even noticed how we felt about each other.'

'We? At this point, it was pretty one-sided.' Said with a rueful smile.

'I don't think it was ever entirely that way,' I mull out loud. 'Maybe I was just a bit blind, that's all.'

'Anyway,' brisk and dismissive, 'that's ancient history.'

'Is it?' Two words weighed down with meaning.

A lull. But I find myself gripping the handset as I hold it to my ear and imagine her thinking hard at the other end.

'What characteristics do you want to know?' she probes. Distracts. 'From the skeleton.'

'Man or woman. Age, if possible.'

'For age, in children the best indicator is the teeth. Plus, bone development, from the fusing of the cranial sutures to progression of each individual bone. For instance, the clavicle is the last bone to be fully formed.'

'What about for an adult?'

'Then you're looking at bone remodelling, a cross-section of the bone to see the size and number of the osteons, the blood vessels in the bone.' I must have made a noise of irritation in my throat because she changes tack. 'You want something more superficial?'

'Can you tell age from the wisdom teeth?'

'To a degree, though it's not exact.'

'Then, what?'

'Maybe the cranial sutures: they become less obvious the older we get. Or general wear and tear, arthritis in the spine and joints. The rib ends are often a good indicator.'

'OK.' Give up on that. 'What about sex?'

'In general terms, you're looking at overall size and sturdiness of the bones, the level of bone development where the muscles were attached. More specifically, you'd assess the pelvis to see how open or closed the pelvic inlet is, the flaring of the hip bones, the subpubic angle.'

'I'd need someone who knows what they're doing for that. What else? What about height? I remember something about measuring the femur?'

'There's a specific ratio but it differs for men and women, so you'd want to have a good idea what sex you're looking at to begin with.'

'What's the formula?'

'I'd have to dig it out.'

'Can you get it for me?'

'Now? Seriously?' She huffs but I hear her drop the receiver and move around her flat as she hunts down the book she needs. I grab my notebook and pen – and the tape measure – from my bag.

'Here it is. It's in centimetres, I'm afraid.'

'Really? That's not your Dad's old book, then.'

'No, I bought a new one. Recently.' Strange. She's embarrassed to be admitting it. 'OK, for a man, you're looking at the length of the femur multiplied by two-point-two-three then add sixty-nine centimetres. For a woman…'

'Don't worry about that,' I interrupt, scribbling the details down. Because I know what I'm looking at.

'Eoghan, are you telling me you've found a body?'

'A skeleton.' Resisting.

'Then why are you asking me? A pathologist will tell you everything you need to know.' A long pause. She puts the pieces together. 'You have reported it, haven't you?' Another empty pause, mine in answer to her question, then hers as she takes in my response. 'Why not?'

How can I tell her it's because Christiane doesn't want me to. And that means *I* don't want to.

'I just…can't.' God, that sounds feeble.

'You sound like Dad.' That despair in her voice…is that for the loss of him or for me?

'Please, Sam. I have to do this. I need to know.'

I can almost feel the battle of wills down the telephone line. But underneath it, there's more than that: I can feel her concern for me. It makes me feel…loved.

The silence stretches out between us. And I'm aware of her in a different way. How close she feels, even though we're miles apart. Hearing her breathing.

'Eoghan.'

'Hmm.'

'Did you mean it?'

'What?'

She hesitates. 'That it's not…that we're not…ancient history.'

A shot of adrenalin hits my heart first and then shoots through my limbs.

'Maybe…' Nervous suddenly, not knowing how she's going to respond. 'What…'

The pips start sounding loudly in my ear. The phone wants more coins.

I cradle the handset against my shoulder as I scrabble in my pockets. Uselessly, because I know I've already fed all my change into the machine.

'Eoghan, put more money in.' She wants this as much as I. I can hear it in her voice. At least, I hope I can hear it.

'I'm out, Sam.'

A noise of frustration as the pips go on. 'Eoghan, I…'

The line goes dead.

I slam the handset down and stare at the useless machine for long moments. Until I realise I could contact the operator and ask her to take a reverse-charge call.

Immediately I pick up the handset again. But then I hesitate because the moment's gone.

And because I'm afraid to know the answer.

At least she's given me a different one.

I take the bone package from where I laid it on top of the coin box and gingerly open the cloth wrapping so it lies exposed.

Fifty-four centimetres long. Double it – a hundred and eight – plus a quarter – thirteen and a half, so one-twenty-one point five – then add sixty-nine: call it one-ninety. What's that in inches? I could do the maths but it's easier to pull out the dual-scale tape measure.

Six foot three.

Almost as tall as me.

Goosebumps rise all over me. Because I know who this is.

The skeleton is Henry.

Monday

Chapter Fifty-six

Threfield Percy. 20th September 1976

I'm awake before dawn.

My mind is buzzing with thoughts before I'm barely conscious and I keep my eyes closed, wanting to stay there longer. With Christiane. With Sam. They float in and out of my awareness, from one to the other and back again. Blending.

Then I remember the site and open my eyes to a focused alertness, every trace of sleep disappearing in that instant.

It's time.

I feel the words everywhere. In my head. In my ears. In the air around me. And my body vibrates in resonance, tingling through my legs and arms, moving through my chest, up my neck and across my scalp.

It drives me out of my makeshift bed, and I've got my boots and coat on before I can blink. There's a new food parcel on the hood of the car, a fresh thermos of tea. I throw them in my bag with my toolkit.

The bone I treat with more care. Somehow, now I know who this is, that superstitious reticence I felt has gone. Instead, there's a closeness. A kinship. A reverence.

Bird calls fill the air as the sun lightens the horizon. The dawn paints the sky in vibrant reds and oranges, gilding the edges of small clouds in brilliance. In fact, the whole world has become an intensified version of itself and each of my senses sings with its symphonic reverberations. The air is sharp and fresh in my nostrils; the cold is bright and energising on my skin; the calls of the dawn chorus are precise and crystal clear in my ears; even the river's bubbling flow and the wind's rustling hand add harmonic bass lines to their melody.

The familiarity of the walk across the bridge, left down the short path and to the standing stone draws me in, each ridge or divot in the earth, the shape of each tree or shrub in the hedgerow, each mark or erosion in the sandstone block so known and recognisable that they seem a part of me.

The village embraces me as I step over the boundary line. And joy sweeps through me from my head to my toes.

My surroundings fill me as I walk the lower path. And though I can't see them, yet the structures and landscape of her time are as present to me as those in mine, so that the two environments overlap and coalesce. And when I reach the church, I feel the blending of both, like two complementary tunes that merge into a single refrain. Until I reach the site and stand astride two eras as one, a connecting thread of time.

My first instinct is to reunite the femur with the rest of him. Depressions from its long rest in the earth are still discernible, even after I disturbed them, and I replace the bone in its exact position, enjoying the wholeness of it again.

I get a flash of Henry as I last saw him, standing on the upper floor in this very spot. A man who, though only eighteen, was already an experienced warrior. Strong, lean, bulkier than I am and almost as tall, though I'm broader in the shoulder. Red hair, fair beard. Blue eyes, like her father's. And like mine. I have his nose too and his jawline.

Removing the rest of the tarp, I squat down to contemplate the site.

What happened here, Christiane? Why is your son's body buried here?

My hair moves, as if ruffled by the wind, and that strange energy ripples through my skin.

OK, there's only one way to find out: keep digging. So, where now?

The answer comes with pristine clarity, and I drop down on another area where the students were digging down before.

Beside the steps at the entrance to the tower.

Chapter Fifty-seven

Threfield Percy. August 1347

The first whispers of it come on an ill wind.

Just as they are bringing in the wheat, the wind turns against them, swinging round to come from the north and bringing with it driving rain. Days and days and days of it. Each morning they look out with hope of a let-up overnight and each morning their hope sinks deeper beneath the waters until dread takes hold of their hearts.

She's standing inside the open barn doors, watching three of the most experienced women thresh a bushel of wheat, their flails moving rhythmically in a dance-like rotation, one, two, three, one, two three. After several days in the barn, the crop has dried somewhat but not enough.

When the rain first started, they waited, praying for a break in the weather, believing that at some point the sun would shine and the harvest dry. In desperation they brought it in still wet, more afraid of losing the whole crop by leaving it longer in the fields.

It's still raining now: an unremitting downpour from leaden skies, sustained since before light. What started as rivulets of water across the yard have turned into heavy streams, carving their way ever more deeply through any slopes and undulations in the earth.

'How bad is it?'

Philip of Ghent stands beside her, surveying the scene with a frown that cuts two deep vertical lines between his brows. The replacement steward, competent but not well-liked. His accent makes him stand out and his stilted English is difficult to understand at times. His skills are in managing, not farming, and she's wishing Richard were here; she misses that natural sympathy they shared, that quick understanding he had of whatever she was dealing with.

'I've seen it like this once before,' she admits. 'Many years ago, when we lost three successive harvests to rain. It led to the Great Famine.'

And to her father's rebellion. She doesn't say that; coming from Flanders, Philip probably hasn't even heard of it, and she isn't about to enlighten him. It's a lifetime ago.

'Will it dry?'

She shakes her head. 'Never as well in the barns as it would in the fields. We'll lose a large part of this.' She sighs. 'We had such hopes of a good yield this time.'

'Too dry one year, too wet the next,' he responds, and his voice is weighty with despair.

It hasn't been easy for him since he arrived four summers before. She tried to manage on her own after Richard died; it was Hughes who insisted she take someone on, Hughes who, when she showed no sign of listening, sent her his most able administrator. Their years of friendship have been conducted almost entirely at a distance, and yet he seems to be more concerned for her than those up close.

'We'll get by.'

She says it because she has too, not because she believes it. She knows how many of the villagers will struggle to get through a second year like this; what stocks they had were all but used up last winter.

'And there are some who will always thrive in the worst of times,' he raises, cynicism in his tone. 'I'm hearing the reeve plans to enforce the debts of two more households at Michaelmas.'

She grimaces. 'I feared as much. They were relying on the harvest to repay him. They'll be lucky to get two-thirds of what they expected, even if they sold everything they've grown. Gilbert Wragge will manage well enough; he has sufficient land to sell to cover the debt and still support his family. But I worry for Will Hering; his situation was all-too-vulnerable to begin with.'

'Meanwhile, Simon Reeve becomes ever more powerful at the cost of those he should serve.' Philip has a black-and-white sense of justice. She smiles wryly to herself; she was that way once.

If she could, she would quietly provide the monies to Will herself. But what she gets from her dower lands has already gone on repairs the tenants couldn't afford, and more won't be forthcoming until after Michaelmas; by then it will be too late. As it is, there are several more houses in the village where repairs have been delayed and delayed, and she knows they will provide inadequate protection should the winter be a hard one.

She's worrying about how much power the reeve now wields on the manor. Half the tenants have borrowed from him this last year, more will no doubt do so as a result of this harvest. Borrowing from one another is a staple way of life for the villagers, but this has become disproportionate. It's Amicia's self-serving ways that have so lined the reeve's pockets that it has skewed the balance of power on the manor; the bitter irony is that, at this rate, he could end up carrying more weight than she.

Philip uses her thought-filled silence to change the subject. 'I have news I must share with you, my lady.'

'Indeed, Master Steward?'

'Master Hughes writes that Calais has surrendered. The truce has yet to be negotiated but the siege is over.'

'Thank the Lord!' she breathes. 'Then the men will return. It has been a long year without them. And they departed again so soon after returning from Crecy that it feels they have been away even longer than that.'

'Master Hughes says the king has expelled the French townspeople and is enticing Englishmen to populate it instead.'

That erodes her joy a little. 'Incentives from the king will be very attractive to some,' she worries. And what do we have to offer them here? she wonders. Little food, poor housing, low wages for their labour and high prices for food, which will only worsen now with this disastrous harvest.

She becomes aware of Philip's continuing discomfort.

'You have more bad news, Master Steward?' she surmises.

'Master Hughes mentioned another concern that he said I should raise with you.' He seems reticent.

'What is it?'

'It may be nothing,' he caveats. 'Perhaps he overstates the case.'

'Spit it out, Master Steward,' she encourages.

He relents. 'He has received word of a pestilence in the East.'

'Of what kind?'

'He does not give specifics.'

'And why does he believe I should be aware?'

'He says it is being carried along the great trade routes. It struck Constantinople in the spring and has ravaged the city. Merchants are returning with rumours of thousands of people dying.'

Constantinople. The gateway between the East and the Mediterranean. Before, the name conveyed an idea of a place so remote, so exotic as to be meaningless to her. But as a barrier, a boundary between them and a new disease, it suddenly seems so much closer. On the threshold of the European world.

A gust of wind whips around her, driving rain into her face with a surprisingly biting chill. She shivers, half from the sudden cold, half from an unexpected foreboding.

'Does Hughes advise any measures we should take?'

Philip shakes his head. 'None, yet. He pledges to keep us informed of what he hears.'

'We should keep this to ourselves for now,' she decides. 'No need to concern others with a threat that is not yet real to us. Particularly not the lady Amicia.'

But it's too late for that.

* * * * * * *

'Good, you're here. Perhaps you can talk some sense into him since he seems to have left whatever he was born with at the door!'

Amicia's tone is acidic and Father Peter's face flushes with humiliation and frustration. Extreme agitation shows in the frantic clasping and unclasping of her hands.

Christiane sends a questioning glance to Father Peter where he sits, awkwardly hunched on a stool too low for his angular frame. He grimaces in response with a helpless shrug that bespeaks his long pains in dealing with Amicia.

'What is the matter, my lady?' she enquires, adopting the steady tone she tries to maintain with Amicia; she learnt long ago not to let herself be drawn into Amicia's moods, erratic at best, violently volatile at worst.

'This! This!' she barks angrily, snatching up a letter from the table and thrusting it in Christiane's face as if she were an imbecile for not knowing. 'It is coming,' she mutters darkly, though more to herself than to them. ''Tis as I have always feared. We must protect ourselves!' she demands suddenly and loudly, staring at the two of them and pointing a shaking finger.

It is a moment's work to scan the letter and understand her fear: Ralf has written to warn his mother that a pestilence threatens to reach the Mediterranean coasts.

Foolish man. Did you think to help her with this news? Christiane chastises. Do you know your mother so little that you think this a loving act? This will only spark the terror you hope to forewarn against.

'Calm yourself, my lady,' she counsels Amicia, taking a seat. 'My lord seeks only to keep you informed. The pestilence is nowhere near, not even on English soil.'

'Stupid girl!' Amicia lashes out. 'You think you know of what you speak? You know nothing and yet you always command me as if you knew better than I what is happening.'

'There is always pestilence in the world,' Christiane defends. 'He does not say we should be concerned at this point.'

'But he knows,' she disagrees, with a whispering tremor in her voice. 'He knows, and you do not.'

'Knows what, my lady?' Christiane asks, though she guesses the answer: this perturbation of mind comes from Amicia's fear of the prophesy, the old woman's curse.

'He knows,' she repeats, visibly trembling now. 'He knows how I must be on my guard.'

Christiane reaches across to take her hand, hoping to comfort her. 'May I not help you, my lady?' she offers.

The old woman searches her face, almost desperate in her need for reassurance.

'We must protect ourselves. You must protect me,' she pleads. 'All of you. Call everyone to the church,' her eyes straying to Father Peter with the instruction. 'Tell them. Tell them what is coming. Tell them my life is in their hands and their duty is to protect me.'

'What would you have them do?' Christiane asks.

'No one can leave the village.' Her voice rises with the panic in her eyes. 'Not to the market. Nor to the fairs. And no one can be allowed to enter. Tell the idiot Walter: no one comes through that gate!'

'We should not frighten them unnecessarily,' Father Peter interjects. 'They already have enough to worry about, what with the poor harvest and the prospect of a second winter with too little to eat.'

'And,' Amicia carries on as if she hadn't heard a word, 'those who are already absent, they are not allowed to return. They will be our greatest threat, those who come from foreign lands. They must keep their distance, for they are sure to bring the very thing we fear to admit.'

'You cannot mean that, my lady,' Christiane defends, going cold at the thought of having to turn Henry and Dafydd away. 'We cannot refuse our men when they return from Calais. Your own kin will be among them; for sure you would want to see them? And for the others, don't they deserve to be allowed home after the service they have given to our king and to England?'

'See!' Amicia exclaims in frustration. 'You have no idea what is at risk here or you would never dispute my orders like this. It's so typical of you,' shaking Christiane's hand off angrily. 'You have never understood me.' Her face is warped with aggressive spite as she stares her down. 'You have never sympathised with what I endure, the pain and terror that dogs me daily. I feel so alone,' her voice catches on a sob. 'And you stand by and do nothing to help.'

At the iniquity of her charges, Christiane struggles to force herself to be calm; she clamps her lips shut against the rebuke she would speak and closes her eyes against the stirring of her own anger. The gentle touch of Father Peter's hand on her shoulder silently communicates his fellow-feeling.

'This makes no sense, my lady,' Christiane breathes through her anger, her voice controlled and quietly insistent. 'Father Peter's right: they'll be more concerned about how they're to meet this quarter's financial obligations.'

'All the better. Their debts will make them more obedient,' Amicia bites back.

'Many will wonder why we're raising concerns about something happening on distant shores,' Christiane cautions.

'Forewarned is forearmed,' Amicia opines sanctimoniously.

'Such demands will not be taken seriously,' frustration increasing within her. 'They will see there is no immediate threat and will not obey.'

'Then you shall make them! With whatever punishments it requires.'

'Please, my lady, see sense. We cannot punish them at a time like this!' Christiane begs. 'They are facing the prospect of starvation this winter. How can you threaten them with this danger too?'

'You have ever been too lenient with them,' Amicia accuses. 'Always advocating that we show mercy, hectoring me to take their pathetic little circumstances into account. Are you surprised that they offer us disrespect and disobedience in return? I will not have it! I am their lady, and they will do as I say!'

Both women turn away from one another, knowing they will go too far if they say more. A long and intensely uncomfortable pause ensues, Amicia's shoulders rigid with rejection, Christiane torn between guilt for giving her pain and her sense of obligation to their people.

Eventually, the priest breaks the silence. 'Perhaps,' he ventures, 'perhaps we might wait until the Michaelmas court? Another few weeks should make us better informed about this situation. It is far enough away to give us time before we must decide how to respond, should we need to respond at all.'

Christiane sighs with relief. 'Your advice is sound, as always, Father.'

Amicia sits back heavily, her head bowed as she gives in.

'That is tolerable to me,' she begrudges. 'But,' raising her eyes so both he and Christiane see the bleakness within, 'what if it's too late by then?'

Chapter Fifty-eight

Threfield Percy. 20th September 1976

Plague.

The very word fills me with dread.

What it is to know too much. To know what she is about to face before it happens.

Not just a disease: the greatest epidemic in history. They called it the pestilence. We call it the Black Death. The plague bacterium, carried by rats, transmitted by their fleas.

This is it.

It's sickening to feel it so close, surreal to feel it almost before me, as if I were about to live it myself. Rationally, I'm detached because I know it's not a risk to me but, emotionally, I'm appalled because I know what kind of risk it is to her.

Is this why I'm here? Can I help?

What could I possibly do?

And yet, why else would I be here? Why would we have this connection? Is there any way to communicate to her what this means, to help her protect herself, if not the village?

I'm not sure there's much she can do for the rest of them, but could she avoid it herself? Get as far away as possible from other people, from wherever the infection is.

I'm being irrational. I know what this means. In places, half the population dies, particularly in the towns. Those who catch the bubonic form stand a sixty per cent. chance of dying. Those with the pneumonic form die ninety per cent. of the time, and fast.

Even if I could intervene, would it change anything? Can you change the past? The laws of physics would say not.

So, why am I here, Christiane?

As the thought forms in my mind, I feel a prickle of awareness tickle across my skin.

Christiane.

She's here. How is she here?

Eoghan?

Her voice is in my head.

And, somehow, I'm seeing my world, my time as if she's seeing it through my eyes. That sounds absurd but it's the only way I can describe it to myself. I'm seeing through my eyes and *she's* seeing through my eyes too. And I'm aware of both.

I can see the walls of the tower bedroom all around me and yet I'm seeing their absence in my time too. More than that, I'm seeing *through* it all: the intricately carved stone blocks that make up the wall and the lime-plaster on top and the whitewash on top of that and the tapestries on top of that; yet I'm also seeing the remnants of the rubbed-out walls in my time, emerging from the ground like worn-down stumps of teeth, encroaching grass on one side, darkened soil on the other.

And I…we…see beyond, too. To the woodland: to her, a dense, dark backdrop of mature trees, well maintained for a source of firewood and timber for construction; to me a thin and scrappy shadow, self-sown silver birches, spindly and etiolated. To the fishpond: a large flat expanse in her time, clear water reflecting the blue and white of the sky; a reed-choked morass in mine, sharp green spines projecting skywards. To the church: bright and vibrant in its young stone and multi-coloured adorned windows; pocked and eroded in mine, a partly decayed corpse, its windows like empty eye sockets, its half-collapsed bell tower slumping down like stacked vertebrae without a body to hold them up.

I can feel the shock in her at seeing all this and recognising it.

Where are you?

What she means is "when", but she hesitates to ask it. The idea of encountering someone out of time must be incomprehensible to her.

She…we…look down at where I'm digging. And she can discern where she is, but it's disorientating because the level of the soil in-fill means it's akin to her standing in mid-air in the lower storey of the tower, at about the level of the bed's mattress.

She turns to look over her shoulder at the area I've covered with the tarp.

Henry.

His name comes to me instinctively and impulsively.

And immediately I wish I could take it back. How will knowing that make her feel?

But there's no feedback. Nothing to say she's caught my thought. Thank God.

I do pick up a flash of curiosity that crosses her mind, but it's as though she intuits that she doesn't really want to know what's under there, because she releases the impulse and looks away.

This is Amicia's home, she reflects, frowning. *What are you doing here?*

This is what I do. I dig to find answers.

I sense her concentrating, wanting to see if she can hear my thoughts.

What happened here? How did the building come to be like this? And the church?

She tries to listen, waiting for something to come through. When it doesn't, her frustration is evident. Wanting to understand but unable to. I focus with her, trying to communicate. Holding to thoughts about what I'm doing, what I'm looking for, in the hope that she'll pick something up.

But something's in the way: I'm receiving her thoughts, but she can't connect with mine.

Impatiently, she stands. And an overwhelming impulse forces me to stand as well. She looks along the lane, beyond the church.

The houses have gone. The gate too. There are no animals. No people.

What's happened to my home?

Her potent distress becomes my own a split second after I feel it wash through her, and the compounding effect of one on the other floors me.

In that instant, she's gone.

And I'm left feeling entirely empty. Hollowed out. A shell with too much room for just…me.

Chapter Fifty-nine

Threfield Percy. August 1348

Amicia's fears prove unfounded. For a year.

Against Christiane's misgivings, she forces them to tell people at the Michaelmas court. That's a dark day: announcing an incomprehensible threat amid the annual reckoning that shows them all, with parchment and ink, how stark their situation already is. A quarter of the crops have been lost to the August rains, leaving a yield almost as low as from the prior year's drought.

And yet, they make it through the winter. Most of them. The weak and the old bear the brunt of it, and there's little Christiane can do to alleviate their suffering. Life becomes more precarious even among those who remain; almost a third of householders part with land to meet their debts to the reeve and as many again remain under contract with him a year later.

When the steward relays news of the pestilence, a disquiet ripples through the village that takes many weeks to subside. For a while, they adhere to Amicia's strict demands; Christiane aches to see the fear that makes them so suspicious of others, so reticent to venture beyond the safety of their own borders.

But normal life tentatively resumes, with day-to-day difficulties and joys too present to let fear of a distant disease preoccupy them overly long.

It helps that they hear little more in the ensuing months, beyond occasional third- or fourth-hand stories from murmuring merchants in the towns. While it's beyond the sea, the threat seems well out of reach.

That is until one Sunday at mass when Father Peter, ashen-faced and clasping a parchment in trembling hands, ascends the pulpit.

The church is crammed with bodies; the word was sent out that everyone is expected here today.

For once, he doesn't resent the usual babble of gossiping at the back of the nave. Today, it has the reassurance of a world not yet changed, of simple faith in the continuity of lives taken for granted in their unvarying rhythms.

But eyes are drawn to him, and whispers hush the chatter; they know him well and their shock at the distress in his face changes the mood in a moment.

Nausea churns in the priest's stomach; he's sickened to know that he must shatter their fragile resilience, just when they had regained some semblance of equilibrium.

He looks over the faces he has known either for all of their lives or for most of his. How many will survive? Will he?

Amicia coughs deliberately from where she is seated at the front, charging him to get on with it. Everyone else stands in the nave, even the most elderly. Even Christiane. She stands with her people.

When the letter arrived from the archbishop, his first instinct was to turn to Christiane. He, like all of them, has come to rely on her over the years. Amid the chaos centred on Amicia and the darkness she draws to herself, Christiane is their calm haven of light. Her head is bowed as she prays silently for God's strength for all of them this day.

Though, he recalls, even she can be drawn into that maelstrom on occasion, reflecting on tense words between Christiane and Amicia last evening as they discussed how best to share the contents of the letter. Those difficult episodes happen more frequently now; perhaps it is unsurprising when she commits so much of her time to caring for and distracting the older woman. As he knows himself, it's hard not to get sucked into the eddies of her mania.

He raises his eyes from Christiane to the bright painting on the west wall portraying the Day of Doom and what awaits those who die without repentance, without purging their sin. He breathes deeply, trying to draw succour from his faith, reminding himself to accept God's great plan.

At the clearing of his throat, the church stills.

'It is my duty today,' he starts, 'to relay to you some words from my lord the archbishop of York, who has written to every parish and who instructs me to read this to you, his flock.'

What he knows, and they don't, is that this has happened in other regions when the pestilence is closing in. First in the southwest, when the Bishop of Bath and Wells exhorted them all to pray as the pestilence hovered on the northern edges of France. And more recently in the great capital, under the Bishop of London.

Now, Archbishop Zouche has distributed his guidance from York; it is shocking to know even the northern reaches of the realm now have to ready themselves.

'*In so far as the life of men upon earth is warfare,*' Father Peter reads, '*it is no wonder that those who battle amidst the wickedness of the world are sometimes disturbed by uncertain events; on one occasion favourable, on another adverse. For Almighty God sometimes allows those he loves to be troubled while their strength is perfected in weakness by an outpouring of spiritual grace.*'

He glances at his congregation: they are not used to such convoluted language and are struggling to follow. But what ensues will not be misunderstood.

'*Everybody knows, since the news is now widely spread, what a great pestilence, mortality and infection of the air there are in diverse parts of the world and which, at this moment, are threatening in particular the land of England.*'

So many gasps arise at once that it's like a collective intake of breath; the archbishop has assumed this is well known in the world, but that is not the case here. This is the moment that it becomes real to them.

'*This, surely, must be caused by the sins of men who, made complacent by their prosperity, forget that such bounty are the gifts of the most high Giver. Thus, the inevitable human fate, pitiless death that spares no one, now threatens us...*'

Mutterings start.

'...unless the holy clemency of the Saviour is shown to his people from on high, the only hope is to hurry back to him alone, whose mercy outweighs justice and who, most generous in forgiving, rejoices heartily in the conversion of sinners...'

He raises his voice as the hubbub below grows louder.

'...humbly urging him with orisons and prayers that he, the kind and merciful Almighty God, should turn away his anger and remove the pestilence and drive away the infection from the people whom he redeemed with his precious blood.

'Therefore we command...'

He stops, hardly able to hear himself, and knowing they are no longer listening but reacting. He waits, allowing them to regulate themselves; in a few moments they start shushing each other.

'Therefore we command,' he continues, *'and order to let it be known with all possible haste, that devout processions are to be held every Wednesday and Friday in our cathedral church, in other collegiate and conventual churches, and in every parish church in our city and diocese, with a solemn chanting of the litany, and that a special prayer be said in mass every day for allaying the plague and pestilence...'*

That sets them off again. Never in their lives has such an instruction been made by the Church and they feel the import of it, a weight reinforced by that unity with other congregations, from their lowliest parish church to the great minister in York; what is meant to give them a feeling of togetherness brings home to them the scale of the threat that is approaching.

'...and likewise prayers for the lord king,' he's almost shouting now, eager to get the rest over and done with, *'and for the good estate of the Church, the Realm and the whole People of England, so that the Saviour, harkening to the constant entreaties, will pardon and come to the rescue of the creation which God fashioned in his own image.'*

He halts again, holding up his hand to encourage silence; it takes a long time for them to settle enough for him to be heard, and he keeps his hand raised for emphasis to show them they must give their attention to this part.

'And we, trusting in the mercy of Almighty God, and the merits and prayers of his mother, the glorious Virgin Mary, and of the blessed apostles Peter and Paul, and of the most holy confessor and of all the saints, have released forty days of the penance enjoined by the gracious God on all our parishioners and on others whose diocesans have approved and accepted this our indulgence, for sins for which they are penitent, contrite and have made confession, if they pray devoutly for these things, celebrate masses, undertake processions or are present at them, or perform other offices of pious devotion.'

He feels immense relief by the time he is done, released from the heaviness of the news and his own part in conveying it to them.

And he waits for the world to come crashing down.

Chapter Sixty

Threfield Percy. August 1348

There is silence.

As each of them struggles to take the news for themselves, they look to one another to know how to react. Finding their worst emotions reflected in each other's faces, their bewilderment rapidly spirals down into doubt then blame then anger.

'Why should we believe you?'

It's Henry Child, so often the spokesman for the tenants, who starts to question the priest.

'What's that you say, Master Child?' Father Peter responds, mainly to take time to gather himself.

The other men give way to allow him to come to the front. 'I said, why should we believe what you tell us, Father?' His tone remains respectful, but he questions with the authority of both age and standing. 'You warned us about this a year ago, yet nothing happened then. It put us through weeks of worry for naught. Why should we believe you now?'

'I'm not asking you to believe me,' he defends. 'This comes from Archbishop Zouche himself. He would not mislead us.'

'Aye, we can believe the archbishop,' Robert de Windt contends. 'I fought alongside his men at Neville's Cross, and he didn't lead us wrong.'

'Does it follow that we should trust what he says on this?' Reginald Ketel doubts. 'What does he actually know about this pestilence?'

'Is it even in England yet?' Gilbert Wragge leaps in. 'The last we heard it was plaguing the French. With every justification!' he jokes.

''Tis said this was a punishment for the Cathars and Tartars,' Joan Hering inserts. 'Why would God curse good and true Englishmen with such a disease?'

'Where is the pestilence now, Father?' Anne Wragge pipes up, hopefully. 'Does the sea yet stand between us and it?'

Father Peter's blood chills. 'It has not been confirmed…'

'Tell us the truth!' Reginal Ketel growls. 'No covering it up, Father!'

'Peace, Master Ketel,' Henry Child urges. 'Let the priest be heard.'

'I have not had official word,' Father Peter starts again. 'But there is talk…some say…'

'Out with it, Father,' Hilary Ketel cajoles, as forthright as her husband.

'Some may have been infected in the south-west,' he admits heavily.

'In the south-west? But that's miles away. It may never reach us,' Elias Gamel hopes.

'Fool!' Reginald turns on him. 'We said it would never cross Europe. We said it would never cross the Channel. What makes you think it will stop now?'

A woman cries out at the back of the nave and others start whimpering and lamenting with her.

'Stop that!' a man's voice appeals. 'You'll scare the children.'

'And why shouldn't they be scared?' Letitia Fraunceys staunchly supports her. 'That's a death sentence the priest has just read.'

Even Henry Child blanches as her words hit home.

'Father, what must we do?' she turns to him, imploring some relief. 'How can we avoid infection?'

'Are there treatments that can heal?' chimes in Mary Hering, already thinking ahead to what herbs she might need to gather.

At a loss, Father Peter looks to Christiane for guidance, but she stares helplessly at him. Neither knows enough to reassure.

'Can we keep it out if we close our gates and doors?' Henry Child intervenes.

'For sure, if we stop anyone coming in, no one can bring it to us. Can they?' Anne Wragge posits.

'We must be more vigilant. Less people coming and going,' her husband enjoins.

'I pledge to do my level best,' Walter atte Gate proudly turns towards the crowd to assure them.

'And how will *you* keep them out if they insist on coming in?' Reginald Ketel disdains. 'No, we shall appoint a watch, men to stand guard day and night. Master Reeve can organise us.'

The reeve looks sick at the thought, his skin as grey as ash.

'If,' a hesitant voice interjects from the back, 'if, as the archbishop says, this is the fault of those who have forgotten from where their good fortune comes, how is it that we who are so poor can suffer the same?'

'You think yourself so poor, do you, Mistress?' Amicia intervenes, her voice acid with scorn. Though she does not stand, does not even turn to face them, the shock of hearing her speak stills the crowd. Shrouded in black and with her ghostly pale sun-deprived skin, she casts an unnatural chill over the church. 'Do you not have a roof over your head? Do you not have food in your bellies? And land and animals enough to feed your families? How dare you count yourselves as not among the prosperous, you ungrateful swine?'

In the aftermath, none dares speak; eventually, old Agnes breaks the silence.

'Why would God punish us so, Father? What have we done that has made him so angry?'

Father Peter has struggled with this himself, praying for God's patient guidance. He rolls around the words he practised in his head earlier. 'It may not be that He is angry,' he suggests. 'This could be His blessing, a call to repentance. Think of it as an opportunity to reflect on our own lives and to come into His grace.'

'A blessing?' Gilbert Wragge scorns. 'That's stretching it, even for you, priest!'

'What must we do, Father?' old Agnes persists.

'The archbishop has guided us: I shall organise processions every Wednesday and Friday, and as many should join as are able. We will walk the boundary of the village, chanting the litanies. And I shall lead additional prayers each day at mass.'

'You must do more than that,' Amicia intervenes, reprising arguments she made to the priest the night before and ignoring the resistance he expressed then. 'Such obeyances have been used elsewhere and have been insufficient. But you are better placed than most,' she opines self-righteously. 'Pray God will spare us in return for my long suffering in his name. But each of you must also adhere more closely to his law: there shall be no more playing music or gambling with dice.'

Murmurs – outraged yet afraid to dissent – ripple through the crowd. She ignores them.

'Those who can should give alms,' Father Peter suggests. 'We must be ready to help one another, to feed the hungry, to clothe the naked. And continue to visit the sick.'

'We must all give money to expiate our sins,' Amicia overrides him. 'But they should be to enhance the church, to glorify Our Lord. Surely then He will not want to punish us. Father Peter,' ignoring the resentment she knows is within him, 'you shall gather the money and I shall plan how it can be used.'

At that, the crowd's tone starts to turn ugly. Until Amicia stands. Leaning heavily – dramatically – on her stick as if to emphasise the illness she endures, she turns to confront them. She almost smiles at the nervousness they show, seeing several of them fall back a step.

'And no one,' hardly raising her voice since an anxious silence has descended, 'no one is to leave the manor. No markets, no fairs. I have permitted you much liberty this last year...'

'It was either that or starve!' a voice mutters from the back.

'Then thank the Lord it is no longer necessary,' Amicia rebuffs. 'The harvest is good this year; make do with what you already have. Do not leave the village. Any who does puts all our lives at risk. You know the threat that hangs over me,' and her voice trembles at the words. 'Each and every one of you holds my life in your hands. It is your responsibility now to keep me safe.'

There is anger and belligerence in the faces of many, but their voices are stoppered; none will gainsay her to her face.

Father Peter raises his hand to call their eyes from her to him, hoping to distract them.

'Although God often afflicts us to prove our patience and justly to punish our sins,' he warns, 'it is not in man's power to judge His divine counsels. We have been guided how to avert this doom, so let us join the processions and pray together at mass. And we shall ask God, in his infinite and ineffable mercy, to lay his hand over this manor and bring us safely through the other side.

'Now go,' he dismisses them before the situation can deteriorate further, 'and may God's blessing be with us all.'

Chapter Sixty-one

Threfield Percy. 20th September 1976

I've never seen him struggle so much.

Her words jolt me back to my time. Because she's said them to me, directly.

Christiane?

Father Peter. She's thinking aloud and I'm catching her thoughts. *There's almost a physical sickness in him at the fear of what's coming. He's worried he's not strong enough to guide them through these times.*

I think he's saddened by how much he's weakened in the years he's been Amicia's priest; his passion for his ministry is a faded shadow of what it once was. He blames himself for allowing her to control him, to dictate to him, and yet he has no moral strength to pull himself out of the mire and do what he knows he should.

And he'll rely on you to make up for his weakness, I reflect. Just like everyone else does.

Kneeling on the ground, I lean back on my heels as I stretch the ache out of my back and neck. It's mid-morning. The air is fresh, but the sun is warm on my skin, and I feel an unexpected sense of well-being and ease. For a moment.

You know what's coming, don't you?

The bleakness of her words is a sharp contrast with that momentary ease.

How long before it reaches us?

There's a pause, as if she's listening for my answer. I wish I could tell her. I wish she could hear.

You know what it is, don't you? I wish I could know what you know.

Another pause.
How do I help them, Eoghan?
Her tone has an edge of desperation to it.

How is it spread? What can I use to treat it? What symptoms am I looking for?

You'll know that soon enough, I think. The word of the buboes will spread even faster than the disease. You'll hear stories so horrific you'll immediately regret the hearing. The excruciating pain of the buboes, the stench of suppurating flesh. The terror of mortality rates so high as to seem incredible. The helplessness of not understanding how it's transmitted. The horror of seeing those first symptoms emerge in someone you love. Of knowing there's nothing you can do now but ride out the storm, whatever it brings. For them. Or for you.

You're afraid. I can feel it. I can feel your fear.

And I can feel hers notch up in response to mine.

Why can't you tell me? she demands angrily. *I'm begging you, just tell me!*

And suddenly I can see her. Standing in front of me. Looking down at me where I'm kneeling in the dirt. We're face to face across the centuries. She's so close to me I feel I could reach out and touch her. And the desire to do so is painful.

'I would tell you everything, if you could only hear me.' Desperation floods through me at the thought. 'Why can't you hear me?'

She stares for a long moment, but then it's like she reads something in my face, and her expression softens. *I think you would tell me everything, if you could, wouldn't you?* she judges, coming half a step closer to me. She shakes her head regretfully. *Why can't I hear you?*

Chapter Sixty-two

Threfield Percy. December 1348

We're in the main room of the solar.

It's dark outside and there's a bite in the air; a large fire is lit, with plenty of logs set by to keep it going until they retire. Beyond the open door to the Great Hall, the usual evening noise continues; the hubbub of latecomers finishing supper while others clear away and settle down for the evening.

I've been summoned. And I'm not the only one: as I arrive, so do Father Peter, Philip of Ghent and Simon Reeve. At a nod from her, the servant departs, closing the Hall door behind him.

She's standing by what she still thinks of as Geoffrey's chair, though it's more than twenty years since he died. Maybe Ralf hasn't been here enough to override that claim; maybe it helps her to feel his fatherly presence still with her. Whichever, she's taking support from that connection with him tonight.

It makes me realise how little those around her perceive. They do not see how she strives to maintain a façade of normality while presiding over supper; even now, none of them registers her inner preoccupation as she tends to her guests, guiding them close to the fire.

She remembers to herself how Richard Prudhomme would pick up on her moods, then smiles ruefully. First Geoffrey, now Richard; her mind is haunted by ghosts tonight.

She invites Philip to pour them each a goblet of wine. Elias picked out for her the best from their dwindling stock; shipments from France are few and far between now, with merchants less inclined or able to maintain their usual activities. It concerns her that many weeks have passed since she last heard from Hughes. The usual patterns of the world are unravelling. How much we rely on those for our sense of well-being.

Perhaps that's why, after an initial spate of enthusiasm, the level of attendance at daily mass has ebbed to what it was before; even the weekly processions now attract only a threadbare group from the same handful of stalwarts.

Maybe that's human nature: after four months of waiting for the plague to arrive, they've reverted to their old behaviours. It's difficult to sustain a heightened level of anxiety about a faceless threat.

Father Peter looks tired. Unlike his flock, he has maintained all those additional duties and imposed on himself heightened attentiveness to each and every soul. For him, the threat has brought home the fragility of life and the responsibility he bears for their redemption; he takes it hard that most of them seem so little concerned for themselves.

The reeve is nervous: Christiane sees a mustard-yellow tinge to his aura, which is also opaque and strangely sluggish. He's always agitated around her now and avoids her whenever he can. The way he takes advantage of others' difficulties sits badly with her, though she's not spoken of it to him, yet. He's fretting about why she's called them together tonight.

For a few moments, they talk of preparations for the Christmas festivities. If she can, she will make this season feel as normal as possible; she can't overturn Amicia's ban on music, but there can still be games and other entertainments.

But there's no escaping the fact that the revelries have an unreal quality to them this year.

'Anne Wragge tells me Gilbert is refusing to attend,' Father Peter remarks. 'He's insisting the whole household stays away from any of the feasts.'

'It's Mistress Wragge's own fault,' Simon Reeve condemns, 'for listening to tall tales. She's been telling everyone about that black-clothed preacher she heard in Malton market square. She threatens all of them with agonising deaths that will carry off half the village and repeats his warnings that it takes many so fast and so suddenly that they die unshriven, facing centuries in Purgatory if not an eternity in Hell.'

Even the priest shivers at that one.

'Whatever the cause,' Christiane cuts in, 'Master Wragge hasn't left his house in days, except to tend his fields and animals.'

'It is hard to watch, and yet we must respect their decisions,' the priest advises. 'Each is choosing their path based on their personal concerns.'

'I have asked Elias to prepare enough food for all and to allow them to come to the kitchens to take their share if they will not join us in the Hall,' she affirms.

The reeve tuts; it's an habitual judgement that escapes him thoughtlessly, and he flushes red at his indiscretion. 'Master Reeve?' she questions his intervention.

He hesitates but, in his nervousness, he has drunk the strong wine too fast, and it loosens his tongue. 'Such indulgence encourages disobedience,' he grumbles. 'And I am always the one facing the sharp edge of that blade.'

'These are unusual times,' she consoles. 'A little kindness will go a long way.'

''Tis weakness,' he maintains, sullenly.

'Maybe, Master Reeve,' Christiane rebuts. 'But what we do today sets a standard for how we shall respond to this challenge when the time comes.'

At those words, a new seriousness settles over them.

She takes a deep breath. 'I have a letter from Dafydd to share with you.'

In fact, she has written to all three of her men. Reluctant to rely on local gossip and rumours, she sought what they know of this disease, hoping their positions in the world will give better insight. And at the same time, softly reminded them of their duty to their own people.

A rare – and, for that reason, acute – anger simmers within her at how Ralf responded: he flatly refused to return to the manor or to raise a hand to help, insisting he was essential to holding the peace on the Scottish border. With hollow flattery about her ability to manage without him, he washed his hands of them.

The pain caused by her elder son she buries deeper: her heart aches at the curt lines of refusal, so self-serving, so careless of others. She's disappointed that Henry has turned out so much like his father and blames herself for the failure.

Though there is a worse niggling thought worming itself deep in her mind: what if she has already seen her son for the last time?

There is, however, one letter she holds in her hand. It has taken some weeks to reach them. As I look at the weather-stained parchment, I sense its journey, being passed from hand to reluctant hand, reliant on the thinning numbers who are still willing to travel England's roads; messengers are almost impossible to find.

Ah. Now I know why I'm here.

As my awareness tunes in to her, I feel her focus encompass me.

She passes over Dafydd's introduction, private words couched in accepted phrases – a respectful opening, wishes for her well-being, promises of aid in whatever way he can give it – but which resonate with a deep love.

He, too, is unable to come home: the earl of Lancaster will not release him, nor any of the retinue, while the king remains at Westminster. Parliament continues to sit: the barons will present a semblance of normality, offering a visible leadership to the country for as long as they can.

The four of them must do the same for the people of Threfield Percy.

'I believe the more we know the better we can prepare,' Christiane starts, holding each man's eyes in turn. 'But this is heavy knowledge to bear, so I ask you not to share too much with our people just yet for fear of overwhelming their hearts. In time, we will not be able to keep this from them, but we might give them the blessing of living with the painful anticipation for as short a time as possible.'

The priest and her steward look grave but ready. The reeve looks heartily sick; it is he she most worries about but to exclude him from this, given his status and influence, could do more harm than good.

She reads.

All reports confirm it is a pestilence of unprecedented ferocity. It started in the East some two or three years since and spread across the Levant. At the Michaelmas before last, it leapt to Sicily, and from thence moved swiftly to the mainland and other islands.

Throughout the winter, it continued to extend around the Mediterranean and entered via the great ports into France and Spain. Marseilles sent Genoa's ships away, but too late: they had already let the pestilence in.

Even Avignon, that great city with its abundance of holy men, has not been immune. If the most powerful prayers and penitential processions are not sufficient to appease God's wrath even in the Pope's own city, what hope can there be for the humblest of men?

News reaches us daily of the toll it is taking on France and the Low Countries; there are tales – though it is not possible to know the truth of this – of cities where barely one-tenth of men remain alive.

For two months now it has been creeping inland from our western and southern shores. We cannot deceive ourselves: this scourge has never weakened nor ceased its determined progression elsewhere, so why should we be spared?

You ask what we might do to avoid infection. The only answer seems to be to stay as far from other beings as possible. We prayed the Channel might keep our island kingdom separate but that was a vain hope; this pestilence has already crossed far greater seas than ours. In Parliament, many called for us to turn all ships away, yet such a response is impractical, and the king is too reliant on revenues from the merchants to refill his coffers after the war in France. Nor should he: is he not king to more than the English? Has he not the same duty of care to those in Calais, the Agenais and Gascony as he has to his people here?

Would that I could give you reliable guidance on what you should expect or how to protect yourself and others, my beloved mother. Some say it is spreading as a miasma in the air, a poisoned cloud that drifts wherever the wind will take it. Others disagree and insist it moves from man to man; they advise not to look in the eyes of one sickening or dead from the disease as being the route by which it is communicated.

In truth, no physician seems to know how to heal or to prevent transmission, though many profess their knowledge loudly enough. Indeed, even the symptoms create confusion. Some cough up large amounts of blood and die within two days; any who looks on them becomes infected, and none survives the experience. Others linger longer and show hideously blackened and foul-smelling swellings in the armpit or groin or neck; I hear word that some survive if the boils dissipate, though they are but few.

You asked for the truth, my dearest lady mother. I would hesitate to write such blunt realities to any woman but you, yet I know your inward strength and I trust you have those around you who might prove themselves worthy by supporting you.

I shall write again should I receive any insight I believe can assist you. I pray daily that our beloved Holy Mother will protect you and live in hope that I may see you again in better times, God willing.

Your loving son, Dafydd.

As she puts the parchment down on her lap, there is silence in the room, punctuated only by the pop and hiss of a damp log on the fire.

She's watching for their responses.

And she's feeling for mine.

I'm cursing myself for not having read those two books in Michael's library. I took them off the shelf, even sat down to read them. But I got distracted.

I'm perpetually immersed in periods of history and surrounded by inordinately insightful historians, and yet my knowledge of the Black Death is little more than that of an average schoolboy. Perhaps I should go to the flat? There must be something more relevant than talk of disease clouds and avoiding eye contact. How is it spread? Black rats and fleas, I know that much. The bubonic form – the black buboes in the lymph nodes that they talk about – and the pneumonic form that hits the lungs. Fleas jumping to human hosts after they decimate the rat population. Transferred in infested cloth too.

I notice that Christiane's sitting incredibly still, as if she's listening intently though the room remains silent; I think she's trying to pick up my thoughts. Even if I knew enough to help her, would I be able to communicate it? Could she receive it?

But then I catch an image that flashes through her mind. She sees the village's gate barred and manned, the doors and windows of the houses shuttered and closed. An eerie stillness in the village, each family closeted away from the next.

Is she getting that from me?

My fingers tingle: it feels like hope.

Dafydd's right: isolation is their best answer. Can they stop it coming here? Can they stop it spreading?

'When the time comes,' Christiane turns to the three men before her, 'we must use our isolation to our advantage. Our best hope is to prevent anyone coming in who might already be infected.' The irony that Amicia's paranoid precautions may be their best defence is not lost of any of us.

'When the time comes?' the steward probes.

'The pestilence does not leap unaided from one location to the next,' Christiane reassures him. 'It is carried in some form, and though we don't know what that is, yet we will be able to see it nearing for there are sure to be cases in the area before it reaches us. That may be weeks or months. We must be watchful and ready.'

'But what if it is spread in the air?' the reeve agitates.

'Then there may be little we can do.' A tetchy answer born of a long frustration with him. Then she corrects herself with a sigh. 'We shall encourage people to stay in their houses and to burn fires to purify the air.'

'We must ensure everyone has sufficient food and fuel,' Philip remarks.

'And support for the sick. I'm concerned we're already seeing neighbours shunning one another when illness is rumoured,' Father Peter mulls. 'It is our duty to help those who cannot help themselves.'

'I disagree,' Simon Reeve inserts. 'Each must look after their own. They must close their doors and take responsibility for themselves.'

'We cannot leave them to suffer unaided,' Philip of Ghent disagrees, shocked by the reeve's callous lack of concern.

'No, we cannot,' Christiane reinforces before resentment can be returned; she needs unity between the four of them. 'Let us agree what practical steps we can take now.'

'I shall review our food stores,' the steward offers. 'And see if we might acquire some additional supplies, just in case.'

'Perhaps you and Master Reeve might make careful enquiries, thinking about any household that could struggle if they should have to be contained?' Christiane suggests. He nods.

'I must reiterate our responsibilities to one another in this season's sermons,' Father Peter muses. 'And I shall redouble my efforts to encourage people to confession.'

It makes Christiane wonder what would happen if the priest were one of the first to die; who then would hear their confessions or administer the Last Rites?

'I will enforce the demesne responsibilities at the court next month,' the reeve opines. 'Master Wragge has twice failed to turn up this week, and his punishment will stand as a clear warning to others.'

'I'm glad you have raised the subject, Master Reeve,' Christiane broaches. 'I was thinking we must be charitable in how we respond to such breaches at this time.'

'There are several who have not fulfilled their demesne obligations this quarter,' he asserts. 'Not just Master Wragge.'

'Maybe so, but…'

'And to show lenience would be taken as weakness,' he interrupts.

'Where breaches are clear and deliberate,' she accedes. 'But where neglect has been born of fear or motivated by self-protection, can we not extend some compassion?'

'We are coming up to a critical time of year,' he points out forcefully, as if she weren't sufficiently aware for herself. 'Would you put the harvest at risk for lack of sufficient labour now?'

'I am asking you to tread a fine line, Master Reeve,' she asserts, irritated by his highhandedness. 'And I am suggesting that a quiet word might carry more weight than a public punishment in some instances.'

His resistance is almost palpable. 'My lady expects heavy fines from the next court,' he objects.

'After all these years, Master Reeve,' she criticises, her patience stretched thin, her words clipped with barely contained annoyance, 'how is it you are still not aware that when my lord is absent it is to me that his responsibilities and power fall, not his lady mother?'

The barb stings and his face reddens in response. He stands, though he has not been dismissed.

'We are not finished, Master Reeve,' she halts him as he heads for the door. 'I am also concerned about those who are financially vulnerable at the moment.'

'And why are you raising this with me?' sullenly.

'The court rolls make it clear many of their debts are held by you. I would ask you to give them some leeway.'

'Leeway?' The word is like acid on his tongue. 'What I demand is only mine by right.'

'That is not in dispute,' she pursues. 'However, I have particular concerns about Hugh and Anne Miller.'

'Who have long been beneficiaries of your attention,' he points out.

'They are far from being alone in that, Master Reeve,' she justifies, an icy edge of warning in her voice. 'I am aware they have sold most of their land to you and in defaulting at the next payment will forfeit the rest of their property.'

'You seem to know much,' he resents.

'A man without land has little to keep him here,' she persists. 'I would not want to see the Millers decide to leave Threfield Percy. We have already lost too many men…'

'That is not my concern,' he interrupts.

'Then it should be!' she argues angrily. 'You have benefited mightily from this manor over the years. And I shall no longer stand by while you milk it dry for your own gain!'

She catches herself, too late. She has gone too far, stirred by his selfishness.

'You will find that every contract is writ tight and every term is clearly set out. There is nothing you can do. *My lady*,' with disdainful emphasis.

'Let me be plain, Master Reeve.' She stands to confront him head-on. Small man that he is, in body as well as in spirit, she can easily look him in the face. 'We have no idea when this pestilence will reach us, nor how badly it will affect us, nor how many of us will survive.' He whitens at her words and his aura turns a deep shade of grey with fear. 'I have tolerated your self-serving ways for the sake of harmony on the manor. What little I ask for Anne and Hugh is well within your scope to provide.'

He contemplates her, thinking hard, trying to wriggle around her request. 'And what if they should die of the pestilence in the meantime? You know their debts die with them.'

'Then I will personally honour that debt,' she avers, lifting her chin determinedly.

He meets her gaze. 'I will have that in writing, my lady,' he demands.

'Draw up the agreement,' she accepts. 'And I shall sign it. Now,' fighting down her own anger at his insulting treatment, 'you may leave, Master Reeve.'

Her heart is beating hard as he gives her one last spite-filled look.

As the door closes behind him, she takes a deep breath and curses herself for allowing him to goad her into such rashness.

That was a mistake.

Chapter Sixty-three

Threfield Percy. 20th September 1976

Time is slipping.

I find myself back in my own present. The sun has climbed high overhead; a morning's work is done, but all that painstaking scraping has yielded little beyond more charred material and the substance of the stone steps that lead down from the door into the bedchamber.

Though I'm back in my own time, I'm still aware of her.

I can hear her fretting about that argument with the reeve. It's left her feeling unsettled. Vulnerable, almost. She's never trusted him, but she's never given him a reason to turn against her. Until now.

As her mood calms, I sense her attention switch to my time, as if she's with me while I work, watching what I'm doing. I like it. I like her company.

Her mind quiets in focusing on my careful action, just as mine does in becoming absorbed by the task.

She spots the artefact in the same moment as I do, and I feel a rush of interest flash through us simultaneously.

What is it?

The long, thin piece of metal broadening out into ornate filigree, flower-shaped and substantial, claws holding a dark stone.

I feel her at my shoulder, watching intently. Watching with intent. Because she's not waiting to see what it is, as I am, she's waiting to identify it.

It belongs to Amicia.

Geoffrey gave it to her the year before he died. I just put it away...

She replays that action in her mind, turning as if to look for the box she's stored it in. Remembering the weight and shape of it in her fingers, the nap of the velvet cloth she wrapped it in, the smell of oak and leather and cloth that rose as she opened the jewels case. The attention with which she tucked it among the other wrapped items, in its usual place to be easy to retrieve next time. She's even recalling the intricacy of the silver key, the smoothness of the mechanism as she locks it and Amicia's possessive expression as she holds her hand out to retrieve the key, not trusting Christiane with it, even now.

We feel the disconnect between that small act and the position and condition of the pin now. Tarnished to black and with the brilliance of the ruby and the detail of the silverwork dulled and muted by dark, fire-filled soil.

She shivers. She senses it, just as I do.

What happened here?

The air around me is changing: the sun has disappeared behind a blanket of cloud, overlaid with faster-moving, greyer ones that threaten rain; the warmth of the day has gone.

Someone's here.

My hackles go up as I hear Christiane's words and I raise my head to see a small, squat figure some twenty yards hence.

Who is she? A frown of concentration.

The farmer's wife. She sees me looking and gestures towards a packet she's left on the grass: more food. Even from here, her resistance to coming any closer is strong. As if she's fulfilling an obligation to be here, to help me, but would rather be a thousand miles away.

And I wonder suddenly if her reticence comes from more than the local superstitious fear.

Because her eyes are fixed and staring. But she's not looking at me.

Chapter Sixty-four

The Savoy Palace. January 1349

My well-beloved lady Mother, I recommend me to you, with such tidings as I have to share.

Our lord king has, at last, decided to prorogue Parliament and will delay its next sitting until after Easter in the hope of evading the pestilence that is now rife in the capital. Though I hear evil cant from those who know no better, none should doubt the king's courage in the face of this terrible threat; he has remained in London longer than many of his nobles, which has for certain helped to sustain a measured rule amid the unprecedented fear and uncertainty that surrounds us all. And this despite bearing a close and personal grief from losing his beloved daughter, Joan, to this plague at Bordeaux last June.

The king and queen will sojourn at Windsor, where the cleaner air, it is believed, may protect their royal personages and, God willing, bring them through the crisis safely.

Many others did not wait for the king to lead the way but departed as soon as the Christmas festivities were over; distant manors that have seen neither hide nor hair of their masters for many a year are now home to the country's greatest lords and ladies, hoping to hide away where the pestilence cannot reach them.

With Parliament suspended, my lord the earl of Lancaster will now return to his estates. I pray that you, gentle Mother, will find it in your heart to understand when I tell you that I have chosen not to leave when he does.

From what I know of your caring nature and dutiful service, I believe you, of all people, will reinforce my decision when I tell you what we are facing.

As many as sixty deaths a day are being recorded in the City of London; if experiences in Paris and other great cities are to be believed, we can expect that number to exceed two hundred a day in the coming weeks. Indeed, Bishop Stratford has consecrated ground at Smithfield for a new cemetery, the second such new site, as the existing ones will soon be full.

Any who has somewhere else to stay departs, but that is not a choice open to multitudes of people, who are left to fend for themselves in these filthy streets and dank air, often without any to lead them or even those who can treat or tend to them. The Church has ordered the priests to remain in their parishes and administer to their flock; while many do, they are often themselves among the first to die, exposed as they are to the sick in ministering to their departing souls.

I hardly know how I may help, yet I cannot deny the calling within me to do so. I do this in full knowledge of what it likely means and can ask only that you will pray for us all, beloved Mother.

By your obedient son, Dafydd.

Chapter Sixty-five

Threfield Percy. January 1349

It has taken the best part of a month for his letter to reach her.

He could already be dead.

Her mind rushes to protect her with denial of that appalling thought.

For so long she has faced the thought of losing her husband or her elder son, martial men both, but she has not prepared herself for losing Dafydd. Not this gentle man, this thoughtful, intelligent, deep-feeling boy who is not even yet of age.

But there's no time to think as Philip of Ghent arrives to escort her into the Great Hall: supper is over, and the restless crowd is impatient for the manor court hearing to begin.

She takes the central chair on the dais, nods to the reeve to start proceedings and tries to ignore thoughts that would drag her mind away.

The Hall is heated, both physically and emotionally. Since the turn of the year, the mood has shifted like the wind, becoming increasingly ugly and divisive. Few are absent tonight: it is ironic how conflict brings this community together.

Despite her appeal for caution, it didn't take long for news of the outbreak to spread. Once out, word travelled as fast as fire. She can't help but suspect the reeve has deliberately gone against her in this; she guesses too that he has seeded doubts by implying she wanted to keep this knowledge from them.

The range of reactions to the threat is telling.

For some, the heightened carousing of the Christmas season continues unabated. At this rate, many will not have enough food to get them through the rest of the winter and care even less. If death is coming, they argue, what merit is there in restraint? Life must be lived to the fullest when the end is in sight.

At the other extreme are those whose entire focus is the strictest adherence to God's laws. How else might they stop the pestilence arriving but by the grace of God? She has some sympathy with their stance, finding a reassuring calm in her faith, but not with how quick they are to blame and chastise others. What if, they argue, those who carouse and fornicate and make a virtue of every possible sin bring the plague to their very door? It is one thing for others' licentious behaviour to call down God's pestilential punishment upon themselves, but quite another to put others at risk.

Together, they turn against one another, self-righteous, convinced and condemning.

Mercifully, there yet remains a measured majority, those whose comfort comes in maintaining life's habits, reconciled to facing whatever comes and whatever remains thereafter. It is they who continue to farm the land, to tend their animals, to support their families and neighbours. But there is a wariness even among them, an increased suspicion of strangers and of those who break Amicia's embargo to sneak out to the towns, afraid that they might be the ones who bring the plague back.

A few of them talk about undertaking a pilgrimage to Our Lady of Walsingham in Norfolk or even to St Thomas a Becket's grave in Canterbury. Christiane sympathises but she knows Amicia will never allow it. Father Peter has tried to argue, disputing that no one has the right to prevent a pilgrimage by any who is genuinely called to it, but he is shouted down.

The reeve takes a seat in front of the dais; how he does love to preside over these occasions. He has always held himself superior to those he lives amongst. He revels in his position, in his ability to impact and manipulate their petty lives. They mistrust his closeness to Amicia but fret about it at the same time, and in the gap between he finds a power over them. Of late, he has taken to dressing in black clothes, rich velvets that proclaim his wealth but also emulate her appearance; he is becoming her physical manifestation before their eyes. Though she is ever-absent, yet everyone feels her skeletal fingers reaching into the room.

As Christiane watches him instruct the clerk – an absurd title that is nothing more than exaggerated ceremony, for Gilbert Beadle's son knows little reading or writing, and any records of the night's proceedings will be produced and carefully controlled between the reeve and Amicia – she assesses the man before her.

She has had few reasons to be near him since their disagreement and has assumed he is avoiding her as much as she is he. But now she notices with deep misgiving that something has been changing, that tones of a deep red are pushing into the fringes of the grey-brown hues that usually surround him. To her, it's a dark and hidden force that is contained behind an invisible membrane, but which is trying to push its way through the barrier. It is a colour she associates with Amicia.

The hearing starts with a long list of trespasses by one tenant against another; many illustrate a disturbing carelessness, with multiple claims for damage related to inadequate control of their animals, from cows and foals to geese.

After a drawn-out hour of one neighbour pitted against another, they exhaust the list, and the reeve turns to infringements against the manor itself.

Since Christmas, there has been a spate of thefts from their properties: straw from the hayloft; vegetables from the kitchen garden; pies and wine from the stores. The straw and vegetables are petty crimes motivated by need not malice, but the food and drink concern Christiane more, both for who is involved and for the manner of the act.

Elias Gamel, the cook, is called to the front with his co-conspirators: Reginald and Hilary Ketel; and Hugh, the husband of Anne Miller. Called as witnesses are Joseph Crow, an elderly and rheumatic servant who sleeps near the kitchen fires for warmth, and the Ketels' neighbour, Alice Beadle, who saw them returning to the house, noisy and disruptive, with their spoils late one night.

For those determined to drink their way to the end, the alewives can hardly brew their batches fast enough. Hilary's latest supply was so deeply consumed one evening that Elias, significantly the worse for wear, suggested they replenish the gathering using the manor's stocks. Some balked at the idea and wisely elected to disperse, but the accused – who are among those most determinedly enjoying themselves in these strange times – readily agreed. Once they had drunkenly and none-too-stealthily made their way from the Ketels' cottage to the manor house, Hugh Miller cajoled them into escalating their intent from ale to wine and supplementing it with meat pies from the pantry.

The jury, finding the witnesses' testimony reliable, consults with the reeve on a suitable punishment: Hilary is barred from selling ale until Whitsun and she and her husband are fined the value of what they consumed; Elias is fined more heavily but takes his punishment well, relieved to have held onto his position after such a breach of trust; but Hugh Miller, whose fine is the lowest for being least able to pay, bears it worst, with resentment written all over his face.

Nor is his pain over. As the penitents disappear into the crowd, Hugh is ordered to remain where he is as the reeve brings further charges: that Hugh the Miller is in default of the service he owes to the manor having refused to grind grain for the kitchens on two occasions and been absent from ploughing on the requisite days.

The reeve takes a high-handed approach, aggravating Hugh Miller's belligerent mood as he calls on witness after witness, including Elias Gamel, who apologetically gestures at his friend when he's forced to confirm his failings.

'What say you to these charges?' the reeve eventually offers Hugh the chance to plead his defence.

From where she sits, Christiane has a view of Anne at the back of the Hall, her arms folded defensively across her body, a frown on her face; her gaze slips away quickly as she catches her lady's eye on her.

Hugh's muttered response is inaudible.

'Speak up, man,' the reeve demands. 'How do you justify your crimes?'

'I said, why should I waste what's left of my life working for you?'

He's looking directly at Christiane as he says it.

Though surprised murmurs ripple through the Hall at his contempt, the reaction is less than she might expect. How many of the others are thinking it, even if only Hugh dares say it?

She knows she shouldn't react but the barb stings and she leaps to defend herself.

'Have I not always done my best by you, Hugh Miller?' she hits back. 'Have you not had additional food when needed? Repairs to your roof this past summer? A responsible position in the manor?'

He pales, knowing the truth of what she says, but his embarrassment makes him strike back. 'And why would you do these things,' he challenges, his voice rising in anger, 'but to relieve your guilt towards myself and my family?'

He dares not speak his grudge explicitly but there are few here who do not understand his meaning. Never mind that she has been wronged as much as he, yet they would hold her accountable for her husband's actions.

'I hope there was more charity than guilt in my heart, Master Miller,' she reacts. Though he falls silent, his face continues to reflect his resentment.

The discussion between the appointed jury and the reeve drags on for some time; as it does, the crowd becomes more restive, but she struggles to pick out what they're saying about the outburst.

Eventually, Henry Child, as spokesman for the jury, announces the punishment, but his face and others' betray considerable reluctance. They fine the miller the equivalent of half-a-year's profit and demand he serves twice the lost time in the fields. The remedy, unprecedented in its harshness, sparks outrage among many tenants.

As the noise levels rise in the Hall and the steward steps in to bring calm, Christiane calls the reeve to her.

'Master Reeve,' she admonishes. 'I asked you to show consideration towards the tenants during these difficult times. Handing down such a heavy punishment is hardly that.'

The reeve's face offers her a mask of surprise, but he can't conceal the manipulation behind his eyes.

'My lady,' he returns easily, as if prepared with his answer, 'would you show leniency to one who has so disrespected you before your people? Look at their faces,' he demands. 'See how deeply this decision is affecting them. Then consider how you will maintain control if they believe their transgressions will be only lightly punished?'

'What I see is anger, Master Reeve,' she retorts, knowing full well she sees their emotions much more clearly than he. 'How is that intended to help the situation?'

'You are mistaken,' he corrects smoothly. 'What you see is fear, which will control them very effectively. Moreover,' pouring oil on troubled waters, 'my lady Amicia instructed that we make an example of either Master Miller or Master Gamel to show that those in privileged positions are held to account. I did, of course, explain the stance you had asked me to take, but she reiterated that she expects substantial fines to be imposed tonight. As I have shown clemency elsewhere, I must balance that out somewhere,' he argues, his tone greasy with reason.

Christiane grits her teeth, furious that he has gone behind her back and empowered himself with Amicia's contrary instructions. He is making it impossible for her to challenge the ruling. She sits back, infuriated.

The reeve barely hides his smug smile as he retakes his position in command of the court, raising his hands to call their attention to him and demanding that order be restored.

Hugh Miller skulks away, disappearing into the shadows near the door, dragging Anne with him.

The reeve is not done yet.

Next, the clerk calls forward Thomas Terwald and Eleyne Marshal.

Christiane watches Henry Child's face register surprise and then suffuse with embarrassment and anger. He has always taken his standing in the village very seriously, leading by example, careful to uphold the law and respecting his neighbours' rights. Eleyne is his daughter, and it humiliates him to see her brought to task like this; he's angered too that no one did him the courtesy of forewarning him.

'Who brings this complaint?' the reeve intones.

To Christiane's eyes, this has something of the play about it, but she can only wait for the performance to unfold.

'I do.' Gilbert Wragge moves to the front of the gathering, his wife Anne alongside, standing in solidarity with him.

'Speak your concern, Gilbert Wragge,' the reeve orders him.

'That Thomas Terwald and Eleyne Marshal, in contravention of God's holy law, are living as husband and wife even though they are neither betrothed nor married and Eleyne Marshal has a husband yet living in a village not three miles from here.'

'This is hardly news,' Thomas objects. 'Why raise it now?'

'The fact of its longstanding does not make it right, Thomas Terwald,' Gilbert opines.

'How can she return to her husband?' he persuades. 'You know full well he has discarded her.'

'It is her duty to be with her husband,' Gilbert Wragge stubbornly holds his ground.

'But he has been living these many years with another woman as his wife!' Eleyne resists, blushing.

'And does his wrong thereby make yours acceptable?' Anne Wragge intervenes alongside her husband, her voice tense with anxiety. 'Do you not see that God is sick of such sin? That this pestilence is His punishment for a world that has become so corrupt that the very air is polluted?'

'Aye,' Roger Fraunceys calls, stepping forward too and shaking off his sister's hand as she tries to stall his intervention. ''Tis clear to any with eyes to see that we must act now to prevent this pestilence knocking on our own doors.' He turns to appeal to the wider audience and muttering agreement murmurs around.

Eleyne looks to her father, but he shrugs helplessly, knowing he cannot speak on her behalf, that they have no defence.

Christiane frowns. This situation has been known and tolerated for many a year. When, childless and too old to conceive, her husband pushed her out of their home and took up with another woman, Eleyne returned to Threfield Percy for work and shelter, becoming housekeeper to her father and, subsequently, to the bachelor Thomas Terwald. Quite when the two became as husband and wife is unclear, but it is widely acknowledged, and all were happy to turn a blind eye. Until now.

Father Peter leans forward from his seat on the dais, concern creasing his forehead. 'This matter is for an ecclesiastical hearing, not this court…' he defends.

'Then why have you not dealt with this before now, Father?' Letitia Fraunceys intervenes, calling out from beside her brother's shoulder.

A surprising number of voices cry 'aye' in support.

The reeve steps in. 'If such an ecclesiastical hearing were likely to be convened in the coming weeks, we would for sure defer to it,' he opines, sanctimoniously. 'But in the current circumstances,' he raises the spectre of the threat and lets it hang over them all for a long moment, 'when we know there is one rotten apple that could taint the whole barrel, would we not do better to remove it ourselves than to wait for the proper authorities to do it? Moreover,' smoothly turning to appeal to Christiane, 'can it not be argued that this is an issue for the manor and therefore for the manor's court? After all, the accused are her ladyship's tenants. I am sure she would not condone the continuance of such sin in her own property, the more now that we can all see how concerned others of her tenants are by these circumstances.'

Christiane holds his gaze steadily, outraged by his manipulation.

'We shall, of course,' the reeve resumes smoothly, 'look to you, Father, to guide the jury in what the judgement and punishment should be.'

Backed into a corner, the priest has no choice but to fall into line. 'If they are unable to marry, they must break off the relationship,' he confirms, casting a regret-filled look towards the victimised couple.

'Show some pity,' Eleyne whispers, her face distraught as she hangs on Thomas's arm and looks in all directions for support. But care and mercy have fled this night.

They have been played.

Christiane surveys the wreckage the reeve has created: her own position and Father Peter's undermined; Hugh Miller enflamed with hatred; and neighbour turned against neighbour. With mealy-mouthed and cold-hearted manipulation, Simon Reeve has riven deep fissures through their lives.

While she does not trust the reeve, never for a moment has she considered such an organised move would be made against them. And to what end?

The great door, forced ajar then caught by a high wind, slams back against the far wall and all eyes turn towards the interruption. Little Robert atte Gate, Walter's eldest boy, staggers in, trying to catch his breath enough to speak.

'Come quick,' he calls, signalling frantically. 'There's a crowd of itinerants at the gate and they demand entry. Please,' he cries as they hesitate, 'my father needs your help to stop them!'

For a moment, they look from one to the other, and then the impossible happens: they turn to the reeve for guidance.

'What are you waiting for?' the reeve instructs them, his voice strangely high with excitement. 'Grab your weapons! Defend us all!'

'Wait!' Father Peter calls, holding his hands up. 'They may need our help. Show some care...'

'Nay, Father!' Robert the blacksmith counters. 'We've had our orders from the lady Amicia, more than once. No one in, no one out.'

'Do you even care that they could be bringing the pestilence, Father?' Roger Fraunceys cries. 'Why do you put their well-being ahead of ours?'

Numerous voices murmur their agreement. Defeat clouds the priest's face, and he sinks into his chair.

'To arms!' Gilbert Beadle rallies them, memories of his fighting days with Ralf sparking fire in his eyes.

Pulling torches from the sconces, the men rush to recover their blades by the Hall entrance. They hurry out into the inky, starless night, the squally winds throwing their flames into the darkness, their women close behind them.

In moments, the Hall empties.

The reeve sends a long look towards where Christiane and the priest still sit, taking in the steward standing behind; he makes no attempt to hide his satisfaction.

As he turns to leave, Eleyne and Thomas cross the Hall to join Henry Child, a bewildered and angry family. And Hugh Miller steps out of the shadows to accost the reeve at the entrance.

'Not here,' the reeve chides, trying to shake off the miller's hand where it grips his forearm.

'I did what you wanted,' Hugh hisses. 'I want to know you'll keep your end of the bargain.'

The reeve laughs. 'You are a fool, Hugh Miller,' he mocks, cruelly. 'Did you really think I could overturn the court's ruling? It's in the records now and you will be held to account.'

Hugh's face suffuses with blood. 'But you swore...' he stutters. 'How do you think I shall pay such a hefty amount?'

The reeve leans in, close to his face. 'I am your friend in this, Master Miller,' his tone suddenly warm and cozening. 'And should you need to borrow money, you know where to come.'

'You deceitful...' Hugh flares up, enraged by the trap he has blindly been led into. 'And you would have my cottage and land too, would you, you greedy toad?'

He violently shoves the reeve away and disappears into the night.

Their words carry to the silent watchers on the dais, but then they have made little effort at concealment. The reeve glances towards them, a thin smirk compressing his lips. Then he too leaves.

Shock incapacitates Christiane and it takes the steward's intercession to stir her. 'My lady,' he urges. 'We should follow them.'

She stares at him blankly; it is long moments before her thoughts clear. 'Yes,' she nods. 'We must go. Father,' turning to the equally stunned priest, 'we must stop this.' He hardly responds. 'Father Peter!' As she shakes his arm, his eyes finally shift to meet hers. 'We cannot stand by and allow the reeve to drive the people to violence this night!'

'This is not just the reeve,' he warns, wearily. 'We have all been complicit in this.'

'All the more reason. Stir yourself, Father!' she demands urgently.

The steward reaches for his blade. 'No weapons, Master Steward,' she negates. 'I want to avoid bloodshed, not to increase the chance of it.'

Edith throws a cloak around Christiane as she hurries towards the door; Philip snatches up a flaming torch to light their way.

From the top of the ridge, they can see the rabble has already reached the lower path, with a wide group of torches gathered on the village side of the gate. Christiane starts to run, slipping on the slope in her haste, the priest and the steward at her side.

Voices are raised as she nears. They are crowded around the closed gate, the largest and strongest men at the front, hanging over the gate, shaking knives and sticks at people huddled together. Robert the smith is at the centre and seems to be the only one trying to calm those on both sides of the divide. Walter has been pushed to one side, his face white, Margery and little Rob hanging on his arms. More join the crowd even as they arrive, bringing farm tools as makeshift weapons from their cottages.

'Make way!' Father Peter forces himself through with Christiane close behind.

'What is't, Robert?' she asks. 'What do they ask for?'

'They seek food and shelter, my lady,' he confirms. 'Only for the night, they claim, though I doubt the truth of that. They carry so little with them,' nodding for her to look for herself, 'I suspect they are fleeing from something.'

A score of travellers, shrouded in hoods and cloaks against the night, herd together several yards distant from the gate, lit only by the torches held aloft by the villagers. By the height of them, many appear to be women or children, with only a handful of men who stand to the front, sheltering the others behind them. The smith is right: there's no sign of baggage, no beasts bearing possessions, only what they can carry in their hands or on their backs.

'You need to leave,' Robert Smith advises, the calmest of all the voices but the most imposing presence at the gate.

'How can we?' one man – their leader, it seems – tries to reason him. 'With night upon us and the road so dark we can scarce see where we tread?'

'You should have thought of that before now!' a woman's voice shouts from behind.

'My lady,' he appeals to Christiane,' our lord has driven us off his land. He has fled there from London and says he'll have none but his own villeins there until the plague is done.'

'That's a lie!' Reginald Ketel accuses. 'What lord would turn away good labour at this time?'

'Please! We ask only a roof for the night; a barn or byer will suffice,' pleads the man. 'We have nowhere else to go!'

'That's not our problem!' Gilbert Beadle shouts, pushing forward and brandishing his knife; his blood is up and he's spoiling for a fight. The crowd heaves forward and Christiane presses her hands against the gate to avoid being crushed as they jostle and push her, oblivious to her status amid the mob.

'Pipe down!' the smith chides. 'Let's hear the man.'

'Tell the truth,' the priest intervenes. 'Are you fleeing the pestilence?' Nervous glances are exchanged by some of the travellers, but their leader speaks clearly.

'Nay, sir,' he assures. 'We have come across no one with symptoms.'

'Lies! All lies!' Anne Wragge screams, spraying spittle with her vehemence. 'Send them away!' she demands of her husband, shoving him forward abruptly.

'In God's name, you have to help us!' the man implores. 'There are women and children in need of shelter…' encompassing them with a sweep of his arm.

'Open the gate!' a voice demands, one of the kitchen lads, perhaps. 'We'll chase them off at the tip of a blade!'

'Open the gate! Open the gate!' others take up the chant, dragging Walter forward as he fumbles with his keys.

'You'd best be away,' the smith warns their leader, shouting over the crowd's noise. 'Once they open this gate, I can't be held responsible for what they'll do to you…' He turns to Christiane. 'And you'd best get of the way, my lady,' quietly manhandling her to one side.

'We cannot let this happen,' the steward appeals to those around him.

'Stay out of this, Philip of Ghent,' Gilbert Wragge warns.

'Aye!' Gilbert Beadle chimes in. 'Think yourself lucky we don't send you away with them, Fleming!'

Christiane's heart chills at the hatred in his words. 'Stop this, Robert Smith,' she orders. 'These people deserve our charity.'

'Too late for that, my lady,' he disallows, grim-faced. 'Their blood is heated. You'll get no sense from them now.'

The travellers start to back away. The lead man stands, helpless, hopeless, staring the villagers down for a few moments more, then a woman snatches at his arm and tugs him away.

''Tis the devil's work you do this night,' he chides them, throwing the words back over his shoulder.

At that, Gilbert Beadle grabs a stone from the path and hurls it in their direction. A yelp of pain and indignation is heard as it catches the man on his back, and more villagers snatch up stones, pelting their departing backs with deranged shouts of rage. The travellers run into the night.

A rough cheer goes up all around, with cat-calls and taunts thrown in the direction of the empty path. Clapping each other on the back, they issue cheery invitations to a mug of ale, elated at their success.

Christiane shakes her head in disbelief. Father Peter stands at her shoulder, Philip of Ghent beside him.

'How did it come to this?' she wonders aloud.

As the villagers disperse, she sees the reeve at the back of the crowd; he has kept his distance all this while.

He shrugs at her, as if to say, "What could I have done?". But the feigned bemusement is replaced by a smirk that creeps across his face as he turns to follow the crowd.

They are three against many. The divide between herself and her people has never felt so great, not even in those early days when they looked on her with such suspicion, an outsider in their midst.

Out of the black and laden sky, heavy rain starts to fall.

Chapter Sixty-six

Threfield Percy. March 1349

Will it ever stop raining?

Christiane's exasperated exclamation is so clear it's like she's standing right next to me.

I'm back at the site again. Still digging down, though I hardly know what I'm doing now. Each time I return like this, there's more that's been uncovered but I don't remember any of it.

The stone stairs from the door are largely cleared: I can see the outline of three steps, but I know there's a fourth. Beside it is an excavation pit, six feet wide, half as deep so far.

To judge by the sun dropping lower against the horizon, it's now late afternoon. The sky is a picture of contrast: clear blue and sun-filled in the west, dense dark clouds threatening in the east. I glance at the discarded tarp, but a second thought immediately counters the impulse: it could be hailing, snowing or thundering and still I would stay. I'm not leaving while there's light to see. Maybe not even then.

Christiane is pacing Amicia's lower chamber like a caged animal. 'Can we have just one day without rain?' she implores, raising her hands heavenwards in supplication. 'Just one? It's been two months since I saw the sun!

'Everywhere stinks of wet clothing,' she complains. 'The moment I step outside the door, I'm soaked again. And Amicia doesn't care that she has me forever running between here and the Hall. It happens so often now that I can't help but think she does it on purpose!'

Growling in the back of her throat, she flops down on the bed, watching me scrape away at the soil while she fretfully picks at the velvet coverlet.

'It reminds me of the Great Famine,' she worries. 'The relentless rain. Only then it was so cold that the rivers froze. This is just unending wet. But the sheep have started dying and the cattle are sure to be next. And the seeds will have washed away in the fields so who knows what crops we can expect.'

She leaps to her feet again and resumes pacing.

'Can you believe there are carcasses rotting in the fields, so diseased that neither beast nor bird will approach them? Yet none of the tenants will stir to clear them. Half of them are too busy mortifying themselves and the other half are so determined to live only for pleasure that they neglect their every duty. And I swear either side only lets up to chastise the rest. I'm at my wits' end trying to keep order.'

She stops talking and stands, arms folded, watching me with interest but also with a bemused frown: why would I be digging this corner of the room? There's nothing here, not even one of the multitude of chests that skirt the rest of the wall. I wish I could tell her why, but I don't know either. Except that I can feel something beneath the soil that I can't yet see. It's not a good feeling: it's a sinking in the pit of my stomach, not nausea so much as a weighty dread. I fear to go on and yet I can't stop; the compulsion is too great.

Her mind wanders. Amicia is dozing in her chair upstairs by the fire, and she has a rare few minutes' respite. She worries about how few lambs there will be this spring, about the mould they've found in the grain where damp has seeped into the store and about on what's happening in the village.

'I saw Mistress Wragge yesterday,' she recalls. 'Since she took to wearing her roughest, plainest clothes without any linens beneath, her skin has turned red raw. And she shows the multitude of bites to all and sundry, heralding the suffering she endures as a source of salvation for them all. 'Tis so long since she or her husband washed – either themselves or their clothes – that none can stand to come near for how rank they smell. When did washing become a mortal sin?' she appeals to me. 'I fear the world has gone mad.

'Do you know, she and Mistress Ketel have taken to wearing wax amulets around their necks? Master Ketel proudly claims they're made from stumps of candles used in high mass at York Minster.'

She crosses the room and perches on the steps beside me, sighing in exasperation.

'And Father Peter can hardly keep up with the demand for holy water. They sprinkle it everywhere: on food, on themselves and their animals, on the doorways of their homes. The only ones working as hard as he is are the ale-wives: they can scarce brew fast enough, and the ale-houses are rarely empty, day or night. That just leads to fighting and more broken heads and bones.

'And yet, every one of them is going to confession practically every week, they're that afraid of dying. And I've never seen such attendance at mass as since the start of Lent.

'Maybe Amicia was right,' she muses, heavily. 'Maybe this is the end of the world, heralded by pestilence and famine.

'And yet, it can't be, can it?' she realises. 'It can't be the Apocalypse. Because you're here.'

I look up and her proximity intensifies the electricity until it almost zings between us. Can she feel it too?

A loud thump on the door makes both of us jump. She laughs nervously, her gaze still holding mine, her hand on her chest as if to still the sudden racing of her heart. She gives me the slightest smile, rueful, amused. And my heart thumps hard too. It's hard for either of us to look away.

Repeated knocking fractures the moment.

Pushing herself upright, she turns the heavy key and heaves open the door.

'My lady, a messenger…' Margery, Walter's wife, hesitantly holds out a packet, anxious to fulfil her duty, but equally anxious to be gone; none approaches Amicia's tower without trepidation.

'Thank you, Margery. The messenger did not wait?' Christiane asks.

'I offered him food and rest, my lady, but he wanted to be on his way. Said he'd heard about the welcome strangers receive here.'

Margery blushes with shame. Christiane grimaces and releases her with a nod, re-locking the door behind her.

'What is't?' Amicia demands from above.

Short on patience, Christiane ignores her and breaks the seal on the letter.

I feel her attention shift, and she becomes less present to me.

But I'm also strangely distracted, suddenly more interested in where I'm digging. I'm being called into my time and, as I am, I notice that the air has turned chilly and a brisk wind is riffling through the treetops, making the leaves rustle and the branches swish, bowing down before the heavier gusts. The black clouds are much closer now.

'Eoghan…' Her voice is distant. 'A letter…'

I try to focus on what I'm doing but the locus has swung and now I'm being dragged into her world; it's a push and pull of conflicting energies, splitting my attention. It's disorientating.

I close my eyes to help me focus on her and slip into her mind so seamlessly that the elaborate script and medieval French become comprehensible to me.

And somehow, I also intuit insight about the letter itself: I can see Dafydd as he wrote it, shut away in small, ill-lit room at the Savoy, the great palace eerily quiet without Lancaster and his retinue. Among the few who remain, the same drunkenness dominates as in the village, each desperate to blot out their fear in unawareness.

I catch snatched memories, images of what he's witnessed, and feel him consumed again with horror as he recounts it to her. And I sense the dread that builds within him, knowing he must go out into that world, but also his resolve, the responsibility he bears and a clear-minded determination to help.

My beloved lady Mother,

The pestilence has raged through London these three months, and I do not know how many are left for it to claim. If half the population should survive the summer, we shall count ourselves blessed.

Each day, unimaginably large new graves are dug and, each day, they are filled with layer upon layer of bodies. It is beyond pitiful to see fathers and mothers carry their children to the graveyard with neither ceremony nor ritual or fling those small bodies onto the grave diggers' carts as they are hauled through the streets, piled high with corpses. Almost as bad are the houses where none is left alive to dispose of the dead, where only the stench of their rotting flesh tells their sorry tale. It is a foul stench indeed to be distinguished from the stink of our unkept streets.

Desperate steps that would have been unimaginable before now have become essential measures. So many priests have died that the Bishop of London was forced to accede that confession could be received by any who is near, even a woman, better than to die in the burden of sin. One of the most sacred acts made profane by these dire times.

The food supply has collapsed; bread and meat and ale are become treasures almost beyond price while there is a great cheapness to all other things. Those in the country who bring food to market have stayed away but their efforts are in vain for so many are driven to venture outside the city in search of food that they carry the pestilence to those who thought to avoid it.

I know you would adjure that I flee London as so many others have, but I cannot leave. Inside the Savoy Palace, we are somewhat protected, we few who remain; outside, though, the city has become lawless, and our people wander blindly in the wilderness. But we must persist: the dead must be buried; the sick must be succoured; the hungry must be fed.

I hope you are not alone. And if you are, I pray that our Beloved Lord supports and guides you.

I commend myself to you, beloved lady, and my soul to whatever our Lord and gracious Father wills.

Your loving and obedient son, Dafydd.

If he wasn't dead before, he surely is now…

For the time it took her to read his words, her beloved son was returned to life; now he's been wrenched from her again. Her body fills with a grief so intense that it shocks through me too. I ache to take her in my arms, to hold her until the pain eases, and then for a long, long time after.

But even as I feel her drawing me to her, needing me there, needing my support, simultaneously something is dragging me back to my own time, a force so undeniable that I'm almost physically pulled forward by it.

That…thing…in the soil. I sense it so strongly.

Dropping to my hands and knees to get more leverage, I gouge at the ground with my trowel, haphazard in my desperation to get deeper. Great chunks of earth come away and scatter carelessly around me.

I'm still aware of Christiane's distress, but it's muted, muffled by time. The sky has darkened around me, almost like night.

Now I can see something. Pale against the soil. Even before I unearth it, I sense what it is. And why I'm being pulled in two directions.

I jump as lightning flashes and, in the same instant, deafening thunder cracks right overhead, so loud that my ears ring.

Out of the black and laden sky, heavy rain starts to fall.

Huge drops splash against my skin and hair. Within moments, it becomes a deluge. It soaks the soil and is so heavy it starts washing away the top layers. I don't even have to dig any more. The air is thick with static and the hairs on my arms rise as it moves up my body, through my neck and prickles painfully on my scalp.

Where the soil is being eroded by the rain, that ghostly thing is starting to emerge. I grab my trowel again and gingerly probe around more resistant parts of dirt. I'm trying not to touch it because every instinct screams that at me. As I prise pieces loose, the rain washes it clean.

She's with me now. It's holding both of us here, tight and tense in the moment. She's afraid of it. And her fear infects me until I shake with it.

Lightning flashes, its brilliant luminescence brighter than day. Half-dazzled, I lean forwards to ease more of the earth out of the way, the rain a partner in my work. Until it turns against me and starts pooling in the bottom of the trench. Frustrated, I scrape harder at the mud, desperate for answers before it's submerged. The trowel slips and splashes in the water: I'm finding it harder to get purchase. Angrily casting it aside, I go in with my hands, sinking my fingers into slick mud and gouging it out of the way, pooling the rainwater in my hands to bail it out of the hollow. I'm fighting the conditions…until an inspiration has me reaching for the trowel again and I start cutting a channel so that the water can flow away.

Another flash of lightning illuminates the darkened site. And what the rain is now rapidly uncovering.

A dome. Two hemispheres fused along a central line. Delicate ridges curving above two dark orbits; where earth now fills, green eyes once smiled.

A painful buzzing starts in my right ear and tingles as it moves over my scalp until it reaches the left. The thunder becomes muffled, held at a distance by the dominant buzzing inside me, but I still feel it as vibration all through my body. Pressure is building in my head, across my temples, behind my eyes. Pinpricks of light dance across my sight and darkness crowds from the edges of my vision until all I can see is the thing in front of me.

Something makes me put out my hand. I don't want to. She doesn't want me to. But I can't stop it. As my fingers near, the buzzing rises to a high-pitched whine and my whole body seems to judder as the vibration accelerates.

Lightning flashes. I'm blinded. Everything is pitch black.

And I feel my fingertips connect.

The whining sound becomes a piercing scream, engulfing my whole head and merging with that uncontrollable power. The world is spinning though I can't even see, and I feel that energy yanking me forward, sucking me into a swirling vortex until I hardly know up from down. And I hold onto the only thing that's still real for me, screaming her name in my mind.

Christiane!

Easter Day

Chapter Sixty-seven

Threfield Percy. Sunday, 12th April 1349

He's here. How is he here?
'Eoghan?'

It's not much past dawn. Though there's still a slight haze in the new day's light, spring's warmth is evident in all the fresh growth around me.

She's surrounded by her people, nearing the church at the end of their procession around the village, and the air reverberates with the hymn they've just finished singing. They smile to one another, briefly finding unity in worship. She finds it a joyful contrast with the solemnity of the previous three days, with the church stripped bare on Maundy Thursday, stark and cold, and intense mourning on Good Friday. Many performed the Creeping to the Cross with shows of heightened emotion, the reverence and humility of their approach – barefoot and on their knees – augmented by both penitence and supplication. Alice Beadle prostrated herself before the Cross, sobbing fit to die, and had to be supported away by her husband.

As they head into the church, they glance askance at her because she's suddenly stopped dead on the path.

Her surprised smile is so entrancing, I catch my breath.

Now, in her middle years, she carries her authority naturally, lightly and with a deep warmth and caring. Her face is lined, but those lines bear testament to her temperament, carved by frequent laughter and constant love. The busyness of her days keeps her slender, but the curves born of three pregnancies make her beautiful.

It's a glorious day, and my heart lifts to feel the caress of sunshine and a gentle breeze on my face.

The rain has finally stopped, then.

On Good Friday. Two days ago.

I smile as I catch her reply. Which turns to surprise as I realise…she's heard me.

She mirrors my surprise for a moment, then that gentle smile broadens with joy.

Because I'm here. I don't know how, but I'm here.

I turn to take everything in; each sense is acutely heightened, almost unbearably so. Every colour is more vibrant: the green of the grass is fresher; the blue of the sky is deeper; the yellow sandstone of the church is richer. The air is so clean it's sharp in my lungs, and I distinguish the scents of hearth fires and livestock, of damp earth and new growth, of blackthorn blossom in the hedgerow. The woods behind me are alive with the chatter of birds, more varied than I've ever heard. And now the church bell is ringing, a monotone clang that's ever so slightly out of tune.

It's been like that since the day the earth shook.

I look at her again in disbelief. I'm here.

You're here.

Christiane.

I feel a compulsion to see if I can touch her. But as I put out my hand, something makes her take a step back.

Don't, she warns.

Father Peter approaches. This is so real to both of us that we half-expect him to acknowledge me.

'My lady, everyone is ready. Will you fetch the lady Amicia so we may start the mass?' He frowns as he looks at her; it's not easy for her to focus on him. 'My lady?' he prompts.

She nods distantly. 'Yes, Father. Of course.' *Come with me?* she asks. I go with her.

Walter atte Gate is leaving the tower as we arrive and stands aside to let his mistress pass.

'Walter? What do you here?' she enquires.

He falters, a typical Amicia-induced uncertainty passing across his face. 'I cannot say, my lady,' he apologises anxiously. 'The mistress bade me not tell. But 'tis a welcome surprise that awaits you inside,' he hints, smiling shyly.

Shaking her head, she locks the door behind him.

After the pleasing softness of the day outside, it's a furnace-like heat in here, with a large fire blazing in the downstairs hearth and no doubt another in the upper chamber too.

I frown in confusion at my own clothes, bemused to find myself overdressed for the conditions in a waxed jacket and sweater, and only distantly recalling I needed them for digging. I shed both as Christiane leads me up the steps; it's strange to hear my footsteps on the stairs and feel the wooden tread give beneath my weight. It's so real.

Amicia looms at the head of the stairs, making both of us look up. Is it my imagination, or do her eyes, just for a moment, flick beyond Christiane? My heart jumps: can she see me?

She backs away as Christiane approaches, and whatever was in her eyes before, now she looks like a naughty child caught in some mischievous act.

She plants herself between Christiane and her usual chair, belligerence settling on her face.

'I don't care what you think,' she starts, holding her hands out defensively. Absurdly. Because, small as she is, Christiane could sweep this fragile, ageing woman aside easily.

'What in Heaven…' Christiane breathes.

There's a form slumped in Amicia's chair: a man, his face turned away from her.

'Henry?' she starts, strangely uncertain of her own son.

Though perhaps that's understandable. Because he's a gaunt, shrunken-in version of himself.

And a chill premonition slices through me.

Delight propels her across the floor before I can stop her and she falls on her knees beside him, turning his face towards her with a gentle hand.

'My son,' she murmurs with deep pleasure, her eyes traversing his face. 'It has been so long…' Her voice fades away.

A sheen of sweat stands out on his brow but his skin is ice-white and cold.

'Mother...' appeals to her, his eyes searching hers. 'Have pity,' he implores. His eyes tell her how scared he is; his aura tells her how much he should be.

I see her close her eyes, controlling her breathing as her mind reaches out for mine.

She holds both of Henry's hands in hers and carefully turns to look over her shoulder, seemingly towards Amicia but, in reality, beyond her to me.

Her gaze is steady, but her eyes fill with the horror of my knowing.

Plague has arrived.

Chapter Sixty-eight

Threfield Percy. 12th April 1349

She's so still – crouched before her son, her hand on his arm – that time seems frozen.

Inside, though, thoughts are hurtling through her mind, fleeting answerless instincts that flood one after another.

What symptoms has he got? How can she help him? Does Amicia realise? Has he infected anyone else? How can she stop this spreading? *Can* she stop it? Will he survive?

Emotions chase on the heels of the thoughts: overwhelm, worry, fear. And grief.

Her mind reaches for me. *What do I do?*

Isolation.

Because amid all that turmoil, the strongest instinct within her is to protect the rest of the village.

It may be the plague, it may not: they must watch and wait. If it is, there's a good chance he didn't infect anyone else.

What about Walter?

Even as the thought forms in her mind, she's on her feet and fleeing down the stairs. Flinging open the door, she catches sight of his awkward figure just beyond the church.

'Walter!' she cries, her voice rising in panic. 'Walter, wait!' she orders. Turning, he sees her and walks back down the path. When he's yet some feet distant she holds up a warning hand: 'Stay there.'

'My lady?'

'Walter,' she drops her voice, though everyone is in the church and the path is otherwise empty. 'Master Henry is unwell.'

'I thought so,' he sympathises. 'He seemed unlike himself.'

'It may be nothing,' she hesitates, uncertain how to reassure and at the same time convey the weight of the situation without panicking him, 'but we must take great care in these...difficult times.'

He frowns, then understanding slowly forms.

'You think...' he starts.

'I know not,' she hurries. 'But we must be careful. For everyone's sake.'

He takes a deep breath, his sense of responsibility to the village overriding any concern for himself, and she finds anew her appreciation for this stalwart man.

'What would you have me do, my lady?'

'Go straight to your cottage, Walter, and stay there. Do you understand me? Do not leave the bounds of your toft. Speak to no one, let no one come near. Not until we know you are safe.'

'What about Margery? And the children?'

'Were they there when you saw Master Henry?'

'Nay, my lady!' and she hears the relief in his voice.

'You're certain?'

'For sure. They joined the procession.'

She nods, remembering. 'Then they must not come home after mass. I'll have Mary Hering take them in.'

'Thank you, my lady.'

'Go, now,' she encourages. 'I'll send Father Peter to you. We'll take care of you, never fear. God be with you, Walter.'

'And with you, my lady. I pray Master Henry be well.'

She closes the door and leans back against the inside.

And then the anger comes. That Amicia – this thoughtless, selfish, blinkered woman – has allowed this to happen. She can't blame Henry for coming here. But Amicia? After everything she's said, the restrictions she's imposed, the guilt she's laid on all of them. And now, she's the one...

She grips her hands in fists to stop herself. This isn't helping.

A foot on the stair makes her look up; Amicia descends.

'Where are you going, my lady?' Christiane challenges, aware her voice shakes with anger.

'To mass, of course.' Her dismissive look riles her more.

'No.'

Amicia halts halfway down the stairs, checked by surprise at Christiane's flat denial. 'Don't be absurd. It's Easter Day.'

'You can't go. Not now.'

'You don't tell me what I can and can't do.'

Christiane shakes her head in disbelief. Is she so consumed with herself that she's blind to what's happening before her?

'Henry is sick.'

'It's just a chill,' dismissively.

'It's not,' frustratedly. 'Open your eyes!' *No, stop,* she tells herself, knowing a panic-stricken Amicia will only make things worse. She sighs. 'We don't know what it is. But we need to be sure it's not…' she's reluctant to voice the words, 'what we fear.'

Finally, Amicia blanches. 'Why would you say that?' she whispers.

'Let's speak upstairs,' she suggests. 'You will be more comfortable there.'

There's a moment of resistance as the two women stare at each other; it's Amicia who concedes and retreats.

Christiane removes the key from the door and puts it in the pouch hanging from her waist. Her heart is thumping hard as she looks at me.

In all the worry for others, she has barely stopped to think about herself. She's not safe here.

But I can't leave, can I?

She's extraordinary: there's barely a glimmer of fear in her, just calm, clear determination.

But this is what I've dreaded: being confronted by losing her.

Her eyes hold mine. So steadily.

* * * * * * *

Amicia is perched on a stool, seemingly as distant from Henry as she can place herself.

'Henry?'

Christiane stands before her son; his glazed eyes slowly focus on her.

'I need you to remember,' she urges. 'Other than Walter, did you see anyone on your way here?'

'In the village?' he clarifies. 'No.'

'You're certain?'

'He's already told you,' Amicia inserts sulkily. 'Leave the boy alone.'

'I need to know,' turning towards the old woman. 'Lives may rest on it.'

'You're making too much of this,' accusingly.

'How can you say that,' Christiane proclaims, anger simmering again, 'when you have demanded such vigilance from all of us?'

'That's only right,' Amicia objects. 'You should want to protect me!'

'And you should want to protect our people!' she rebuts.

'What would you have me do?' spitting with righteousness. 'Turn him away? He's my grandson. A Percy in all but name!'

'Cease!' Henry demands, holding his head in his hands. 'I can't stand the noise!'

Christiane crouches down by his chair, resting her hands on his knee.

'When did the illness start?' she asks gently.

He lifts his head to look at her.

'Yesterday evening.'

'What symptoms?'

'Aches, chills. Such a heaviness in my head.'

'Any sign of carbuncles?'

He shakes his head but there's intense fear in his eyes at hearing her express what he's tried to hide from his own mind.

He knows what he's got. And he knows it's likely to kill him.

'I didn't know where else to go.'

He looks at her helplessly and her heart aches for him. She's reminded of how he was as a small child: determined and fearless, almost domineering, until he hurt himself and then, just for a moment, he'd look to her for reassurance with that same wan look, unable to marshal his emotions...only to push her away again as his vulnerability ebbed.

You see why I can't leave?

I do, of course: she's a mother as well as lady of the manor.

My only living child. Her heart aches more, with the emptiness of two she has lost as well as the danger to her first. *I wouldn't be anywhere else.*

Amicia whimpers, staring at Henry; the truth rises behind her eyes and horror closes in behind.

'Get him out,' she whispers, unable to look away from him.

'We can't,' Christiane denies.

'Get him out,' she demands, louder now.

'My lady,' moving to stand between Amicia and the focus of her gaze, 'you don't understand. Henry cannot leave this place: if he's infected, we can't risk the pestilence being passed to the villagers.'

'And yet you would let him infect me!' she cries, panic setting in.

You let him in!

How much she wants to say that.

'I told you, get him out of here!'

Christiane turns her back.

'Come,' taking Henry's arm and encouraging him to rise. 'You should rest. You will be more comfortable in bed.'

'Not in my bed!' Amicia panics, also rising to her feet and trying to block their way. 'I want him out. Get him out, get him out!' she screams, scrabbling at Christiane's arm.

'Madam!' Christiane cries, feeling the old woman's nails dig into her arm. 'Enough!' Amicia falls back, shocked into acquiescence. 'Come, Henry,' more insistent, a hand on his broad back to direct him towards the stair.

As he reaches the bed, he falters and halts, apparently unable to move further. When she turns to face him, his eyes stare blankly, looking down at her but not seeing.

'Henry,' she murmurs, touching his face. He blinks.

'What is going to happen to me?' he whispers.

'I know not, my dear son,' she admits. 'We will do what we can.'

Yet a cold expectation runs through her.

And I have no consolation to give.

Chapter Sixty-nine

Threfield Percy. 12th April 1349

Exhausted, Henry falls asleep in moments and sleeps so heavily that the knocking doesn't wake him an hour later.

It's the priest.

Christiane glances at me with a frown.

How do you know that?

I shrug. Because I can see through walls.

The villagers are still milling around the church after mass; they're suspicious of her absence and are waiting to see what happens next. The priest looks worried.

From behind the closed door, she calls out to Father Peter.

'I'm here, my lady.' He waits for her to open the door. When she doesn't, his worried expression worsens. 'My lady, what's amiss?

'Father, is anyone near who can hear me?'

You're safe to speak, they're keeping their distance.

She notes my thought with a quick nod.

'Nay, my lady.'

'Henry is here, Father. He's sick.'

The priest receives the news in weighty silence.

'Is it…?'

She glances at me: she knows I'm convinced it is plague, but she worries about the effect of confirming that to the villagers, the more so when she can't be there with them.

And we may yet be able to contain it.

Ever hopeful.

'I can't say for certain, Father,' she evades. 'Not yet.'

'He hasn't the boils?'

'No.'

The priest is thinking hard. 'What would you have me do, my lady? Talk is already rife among the villagers because of your absence, and they'll want to know what I've learned here.'

'Tell them Henry has arrived and we're keeping our distance for a few days, just to be sure he's safe to move among them. No one is to come in here and the lady Amicia and I will stay with him. I've told Walter to do the same because he met Henry at the gate: he must keep to his cottage. Margery and the children weren't there, so they're not in danger. Will you see if Mary and Will can house them for a few days? If not, have them accommodated in the Hall. Make sure Walter has enough food and ale. If you must converse, do it through the door as we are now. I pray he's safe; he wasn't with Master Henry for long, but we need to be sure.'

The priest seems to be considering. She looks to me for guidance.

Do you think he understands me? Does he know important this is?

From his expression, I'd say so.

'And what do you need, my lady?' Father Peter offers.

'Have Elias Gamel send some tempting morsels for the lady Amicia,' she requests. 'Perhaps some broth or pottage for Henry. Some good wine, too, to strengthen him. Tell Elias it must be left outside: the door is locked and will remain so. They should knock and immediately depart. I will deal with the food. And I'll need some fresh water and cloths.'

'It shall be done.'

'And, Father, I need you to tend to the villagers for me. I can only imagine how this will affect them. If it is the pestilence, all I can do is keep them away from it. Whatever it takes.'

'What about today's feast?'

'That can go ahead: the steward and reeve should oversee it. Make sure everyone is well fed and give them plenty of wine; it's best we keep them busy.'

* * * * * * *

Henry slumbers on through the morning.

From her stool by his bedside, she follows the pattern of his breathing, listening for any slight change.

She watches him. And I watch her.

This remarkable, strong, beautiful woman.

Her mouth twitches with a smile.

You know I can hear your every thought now?

My smile matches hers.

The beams overhead creak and we can hear Amicia pacing again. She's been doing it on and off for the past two hours; it's putting both of us on edge.

It feels isolated down here at the tower, cut off from everyone. There's little noise from outside; up at the Hall, they'll be playing games and chatting while the kitchen staff prepare a small mountain of food.

The Easter feast is one of my favourite times of year. A time to celebrate the village's life together, to thank God for getting us through the winter and for the start of spring with all its hopefulness and promise.

But what will it be like today? As the news circulates and speculation starts, how will they respond to the pariah in their midst?

Don't go getting maudlin, she chastises, stern but teasing. *I get enough of that from Amicia.*

The pacing pauses briefly, as if she's heard. Then starts again.

I must check on her.

'It's about time,' Amicia sulks as Christiane emerges on the upper floor. 'How much tending does a sleeping man need?' Christiane's frustrated look is wasted on her. 'The fire needs more wood,' Amicia instructs pointedly.

'It's so warm in here already,' Christiane observes. 'Are you sure you need it?'

'How can you ask? After all these years, do you still have no concern for my health?' She stands over Christiane as she adds logs to the fire, supervising. 'When is food coming?' she grumbles.

'Soon. I'm sure they will send someone down before they start the feast.'

'I should hope so! They could hardly feed the tenants before me.'

'Would you like me to read to you while we wait?' Christiane seeks to distract her.

'No. I'm too restless.'

Christiane sits at the table, one eye on the older woman as she starts pacing again, marking the short distance from one side of the room to the other. Her anxiety is high.

'How is Henry?'

'He's sleeping well, which is a mercy.'

More pacing. The flooring creaks beneath her weight; not that there's anything of her, barely a sack of bones in a dress that's too big.

That fitted her last Easter. 'Tis her favourite, but she's much diminished this past twelvemonth.

I'm astounded that she can still feel pity for this difficult woman.

She's not well. Show some kindness.

'What if it is the pestilence?' Even under her paper-thin, yellowing skin, Amicia looks sallow with dread. She stops in front of Christiane, and her fidgety hands betray her tension, the heavy rings loose on her fingers, held in place only by swollen joints.

What do I say?

How can I answer that? Whatever I say applies as much to Christiane as to Amicia.

As if I didn't I realise that.

'We are in God's hands,' Christiane allows softly.

That stops me in my tracks: feeling the power of her faith, the resonant vibration that fills those simple words. I was raised in the same religion as she, but I've never felt belief such as this: that total trust in a higher being or a guiding force in the universe. And there's something not just reassuring but strangely empowering in her acceptance.

By contrast, tears of hopelessness spring to Amicia's eyes; this woman, obsessed with herself and consumed by health concerns most of her life, is cut off from that life-affirming connection. What I see is her fragility as a mortal body, any eternal essence in her dimmed beyond recognition.

'I am so weak already,' her voice falters. 'It will be too much for me.'

'You must stay up here,' Christiane advises. 'Keep your distance. I'll tend to Henry.'

'You must not look in his eyes,' Amicia begs, moving uncannily swiftly to clasp Christiane's hand. 'Remember what Dafydd wrote? How it passes from one person to another, leaving one when he dies to find a new victim.'

''Tis not how it works…' Christiane protests, discomforted by the unexpected contact and unsettled by her assumption that Henry will die.

'Promise me!' Amicia cries, her bony hands squeezing hard.

'But…'

'I said, promise me!' she demands, desperation in her eyes.

Instinctively, Christiane breaks away and retreats across the room. 'He is my son,' she voices with a rarely heard determination. 'I will do what I must for him.'

Silence falls between them. In the stillness, only the crackle of the fire is audible.

'When is Ralf coming? I want to see my son.' She sounds as sulky as a child.

'He isn't coming,' Christiane informs her flatly; Ralf's neglect still stings.

'Nonsense, he will, for me. You must write to him. Tell him to come.' She's on the verge of tears again.

Christiane sighs, her innate compassion reasserting.

'Come, sit, my lady. You will wear yourself out with all this pacing.'

She does sit but her agitation does not abate.

'He's sure to come,' Amicia claims. 'He knows how much he owes me, not only in his duty to his mother but also for how much I have sacrificed for him.' She looks at Christiane, ready to tug on the heartstrings once more, to regain the sympathy she survives on. 'I never told you how unwell I was when I carried him?' Christiane shakes her head, though in truth it is a well-trodden path. 'For five months, I was not allowed to leave my bed, I had to stay as still as I might until he was born. The midwives insisted it was the only chance for him to live and I would not do anything to endanger him; I loved my child long before he was born. Five months I lay in that bed. Thank the saints I had returned to Topcliffe when I knew I was with child. I could not have borne such a burden had I been here, with no one to care for me, no one to lighten my darkest moments. At least there were other women of my standing who would sit with me. Though, selfish as they are, they were not always as considerate towards me as they might have been.'

'Topcliffe was your childhood home?' It is a question to which Christiane already knows the answer, but little distracts Amicia so much as to talk of living in her cousin Percy's home.

'I was a favourite from the first with all the women there,' she reminisces. 'Being motherless and such a pretty child, they doted on me. And my father was much admired as a warrior: they talked endlessly about his strength and skill. 'Twas a shame we saw him but seldom, but he was ever in such demand as a fighter and often abroad fighting infidels and Moors. As a young man, before I was born, he even fought in Prince Edward's crusade.'

'Did you not prefer to have your own home after you married?' There's genuine curiosity in Christiane's question.

'Perhaps if it had been a richer manor I might have, but such a paltry place as this is hardly worthy of me. They should have let me stay with Percy; I had no need of marriage, and I would have been no trouble to my cousin. I might even have spent time at court,' she muses wistfully. 'Perhaps then I should not have become so ill. Perhaps then I might not have lived out my days confined to this Godforsaken place,' resentment rising in her voice.

'You have ever borne it patiently, my lady,' Christiane soothes.

'I have,' she preens. 'Though how I hated this place in those early days. At once my shelter and my cage. I cannot stand the sun and yet I have an unbearable desire to feel its touch on my skin.'

For once, I find her regret strangely poignant.

'My lord did much to bring a little joy into your life,' Christiane advocates. 'The delights and trifles he brought you from each trip, the expensive and rare gifts.'

'Those were but a sop to his conscience,' Amicia sulks, 'knowing how he had destroyed my life. You cannot know…no one knows what it is to be blessed with a child only to find the price is to lose one's own self. I have lived but half a life,' she utters, 'forever in the shade!' She stands and starts pacing again, then stares moodily at the heavy coloured glass of the west windows.

'I am not ready to die!' she declares violently. 'Do you see how life clings to me?' turning to Christiane with unnatural colour flushing her cheeks and fire in her eyes. 'No matter how weak and pathetic my body becomes!'

Suddenly, she goes rigid, staring at the far wall, where I sit. A frown of concentration carves deep lines in her papery thin skin.

'What is it, my lady?' Christiane probes, startled by the change.

'My eyes fail me…' she murmurs uncertainly. 'Over there,' pointing with a shaking hand. 'It cannot be…yet however I look…I see a shadow…'

I stand up.

'There! It moves! Do you not see?' she cries plaintively.

'There's nothing there,' Christiane reassures, though there's hesitation in her voice.

'I may be old but I'm no fool!' she bites back. She sits down heavily, hardly able to take her eyes from me. 'It cannot be...' she moans anxiously. 'And yet death feels so near...' Amicia's eyes become unfocused, as if she's seeing something other than the physical world in front of her. 'Geoffrey?' she whispers in confusion.

Goosebumps chill across my skin; I almost look over my own shoulder.

Christiane starts. 'That's the first time you've said his name in years,' she highlights. 'Perhaps even since he died.'

'Nonsense,' Amicia disregards.

'How is it you never speak of him?' she pushes.

'Why should I?' Amicia shakes off whatever is gripping her. 'He was but a means to an end. Beyond that, he was nothing but a disappointment. Imagine,' scathing, 'me, a Percy, married to a mediocre merchant!'

'He gave you a good life!' Christiane defends.

'A good life?' she laughs caustically. 'He took my health and shut me away in this prison!'

The injustice is breath-taking, and it grates against the deep appreciation Christiane still has for this man. Unable to contain her emotion, she crosses to stand by me, turning her back on Amicia.

Her mind has become as twisted and tortured as her body.

Her mind? Or her spirit?

Christiane gives me a curious look. She turns back towards the old woman, who has picked up a book from the table, though she cannot read.

'My lady,' Christiane calls her attention. 'Have you made confession for your role in his death?'

'What are you talking about?'

'If we are...if Henry has...' she hesitates in broaching such a sensitive subject, but they are facing death and she fears for Amicia's soul. 'Should any of us become ill, we must be...prepared,' she finishes weakly.

'My conscience is clear,' Amicia disdains. 'Is yours?'

'What I'm asking is if you have confessed to Father Peter and made amends?'

'For what, girl?'

'For the part you played in Geoffrey's death.'

'I don't know of what you speak,' high-handedly.

'Of what Ralf did?' Christiane prompts.

'Did? Did what? Geoffrey died in his bed, an apoplexy in his sleep.' She's becoming agitated now, frowning in confusion. 'What did Ralf do?' Christiane cannot bring herself to answer.

Does she not remember what she did?

Christiane looks at me in disbelief. *Has she really convinced herself of that?*

Perhaps her mind has blocked it out.

Is that possible?

It's been known in cases of trauma.

'And what is it that you think I did?' There's a tremor of worry in Amicia's voice now, as if she's becoming less certain of herself.

Christiane hesitates. 'Ralf took his...encouragement...' she wants to say "orders", '...from you.'

'Geoffrey died in his sleep,' Amicia repeats faintly. 'And I was here. How could I have had any hand in it?'

If the unsureness that's painted on her face is fake, she's an unparalleled liar. If she's deceiving herself, it's because she can't face the truth. Remembering may do her mind more harm than good.

But forgetting will not gain her forgiveness.

Christiane's distress is real.

I must help her. If she dies without having admitted her sin, she will be damned.

But what can you do?

'You don't know what you're talking about.' Angrily, Amicia cuts off the discussion and distractedly starts picking her way through her jewel boxes, pulling pieces out and casting them over the table. Agitated, she tips the contents of a whole box out and noisily rifles through the items.

'My lady…' Christiane tries again.

'Here,' she demands, ignoring Christiane's words and holding something out to her. 'Come here and help me put this on.' She turns and points to where she wants it to be fixed. 'Here. Put it here,' and lifts her chin arrogantly. Yet there's still a tremble in her lip and her eyes glitter with tears held back.

'Are you sure you want this one?' Christiane suggests, dispirited. 'You know how the fastening is unreliable.'

'Stop it,' Amicia rebukes, her eyes distraught. 'Stop challenging me on everything! Just once, will you do as I ask?'

Christiane sighs as she takes the pin from her and carefully, tenderly almost, fixes it to Amicia's dress. 'There,' she says, giving her a reassuring smile.

Then, stepping back to see it properly, the smile vanishes, and she suddenly looks up at me.

Intricately shaped silverwork and a large, rich ruby.

Shock reverberates through her, and I get a chilling flash of déjà vu.

That's the pin I've just dug up.

Chapter Seventy

Threfield Percy. 12th April 1349

A loud rapping at the door makes all of us jump.

A truce-like silence has settled uneasily over the room. Amicia sits staring moodily into the fire, her back rigid, her hands tense. Negative emotions follow one another across her face: anger, worry, doubt, resentment, fear. Christiane embroiders at the table; her mind keeps straying back to why that pin has appeared now.

It's the priest. And someone's given him one hell of a shiner.

That raises a quizzical look. Amicia pointedly ignores her as she heads down the stairs.

'Is that you, Father?'

'My lady, I must speak with you. Open the door, I beg you.'

She glances towards the bed where Henry turns his back childishly, pulling the sheets up around his head. 'You must keep your distance, Father.'

'I shall,' he promises, rougher of tone than is his norm.

She looks to me and I nod when the priest has moved several feet back up the path. She drags the heavy oak door halfway open.

'There's food and drink,' he gestures abruptly. 'And a vial of Holy Water.'

Anger simmers within him, and his attempt to suppress it makes him awkward in both movement and word: his body is half turned away from us, his jaw's clenched and his arms are folded protectively across his body.

Not just anger: he's vulnerable and afraid.

'Thank you, Father. You didn't have to come yourself.'

He's hesitating, torn now between telling her the truth and protecting her from it. And she senses it.

'What is it, Father?'

In response, he turns the hidden side of his face towards her so she can see the pummelling he's taken. And I realise his arms aren't folded: he's cradling one with the other. Pain is etched in his beaten face.

'They turned on me. My own flock.' Delayed shock surfaces within him and this simple, stolid man finds tears on his cheeks.

'Why?'

'They beat me to find out if Henry has the pestilence. I told them we don't yet know but they didn't believe me. And they beat me to make me tell. But I'd already told the truth!' His voice rises in distress.

'Oh, Father,' she sympathises.

His arm is broken.

What?

The way he's holding it: his arm is broken.

'You must have someone tend to your arm,' she voices.

He grimaces. 'And who will do that, my lady? They're too busy filling themselves with your wine. Elias tried to stop them breaking into the buttery,' he expands, 'but they beat him too.'

'Who?' she demands. 'Who did this to you?'

'All of them.'

'All?'

'It may have been Robert de Windt and Gilbert Beadle who struck the blows, but the rest stood by. At least,' he checks himself, 'those who have not gone into hiding. Many have not appeared for the feast.'

'Where is the steward?' she demands. 'Or the reeve? Why are they not dealing with this?'

A shadow passes over his face. 'I would question Master Reeve's motives in this,' he comments bitterly.

'Speak openly, Father,' she commands quietly.

'I can't help but think he encouraged the attack,' he accuses. 'It's the way he stands by, watching. As if he's overseeing his handiwork. His hands are clean, but all it takes is a word in one ear and then another. And the steward has gone.'

'Philip's gone?' That shocks her.

'I cannot blame him,' he caveats. 'A foreigner in their midst? Simon Reeve would ensure they turned on him next. I am sore tempted to leave them to it myself,' he admits angrily. 'To pick up my things and head for Wharram to be with my family. My daughter would make room for me, I'm sure.' He almost smiles, wistful of a sudden. 'It would be pleasant to bounce her young ones of my knee once more.'

Christiane feels empty at the thought of losing him and it conflicts with her innate human sympathies. 'I shall not blame you for going, Father.'

He holds her gaze, seriously considering. To her relief, he shakes his head. 'Nay, my lady,' he sighs, 'I shall stay. Mayhap if my Joan had still been alive, I would choose differently. But my Thomas and Mary have enough to worry about with their own families; I would just be a burden to them. At least here, I may yet be of use.'

'They must be very afraid,' Christiane sympathises. 'They have faced many a crisis in their lives, but this is too far outside their experience.'

'I had little realised how important your presence was in maintaining order,' he divulges. 'Without you there, they're behaving as lost sheep, swinging this way and that, following whoever bleats the loudest.' Reticence to pile on the bad news makes him pause before admitting the next. 'They have barred the doors and windows at Walter's cottage. Nailed timbers across all the openings.'

'Barred?'

'Simon Reeve had Robert Smith arrange a watch, three men, day and night. I don't know how we can get food to them.'

'Them?'

'It's not just Walter, my lady. They forced Margery and the children inside.'

'That makes no sense!' she argues. 'They weren't there when Henry arrived.'

'What do they care? Reason has fled,' he warns bleakly. 'And I believe they would do the same here were they not so afraid of approaching while a sick man lives inside. Harsh thoughts are being spoken; they blame the lady Amicia for allowing your son to walk into their village.'

'*Their* village?' she echoes weakly.

'That's what they said.'

She absorbs his words in silent stillness, staring beyond the priest to the lane that connects her to the rest of the village. She reaches out to feel for them. Her own people. She has loved and supported them almost her whole life. Her every instinct when this started was to protect them, to keep them away from the danger Henry has brought to them. She can sense their emotions: the creeping terror of those who shut themselves away, the confusion of the many, the growing antipathy of those who are turning against her.

'My lady?' uncertainly.

She turns her eyes towards him, but her gaze is distant now. 'Thank you, Father,' she dismisses him. 'We are in God's hands now.'

She feels his bewilderment as she closes the door, but their energies are crowding in on her, overwhelming her, and her capacity to reassure him is diminished.

Turning the key in the lock, she tries to keep despair at bay.

I shut us away in here to protect them. I little thought it would be needed to protect us.

Chapter Seventy-one

Threfield Percy. 12th April 1349

'What are you going to do?'

Henry is propped up on his elbows.

'What can I do?' she asks.

'You can't let it lie!' he demands. 'They must be punished.'

'How would you have me act, Henry?' she queries. 'I have no steward; the reeve serves his own interests, and I cannot leave this place.'

'But such disobedience cannot stand!' he demands, every inch his father's son. It's too much for his lungs, though, and a fit of coughing overtakes him. She hurries to his side but can only wait for it to subside.

He collapses back on the pillows, his chest heaving as he struggles for breath. 'I'd do it myself,' he pledges, 'but I feel as weak as a new-born lamb.' His lids close and he seems to sink deep into the mattress. 'My head is so heavy I can hardly keep my eyes open.'

She doesn't need to touch his forehead to know he's feverish: sweat stands out against his skin, and he shakes as with ague.

'Are you cold?' He nods feebly, so she digs into one of the chests for the winter blankets and throws them over him. He's so tall, he has to draw in his knees to fit in the bed. 'Can you take some food?' she suggests.

'I'd prefer wine,' he comments wryly.

'Try the broth first.' He opens his eyes and gives her a begrudging look that comes straight from his childhood.

She takes the trenchers of food up to Amicia then sets down bowls of broth and water, and a goblet of wine on a chest beside the bed. Perching alongside him, she cradles his head and shoulders to bring him upright enough to drink from the bowl.

He must be twenty-one but to my eyes he looks much older. His face has the leathery look of an outdoor life and his jaw – which carries two days' stubble – has firmed up and filled out since I last saw him at sixteen.

I remind myself he was heading to his first battle then. When I was that age, I was chasing girls, listening to records and sneaking underage into the pub; Henry was fighting hand-to-hand at Crecy.

He splutters as the soup goes down the wrong way and it sets off another bout of coughing. Coughs that wrack his whole body and double him up in pain. In the moment it subsides, he fights to draw air into his lungs with shallow, rasping breaths.

He wipes the back of his hand across his lips; there's blood on his skin.

Dread drops into her heart.

And into mine: she's too close.

And she knows it.

But instead of moving away, she reaches for a cloth, dampens it and, without a word, wipes the stain from his hand and his chin.

'It means nothing,' he negates, reading the look on her face. 'I'm young and I'm strong. I'll get through this,' he determines.

'I'm sure,' she accedes. 'Now, settle back,' bolstering pillows to prop him up. 'That's better.' She hides the reddened cloth behind the water bowl. 'Your father wrote of your successes in France. At Crecy. And Calais.'

'He did?'

'Of course. He's proud of what you've achieved,' she asserts.

'Glory at last!' he exclaims. 'I said there would be. Father doubted I should go but I was right.' His eyes fire with self-assertion. 'My efforts were noticed too. I'll win my spurs someday soon. I can't wait for this to be over so we can return to war!'

'That may be some time,' she counsels, frowning.

'Nay, this is sure to be over in a few weeks,' he hopes. 'In most places the worst of it passes within a few months.'

'So many people are dying…' she starts.

'People die all the time, if not of this then of something else. And I need to make more money. Most of what I had is gone.'

'What money?'

'From France. I had thought myself well set with what I made from the war, but it's gone.'

'Gone where?'

'Women. Wine. Dice,' he shrugs. 'Time weighs on a soldier's hands when he has no fighting to do.'

He reminds her so much of Ralf.

'I thought you were in the north with your father, defending the border?'

'I was, but it hardly needs defending for now. This disease has people so pathetically scared that even the Scots won't step out. They're convinced it's God's punishment for the English, and yet they're not brave enough to risk so much as a raid.'

'You speak so carelessly of it,' she considers. 'Most people are very much afraid of it.'

'It felt quite distant when I was in Berwick,' he discloses. 'Everything carried on as normal. It may have been a little quiet, but that's all. It was only as I entered Lincoln that it became real...' he shudders at a memory.

'Why were you at Lincoln?' she probes.

He shakes himself and resumes. 'Percy had been called to Windsor. The king is holding a great tournament on St George's Day.'

'You were on your way to compete?' she surmises.

'Nay!' he raises in surprise. 'To claim my inheritance!'

'Your inheritance?' She stops short and stares at him.

'Of course.'

'But your father...'

'...is dead, yes.' He takes in her confused stare. 'You did not know?'

She shakes her head, stunned into silence. I feel her distress and instinctively move closer to her. She turns her head towards me, sensing my presence and needing its comfort, but she does not look up.

'I thought you must know,' Henry defends, discomforted. 'Someone must have sent a messenger...' he concludes feebly, knowing now he has shirked what should have been his responsibility.

'When...? How...?' Her mind struggles to land on a thought.

'A week since. But he had been ailing for months. His wound never healed properly...'

'Wound? What wound?'

'From when he was stabbed last year.'

'Stabbed?'

'You didn't know any of this?' incredulous. Another shake of her head. 'No one saw it happen and my father wouldn't tell. They found him in an alley in the town. Some said it was the husband...' He stops himself. 'He must have chosen to keep it from you.'

'I'm bored. I want you to read to me!'

None of us has heard Amicia's footstep on the stair.

Unthinking, we turn towards her, and she immediately catches the mood.

'What is it?' she demands. 'Something's wrong, I can tell. What is it?'

'My lady...' Christiane moves towards her. But she's not quick enough: Henry, thoughtless, careless, leaps in.

'Father's dead.'

'Don't be absurd.' she flatly denies. 'If Ralf were dead, Percy would have sent a messenger.'

'Consider me that messenger.'

'It cannot be,' she refutes. 'I gave birth to him. If he were dead, I would know.'

'None the less...' Henry tries to dispute.

'Why is there no message from Percy?' Doubt creeps in.

'It's not easy to send messages at the moment...' Christiane starts to explain.

Amicia stares at her, desperate for her to contradict the news. 'You can't believe it's true?' she beseeches.

'If Henry says so…'

A strange tight sound forms in the back of her throat, a strangled, animalistic noise of a pain too great to bear. 'No,' she whispers. 'No, it cannot be. Say it isn't so,' pleading now. 'Say he's coming to see me.'

The distress is too much for her fragile body. She seems to crumple from within. As the heart of her vanishes into a dark void, the rest, with a cry, collapses too.

Chapter Seventy-two

Threfield Percy. 12th April 1349

Christiane almost carries her back upstairs. She weighs next to nothing and is so fragile she's afraid of crushing her; deprived of sunlight, the bones have become dangerously brittle, and the body is painfully thin, barely a skeleton held together by papery skin. It's hard to know how she has survived this long.

She settles her in the chair and pulls a fur around her. Amicia's eyes are glazed and unseeing. Christiane crouches before her, rubbing her cold hands and looking into the embittered face.

Slowly, the old woman refocuses on her.

'Go back to him,' she mouths. 'Tell him he's wrong.'

'How about some wine, my lady?' Christiane encourages.

'Tell him he's been misled,' she pursues. 'Tell him it's not true. It can't be true.' Her voice breaks. 'Not my son…'

She buries her face in her hands. But an instant later, she jerks upright.

'Bring my cloak,' she demands, pushing Christiane away so she can stand. 'I'm going to the church to pray.'

Christiane stands but does not move away. 'My lady, you cannot leave…'

'Nonsense. I'm only going to the church. They can all keep their distance from me.'

'You don't understand…' Christiane tries.

'No!' she turns on her violently. 'You don't understand. I need to intercede with God. To ask his forgiveness.'

'So, you do remember?' Christiane hopes.

'Not for me, idiot girl!' Amicia scorns. 'For Ralf. If what you say is true and he hastened Geoffrey's death, I need to pray for his soul.'

'You can do that just as well here, my lady,' she reasons, gesturing towards the prie dieu.

'No,' Amicia disputes. 'It needs to be in church. I feel it must be there. God is calling me there…' she falters, 'to save my son.' Her voice catches on a choking sob; overwhelmed, she sinks back into her chair. 'I can't believe he's gone. Please,' she begs, catching Christiane's hand in supplication. 'Please, I need to be there. I need God's comfort.'

'I wish you could, my lady,' Christiane appeases.

'You don't understand, do you?' Amicia challenges. 'How hollow my life is without him to love me.' Tears flow freely down her cheeks. 'What's the use of me, of this existence,' with a raise of her chin indicating the room before her, 'if he's not here?'

'Sweet lady,' Christiane empathises, her heart aching for her. 'God sends us burdens to test us, but he also gives us the strength to see them through.'

'Do not counsel me to endure this,' Amicia spits. 'You cannot understand. You do not know what it is for a mother to lose her child.'

What breathless insensitivity.

She's in pain.

So are you.

Christiane pulls away and turns her back on both of us.

'I know you are hurting,' she speaks, her voice tight with self-control, 'but you cannot leave this place, not even to go to the church. I will not risk the rest of the village being infected.'

'Infected?' Amicia goes rigid. 'So, it is the pestilence?' accusing. 'But I heard you saying he has no carbuncles.'

'It's not that simple,' turning back to face her. 'The pestilence has other symptoms…'

'Will he infect me?' she interrupts. In moments, she swings from incapacitating grief to gripping terror.

'It's best you stay away from him,' Christiane reiterates.

'But it moves in the air!' she screeches. 'A miasma…'

'That's not how it works…' she contradicts, feeling for what I know.

'I want him removed,' Amicia commands, standing to confront Christiane. 'Now.'

'No.'

'I don't want him here!' she fights. She's becoming hysterical. 'Get him out!'

'I can't do that.'

'Oh, my heart…' Amicia presses a hand to her chest. Her breathing is quick and shallow. 'Can't you see I need peace?' she blames Christiane. 'I need to be alone to grieve. My son. Oh, my beloved son!' She hides her face in a show of agony again.

When she raises her head a second later, her eyes are wild and she staggers toward Christiane, one hand outstretched to grasp her wrist.

'What if I die?' she shudders.

'Stop, my lady!' Christiane protests.

'I must see the priest,' she implores, gripping Christiane's arm. 'I must confess…'

The façade has fallen away. The look she gives Christiane is bleak.

'Confess?' she hopes.

'Geoffrey…' Amicia whispers.

Christiane goes cold; she's torn between saving the lives of the many and the soul of the one.

'Perhaps Father Peter can come to the door…' she suggests.

Amicia shakes her head, her face aghast. 'What if that's not enough?'

'I'm sorry, my lady,' she reiterates, 'but you cannot leave.'

'You cannot stop me,' she resists and starts scrabbling at the pouch hanging from Christiane's waist.

'My lady, what are you doing?' feebly trying to thwart her but afraid to be too hard with her. Amicia palms the key. 'Nay, my lady…' she discourages.

The speed with which Amicia moves is astonishing. Caught unawares, Christiane is a second or two behind her as she chases down the stairs.

'I'm going,' Amicia insists, fumbling to get the key into the lock. Christiane comes up behind her and grabs at her hand. The key drops to the floor with a heavy clang. Swiftly, Christiane picks it up.

Amicia scrabbles at her hands to get it back. 'Give it to me!' she demands, half sobbing, half enraged. 'Give it to me!' She digs her nails into the back of Christiane's hand and pulls hard and viciously. Christiane yelps in pain and pulls away; she cradles one hand with the other against her breast, her fingers closed tightly around the key.

'No, my lady!'

'God curse you!' Amicia yells, her face wild with rage. Then she sinks to the floor and screams her tears.

Christiane's shock is mirrored in Henry's face. She stands still, frozen, for a long moment. But her mind is racing.

She turns and runs up the stairs.

I need somewhere to hide it.

She looks around the room. At the jewel caskets. The chests filled with clothes. The books. The tapestries.

There must be somewhere! I can't tend to Henry and keep an eye on her. But she'll keep looking until she finds it.

Under the floor?

There's no time.

Can't you keep it on you?

What if she waits until I'm sleeping and steals it?

She won't get past you if you're downstairs.

But this could go on for days. I need to sleep at some point.

The instant the thought occurs to her, my blood runs cold.

No!

Ignoring me, she moves across the room and opens the west-facing window. *I have to.*

You'll need to get out at some point.

Perhaps not.

Even if you're not infected, you haven't enough food to survive.

We can't expect much help from the villagers anyway.

You're condemning yourself to die. All three of you.

Yes. But you've seen Henry: he's dying anyway. And it's likely Amicia and I have already been infected, isn't it? Do you think she will survive it?

No. But you could.

There's total acceptance in her face.

And then she looks at me with the most curious expression.

But from where you stand, I'm dead already, aren't I?

The thought gives her a strange sense of detachment, a calmness that settles over her. I have no retort.

My death is inevitable, it's only a matter of timing. To you, it's already happened. Does it really matter when or where?

Not like this. Please.

She takes a step closer to me. We're only inches apart and she looks up at me with such knowing.

'This is what I have to do,' she murmurs softly, and my spine tingles. 'And now I know.' She's filled with sureness. 'I know why you're here. To give me the strength to do this.'

Drawing back her hand, she hurls the key out of the window.

I hear the splash as it hits the fishpond.

Chapter Seventy-three

Threfield Percy. 12th April 1349

Hours pass.

I'm sitting on the rough floor of the bedchamber, my back propped against the wall by the steps, watching Christiane tend her son.

She moves quietly around the room while he's sleeping, sorting through the chests, shaking out and inspecting clothes then refolding them or putting them to be mended.

Amicia is upstairs alone. For hours we could hear her turning out every hiding place, emptying caskets, overturning cushions and books, shaking out tapestries. All the while talking to herself, vacillating between anger and self-pity. Eventually silence settled, interrupted sporadically by a heavy sigh or the sound of something being thrown across the room. Since then, she's only appeared once when she needed to use the garde robe. She didn't speak or even look at Christiane or Henry.

He's weakening, his breathing is painfully laboured; I suspect he won't last the night.

When he dies, how long should she wait to be sure they haven't been infected? Three or four days? She can survive that long without food, as long as she has enough to drink.

Stop it.

You could tell the priest about the key. He can get the smith to break down the door.

I know you're concerned but this is not helping.

My chest hurts. I've never known the physical pain of grief like this: the tightness around my heart, the inability to breathe.

How many years apart are we?

She's curious, but I know she's also trying to distract me.

Six hundred and twenty-seven. Give or take a few months.

I imagine your world would be unrecognisable to me.

Images of cars and TVs and aeroplanes and rockets parade through my mind. The moon landing. The Second World War. The holocaust.

But then I think of home, of Cambridge. Of Michael. And Sam.

In some ways, yes. In others, I'm not sure we're so different. People are born, they marry, they have children, they work, they die. There are still wars. And greed. And hatred.

And love.

She sends me such a tender smile that I feel my chest expand and, for now, I can breathe again.

In the stillness, an owl screeches. I start and realise it's deep into dusk outside; in the windowless tower room, I haven't noticed the light going. Within a half-hour it will be fully dark. As I tune to the outer world, I hear steps scurrying along the path, slipping in their haste, and turn to look in that direction.

The priest is coming. I was beginning to think he'd forgotten you.

She checks on Henry's unsettled sleep then makes her way to the door.

'Father Peter?' She raises her voice just enough to be heard. 'Is that you?'

'Aye, my lady. I wanted to bring more food, but they would not allow it.'

'There is no need, Father. The door is locked, and the key is lost, so I could not take it in anyway.'

'Lost? Is there no other?'

'No. There was only one.'

'I will tell Robert Smith. He will be able to do something.'

'Leave it, Father,' she instructs. 'It will sort itself out.'

He does not argue. 'How fares my lord?'

'He sleeps,' she replies, briefly. It pains her too much to say more. And he doesn't ask, fearing to know the truth. 'What brings you here?' she prompts.

He glances behind as if a noise has distracted him, but the path is empty.

'It's Simon Reeve,' he starts. 'He's been found dead in the back lane.'

That's no great loss.

Be kind.

'Dead how?'

'His head was smashed in.'

'He was murdered?' Disbelief rushes through her. *How has it come to this?* 'Who would do such a thing?'

'They accuse Hugh. He was seen arguing with the reeve before the feast and disappeared before the first food was served.'

'Why would Hugh do that?'

'The reeve demanded full payment of his fines this morning.'

'But Hugh hasn't the money for that!'

'And the reeve knows it,' the priest affirms. 'He isn't interested in the money.'

He wants Hugh's property.

She meets my gaze warily.

In the last year, he's taken control of a quarter of the tenant properties in the manor. Of course, he's beholden to me for all of it. No, she stops herself. *Not to me now. To Henry.*

And what happens if Henry dies?

That gives her pause.

Without an heir, the property reverts to Henry Percy. He would decide where to distribute it.

Perhaps the reeve saw his opportunity in Henry's illness. Perhaps he intended to take the manor for himself.

But he doesn't know Ralf is dead. Unless there was a message that didn't reach me?

'What's happening with Hugh?' she calls through the door.

'William Child found the body and raised the hue and cry. But the whole place is in disarray.'

'Where is everyone?'

'Some have taken refuge in the church and are refusing to leave; they say it's the only place they feel safe. Many of the servants are so drunk they can no longer stand, men and women alike. The rest have banded together behind Robert Smith. They were heading for Hugh Miller's cottage. I slipped away to tell you.'

'That's enough now, priest.' A man's voice loudly interrupts. Robert de Windt appears from the shadows of the wood. 'I saw you sneak off into the darkness, Father. I wondered what you were up to while good men are protecting our village.'

'This is no business of yours,' the priest proclaims, but his voice wavers and we can both sense his nervousness.

'What are you doing here, Father?' Robert's voice betrays his drunkenness. 'You wouldn't be thinking of letting them out, would you?'

'Of course not,' Father Peter contests. 'I came only to inform my lady about the reeve.'

Robert laughs. 'For sure, he got what was coming to him.' He stops as lights appear at the top of the path and catch his eye. 'Hoi! Over here!' he shouts, waving them towards him. They break into a run. 'I stopped him helping them escape!' he claims proudly as they near.

'I was doing no such thing!' the priest denounces.

'Take him!' Robert Smith shouts to the men at the front as they skid to a halt. Gilbert Beadle and Robert grab an arm each and pull the priest several feet further from the door. 'What's afoot here?' the smith demands.

'He was planning to let them out!' Robert de Windt proclaims. 'I saw him break away when we were heading to Hugh Miller's house and thought it best to follow him. 'Tis as well I did!'

'He lies!' the priest protests. 'I came only because my lady needs to know about Simon Reeve.'

'You would have done better to stay away, priest,' Robert Smith condemns, frowning.

'What shall we do with him, Master Smith?' one calls.

'How can we trust him now?' another inserts.

'Put him with the others,' the smith instructs, 'where we can keep an eye on him.' They manhandle the priest back up the lane.

'My lady!' Father Peter calls in despair.

'What is happening, Robert Smith?' Christiane calls.

He pauses to consider, then instructs the others. 'Let me deal with this. You go back to the Hall. I shall return shortly. Not you,' he points to two of the stable boys. 'Wait there are moment.'

He approaches the door so he can speak more normally to Christiane through it.

'No doubt the priest told you the reeve is dead?'

'He did.'

'You should know they want to elect me reeve for the meantime. So, I speak for all of them.'

'I accept that,' she acknowledges.

'Hugh Miller has fled. That must bespeak his guilt.'

'Or his fear of what a mass of drunken men would do to him. Do not be too quick to assume,' she counsels.

'It is our concern now,' he resists. 'We will deal with him as we see fit.'

'He is still my tenant,' she reminds him. 'As are you, Robert Smith. Which makes both your lives my responsibility.'

'You shall find we are taking responsibility for ourselves,' he grunts, irritated by her assertion. ''Tis time you and your kind showed some responsibility towards us.'

'What do you mean?'

'I mean,' taking a breath to steady himself, realising he is overstepping the mark, 'some among the village want revenge for the lady Amicia betraying us. For years she has controlled and restrained us. She demanded we stay within the village bounds to protect her. And yet she…' his voice rises on tense anger, 'she is the one who allowed your son free access to the village. She is the one who may have brought Death to our very door!' He stops, his face flushed with rage and rebellion.

Christiane's face is white in the candlelight. She cannot argue with that.

'My lady,' with exaggerated respect and an effort at self-control, 'you need to tell me. Does your son have the pestilence?'

She glances behind her towards the bed. Henry, disturbed by the noise, is sitting up, his face stricken; he's waiting for her to speak the words that will condemn him.

She looks at me, grim-faced, then turns back to the door. 'I cannot tell you that with any certainty, Master Smith,' she responds.

I can tell the smith wants to argue but seeing fear on the faces of the two young men, he chooses not to push it. He carries the burden now of how that knowing will affect those around him, those who are looking to him for leadership.

'Tom, Joe,' beckoning the two stable boys closer. 'I want you to stand guard at this door. None can leave and none can approach. Do you understand?' They nod.

'You need not fear us, Robert Smith,' Christiane asserts. 'We cannot leave here now: the key to the door is gone and none shall find it.'

'Even if I believe you, my lady, that won't do for the rest,' he justifies. 'They have put their faith in me, and I must protect them. I shall send replacements at midnight.'

Christiane leans heavily back against the wall and meets my gaze with even greater concern in her eyes.

Chapter Seventy-four

Threfield Percy. 12ᵗʰ April 1349

'How long does it take a man to die of the pestilence?'

Since the smith departed, it's been quiet outside the door. The two young men start out by taking their job seriously but as time ticks on tedium sets in and the chatter starts.

Upstairs, it's gone quiet at last: Amicia is dozing in her chair before the fire. Down here, Christiane maintains her vigil. It's as she rises to replace the candles that we hear them.

'Four or five days. At least, that's what the old women are saying.'

Our warders make no effort to drop their voices. And the three of us can't help but listen: Henry huddled on the bed and staring blankly at the wall; Christiane sitting on a stool close by, ready to help when she's needed; me by the door.

'Does Master Smith expect us to guard them all that time?'

'No choice, is there? As long as they're in there, we're safe.'

'You sure of that?' one worries.

'Should be,' the other hopes, less than convincingly. 'They say it travels in the air. How's it going to get out if they're shut away?'

'I heard a man dies in agony when he has the buboes,' the first speculates. 'Loses his mind so he hardly knows his own name.'

'Some have been known to try to cut the thing out of their bodies, the pain is that bad,' the second ripostes. 'But when they're as large as a duck's egg and as black as night, you're done for.'

'I heard some just fall down dead before your very eyes. Before you even know they've got it.'

That last piece of one-upmanship silences both of them. But only for a time.

'Did you see old Gilbert has already fled? Packed his whole house into a cart, took his wife and children, and disappeared up the lane.'

'Where's he gone?'

'Into the woods, I reckon. He won't be the last, either.'

'He can't seriously believe he can hide from the pestilence?'

'It's not just that,' his partner elaborates. 'He's disappearing before all hell breaks loose.'

'Meaning what?'

'Don't you realise what trouble there's going to be? Think about it, fool,' now dropping his voice, though still not enough; the world lies silent in the night and there's no sound to smother his words. 'With the priest beaten and the reeve murdered, someone's going to pay.'

'Well, they've got Hugh Miller for the murder,' the other parries.

'That won't satisfy them. And, anyway, are you sure it was him?'

'Why not?'

'Master Miller's not the only one to benefit from the reeve dying, is he?' he rationalises. 'Half the village owed him money.'

'The way I see it, he deserved it. Lording it over everyone, acting like he owned the place.'

'Maybe. But that's not the half of it, is it? The priest is sure to want justice for his beating. And what do you suppose will happen if any of this lot,' with a nod in the direction of the door, 'survives? What punishments are we going to be facing then?'

'They can't blame us for what we've done!' the other ripostes. 'We were only looking to protect ourselves.'

'By breaking into the stores and stealing their food and drink? And since when have they ever seen it our way? No, there'll be hell to pay for this, for sure. Things have gone too far.'

There's a heavy silence before the other replies.

'Then we'd best hope the pestilence takes it out of our hands.'

****

Around midnight, more voices join them. But it's not two replacements, it's five, and the original two seem inclined to stay, drawn by the company or perhaps by the wine they bring with them. And as the group expands, what started as a precaution becomes something altogether meaner.

'They've taken the miller!' One of the new arrivals can't wait to share the news. 'Caught him hiding in the eaves of Henry Child's house. Broke down the door and dragged him out by his hair. Took Master Child too for harbouring him.'

'What have they done with him?'

'He's shut away in a storage room, that one underneath the solar. The cook and Henry Child too.'

'There's a pretty hoard in there!' another inserts. 'You should see the cloth and furs; the women were beside themselves with excitement. The men too when they broke into the spice chest.'

'Such a waste,' laments one of the kitchen boys. 'As if any of them knows what to do with them. They only want to own what they think could be worth something!'

'Doesn't matter if they do or not,' throws out another. 'It's better in our hands than theirs.'

'Hush!' one of the first pair orders, harshly. 'Walls have ears, you fool!'

'What do I care?' the same disputes. 'Have a drink and stop worrying, Tom Tuttle,' shoving the flagon of wine in his direction. 'It's from the store. None of that watered-down rubbish for us tonight!'

'Live for today!' another reinforces. 'Let tomorrow take care of itself.'

He raises a cup and Tom, throwing off his reluctance, matches his toast. They settle on the ground in a loose circle, some leaning back against the wall, Tom on the step by the door.

It's descending into anarchy out there.

Shock shows on Christiane's face.

'Sweet Christ but it's cold out here,' one grumbles after a few moments, pulling his cloak closer around his chest.

'We could light a fire,' another suggests.

'I don't see why not,' Tom concurs. 'Fetch some logs and kindling. And bring plenty,' he calls as two disappear towards the wood. 'It could be a long night.'

Christiane looks at me.

What should I do?

I shrug, helplessly. What is there she can do?

Suddenly, Henry starts coughing and once he starts, he can't stop. He strains upright, struggling to regain control but the fit overtakes him until he's almost retching from it. I see the lads outside exchange worried glances at the noise.

When it finally ends, he falls back, drained.

The fever, which had abated for a few hours, has returned and a fierce heat radiates from his sweat-soaked skin. As he collapses on the pillow, she applies cold, wet cloths to his face in a vain attempt to bring his temperature down. He splutters another cough, his shoulders juddering upwards and blood-stained spittle emerging from his mouth. She wipes around his beard, then reaches for a cup.

'Drink, Henry,' she urges. But he gives the slightest shake of his head, as much as he can bear to move.

He's stopped taking food or wine.

And his breathing has an ominous scraping sound to it; his lungs are failing.

A loud hammering starts at the door.

'What's happening in there?' Tom cries out. 'We can hear the coughing. Is that him? Is he dying?'

'You can't ask her that!' another hisses. 'That's her son you're talking about.'

'But it may be the pestilence!' he argues. 'We have a right to know if he's going to infect the rest of us with it!'

'You told me he couldn't if we kept them inside,' Joe butts in, horrified. 'Which is it? Are we safe or not?'

'Do you think he knows?' another voice mocks. 'He's full of it, always has been.'

'Stop it, all of you,' Christiane orders, crossing to the door and pressing a hand against the wood. 'Calm yourselves. You are safe as long as you stay out there.'

'You have to tell me if he dies,' Tom demands.

She fights to suppress the anger that pushes as her self-control. She rests her forehead on her hand as she speaks, and I realise how exhausted she is. 'I am doing everything I can to keep you safe, Tom Tuttle,' she pledges. 'All of you.'

'Please, my lady,' his voice softens. ''Tis Master Smith's instruction. He will want to know.'

She closes her eyes in anguish. 'I will tell you if anything changes,' she promises.

****

For the next two hours, Henry drifts in and out of consciousness, but it's a disturbed mind that surfaces in those early hours. Memories are bothering him: he begs someone not to leave; reacts to another with the terror of seeing a ghost.

He talks coherently at times, just for a few moments together. He rehashes childhood moments with Dafydd and the early days of his squirehood. But when thoughts of his battles come up, he shies away from them, from remembering those he's killed.

She sits on the side of the bed to listen to him, taking in every moment with him while she can.

'I'm glad you came here,' she tells him, placing one hand on his, 'when you fell ill. I'm glad you came to me.'

He looks at her weakly. He knows the danger he's put her in.

'I got as far as Lincoln,' he recalls. 'The inn I stayed in…I should have known. At the city gate, they were so wary about letting us in, they insisted we stop at the inn just inside the wall. They looked at us with such suspicion. You could feel it in the air.

'The inn was almost empty, yet the landlord insisted that I share a room with two other travellers. Reluctant to take us in at all. Getting ready to shut his doors: they'd had word of pestilence in Boston and Bishop's Lynn. "If it's there, it's coming here," he said.

'One of the other men died during the night. He was dead in his bed when I woke; I could see his staring eyes. I didn't even wake the other man, I just got out. I crept down the stairs and out of the door before anyone else stirred. They'd have locked me away had I stayed. I fled. I fled to you. Three days on the road, avoiding everyone.'

His mind wanders. His eyes close and he drifts towards sleep.

'Have you heard from Dafydd?' he asks, his voice drowsy.

'I had a letter a fortnight since.'

'He's probably dead already then.'

'Yes.' There's acceptance in her tone, as well as deep sadness.

Henry half opens his eyes.

'That means it's just the three of us,' he observes quietly. 'You, me and a mad woman. We're all that's left.'

Chapter Seventy-five

Threfield Percy. 12th April 1349

He sleeps.

The noise outside gradually abates. We can still hear the lads chatting, but it's more subdued now they have settled down around the fire.

She rises from the bed and comes to stand before me near the door. She holds my gaze and, in her eyes, I read the many layers of emotion that fill her: love, sadness, pity, regret, concern, acceptance.

I think I must reflect them back to her because she watches me closely, and then, with a silent nod, comes to sit down opposite me on the floor, leaning back against the foot of the bed.

Though she's several feet away, she feels so close to me with what connects us, holding us to one another.

I'm glad you're here too.

I don't think I had a lot of choice in the matter. Wryly, I raise an eyebrow at her. She smiles; the softest, sweetest smile.

Do you know what it's been like for me, having you in my life? You've been more of a constant than anyone else. More than my parents, my husband or my children.

Her gaze is so direct.

You know everything about me. It's so strange to think that no one else knows about you.

I thought maybe Amicia saw me earlier.

It wasn't you. Someone else was there.

Geoffrey?

Maybe. It was just a shadow. She pauses, considering. *You haven't eaten all day. Are you not hungry?*

I hadn't stopped to think about it. But, no, I'm not. I think it's because my body is still in my time and time is passing differently for me there.

That makes her pause.

How much time has passed for you…since you first saw me?

I don't know. Nine…ten days? I'm not even sure what day it is. That makes me pause. I'd better find out: it's Michael's funeral on Thursday.

Who's he?

An image of Michael flashes into my mind: sitting at his desk, surrounded by papers and cups of tea.

Is he your father?

My friend. My teacher.

You're sad: I can feel your grief. He's gone?

A few days ago.

Of course, that makes me think of Sam, which is painful to do. Because of the guilt that I've let her down again, that I've left her to bear her grief alone. Or maybe she's not alone. Maybe her husband… Jealousy sweeps away the rest.

She's looking at me oddly; it's a strange, assessing kind of a look, like she's listening to me. Like she can see right into me.

I've seen her before. I've seen them both.

When?

I've seen the man a few times: at the Hall, in the fields, by the church. He always looked a bit lost. I could tell he was searching for something. He was content but not happy.

And Sam?

When I was a very young child. I remember the red hair, like mine. And her energy: a healer. It must have been on the day I arrived here. The day I realised you were real.

Real?

You were there when my father died but I didn't understand who you were at the time; you were just one amongst the throng. When I came here and you were here again…it was then that I realised you were different.

You accused me of being the cause of bad things happening in your life.

I know. But I was in distress. She smiles ruefully. *And you've forgiven me.*

How is this happening?

She looks at me with that clear-sighted, penetrating gaze of hers.

I can't say. All I know is that something connects us in a way that I can't explain or even describe. Something bigger than either of us.

But how?

I don't know. It was never something I was aware of before it happened; you were just…there…at the right moments. When I was younger, I used to wonder if my father had sent you. She smiles. *You look like him, you know.*

Who?

My father. So does Henry. She frowns, thinking. *You're a Bren too, aren't you? Perhaps that's how, then.*

She hugs her arms around herself as she contemplates me.

Whatever the reason, thank you for being here when I've needed you. I can't tell you what it's meant to me, having you with me. Even when I couldn't hear your words or read your thoughts, I could still feel the essence of you. I could feel your strength and that gave me strength.

She holds my gaze steadily.

I need you to be strong again. For both of us.

We both sense it: she's getting ready to let me go.

Chapter Seventy-six

Threfield Percy. 12th April 1349

An hour later – somewhere around three in the morning – Henry starts coughing again.

And he can't stop. With every exhalation, he becomes weaker. He can't take in enough air and panic shows on his face as he struggles to breathe. Blood stains his beard and shirt.

His face is strained as he collapses back on the pillow.

'Mother.' His voice is so faint she leans in to hear him. 'I need to confess.'

'They won't allow Father Peter in.'

His eyes open wide with fear; he hadn't realised.

I remember Dafydd's letter saying laymen and women were allowed to take each other's confession.

She looks at me, assessing, then hurries to the door and thumps on the wood.

'Tom Tuttle,' she calls. 'I need to speak with you.'

She looks to me for guidance. *Is he still out there?*

It's only then that I realise I can't see outside anymore. That sometime in the last few hours, I've become even more grounded in this time.

How did that happen?

'My lady? Tom Tuttle has gone.'

'Is that you, Joe Crow?'

'Aye, my lady.'

'Joe, I must speak with Father Peter. Can you fetch him for me?' She senses his hesitation. 'I only want to speak to him through the door. I beg you, for my sake do this for me.'

As she turns back to the bed, Henry is trying to rise. Throwing off the covers, he attempts to stand but his legs give way, and he falls forward. She catches him with her shoulder under his arm and her arms around his chest.

'Too hot,' he complains, pushing her away. 'I can't stand it.' His clothes and hair stick to his sweat-slick skin, and it runs down his face, into his beard. 'The river. Must get to the river.'

He's delirious.

Somehow, she gets him back into the bed. He throws the sheets off when she tries to cover him, but less than a minute later he's shaking with cold, and she pulls them back over him.

Someone thumps the door. 'My lady.' It's Robert Smith.

'Master Smith,' she comes to the door. 'They didn't need to bother you. I only wanted to speak with the priest.'

'He won't be coming, my lady,' he refuses.

'Please, Master Smith,' she implores. 'I must know what to do about my son's confession.'

'You'll have to make do without him,' he disagrees. 'I don't trust you. Or him.'

'Then stand by so you can hear everything we say!' she rationalises. 'I beg you, Master Smith. Do this for the sake of my son's soul.'

'And why should I do that, my lady?' he queries. 'What has he ever done for us but bring the pestilence to our door!'

She looks at me, with despair in her eyes.

'Then,' she hopes, 'do it for me, Master Smith?'

We can hear his heavy sigh. 'My lady, am I not already doing all of this for you? Is it better to imperil your son's soul or to endanger the lives of all these people?' She falls silent. He waits for a long time for her answer. 'My lady?'

'You are doing what you feel you must,' she grants.

'Thank you, my lady.' He clears his throat where sadness catches him. 'Then I hope you will understand when I say…' He stumbles and stops. This hardened man struggles against his emotion. 'My lady…'

'Say what you must, Master Smith,' she forces.

'When your son dies, we won't be letting you out.' They are the hardest words he's ever spoken.

'I understand, Master Smith,' she absolves him, her voice much steadier than his. 'Then you need to know that my husband is dead, and I have to assume that my son, Dafydd, is also.'

'My lady…' he starts to sympathise, pity finding its way through now he's delivered his fatal decision.

'If you can,' she interrupts, 'get a message to Lord Percy. He is at Windsor with the king. He needs to know his kin have died. He will decide how to dispose of the manor.'

'Dispose of the manor?' he echoes dumbly.

'You will have a new lord,' she concludes. 'Take care of everyone until then. You are a good man, Robert Smith. Do your best by them and you won't go far wrong.'

She turns away from him.

And the world narrows. As if she's just washed her hands of everyone outside these walls.

You don't need the priest's permission for this.

She nods at my thought.

'Henry.' She kneels by the side of the bed. 'The priest cannot hear your confession, but I can.'

He looks towards her, a doubting frown lining his forehead. 'Are you sure?'

'The Bishop of London gave instruction,' she persuades him. 'So many are dying…'

'Do you remember the words?' he mistrusts.

'More or less,' she nods. 'Pray our Father will make allowances.'

She kneels up so she can be closer to him. He turns on his side, his face close to hers, and she clasps her hands around his.

'Do you believe fully in the articles of faith and the holy scriptures, and forsake all heresies condemned by the Church?'

'I do.'

'Do you know how often, in what ways and how grievously you have offended the Lord your God?'

'I do.' His voice roughens with emotion.

'Are you sorry in your heart for all the sins you have committed against God, all the goodness you might have done but did not do?'

'I am.'

'If your life is spared, are you resolved to amend your life so that you may not commit mortal sins intentionally again?'

No answer. Does he hesitate?

'My son, you must answer.' She touches his cheek, and he seems to come to once more. 'Henry, will you amend your life so as not to commit mortal sins intentionally again?'

'I will,' he promises; tears slide from his eyes.

'Do you forgive fully in your heart anyone who has done you harm or caused you grief, in word or deed?'

'I do.' His lips frame the words, though no sound comes out.

'Will you have all things in your possession given back, and leave and forsake all your worldly goods if you cannot make satisfaction in any other way?'

He gives the barest nod.

'Say it, Henry,' she coaxes. 'Say the words.'

'I will,' he promises.

'Do you believe fully that Christ died for you and that you will only be saved by Christ's Passion, and do you thank God with your heart, as much as you may?'

'I do.' He breaks down and closes his eyes against the free-flowing tears. She leans across and puts her arms around him, resting her forehead against his. She starts the words of the paternoster and, falteringly, he joins in.

Together, mother and son pray.

The world stops and becomes silent. I can't hear anything from outside now, nor from Amicia upstairs. Isolated and separated, it's as if we are the only ones alive in this moment in time. The fire is burning low and there are few candles alight, giving a soft radiance around the bed and deeper shadows at the edges of the room. I draw near her. We feel as one, each other's emotions intertwining and enmeshing until the pain and anguish are held and surrounded by deep love and caring.

He's so still he scarcely seems to be breathing.

She pours holy water in the palm of her hand and, with her fingertips, touches it to his lips, his eyelids, his brow.

'Say the words,' she encourages him, seeing acceptance settle over him.

He looks at her steadily enough, though his voice is broken. 'Into Thy hands, O Lord, I commend my spirit. You have redeemed me, O Lord, thou God of truth.'

'The dear Lord bless you, Henry.' She brushes the hair back from his forehead, as she did when he was a child. 'You are ready.'

'Thank you, my lady,' he murmurs, and closes his eyes.

When the coughing fit seizes him some time later, she holds onto his hands so tightly that her fingers turn white with strain. He hasn't even the strength to raise his body, and bloody spittle sprays over the pillow.

His breath wheezes as he exhales for the last time. As he does, all the fear and anger and pride are released, and I'm left looking at the face of a young man, much younger than the one he presented to the world.

For a long moment, she rests her head against their joined hands. 'I'll see you soon, dearest boy,' she whispers.

Then she stands and turns towards me.

I put my arms around her and hold her close.

Chapter Seventy-seven

Threfield Percy. 12th April 1349

It feels so good to hold her.

Now I know what people mean when they say time stands still. It's a fragment that exists beyond our time and space, a fragment that draws on more than what we are in our lives, more than what we are individually. We're still here, we're still in the now, but we're also beyond. It's a momentary window on the infinite, a potent stillness, shaped with wholeness and unity. A beingness that is us and yet not.

Then she moves, turns her head against my chest. Time reasserts, and an overwhelming flood of emotions hits.

There's relief in knowing his pain is over. Consolation in believing that he's now with God. Emptiness of loss. Of him and Ralf and Dafydd.

A sharp stab of anger at Amicia. And habitual guilt hot on its heels.

A nagging worry about the villagers.

Anxiety about what's coming next, with a burst of fear.

But that's quickly suppressed; there's no changing this, so there's no point in fearing it.

Acceptance.

I can feel her decision to break away from me a fraction of a second before she does.

She crosses to the door.

'Joe Crow.'

A short pause as he comes to the other side of the door. 'My lady?'

'Go to Robert Smith. Tell him that Master Henry has died.' Her voice is strong and clear and true.

'Aye, my lady.'

She turns back to me. 'Help me with him?'

I don't need to ask what she means: our minds are together. We pull back the covers and roll him onto his back, then I lift his still-warm body so she can remove his shirt. She uses the holy water to clean the sweat and blood from his face and neck, wipes the damp cloth over his cooling skin. I lift him again and she slides a fresh shirt over him and we tug it into place. Laying him back down, one on each side of him, we straighten his limbs and fold his hands over his chest. We lay clean linens over him and tuck them close around his body, centred on the bed. She pulls the rich coverlet back over; on the deep red cloth, the blood stains are only darker spots. We straighten the bedding over him and smooth it down.

The church bell starts to toll. I look across at her, and the hold of our gaze is a moment of prayer. In my head, I count each melancholic clang, the off-pitch tone a perfect memorial; one for each of his twenty-one years.

The floorboards above us creak: Amicia awakes.

Moments later, she calls Christiane's name from the head of the stairs.

'Come here!' she demands, her voice still confused with sleep. 'My pin is missing. I need you to look for it. My eyes...' She shuffles halfway down the stairs until she can see Christiane. 'What are you waiting for?' she grumbles. 'Come! I've lost my ruby pin. It was right here...' touching her hand to her breast where Christiane had secured it.

She's upset. About losing a brooch.

Christiane looks at me. And I look in the direction of the steps. We both know where it is.

Amicia stares in the direction of the door. 'Why are they tolling the bell?' she complains. 'It's not time for mass, it's still dark outside.'

She takes another two steps down the stairs and stops dead. In an instant, her face drains of colour.

Christiane moves towards her.

'The bell is for Henry,' she starts cautiously, shielding the body on the bed from Amicia's direct gaze. Not that she needs to because Amicia's gaze is fixed, staring at something…beyond the walls.

Christiane takes the old woman's hand in both hers. 'My lady,' she reinforces, trying to gain her attention, 'the bell is for your grandson. Henry is dead.'

The old woman looks down at where her hand is held then, slowly, almost painfully, her eyes lift to Christiane's. And there is horror in them.

'There's someone over there…' The words come out as a broken whisper.

Christiane frowns. 'Don't worry, it'll just be one of the villagers.'

She shakes her head, a frightened tremble, almost afraid to move. Her eyes are fixed on the distance, beyond the wall of the tower, towards the woods.

Christiane turns her head, but we know she won't see anything.

Can you see?

I look but all I can see is the tapestry-covered wall. I close my eyes and rebuild in my mind a picture of the landscape I know: the copse of silver birch trees, the rough grass that's dry after the long summer, the dog walker's path cutting through towards the lane.

Instantly, I can see a figure standing on the other side of the wall.

Shock jolts through me and I open my eyes.

It's the farmer's wife. And she's looking directly at Amicia.

'Can't you see?' Amicia half-raises a hand, pointing, but also warding her off. Her voice cries for reassurance. Her mind is scrabbling to stay in control, to hold onto a safer reality, to stop the slide into the unimaginable. She turns her face to Christiane. 'Can't you see?' she implores. 'Tell me you can see her?' Inexorably, her eyes are drawn back again with the resistance of one who fears to look but can't not.

Yes, I can see her.

Who is she?

Her husband owns this land.

'Who is she?'

'She's the one…' Amicia's voice falters as her body starts to shake uncontrollably.

Christiane moves in front of her and, taking both hands, guides her to a seat. She reverses down the steps as she draws Amicia on, moving slowly because Amicia can't take her eyes off the other woman.

Watching her, I see the woman's eyes follow Amicia as she moves.

Christiane leads her to the stool and tries to seat her with her back to the bed, but Amicia resists and turns around to keep her gaze fixed forward.

Christiane kneels in front of her, putting herself between Amicia and the woman. 'My lady,' taking the old woman's hands, 'will you not look at me?'

'Why are you here?' Amicia ignores her and addresses the woman directly but timidly; all the usual arrogant command has drained from her tone. 'Why have you come back?'

There's no reply.

'Why now?' Amicia pleads for an answer. And then it's as if understanding dawns behind those staring eyes.

She moves her gaze towards the bed. Towards the still form of her grandson. The knowing slots into place.

And terror with it.

Not just fear. Total terror. As if she's realised she's standing at the gates of Hell…and the gates have just started to swing open.

It paralyses her.

In that same moment, my attention is distracted by what's happening on the other side, beyond the door.

The bell starts tolling again, only now it's calling the rest of the village. No longer a measured, respectful marking of a death but a signal of alarm. A call to arms.

Those who have sheltered in the church emerge by the west door and cluster together, keeping their distance from the tower and from the rest. Others are running down the path, the flames of their torches glowing brightly against the still-dark sky. And it's not just torches they carry; they're armed. Disturbed in the depth of the night, reawakening to the fear they enflamed in one another yesterday, their panic rises.

What is it?

Christiane has sensed my distraction.

You need to see.

I don't have to tell her twice; leaving Amicia frozen, she runs up the stairs.

The window is so narrow and deep-set that it shields her from view. But she sees them. She sees more arrive in every moment, men with blades and bows, pitchforks and scythes, the flickering flames of their torches throwing light on the confusion in their faces. The women follow, banding around the edges of the crowd; she sees their apprehension, their nervousness of one another, their hesitance to approach the tower.

They're demanding an account from the watchmen. The word ripples from one person to another.

Dead. Of the pestilence.

They stare aghast at the silent and threatening tower, at the closed door. Their fear demands a response – fight or flight – but they're at a loss to know what to do. As more arrive and the crowd swells, they turn to one another for guidance. We can't make out what they're saying but we watch the mood shift and turn ugly.

At the sound of Christiane's foot on the stair, Amicia starts and rises up.

'What have I done?' She stumbles forward to meet Christiane, clutching at her hands with fretful fingers.

'What have you done?' Christiane reflects back to her.

She shakes her head, bemused but also denying. 'It's not my fault,' she asserts. 'It is the curse. *Her* curse,' nodding her chin towards the wood. The farmer's wife seems frozen in place too, staring blindly towards Amicia.

'There's no one there,' Christiane tries to reassure her.

'Yes, there is.'

Yes, there is.

Christiane chills at my words and turns towards me.

And just for a moment, the farmer's wife's eyes flick towards me.

She knows I'm here.

'You must be able to see her,' Amicia demands, pulling at Christiane's arm to regain her attention. 'It's her fault!' she condemns. 'She cursed me. All those years ago. And now she's back to make it come true!'

'You're making no sense,' Christiane rationalises. 'What are you talking about?'

'Help me!' Amicia demands, her hands scrabbling at Christiane's arms. 'You have to save me. Whatever it takes, you have to do this for me! It's the curse!'

'What is this curse?' Christiane grabs Amicia's face to make her look at her, though her watery eyes keep darting nervously back and forth. 'Tell me!'

Those cataract-dimmed eyes settle on her. 'She said I would wreak my own destruction.' The dread she has carried all these years plummets through her, making her voice break and her body tremble; she collapses against Christiane.

'Sit,' she soothes, lowering the old woman to the stool once again.

As she does, Amicia's gaze falls on the bed and her throat chokes with anguish.

'It's him!' she points a trembling hand at the bed. 'That's what she means!' She catches Christiane's sleeve again and, with surprising strength, pulls herself upright. 'Can't you see?' she demands, shielding herself by putting Christiane between her and the dead man. 'She said I would bring death to my own door!' There is utter helplessness in her eyes now. 'Please, you must save me.'

'Come away,' Christiane instructs, turning her towards the stairs.

'No,' Amicia resists. 'I have to get out.' She puts both her hands around Christiane's, holding them as if in prayer. 'You have to let me out,' she demands. 'I won't go near anyone, I promise. I'll go wherever you want, but you have to let me out. I can't stay in here with that death-ridden corpse!'

'Neither of us is leaving here.' Christiane's voice remains firm.

'You can't mean that. You are condemning me to die! Give me the key!' she shrieks, her nails reaching for Christiane's face. She's just quick enough to catch her wrists and hold her at bay.

'I don't have it,' as the old woman struggles against her. 'Stop, my lady! The key is gone!'

Suddenly, there's a huge roar from the other side of the door.

What's happening?

She doesn't wait for my answer but runs upstairs to the window again.

They've decided on their course of action.

Purification.

By fire.

A sick feeling drops into my stomach. This is how it ends.

They've already stacked brushwood around the door. Now they're building up the pile.

There are women crying, clutching at one another, and others who are jeering and calling, egging the rest on. Two men move to intervene, to pull away those who are building the pile, to dismantle the wood, but others rush forwards and roughly yank them away, throwing them on the ground, ordering them to stay down. Some still huddle near the door of the church, afraid to approach, afraid to act, appalled not to.

Robert Smith stands towards the back. There's blood all over his face and down his chin; his nose is smashed. The priest is on his knees beside him. Four of our guards crowd around them, arms outstretched one to the next, blocking their way; another points the tip of a knife at the smith's throat, a sixth forces the priest down with a hand on the back of his neck.

More men appear from the woodland at the rear, arms filled with fuel. They throw it onto the pile and another roar goes up.

'It's ready!' Gilbert Beadle cries. The raising of his arm is a signal to the rest and a dozen surge forward with their torches. Cries of resistance are drowned out by shouts of encouragement until the noise pounds the air. The church bell starts tolling faster, an uneven clanging, urging them on. With complicit glances at each other, they lower their torches as one and wait for the flames to ignite.

'Stop!' The cry forces its way out of Christiane. A few faces look up, but the shouting below is too great for most to hear. Robert Smith hears and turns towards her, his face full of guilt and helplessness. 'You don't have to do this!' she cries. It has no effect.

'Amicia...' she murmurs, turning back towards the room.

The bedchamber is eerily quiet; the thick stone walls deaden the chaos outside. But I can already feel heat on the other side of the door as we pass down the stairs.

Amicia is standing on the other side of the room, pooled in light. She's gathered all the candles and arranged them around the bed as if for a vigil; some she's even placed on the bed, propped up against the body of her grandson.

'Stay where you are.' Her voice is unexpectedly determined, and she seems strangely self-contained. She holds the candle up, close to one of the curtains hung around the bed.

Christiane stills. And I beside her.

'Give me the key.' The demand is delivered in crystal clear tones. The ice in her voice chills through my veins. 'Give me the key or I will set fire to the bed.'

'I can't do that, my lady.' Christiane's response mirrors that calm clearness. 'The key is gone.'

'Don't lie to me.' Still steady. Only a slight waver of the candle betrays her.

'I assure you it is no lie. I threw it out of the window.'

'Why would you do that?' A frown steals across her brow.

'So that none of us could leave.'

'You can't mean it.' Faltering now. Fearing.

'We're not leaving here, my lady,' softening her tone as the truth drives home. 'Either of us.'

'You lie.' But it's a pleading whimper now, not an accusation. Her hand is dangerously close to the curtain.

My eyes flick between her face and her hand, and I know the moment she switches from fear to rage.

And loses her mind.

She screams her rage and throws the candle onto the bed, against the body of her grandson, then starts knocking over all the candles she's laid out, tipping them onto the bedding. A few go out in the urgency of her action but most stay alight. In seconds, the fabric catches.

Christiane rushes towards the far side of the bed, snatching up some of the candles, ignoring the burn of hot wax on her skin as she casts them aside.

Amicia grabs another candle and holds it against one of the drapes.

'He must burn!' she screams. 'Fire can stop the pestilence! Let him burn!' she demands, her face contorted.

Christiane tears away the blankets covering her son and throws them on the floor, flipping them over and over, trying to smother the flames. She succeeds and pauses on her hands and knees to draw breath.

The air is shattered by the sound of breaking glass followed a split second later by a whooshing sound; the bed hangings explode in flame. As she turns, Amicia snatches up vial after vial of precious oil from one of the caskets and flings them at the wall behind the bed. They smash, spraying oil over the bed and its canopy. A powerful disorientation assails me as the smell of oud hits.

The flames seem to jump in mid-air, almost leaping from droplet to droplet, then licking up the oil-stained wall and onto the cloth hanging above. In seconds, they shoot along the material and down the drapes at each corner until the bed is framed in flame and the fire starts to reach for the floor joists above.

Christiane falls back from the blaze. Amicia rushes at her.

'Now, give me the key!' she screams. 'It's your only way out. You can die in here or you can let both of us out.'

Bewildered, Christiane stares at her face in despair. 'I have told you the truth. The key is gone.'

'You lie!' Amicia rages. 'Why do you still lie?'

All Christiane can do is look at her, helplessly.

Until, at last, the truth dawns in Amicia eyes.

'It can't be true,' she whispers, hanging onto Christiane's arms. 'Please,' she implores, tears flooding down her face, 'tell me you lied.'

Christiane shakes her head.

Amicia seems frozen for a moment, then she lets out a blood-curdling scream of despair. 'You stupid, stupid girl! You have killed me!'

She spins away and backs against the wall, her eyes fixed on the burning bed. As her back touches the wall, she sinks down to the ground, drawing her legs up to get as far from the flames as possible, trying to disappear into the space where the wall meets the steps.

Christiane hunkers down with her, putting her arm around the old woman's shoulder and drawing her close.

'She said I would bring my death upon me...' Amicia mumbles, hiding her face against Christiane's neck.

Thick, acrid smoke is already starting to fill the room. The heat and the noise are almost unbearable.

I kneel on the ground in front of her.

Outside, I can hear screams. Women screaming at men. Someone's crying that they've murdered their lady. Others call for water from the fishpond. Another shouts that it's too late. Run! Run! There's panic and horror. They flee.

I feel arms come around me and someone's face come close to mine.

I keep looking at Christiane. Holding onto her gaze. Holding onto her.

Someone calls my name. But it comes from such a distance away that I don't connect with it.

I catch a wave of anxiety. But it's not from Christiane. Her face is so calm, her eyes so steady as they hold mine.

It's only a matter of moments. The smoke may do the work before the flames do.

But her eyes slide to my left.

I can see her.

From a place of detachment, I know I'm crouched in exactly the place where I'm digging. And Sam's arms are around me, holding me like Christiane is holding Amicia.

I sense she's shaking me, trying to bring me round. But then she stops.

She's looking straight at me.

She can see you?

She can see me.

How? Even as I ask the question, the answer drops into my mind: because we're all connected.

Christiane's eyes return to mine. She looks at me so steadily.

It's love that lets you in. And it's love that lets you go.

'Please, let him go.' I can hear Sam's voice, and a thrill goes through me.

I have to let you go.

No. I'm here for you.

'He's holding onto you.' There's desperation in her voice and it stirs a deep emotion within me. 'I can't bring him back.'

It's time for you to go.
No.
It ends here. Let me go.
No!

She breaks my gaze and looks directly at Sam. 'Take care of him,' she urges. 'He needs you.'

As her eyes swing back to meet mine, I feel Sam's powerful draw, that visceral connection that's been there from the start. And it's pulling me back to my own time, dragging me away from her.

I don't want to go.

And yet I do.

The noise of the fire and the air blends in my ears into one incredible high-pitched sound, a swirling vortex of energy, a tornado of screeching wind spinning round and round me, sweeping closer and closer, faster and faster, until it's pressing against me from all sides, hammering my skull, crushing my chest so I can't breathe or focus or think, darkness rushing in until it all becomes one pinpoint of intense light and one endless scream.

Tuesday

Chapter Seventy-eight

York. 21st September 1976

'Enough now.'

The voice seems some distance away but the pressure on my hand is rather more insistent.

'Come on, Eoghan. It's time to wake up.'

Another hospital. Late morning, to judge by the light. Too bright to keep my eyes open. My head hurts. My chest hurts. In fact, my whole body hurts.

Her hand is on mine and it presses again.

'We have to stop meeting like this,' I joke, gingerly opening one eye then closing it again, and discovering that my throat is raw and my voice raspy.

She takes a deep breath and lets it out slowly.

'Welcome back. I was beginning to wonder.'

There's a surprising amount of relief in her voice.

I force my eyes to open.

'How long have I been out?'

'Sixteen hours. You were practically comatose.'

'You know I sleep like the dead.'

'Not like this.' She sounds serious and I get a hint of what she's been through. 'And you've baffled the doctors.'

'How so?'

'When you arrived in the ambulance, they were expecting to deal with hypothermia or shock with you being exposed to the storm for so long. Imagine their surprise when they had to treat you for burns and smoke inhalation. Especially when there was no sign of a fire.' She smiles wryly. 'Of course, that became even more confusing when your burns just disappeared after a few hours.'

'Ambulance?'

'Keep up, Eoghan. How do you think you got here?' She's teasing, but I think she's trying to make light of it for her sake as well as mine.

Now that I'm back.

I'm back. And she's gone.

Christiane.

My mind reaches for her but there's nothing there. That door has closed.

I expect to feel bereft, but instead there's a strange sense of detachment. As if everything I've been through, I'm now seeing from outside myself. As if it happened to another person.

Though I don't feel grounded here, either. I'm drifting between two worlds. And the glimpses I catch of this reality are harsh and painful. The grief of losing Michael. The guilt of how I've behaved towards him and Sam.

She looks exhausted: the worry of the last several hours is etched on her face, her clothes are crumpled from sleeping in them, and her hair falls round her face. Yet she's still the most beautiful woman to me.

How do I even start to make this better?

'I'm sorry if I worried you,' I fumble, turning my hand over to take hers in mine. But she withdraws it and sits back in her chair, folding her arms defensively. I try a different tack. 'How come you're here?'

'Mrs Felton called, the farmer's wife. The things she said…she wasn't making much sense…but there was something…' She shakes her head and looks away. 'I just got in the car and drove. I went to the farmhouse first. Mr Felton said his wife had gone down to the site but hadn't returned. He insisted on driving me there himself. When we arrived, Mrs Felton was standing to one side of the mound and just staring at you, like she was in a trance. And you…" The emotion of the memory catches in her voice. "You were kneeling on the ground, soaked to the skin and completely oblivious to everything. Torrential rain, thunder and lightning, and you didn't notice any of it.

'Mr Felton drew his wife away, though she tried to resist him. She kept saying she shouldn't leave you. In the end, I sent them both away to call for an ambulance.

'You scared me, Eoghan,' turning back to me with a bleakness in her eyes that is hard to take. 'I didn't know what to do. I couldn't get any kind of response from you. Not one. I've never felt so helpless as a doctor. I knew I needed to get you out of the storm, but I couldn't move you. And I couldn't leave you.'

'I'm sorry.' Such feeble words.

'And the cold! I've never felt anything like it. When I stepped onto the dig site and crouched down beside you, it felt like the depths of winter.'

I frown as fragments of memories surface.

'But there was a fire…'

She nods. 'I could see it, though I couldn't feel it.'

'It was Amicia. And Christiane was trying to protect her.'

'I know. I saw her.'

'You saw her?' She nods. 'You recognised her?'

'More than that: I felt as if I knew her.'

'She said she saw you. That day you saw her as a child at the site, she saw you too.'

'I got the sense she was an extraordinary woman,' she acknowledges.

'I see her in you. The way you put other people first. The way you understand them, often better than they do themselves. The way you don't judge or condemn. You're very accepting of people just as they are.'

I can see I've surprised her as much as I've surprised myself. She looks at me, remembering.

'She let you go. You only responded to me when she released you.'

'I was there because she wanted me to be. But also because I wanted to be,' I admit. 'I'm so sorry, Sam. I let this…thing…consume me. You warned me. Michael…' my throat thickens at saying his name, 'he warned me too.'

'And no one would have understood better than he,' she accepts.

'I ignored both of you.' The self-blame is coming easily now.

'I don't think it was entirely your fault,' she reflects. 'I felt it at the site, that powerful energy pulling you in. There was something between you and her…'

My heart thumps heavily at the twinge of jealousy in her voice.

'She let me go because of you.' I hold Sam's eyes as I admit it to her. 'When she let go, I didn't want to leave but I couldn't hold on. But then I could feel you calling me back and that was powerful too.'

'Has she gone?'

I nod. She returns my gaze; I wish we could say everything we need to just in that look.

'Did you find the answers you wanted?'

That makes me pause to think. And knowing slides slowly into my mind.

'The villagers set a fire outside, but they only meant the smoke to purify the air. When the fire caught, they thought they were to blame, not knowing Amicia had burned the place down from the inside. Once it burned itself out, they didn't try to find the bodies, they just pushed the stone walls in over the debris and fled.'

'Fled where?'

'Into the woods mainly. Some to the towns or other villages. They ran from punishment as well as from the plague. And from the fear that the plague would be God's revenge for their having killed Christiane and Amicia and Simon Reeve. And Walter too,' I realise. 'Someone let Margery and the children out a few days later but it was already too late for poor Walter.'

'Did no one stay?'

'A few. The priest did. But the plague swept through Yorkshire only weeks later and they all seemed to accept it as their deserved fate.'

'So, the village died out?'

'With no heir, the land reverted to Henry Percy. Perhaps he couldn't find tenants willing to live there. The farmland was eventually taken over by one of the other manors and the village was just…abandoned.'

She shakes her head.

'I wonder what Dad would have made of it,' she ponders. 'Do you think it would have satisfied him, having the answers?'

I shrug. Somehow, the knowing is a bit empty. It doesn't mean as much as I thought it would. Especially now I can feel the hollowness of his absence.

'Sam?'

There's a strong compulsion within me to speak, though I don't know if I have the words to make sense of the thoughts spinning through me.

'Hmm?'

'I think I found other answers. Answers to questions I didn't even know I was asking. More important ones.'

I'm stumbling as she looks at me and I feel tension rise within us both. She waits for me to go on.

'I've seen things I didn't expect to, felt things I can't explain. I've felt her faith, that absolute knowing that we are more than what we appear to be, here and now. I can't shake the feeling of it. What I'm trying to say is, I don't see the world in the same way I did.'

Seeing her frown, I rush ahead.

'I'm selfish and self-absorbed and obsessed. It's who I am, and in some ways, I think it's what makes me good at what I do. But it's no longer enough. My career is important to me, but it's not everything.'

'You are all those things,' she allows, 'but you're also more. Yes, you're single-minded and stubborn and driven, but so am I. And you can also be fun and passionate and caring. I've always known who you are; that was never the issue.'

I take a deep breath; my heart is thumping so fast and so hard I'm sure she can hear it.

'Sam, I've never stopped loving you.' The tiniest movement at the corners of her mouth leads me on. 'Even my anger and resentment were another expression of that love.'

'That's a strange way of showing it.'

'What I'm trying to say is that I think I was changing even before all this happened. I can't promise you it would be everything you might want it to be…'

'It doesn't have to be,' she intervenes. 'When I let you go, I was doing what I thought was right for you. But it turns out it was also the right thing for me, giving me a chance to focus on my career.' She gives me that quiet, considering look of hers and my heart expands. 'We're both different people now.'

'Maybe we've changed enough to give it another go?'

'Maybe. We'll only find out by trying.' She smiles softly. 'It's ironic: I cursed The Woman so many times for what was happening to Dad, but it's Christiane who drew us back together.'

'Giving us another chance.'

'If we want it.'

There is nothing I want more.

I put my hand on Sam's. And, this time, she lets it stay there.

Author's note

While Threfield Percy is a fictional place, it owes much to the remarkable work undertaken at Wharram Percy in North Yorkshire, England by the historian Maurice Beresford and the archaeologist John Hurst. In the 1940s, they began an archaeological exploration of a deserted medieval village that went on for more than forty years. Their pioneering project produced not only unique insights into life in a medieval village but also influential new methods for exploring such a site. To them, to the many people who volunteered with them in those precious weeks each summer to uncover Wharram Percy's tale and to English Heritage who now oversee the site, I give my sincere thanks. And to our parents for dragging us around it as children, little knowing the inspiration it would ultimately provide.

Also available from L. G. Wright

Grace

London, 1919. The First World War is finally over and the lost generation are now fighting to rebuild their future. For Jack Westerham there is no prospect of returning to his sheltered, sedate home in Devon and he strives for a new life in London. Into his ordered existence comes Sarah Samuels, eldest daughter of the owner of Richmond Bank where Jack works, and he finds this considerate, elegant, self-assured young woman turning his world around.

Their lives are affluent, passionate and envied. But there is a darkness at the heart of their lives and Jack finds himself defenceless against Sarah's desperate desire for a child. Her solution to the problem will force Jack to confront everything he believes in.

Straddling war-torn London and the heady world of 1920s New York, this love story twists and turns until the Wall Street Crash brings their world tumbling down and true love faces its ultimate challenge.

Printed in Great Britain
by Amazon